CRASHING THE NET

Seattle Sockeyes

Game On in Seattle Series 3

Includes Bonus Material

CRASHING THE BOARDS

Seattle Sockeyes

Game On in Seattle Series 2

BY JAMI DAVENPORT

Cover by
Hot DAMNDESIGNS
www.HotDamnDesigns.com

This book is a work of fiction. While reference might be made to actual historical events or existing locations, the names, characters, places and incidents are either the product of the author's imagination or are used fictitiously, and any resemblance to actual persons, living or dead, business establishments, events, or locales is entirely coincidental.

Warning
This book contains sexually explicit scenes and adult language and may be considered offensive to some readers. This book is for sale to adults ONLY, as defined by the laws of the country in which you made your purchase. Please store your files wisely, where they cannot be accessed by under-aged readers.

Email: jamidavenport@hotmail.com
Website: http://www.jamidavenport.com
Twitter: @jamidavenport
Facebook: http://www.facebook.com/jamidavenport
Fan Page: http://www.facebook.com/jamidavenportauthor
Sign up for Jami's Newsletter: http://eepurl.com/LpfaL

TABLE OF CONTENTS

Crashing the Boards...5

Crashing the Net 57

CRASHING THE BOARDS (SEATTLE SOCKEYES)

GAME ON IN SEATTLE SERIES #2

By Jami Davenport

Can a party crasher melt the icy heart of a reluctant party guest or will she crash and burn along with her fledgling business?

Professional party crasher, Izzy Maxwell, has been hired to ensure the Seattle Sockeyes team party is a rousing success, while team captain Cooper Black is determined that it will be anything but. Armed with killer heels, a provocative dress, and loads of confidence, Izzy is determined to win over the ruggedly handsome hockey player and save the party and her business.

Seattle Sockeyes team captain Cooper Black can't get beyond his anger over the new owners moving his team to Seattle, the one place on earth he swore he'd never live. Izzy hijacks Cooper, posing as his girlfriend, and his best buddy plays along despite Cooper's protests, but Izzy's persuasive talents, their undeniable chemistry, and a couple of intimate liaisons destroy Cooper's resistance.

But when Cooper finds out Izzy was hired to crash the party, and he's been played a fool, the beginning of something special ends before it starts. Can Izzy convince Cooper to take another chance on her or will they both crash into the boards?

DEDICATION

A special thank you to Cassandra Carr, Toni Aleo, and Catherine Gayle, my go-to ladies for all things hockey.

Chapter 1—Shutdown

Cooper Black skidded across the ice on his ass and slammed into the boards behind the net, taking the puck with him. Stevich, the Boston defenseman, was on the puck like Coop's old tabby cat attacking the neighbors' chickenshit dog. Cooper scrambled to his feet, digging the blades of his skates into the ice, trying to get his balance, only to fall again. Stevich fought like a crazed man, gaining control of the puck, and executing a perfect pass to his center.

If Cooper hadn't been so preoccupied with keeping one eye on the clock winding down and the other on the puck, he might've seen the Russian coming on his blind side. He might have had one more chance on goal, one last desperation shot for a tie to send game seven of the semifinals into overtime.

Only he didn't get that chance.

The final buzzer sounded.

This wasn't how it was supposed to end with Boston celebrating on the Giants' home ice. His five-year-old nephew skated better than he had tonight. Struggling to his feet, Cooper skated around the victors and headed for the locker room with his head down. Boston moved on to the Finals, and his team moved on to prepare for next season. Always next season.

He couldn't avoid the press blocking his exit. Too weary to put up a good fight—he'd left all his fight out on the ice—he patiently answered their inane questions.

How do you feel after coming so close but coming up short?

"How do you think I feel?"

What are your plans for the off-season?

"Take a few weeks off for my body to heal and go back at it."

How many more seasons do you plan on skating?

"Heck if I know."

And so it went, he'd just managed to extricate himself from the bloodsuckers when the Giants' PR guy pulled him off to the side. "There's a group of kids from Make-A-Wish anxious to meet you for pics and autographs."

Cooper almost said no. He was that tired, but he never said no to kids, especially kids with disabilities. He'd never forget his childhood hero walking right past Cooper and his little brother as if they didn't exist despite their pleas for an autograph. They'd waited outside the visiting locker room shivering from the cold for what seemed hours, and the jerk couldn't take one minute to make two small boys' dreams come true, completely destroying Cooper's image of the man. Cooper would never be that guy. As long as a kid wanted a moment of his time, he'd give it.

Several minutes later, he put on his best team captain face and yanked open the locker room door. Despite how miserable he might be inside, he'd never let the guys see him defeated or discouraged. Cooper paused in the doorway and swung his gaze around the solemn locker room. He'd attended funerals more cheerful than this.

"What the fuck is going on? Who died?" Cooper faked a grin he didn't feel and strode into the room, the picture of upbeat confidence. There were too many young guys on this team to let this setback get them down.

No one even looked up at him.

"Hey, guys, we'll get 'em next year. We were that close." He held up his hand using his thumb and forefinger to illustrate just how fucking damn close they'd been to winning that last game and making it to the Finals—the dream that had eluded him for ten years.

Finally, Cedric, his best buddy on the team, lifted up his head and rubbed his beefy, scarred hands over his face. Heaving a deep sigh, he turned toward Cooper. Cedric's stricken expression struck fear deep in Cooper's gut. "They fired Coach."

"They? Who the fuck is they?"

"Our new ownership."

Cooper stared at his friend, certain he'd heard wrong. "New ownership? I've been gone from the locker room thirty minutes, and we lost a coach and gained new owners? You guys are playing me."

Ced just stared at him.

"Right? You're bullshitting me. Isn't he, Crandall?"

Crandall glanced up and then buried his head in his hands again. He turned to the others. The young guys wouldn't even look at him.

A cold shiver sliced through him. They weren't shitting him.

"What new owners?" Sure, there'd been all sorts of rumors, but there'd always been rumors. He'd been with this organization since he'd come up from the minors, thirteen years ago. And he'd heard every rumor known to man until he quit listening.

"The Puget Sound Hockey Alliance."

"That Seattle group that's been stalking every team with a shaky fan base and money-starved owners?"

"The very one."

"They do have deep pockets, so that's a good thing." Cooper forced himself to remain positive. The team's now former owners had been douches that bled the team dry.

"Sure, if you like rain."

Cooper sank onto the bench. "No."

"We're moving to Seattle." Cedric confirmed his worst nightmare.

Cooper's future turned as dismal as a gray Seattle sky. He knew all about Seattle weather. As a kid, he'd been forced to spend a few weeks there every summer with a crotchety old aunt. He hated it there, swore it was one place on earth he'd never live.

He looked at all the down faces in turn, and the truth was reflected in each one. "We're going to Seattle." He said the words with such despair, a guy would think he'd been sentenced to death row. In his mind, he was.

As captain of this team, he should be singing Seattle's praises, waxing poetic over the billionaire owner, and convincing the team this was the best thing that had ever happened to them.

He wasn't that noble. In fact, he was fucking pissed.

Chapter 2—Attacking Zone

Party crashing was an art—if done right.

Isabella Maxwell should know. She'd been crashing parties for years, at first to get a decent meal and later—much later—as a part-time profession with her three younger sisters. She'd never crashed a party she didn't take from dud to memorable in minutes.

Tonight she might have met her match.

She'd done her research and knew the obstacles and challenges, but nothing prepared her for the scene awaiting her on the party deck of the Washington Queen, a local tour boat rented by the Seattle Sockeyes hockey team for an evening dinner cruise around Elliott Bay.

As security checked invitations at the door, Izzy snuck past them and peeked in the doorway, scoping out the scene inside—DJ in the corner, empty dance floor complete with mirror ball and flashing lights, not a dancer anywhere. Hockey players were slouched in chairs clumped around tables, reminding her of pimply faced preteens at a junior high dance. Only these boys weren't preteens or pimply faced. They were a formidable wall of broad chests, muscular thighs, and determined expressions. Each one mirroring the other, but she'd done her research. There was one man she needed to win over to salvage this party, and he hadn't arrived yet.

Her sisters had already boarded the boat, managing to sneak past security, every one of them dressed to kill or at least to charm a professional hockey team. Betheni dazzled her plunging Vera Wang gown and deadly high heels. Emma and Avery, the youngest at twenty-one and identical twins, looked every bit like giddy hockey groupies who'd managed to snag an invite to the party. Standing near the buffet table, they giggled and whispered as they stole glances at the players. Several players stared right back. Nearby, Betheni engaged the team play-by-play announcer in conversation, while he stared at her boobs, but men always stared at Betheni's boobs.

The stage was set.

Time to get this party started. The Sockeyes were going to have the time of their lives if she had to threaten bodily harm with their own hockey sticks.

"Ma'am, I need to see your invitation." A security guard with a receding hairline, the waist of his polyester pants pulled up to his armpits, and a determined set to his skinny jaw, stepped in front of her before she could enter through the double doors.

"Oh, that." Izzy made a show of digging through her saddlebag of a purse, not exactly in keeping with her little black sheath, but it served its purpose. "I know it's in here somewhere."

The security guard wasn't the least bit impressed. He tapped his toe on the floor and took a ready stance as if he expected her to run any moment. Just what she needed, a SWAT team wannabe. She batted her eyes at him and continued to dig in her purse.

"I'm sorry. I know it's here somewhere."

"Ma'am, you'll need to leave the boat until you can find it."

She laughed and rubbed one perfectly manicured finger across his name tag. "Now, Carl, you just hold on one teensy bit. We'll get this straightened out." Izzy slipped into her fake Southern drawl; it brought most men to their knees.

Not Carl. In fact, not one hair quivered on his mustache. "My orders are strict. No one, not even the governor, gets in without an invite." He wrapped scrawny fingers around her arm and pulled her none too gently from the doorway. He might look like a wimp but the guy was surprisingly strong.

No matter. She'd switch to Plan B.

"My boyfriend will be here any moment. He must have the tickets."

As if on cue, her target for the night walked up the ramp and onto the boat. *Cooper Black.* The captain of the newly christened Seattle Sockeyes, and the most outspoken man on the team especially when it came to the team's move and current situation, which he hated—the very man Izzy needed to tame tonight for this situation to turn around.

Judging by the stubborn set of his jaw and those steely blue eyes, this wasn't going to be easy.

* * * *

Cooper stalked onto the boat hefting a boulder-sized chip on his shoulder.

No way in fucking hell would he cooperate at this fucking party.

Not after what the new ownership had done to his team, his coaches, and the staff. It was bad enough they'd forced him to attend, and no one forced him to do anything. Attend was one thing, play nice was another. They'd find that out soon enough.

Oh, yeah, he was in a mood. Not even his buddy Cedric could joke him out of it.

A line of people formed at the head of the dock, waiting impatiently to board the boat. A gorgeous brunette with legs longer than his hockey stick appeared to be holding up the line. She kept digging in her purse and pleading with the rent-a-cop who guarded the door with zealous intent. The guard didn't look the least bit sympathetic or amused. Instead he politely yet firmly pushed her out of the way and began checking the invitations of the couple behind her.

She frowned and did a quick survey of the area. Her big brown eyes landed on Cooper, and she headed straight for him. Confidence oozed out of her, and he immediately pegged her as a spoiled rich twenty-something who thought the world revolved around her. He'd met plenty just like her in his thirty-two years.

She walked closer with the security guard dogging her heels and turned the full-wattage of her gorgeous smile on Cooper, as if she'd been expecting him. He'd never seen the woman in his life.

Disinterested in whatever game she might be playing, Cooper gazed over the heads of the people in front of him, getting the lay of the land in the ballroom beyond. He caught sight of the suits across the room, minority owners of the team, hanging out with the big guys. Next to them stood the majority owner of the Sockeyes, Ethan Parker, the thieving bastard, and the team's assistant director of player personnel turned traitor, Ethan's beautiful fiancée, Lauren Schneider. Cooper frowned even harder. They were the enemy.

Cedric elbowed him then focused his blond, European charm on the woman striding toward them. Good, she could latch on to Ced, and Cooper could get back to his grudge match with the team's new owner.

Only the gorgeous pair of legs glided past Cedric with the grace of an gold medal figure skater. The woman looped her arm through Cooper's, catching him off guard. Ced's grin turned to confusion and his eyes narrowed. He always got the women over Cooper. Always.

"There you are, you bad boy. Shame on you for being late. You know I hate waiting." She tapped his chest and smiled into his eyes. She was tall, but he was taller, and he wasn't buying any of what she was selling. Not tonight. Not ever.

Cooper frowned and narrowed his eyes. He didn't like being touched unless it was his idea. "I don't know you."

"You're such a joker, isn't he, Cedric?" She looked to Cedric for confirmation.

Cooper's best buddy opened his mouth to back him up, only no words were spoken. Instead, his confusion turned to an evil grin, revenge lighting up his pale blue eyes. "Seriously, Coop, You know how your princess gets when you play jokes on her."

"This isn't a joke. I don't know this woman," Cooper ground out the words, his foul mood fouler.

The rent-a-cop, identified as Carl by his name badge, stepped forward. "Mr. Black, I'll have her removed. I can see she's harassing you."

"Carl, I told you, he's my boyfriend. He's just a little upset at me for having my way with him and his credit card. Check your list again, I'm sure my name's on it. Isabella."

"No need to check the list." Cedric held out his arm. "Come on, Isabella, I'll escort you inside if this asshole won't."

Grumpier than ever, Cooper followed Cedric and Isabella into the ballroom. The woman winked over her shoulder at him as she sauntered into the room as if she owned it, a huge purse clutched in her delicate hand and walking with the grace of an athlete on impossibly high heels. Once inside, she extricated herself from Ced's hold.

"Thanks so much, Cedric." She gave him a peck on the cheek, which really annoyed the hell out of Cooper.

"It was my pleasure, Isabella." Cedric dialed up the charm.

"You can call me Izzy. That's what Coop calls me."

"I don't call you anything." Cooper stiffened as she advanced on him, not sure what she'd come up with next. By the twinkle in her dark brown eyes, she wasn't done with him yet. She put her hands on his collar and gazed up into his eyes like a loving girlfriend.

Loving? What the fuck? Feeling a bit claustrophobic, he backed up a step, running into a support post behind him. Her gentle laugh reminded him of the songs of the little birds he fed every day on his front porch. He loved listening to those birds in the morning. Her, not so much. And no way in hell would he be listening to her voice in the morning or any time.

She pressed that sweet body against his in that intimate way lovers had. "I see people I know. I must say hi. You don't mind, do you, darling?" She kissed his cheek.

"Not one damn bit," Cooper growled, catching Cedric holding his stomach out of the corner of his eye. The jerk would be rolling on the floor laughing any minute.

Isabella strolled away, as if she were out for a walk in the park. Cooper swallowed as he stared at that nice rounded ass of hers and briefly wondered what it'd feel like in his hands. She nodded at a few people as if she knew them, and joined a group of men several feet inside the doorway, charming them immediately. Their hearty laughter bounced off the walls of the otherwise quiet room as she told some entertaining story, which must have involved a high heel, a little dog, and a motorcycle judging by how she expressed everything dramatically with her hands.

Despite his best intentions, Cooper was mesmerized, then he reminded himself of his intentions not to have a good time just to prove his point. He didn't know this woman, even though she did attract him on the most basic of levels. But then she'd attract any man as she was drop-dead gorgeous. He'd had any number of gorgeous women on his arm in the past so she shouldn't be anything special.

Tell that to his dick. It considered her damn special right about now, most likely because he'd boycotted everything Seattle since he'd arrived a month ago, including its coffee and its women.

"Your girlfriend is one hot number, Coop. You'd better keep an eye on her or one of these fuckheads will be moving in on your territory. Including me."

"Fuck you. You set me up."

"And it was damn funny."

In another place and time, Cooper would be angling for a piece of that nice ass, but not tonight, not while the new ownership and coaching staff was watching. Cooper Black couldn't be bought, even if they did buy his team.

That coaching staff, led by a young first-year head coach, mingled with the crowd, shaking hands and selling the team since the team currently refused to sell itself. Cooper glared at every coach and staff person stupid enough to attempt to engage him in conversation, and his teammates followed suit, loyal to the last man. So far.

He stiffened and prepared for battle as the man he called the asshole—Ethan Parker—walked toward him, as comfortable in an expensive suit as Cooper was on the ice. Cooper tugged on his collar and loosened his bowtie. He hated wearing a damn tux, wasn't even sure why he'd put it on at the last minute when he'd planned on wearing a Gainesville Giants hoodie. Blame it on his parents. They'd drummed duty and loyalty into his head since day one. His father, a real life Army hero, and Cooper's personal hero, made sure his son did what was expected of him. In Cooper's mind, he was expected to attend this party dressed correctly, and that was as far as duty took him. Fuck the rest of it. His loyalty remained in Gainesville with the fans who'd earned it.

He glared at Parker, hoping to intimidate the guy, but even his best you're-going-to-get-the-shit-kicked-out-of-you glare didn't dissuade the man.

"Cooper." Ethan nodded and then smiled at Cedric. "Cedric. So good to see you, gentlemen. Beautiful Seattle night, isn't it?"

"If you like drizzle and gray," Cooper snorted. The weather was pretty much par for the course, and it was fucking July already.

Cedric, being a loyal friend for once, shrugged and stared at the shoreline.

"Seattle is ready for a hockey team. Did you realize we have the largest adult hockey program in the country?"

Cooper grunted.

"And you'll be natural rivals for the Canucks up north."

Cooper yawned.

Ethan leaned forward, his eyes narrowing to glittering slits. "Listen, Black, if you think your crappy attitude is going to move you back to Florida, you might be right. Only the team won't be going with you. I'm willing to be patient, but only for so long. This team is here to stay, whether you fucking like it or not."

Cooper stared straight through Ethan, forcing his face into stone, but he could feel a muscle jerking in his jaw. Satisfied that he'd made his point, Ethan strolled away as if enjoying himself.

"He's right, you know," Cedric said from next to him.

Cooper whipped his head around. "Right? About what?"

"He can trade your ass any day to a team with no hope of winning, now or for the next decade."

"Maybe I want to be traded."

"No, you don't. Not when we came so close last season." Cedric sighed, as if he was weary of all this but was too loyal to say so. "Don't look now, but here comes your girlfriend."

"Just what I need. And quit calling her that. I don't even know the woman."

Isabella took a detour to the DJ, spoke to him, and continued across the dance floor. She paused, her gaze directly on Cooper. A slow smile crossed her face, and she raised her eyebrows, glancing pointedly at the dance floor, then at him. He frowned so hard his teeth hurt. He was not dancing with her or anyone else tonight.

She graced him with a sexy little smile, one of those come-and-get-me-big-boy smiles. He looked away. Despite the fact that his dick skated into the rink, he was staying on the bench. His little head had never been very smart anyway, especially when it came to women.

The music started, some pulsing, sexy, upbeat dance tune, and Izzy's hips swayed with a seductive, hypnotic rhythm while she kept her eyes on him. Pretty soon a few other women joined her, dancing together as women often did. A set of twins, blond-haired versions of Isabella, gyrated on the dance floor. The uncanny resemblance set off his warning bells.

His teammates leaned forward in their chairs, especially the young guys, probably imagining every guy's most perverse fantasies involving twins. Another equally gorgeous woman with auburn hair joined them, twirling, laughing, having a great time, as if they were the only ones at the party. She, too, could be a sister to the other three. Another weird coincidence? Not a chance. Cooper didn't believe in coincidences.

Regardless, he dismissed his suspicions. So they looked like cloned versions of Isabella. So what? He had bigger problems. He glanced at his guys and sensed a mutiny in the making. Even Cedric's tongue was hanging out. Cooper jabbed him with an elbow and got an "umph" along with a couple "fuck you"s.

One of the twins danced over and grabbed Mike Gibson's hand. The horny rookie just about fell out of his chair.

"Let's dance." The cute blonde never quit moving those hips,

16

not once. Cooper shot Gib a look of pure homicide, and the rookie caught it. With reluctance, he shook his hand from the woman's and pulled away. She frowned at Cooper, then gave him a charming smile; he just glared back. The blonde flounced off in search of another sucker.

Cooper turned toward the rookie. "We all stand together. Remember?"

Gibson shrugged. "The women in Seattle are hot, and this isn't such a bad place. We might as well make the best of it."

Cooper stared him down, and Gibson looked away first. The kid might be formidable on skates, but he was no match for a seasoned veteran like Cooper, on or off the ice.

"There's no disloyalty in dancing with pretty ladies." Drew Delacorte, a second-year guy from Toronto, bravely jumped in the conversation.

"Do I have to spell it out to you? To all of you? Stay away from the groupies."

"You came in with one of them." Delacorte pointed out in a second rare display of defiance.

"She latched on to me at the door. Ced escorted her in as joke." Why the fuck did he feel the need to explain himself?

"He's playing hard to get. Isabella's his girlfriend." Cedric grinned and took a long pull on his beer.

Cooper heaved a sigh, knowing Cedric would keep this up until the night ended, especially if Cooper made a big deal about it. Unsuccessfully hiding his smile, Drew drank his beer in silence, his eyes on the hot women dancing several feet away. Cooper could feel his hold over the team slipping with each beat of the music. Loyalty was a lost art, but not for Coop, which was exactly why the new ownership would not get his cooperation. Instead they'd understand the full extent of his displeasure. So what if they cut him or traded him?

Cooper leaned back in the hard chair, crossed his arms over his chest, and glared at Cedric. Cedric just grinned his trademark shit-eating grin. Nothing got to Cedric. Everything rolled off his back as he went on with his life, doing shit his way.

"They have to be sisters." Cedric's eyes followed the redhead as the song ended, and she strutted off the dance floor, short skirt swaying to the movement of her hips. "I'd like to find out if that one is a true redhead. Only one way to find out." His slow smile said it all. Ced had picked his woman for the night, and he usually got what he wanted.

The song ended and Isabella danced all the way across the floor to his side.

"Fucking groupies," Cooper muttered, pissed that they were wearing down his teammates' resolve.

"Lighten up, man." Cedric chuckled and nodded toward the banquet table. "Besides, they aren't groupies. Take a closer look."

Cooper narrowed his eyes, but he wasn't seeing what Ced saw. "Yeah?"

"See the big bags those twins are carrying? Watch them cram food in those bags when they think no one's watching."

Cooper nodded as it dawned on him. "They're party crashers."

"Damn right."

"They aren't here for the hockey players, they're here for the food." One more reason to hate Seattle. They didn't even have hockey groupies, just a bunch of hot women more interested in grabbing food than horny, athletic men.

"And the entertainment," Cedric added. "It's better than popcorn and a movie any day."

Cooper's annoyance gave way as a plan formed in his mind. A slow smile spread across Coop's face, the first one since this nightmare began what seemed like a lifetime ago. "I wonder how Parker would react if he found out these starving college students or whatever have crashed his perfect little party with his Seattle A-lister attendees, and he's none the wiser?"

"Pretty damn hilarious, isn't it?" Cedric continued to stare at the redhead.

"Yeah, here I thought they were enemies, and they're allies of a sort."

Cedric nodded. "Even if management suspects she's a party crasher, they won't kick her out on the off-chance she really is with you."

"Maybe I can have some fun with them. Make this party crash in style." Cooper's smile spread farther.

"Coop, you scare the shit out of me when you smile like that. It means someone's going to die or get their body slammed against the boards."

18

"No dying, no slamming. At least not physically." Cooper rubbed the stubble on his chin. His gaze was drawn to Ethan Parker, who'd walked across the room and was trying to engage a couple players in conversation. They weren't warming up to the idea. Ethan glanced in Cooper's direction, and their gazes clashed with the intensity of two warriors squaring up on a battlefield. Ethan's eyes narrowed. He'd deal with Cooper later, Cooper was certain of that. Fine, bring it on.

Shaking his head in frustration, Ethan walked away from the table of players and struck up a conversation with his head coach.

"She's heading your way." Cedric jerked his head, and Cooper forgot all about the team owner. Isabella walked toward him with the loose-hipped stride of a runway model. This time he was ready for her games. In fact, he'd play a few of his own, and he played to win.

Chapter 3—Change on the Fly

Okay, this party wasn't going as intended. Isabella caught the eye of the team majority owner, Ethan Parker, who'd hired Party Crashers to do this job. He jerked his head toward the players clumped at tables and looking miserable, not mingling, not enjoying themselves. They'd turned down every advance by her sisters to dance. No results, no money. That was the deal she'd struck with Parker, and they needed this money, not just to pay bills, but to take this business to the next level and move a step closer to quitting their day jobs.

She'd step up her game. And that game began with the guy who called the shots, the team captain, Cooper Black. She strolled toward Cooper, as if she had all the time in the world, even though inside her stomach tied in knots. Cooper glowered at her while his buddy wore the biggest grin, obviously willing to play along with her ruse. Thank God, she could use an ally in this place. Cedric abandoned the chair next to Cooper, despite his buddy's warning scowl, and Izzy sank down into the seat, not as gracefully as she'd like because her feet were killing her in those shoes. What she'd give right now to soak them in a warm bucket of water.

"You're back? Haven't you tortured me enough?" Something in his tone caught Isabella off guard. He sounded almost conspiratorial.

She recovered quickly and wrapped an arm around his waist. "Seriously? Not even close. Let's dance, big boy."

He watched her for a long moment, and she could almost see the wheels turning. His expression made her uneasy. "I know your game."

"Excuse me?" She gazed up at him, an adoring smile plastered on her face, but she could tell he saw through it, maybe even caught her moment of uncertainty.

"Your game. I know what your deal is." His smug smile indicated he thought he had one up on her.

Izzy went all cold and still inside, her smile frozen in place. "My deal?"

"Yeah." He crossed his arms over his ample chest and leaned back in his chair. "You're party crashers. Do you go around to parties just to get free meals and free alcohol, or is there more to it than that?"

"What are you insinuating?" Anger replaced her fear. She leaned forward, a hand on his arm and gave him her patented bitch glare. Bad idea. Touching him was like touching an inferno. The heat from his body set fire to the heat inside hers, and she barely knew the guy. *Get a grip, Izzy.* Obviously, she'd concentrated on her business too long and neglected her sex life, so now her sex life wanted a front row seat on this hunk's lap.

"That you do this pretty frequently." His smug smile slid off his face as he watched her warily. His gaze kept flicking to her hand, as if he felt the heat, too.

"Hey, money's tight. We do what we can." She shrugged and sat back in her chair, taking her hand off him and feeling as if she should dunk it in a glass of ice water.

"You are sisters then?" He almost seemed interested and way too cool and calm.

"That's right. Besides, the twins are huge hockey fans. We couldn't pass up this chance to party with the players and take advantage of the food and drink."

"Opportunists?"

"A little. What about you? What's your story? It's obvious you don't want to be here. Your attitude is ruining the party." She stared into the most piercing set of blue eyes she'd ever seen anywhere, so piercing they sliced right through her tough armor, down to her deepest secrets. Her knees would've given out if she'd been standing, so powerful was his steady, unwavering gaze.

"What do you care?" He studied her, as if reading every line in her heart's history.

"I hate seeing a good party go bad."

"It was never a good party. You and I could have our own party somewhere away from this place."

Panic must have crossed her face because he chuckled.

"Well, you are my girlfriend." He almost smiled.

"I think it's time to eat."

"If there's anything left, the way your sisters have been shoving food in their purses."

"I don't know what you're talking about." In response, her stomach, which hadn't been satisfied in hours, growled like an angry lion. "By the way, I'm Izzy."

"Wouldn't I know that as your boyfriend?" Another smile

tugged at the corners of his generous, very kissable mouth. This man was all kinds of sexy, and she'd bet her grandmother's support hose his body looked as good as his face.

"You would think."

Together they stood, and he escorted her to the buffet table, hand on her elbow, like the gentleman she bet he really wasn't. Especially not in bed.

They loaded their plates and returned to their table.

He eyed her heaping plate of food, equal to his. "Are you really going to eat all that?"

She nodded as she dug in. Being horny always made her hungry when she couldn't satisfy the horny—not that she'd tell him that.

"Where do you put it all?" He stared at her plate in amazement then slid his gaze up and down her slender body.

"I'm active."

"Obviously."

"So, Izzy." Cedric grinned at her as he sat down opposite Cooper. "What are you doing dating this clown?"

"She's not—"

"I like projects, and he's a project. Besides, he has a soft side."

Cooper's teammates at the table elbowed each other and laughed at his expense. Cooper frowned and shot her a warning glare, but she'd never been the type of girl to be silenced by a single glance, despite the dangerous glint in his eyes.

"He does. Really. He writes love songs." Izzy stroked his stubbled cheek, and he sucked in a breath.

"No fucking way? This guy?" The teammate sitting next to Cooper slapped him on the back, causing him to choke on his food.

Cooper swallowed and rose to defend himself and his manhood. "I don't—"

"They're beautiful. He's very poetic, says my eyes are like diamonds in the sky and my hair is like chocolate silk." Izzy gazed adoringly at Cooper. He didn't return the favor.

Matt, a guy she recognized as one of the best defensemen in the league, snorted so loud he could be heard several tables away. "Never knew you had it in you, buddy," he said in this adorable French Canadian accent.

"She's making that up." Cooper looked ready to commit a mass murder and leave no witnesses.

"He's shy about his talents." Izzy patted his arm in a loving gesture and got another deadly glare in response. She was having a helluva good time, even if it was at his expense. "He's such a romantic soul, always leaving me little cards everywhere declaring his love for me. He calls me his little chicken coop. I think it's so cute."

The guys were laughing so hard they were wiping their eyes.

Izzy was just getting warmed up. If he wanted her to stop, he'd have to dance with her. He buried his dark head in his food, shoveling it in so fast she got the distinct impression he wished he was cramming her mouth full of food to shut her up.

"What do you call him?" Matt wiped his mouth with his sleeve; obviously manners weren't his forte.

"Super Cooper or Supe because his ego isn't the only thing that's super-sized." She smiled sweetly at all of them, playing the naïve, innocent thing to the hilt.

Another round of hilarity ensued while Cooper's face turned redder than her cherry bomb lipstick. Finally, as if accepting his fate, he buried his face in his hands and groaned.

She leaned over and whispered in his ear, bringing on another round of hoots from the cheap seats. "You want me to stop then dance with me."

"Not a chance in hell." He lifted his head, his blue eyes burning right through her, and it wasn't just from anger. In fact, that heat zinged right down to her crotch and wet her panties.

"I won't stop until you do."

He studied her for a moment, as if assessing the conviction behind her words. "I don't know you." He turned to his buddies. "Hear me out, guys. I don't know this woman. She latched on to me to crash this party."

"Oh, Coop, don't be an ass." Cedric grinned. "You're just pissed 'cause she's got your dick on a leash and you fucking don't want to admit it."

Several heads around the table nodded in unison. Cedric turned to Izzy. "We love you, honey, even if he's too much of a dick to admit to his weakness."

"Oh fuck." Cooper slammed his fist on the table, drawing another set of head-turning around the room. He jumped to his feet and stalked across the ballroom and out the double doors. Izzy gave the boys a "so sorry" look and ran after him as fast as her heels would carry her, off to do damage control.

Maybe she'd pushed him too far. She desperately needed the man to dance with her. Just a dance or two. Once he hit the dance floor, all his buddies would follow, and the party would be on its way, as would her new business, the very business way too far in debt after her sisters and she purchased clothes and accessories in keeping with their image.

Cooper's broad back disappeared into the men's room, the door slamming in her face. She stood outside, wringing her hands. And they said women took forever in the bathroom? This guy must be reading an entire newspaper in there or something.

Or jacking off. Her brain did a deviant detour to a little fantasy in which she walked in, found him jerking on an impressively large dick and said, "Here, let me help you with that." She had to admit, the man was hot, really hot, and she wanted some of that action in the worst, unprofessional way. She wasn't opposed to recreational sex, but she'd been too busy to indulge, what with getting her fledgling business off the ground, along with her day job as a barista.

Only there was that pact with her sisters, a tiny little roadblock on a highway already riddled with potholes. When they started this business, Rule Number One pertained to never sleeping with the party guests, no matter how delectable.

Cooper wasn't just delectable, he was the definition of sexy. And desperate times often called for bending or obliterating rules. Oh, yeah, she was trying every which way to justify an action which had no justification.

Or did it?

This night would be a disaster if she didn't find a way to rescue it and fast. Despite her efforts, the stubborn man held strong. Too strong. Izzy racked her brain for a different plan, instead that plan kept involving naked skin, sweaty bodies, and a lot of groaning, panting, and sweating.

Holy crap.

Izzy fanned herself and stared at her watch. Bolstering her courage, she pushed the door open and went inside, not certain what she'd find or even what she wanted to find.

Cooper glanced up from washing his hands, shock crossing his handsome features momentarily, followed by a slow, predatory smile. She liked him as a predator, didn't even mind being the prey because that particular role would have its perks and then some.

"Well, honey, this takes party crashing to a whole new level." He propped his fine ass on the counter, crossed a pair of strong arms over his equally impressive chest, and grinned a sexy, lopsided smile that pushed her off balance, but her years of pretending everything was fine when it wasn't came into play.

She smiled right back, refusing to let him see her sweat. "You have to dance with me."

"I don't have to do anything." His sensuous lips turned down and his square jaw set in that stubborn line she'd come to realize meant she wasn't getting her way tonight or in the next decade or two.

Unless she called in the big guns.

Izzy's breath caught in her throat as she put her hands on his belt buckle. She'd never done anything like this before. Never solicited a guest at a party. Never been this bold. But caution escaped her as the full power of his lustful gaze slammed into her. Party be damned, she wanted this man and that insane wanting trumped every other argument her practical side produced.

"Dance with me," she spoke again, this time her voice sounded husky and low.

A muscle ticked in his jaw. "It'll cost you."

Of that she had no doubt, but right now, she was willing to pay the price.

* * * * *

Cooper had to have her. Hell, he'd gone almost three months without a woman, a virtual record for him, and his dick throbbed harder than it had that night in the VIP room of a New York City nightclub while three stunning and very naked women had their way with him and his dick.

Only this was Izzy. Not three nameless, faceless women, and for reasons he couldn't fathom, she did it for him more than a VIP room full of horny, uninhibited women.

Izzy's full lower lip fell in a full-blown sexy pout. He held his breath, waiting to see what those fingers would do with his belt buckle. She parted her red lips and moistened them with her tongue.

He stared at her mouth, forgetting how to breathe. With a sultry smile and deft fingers, she undid his belt and unbuttoned the top button on his dress pants. He sucked in a breath, afraid to move one muscle and destroy the moment.

She was about to go down on him in the men's room of a chartered tourist boat, and he wouldn't miss this experience for all the Cups in the world.

With a sly smile, Izzy slid down the zipper. It was her turn to suck in a breath when his penis sprang free in all ten plus inches of hard male glory. She glanced up at him with one arched brow. "Commando?"

"Always prepared. That's me. Why deal with unnecessary clothing when you can cut right to the meat of the matter." He found himself grinning. Underwear was overrated and got in the way. He hadn't exactly planned on finding a woman tonight and taking her home, but it'd been a possibility he hadn't discounted.

She ran a fingernail over the tip of his penis. He gripped the counter, unable to stand without support. A tortured groan was wrenched from deep in his gut. Hell, he'd been with more women than he could count over the years, from debutantes to anything-goes groupies, but not one had shaken him to the core like this woman with just one scrape of her fingernail across the sensitive tip.

"Fuck me with your mouth, honey." He put his hands on her shoulders with gentle pressure. "Do you deep throat?"

"As big as you are? I'll give it my best." She started to kneel when the door slammed open.

It was Cedric.

"Oh, for fuck's sake, Coop. Get a room, would ya?"

Izzy shot to her feet and ran from the bathroom in a flash of sexy dress and long legs, her deadly heels tapping out a desperate beat on the tile floor. Zipping his pants, Cooper pushed his friend out of the way and sprinted after her. He caught her halfway down the hall and pulled her against him.

She stared up at him in shame, her chest heaving. "I just about gave you a blow job in a public bathroom."

"Yeah, I know." He couldn't stop the grin from spreading. Music spilled out of the party deck doors, pulsing, sexy music. He wasn't going to let her get away this easily. Not when his entire body needed her as much as it needed oxygen.

He grabbed her hand and pulled her along, trying several doors until he found one that wasn't locked. The ladies' room. Somehow that seemed fitting. He pulled her inside and locked the door this time.

Perfect.

Picking her up, he ignored her protests and carried her to the makeup counter. She licked her lips again and swallowed, her eyes locked with his. He kissed her, gently at first until the fire built to an explosion inside him, then he ravaged her mouth like the starving man he was. She wrapped those long legs around his waist and gave as good as she got, not the least bit intimidated by his size and power like some women were.

Her courage and passion drove him fucking nuts.

Cooper pushed her down on the counter and lowered the straps on her dress, revealing the most perfect set of tits he'd seen in a long time, not huge, but not small, just right. Leaning forward, he ran his tongue around one nipple. God, she tasted as good as she smelled, all honey and sweetness with a bit of wicked thrown in. She shuddered underneath him, burying her fingers in his hair.

He drew her nipple into his mouth, sucking hard then holding it between his teeth and tugging slightly. She whimpered, her hips rising off the table.

"You like that?" For reasons he couldn't fathom, her answer was important to him.

Izzy nodded, her luminous eyes full of wonder and desire.

"Some women think I'm too rough."

When she didn't respond, he took that as a good thing and bent down to repeat the process on the other nipple, this time testing her by biting a little harder. She gripped the table with her hands and tossed her head from side to side. He flicked her nipple with his tongue several times as she writhed underneath him.

"Like that?"

"Fuck yes."

Pushing down her dress, he trailed little kisses to her navel, pausing to nip here and there, marking her with his teeth.

He knelt between her legs, pushing aside her G-string. Even in the dim light, he could see her glistening juices. He parted her folds and slipped his tongue inside, pushing as high up as possible. She dug her spiked heels into his back.

He followed his tongue with a finger. Damn, but she was tight. Just like he liked his women, and relatively hard to find among the women he hung with. He slid another finger inside her and pumped, while his tongue worked its magic on her clit.

She arched her back and pressed her crotch into his face, giving him the green light to take her to heaven, and he planned to do just that. With an enthusiasm he'd been lacking lately when it came to sex, Cooper gave her everything he had until she was shaking and screaming his name.

Finally she collapsed, boneless and silent, except for her panting. He watched the rise and fall of her chest and had to smile. Satisfaction surged through him, despite the fact that he hadn't gotten any yet. He loved pleasing a lady, almost as much as he loved a lady pleasing him. The way he saw it, his turn was next.

Oh, yeah, it was going to be a good night.

Finally Izzy's eyes focused on his face. She blinked several times, cleared her throat, and wiped the sweat from her forehead. Glancing around the room, as if to get her bearings and compose herself, she eventually brought her gaze back to him.

"Now you have to dance with me."

"That wasn't part of the deal." It was a token statement of resistance. How did a man turn down an order like that?

"We had a deal." She slid off the counter and straightened her clothing.

Pounding on the door brought them both back to reality. She smiled at him. "I'll wait in a stall for a decent amount of time. You leave first."

"Are you sure?"

"Absolutely."

"I'm not done with you." Cooper gave her a quick kiss, waited for her to hide in the stall, then opened the door. A shocked Lauren Schneider stood on the other side. He smiled at her as if he always walked out of the women's bathroom.

"Oh, sorry. I guess I went in the wrong bathroom. No wonder it didn't have urinals." He saluted her and sauntered off.

She stared after him, her soft laughter following him.

He wasn't fooling anyone, least of all himself.

Isabelle would be his completely by the time the night was over, and he'd savor every moment of it.

Now to find a more romantic, private place than a bathroom, one with a lock on the door. He didn't think he could wait until they got off the boat.

Chapter 4—Body Checking

She didn't know if it was too much wine or Cooper's hot gaze melting her inhibitions or a combination of both, but this man had just driven Izzy to the brink of infinite pleasure and pushed her over the edge. She'd never in her life experienced an orgasm so totally awesome in its power as it swept through every cell in her body and laid waste to all of her past sexual experiences. There wasn't a man on Earth who could equal what this man had just done to her.

And that was only the appetizer. She couldn't wait to see what he did for the main course. Greedy bitch that she was, she wanted more, and she wanted it badly. But she had a job to do, and there was that pesky pact between sisters—no sleeping with the guests. None. Zero. Zilch. And big sister never broke the rules, though she'd stretched them to their breaking point tonight. They had to get off the boat first so he wouldn't be a guest anymore. Then it'd be okay. Their pact didn't extend off the party premises. Or at least, she'd just amended that particular rule.

Izzy walked out of the stall she'd been hiding in, ignoring Lauren's knowing smirk, and acting as if fooling around in the bathroom was something she did every day.

She stood in front of the sink and checked her makeup, washed her hands and straightened her clothes. All the while Lauren watched.

"Your boyfriend is a stubborn man," Lauren noted.

"That he is." It would seem Lauren didn't know about Party Crashers, which didn't surprise Izzy. After all, for them to be effective, everyone should think they were real party crashers.

"Perhaps, you can convince him to enjoy the party a little. He's not doing anyone any favors, including himself, by refusing to cooperate. That is if you really know him."

"Of course, I know him." Izzy put just the right amount of indignant haughtiness in her voice.

Lauren didn't look convinced. "I saw the commotion when you tried to board the boat."

"Just a little misunderstanding."

"I wonder. I really wonder." Lauren looked her up and down as if assessing her. Turning she left the room.

Izzy smoothed back her hair, hoping she didn't look like she'd done what she'd just done. Lauren was on to her, and that was the number one party crasher rule: don't ever let the guests discover that you weren't invited.

Faking a cool, confident smile, Izzy ventured back into the main room. Betheni was on her in a second.

"What the hell happened to you?"

"Building good will with the team captain." She could never lie to Betheni. Her sister saw right through Izzy's every lie. Either Betheni was damn perceptive or Izzy was a damn poor liar.

Betheni's perfectly shaped eyebrows disappeared under her bangs. "Are you melting his icy heart any?"

"Let's say there's been plenty of heat."

"Tread lightly. This isn't what we're about. And you have a tendency to fall in love first and ask questions later." Betheni, on the other hand, did not have that problem. Her heart never seemed to get involved with her dalliances.

"I know, but sometimes a girl's gotta do what a girl's gotta do for the greater good."

"Whose greater good? Yours, his, or the company's?"

Izzy opened her mouth to answer, but Betheni held up her hand. "Do what you have to, but don't compromise what we stand for."

"He's going to dance with me. Once he hits the floor, the team's boycott will shatter."

Betheni almost smiled. "I'll do my part. I've been eyeing that tall Swede all night. Don't do anything I wouldn't do." Betheni winked and sashayed off.

And that left Izzy a hell of a lot of leeway.

Taking a deep breath, Izzy refocused on her job, making this the best party ever. Right now it wasn't. In fact, far from it. The team sulked at the tables in the back of the room, either wolfing down food or guzzling alcohol and ignoring the advances of the women and the attempts of the coaching staff to get them on their feet. Even though some of the younger players looked ready to cave at times, threatening glares from the veterans pinned them to their seats.

She had to take action soon before the players were too drunk to notice and management was too disgusted to care and her fledging business crashed into the boards on its first skate across the ice.

A few couples braved the dance floor, including Ethan and Lauren, while Emma and Avery grabbed mics and sang a popular country song in their sultry voices. Several hockey players licked their lips as they watched the twins. It wouldn't take much to break this party wide open. All she had to do was get the cooperation of Cooper, who currently didn't look the least bit ready to cooperate. He stood in the back of the room, behind the team tables, like a sentinel, in his usual stance of arms crossed over his chest and wearing his trademark scowl. He'd gone back to pissed off mode, despite her best efforts and his.

Time to push him further and see how far he'd go.

* * * *

What a fucking wuss Cooper had been.

Pretty women had been his weakness in the past, and he'd paid dearly for it with expensive gifts, trips, even an apartment or two, and once with his heart. He'd hardened that very heart to women after his fiancée stomped all over it and left the gory remains spread all over Twitter, Facebook, and the gossip sites.

Never going there again. Women were for recreation. That was all. Because in his world, all the good women were married, attached, had kids, or were too young. Cooper didn't rob the cradle. He liked his women mature, sexy, and adventurous. Yeah, like a woman who'd do him on a public bathroom counter.

Now that turned him on, and he'd lowered his guard twice, forgotten his mission, betrayed his former coach and fans, and the charity he'd left behind. Hell, the whole Gainesville community was mourning the loss of the Giants. At least he liked to think they were.

Izzy was a dangerous woman. He'd never felt such instant physical chemistry. Never wanted to fuck a woman as badly as he did her. If Lauren hadn't pounded on that bathroom door, who knows what they'd be doing about now.

He'd be fooling himself if he thought she was done trying to manipulate him into doing her bidding.

Izzy walked toward him, determination etched on her beautiful face. She wanted that dance. And if he danced with her, his teammates would follow. Parker would win, and he'd have betrayed the very city and fans who'd been so loyal to him over the years. Yet, in the words of his take-no-prisoners agent, loyalty has no place in professional sports. This was a business, plain and simple. A guy goes where the money is, or in his case, where the team happened to be moved.

"There you are, honey." Izzy slid up next to him, cupped his face in her hands, and kissed him soundly. Several of the guys hooted and whistled. Cooper stood completely still, arms at his sides, refusing to touch her, even though his fingers itched to stroke that creamy skin. It took every ounce of willpower he possessed and then some. She pulled him to her like the planets were pulled to the sun, and his body definitely wanted to be in her orbit even as his head warned against the idea.

Push her away now. End this stupid charade. Hell, he could report her to management as a party crasher, and they'd lock her up somewhere for the remainder of the cruise.

Cooper stared into her chocolate brown eyes, soulful eyes, eyes that'd seen a lot, and continued to fight. He liked that. He liked her, and he hated himself for liking her because when he liked a woman, he wanted to please her. That was the way he rolled.

And he knew what this woman wanted.

A piece of him. Not just his body but something infinitely more dangerous. And he didn't give that away, not anymore.

Pulling away from her, he headed outside for some air to the deck that circled the entire boat. It was a chilly night, but the earlier misty rain had given way to stars. An almost full moon cast a ray of light across the calm water. It was a beautiful night, and he steeled himself against that beauty.

He heard Izzy's heels clicking on the deck behind him, and he walked faster, hoping she'd give up.

"You owe me a dance," she called out to him. Her heels tapped louder until she grabbed his arm and spun him around.

"I don't owe you anything. I believe I paid you quite nicely already. Seems you owe me something." He stared down at her, vacillating between running like hell and kissing her ruby red lips until they both collapsed to the deck in a tangle of writhing bodies.

"Dance with me." Her chin jutted out stubbornly, and he had to chuckle. She was a fiery female, and he loved women with spunk because their enthusiasm carried over nicely into bed.

"What do you care? You're a party crasher."

She didn't respond, instead she leaned against the railing, shivering and hugging herself. Cooper couldn't staunch the wave of sympathy that rolled through him. He put an arm around her waist, pulling her close, as he, too, stared out at the water.

"So how long have you and your sisters been doing this?" He tried to sound casual, but her hip rubbing against his caused his voice to drop to a husky rasp.

"Crashing parties?"

"Yeah."

She sighed, as if the wind had gone out of her sails. "Since we were kids and our parents would be gone for weeks at a time, leaving us to fend for ourselves after the meager amount of money they gave us ran out."

He frowned, feeling indignant for her and protective at the same time. "What the hell? Why weren't they reported?"

"We lived in a private neighborhood, and we did everything we could to keep from being broken apart into separate foster homes. Our parents aren't bad people, but they should've left the condoms on and not had kids."

"Why did they leave you guys alone? Where did they go?" He really wanted to know. The answer was important to him for some unfathomable reason.

She tilted her head and looked up at him, as if assessing his worthiness to hear the next bit of information. "Ever heard of To the Max?"

"The rock group?"

"That's the one. Rock and Fawn Maxwell are our parents. They've spent their entire lives either chasing the dream or trying to recover it." Something flickered briefly in her eyes, pain, sadness, vulnerability. He wanted to wrap her in his arms and promise he'd always keep her safe and secure. Only he didn't because he couldn't care, shouldn't care. Yet a part of him did.

Izzy stared out at the water, her beautiful face an expressionless mask, but Cooper had glimpsed the truth behind the mask.

"They never recovered their dream?" he asked.

"No, and they still haven't stopped trying, but at least we're not under their roof anymore."

"I'm sorry. That must have been tough."

"It was. Especially when the house got foreclosed on, and we lived in a fifth wheel on their friend's five acres. But as our parents' children, we could sing, dance, and entertain like no one's business."

"So you took those talents to parties?"

"Yes. One night when I was sixteen, we were out and about, looking for a way to score some food, maybe a generous stranger or a shopkeeper who'd hire us for a few hours under the table. We stumbled upon an old house used for weddings and such. There was huge reception going on, and the caterers were bringing in tray after tray of food. We were starving, and the food smelled so good. We looked at each other and decided to give it a shot. Weddings are great because usually one side doesn't know the other side's guests and family. And we were relatively well-dressed in Mom's vintage designer clothes."

"So you crashed the party."

"We didn't just crash it, we made it. It was the dullest party ever, and we walked in and got the party started. Both the bride and groom thanked us profusely, even though I don't think they ever figured out who the hell we were. We snuck out with tons of leftovers and ate off them for a week."

"And so your career started?"

She frowned for a moment. "You could say that."

"Why did you pick this party to crash?"

"Hot hockey players and a cruise on Elliott Bay. What party crasher could turn away from that?"

He smiled. "Your secret is safe with me."

"I appreciate it."

Something seemed a little off with her, as if she weren't telling him the entire story, but he couldn't imagine what else there'd be to tell. She'd been open with him, so why hide anything? Yet, something didn't add up.

"So how about you? Why are you being such a douche about this party? You seem like a nice guy." She leaned her head on his shoulder, and he pulled her closer to his side.

"I am a nice guy, but I don't want to be here. I want to be cut or traded, and I'll take my chances elsewhere."

"Seattle isn't such a bad place. I've lived here all my life."

"You're used to the incessant gloom."

"You'll be playing hockey indoors during the gloomiest months, so what difference does it make?"

He stared into her eyes, and forgot for a moment what difference it did make. "I, uh." He shook his head in an attempt to

35

ward off this weird spell she'd put on him. "I'd been with the team my entire career, loved the city, the weather, the fans, my coaches."

"The fans here are great. Just wait and see. Seattle is going to be an incredible hockey town." Her eyes lit up and the corners of her sexy mouth tipped up into an engaging smile. She almost made him want to believe her.

"Are you a hockey fan?"

"I will be. That's how most Seattleites feel now that we have a team."

He nodded, absorbing her words, and even toying in his mind with the excitement of starting something new and different in Seattle. But those were traitorous thoughts.

"You're hurting yourself and your teammates more than anyone else. You know that, don't you?" She glanced over her shoulder at the party going on inside, or at least attempting to go on.

"I'm proving a point."

"For what purpose? This team isn't moving back to Florida. This is Sockeye country now. Why don't you embrace it? Help us build something to be proud of, instead of tearing it down and undermining it. You're a leader. Lead. Make the best of this situation. Your teammates need you to be that guy. To shuck off your grudges and move forward."

"I'm not holding grudges."

She rolled her eyes. "I've been reading a thing or two about this team. Mr. Parker fired your beloved coach and his staff, only brought a few existing employees with him, including his now fiancée, and he changed the team's entire identity."

"There was no reason to fire our coach."

"I don't know Parker. I don't know his rationale. I did read he wanted a fresh start, and the old coaching staff wasn't going in the direction he wanted to go."

"We were one goal away from playing in the Finals. Parker doesn't know a damn thing about hockey."

"He'll learn. He's got the money, the time, and the ambition. The team's old owners were idiots. They bled the team dry and wasted the meager profits on gambling in Vegas. You know that."

Cooper nodded. She'd done her research, and he couldn't deny the truth. He'd hated the old team's ownership. They'd been slimy assholes who'd used the team as their own private bank account until they'd raided the coffers to the point that the team had fallen deeply in debt.

"Mr. Parker's group is the richest ownership in the league. He's committed to bringing a championship to Seattle and putting the best team possible on the ice."

Cooper couldn't mount a single, viable argument. The words escaped him.

"Have you ever won the Cup?"

"Uh, no." Cooper hated admitting it, but he'd never even played in the Final.

"Isn't it a hockey player's dream to skate for a team committed to bringing one home?"

Cooper shrugged, starting to feel like a stubborn, misguided idiot.

"Did you know that the Seattle Metropolitans were the first US team to ever win the Cup?"

"Uh, yeah, I heard that somewhere."

"Give Seattle a chance, Cooper. Quit shooting yourself and your team in the foot."

"It's a pretty big foot; makes an easy target." He grinned his lopsided grin, the one guaranteed to make any woman forget her name but definitely not his.

Only her lecture wasn't over.

"You need to get over it. You aren't going back to Florida. Build your career here or get traded or cut. Is that what you really want?" She fingered the collar of his dress shirt and tugged on his tie to pull his face closer to hers. "I don't want to see you go."

"You don't?" He stared at her lips only a few inches away, wanting to kiss her, yet holding back.

"No, I don't." She planted a wet kiss on his lips and drew back before he could recover. "Dance with me."

"Why is it so important to you?" His voice was raspy, husky with lust.

"Because it's important to you to move on and embrace your new home."

How could a man say no to a woman who put him first, a woman with beautiful eyes and a delectable body?

He nodded. He couldn't help himself. She'd decimated his resolve, not to mention his stubborn vengeance. He hoped his guys forgave him, but she was right. Nothing he did would move this team back to Florida, a team poised on the brink of success, a team he'd watch grow over the past ten years. It might not be the same location, but it was the same guys.

He was their captain. They trusted him to lead them in the right direction, and he hadn't lately, but tonight would be a start.

* * * *

Izzy couldn't believe she'd worn him down that easily. A man like Cooper Black didn't give up his convictions without a fight unless he believed those convictions hadn't been correct in the first place. When she'd told him dancing was important for him, not her, she'd meant it. To hell with the money dangling on the line for Party Crashers, she wanted Cooper to embrace this city and give his team a fighting chance. For that, she'd do just about anything, and for Cooper, she'd skate into the great unknown or dance in the stars.

Holding her hand, Cooper led her inside to the dance floor. She winked at her sisters over his shoulder as he pulled her body to his. The music pulsed around them in a sexy, sultry beat, while lights flashed with dizzying speed.

Over his shoulder, the shocked, open-mouthed faces of his teammates swam in her vision. Then they broke ranks and flooded the floor, dancing all around them with any available woman they could find. The party had gone from bust to blast in ten seconds.

And Cooper had led the charge. She was proud of him, as if she had a right to be.

The now crowded dance floor with its pulsating lights and club atmosphere afforded a bit of anonymity to the dancers in the crowd. It was hard to tell where one body started and another ended in the mass of wriggling, gyrating hips, waving arms, and flashes of leg.

She glanced over at Betheni dirty dancing with the gorgeous Swede, Cedric. Betheni had always been as daring as her red hair, the wild child of the family, though the twins were a close second. Her sister threaded her fingers through Cedric's hair and kissed the hell out of his mouth, while her hands roamed up and down his back.

Cooper tugged on her hair bringing her attention back to him and his large muscular body pressing against hers. She could feel his erection against her stomach.

"So how the hell did we meet?"

Izzy blinked several times. "Meet?" She tried to switch gears from his dick to his question. It took her a few seconds. In fact, so long he clarified the question.

"Yeah, we've been together for what? A month or so. How'd we meet?" He grinned down at her and his blue eyes sparkled.

Izzy laughed. He might be an ass at times, but he could be a charmer, too. "I swept you off your feet when you came into my coffee shop."

"You own a coffee shop?"

"No, I'm a barista. You ordered a double-caramel macchiato."

"That's sounds like a girlie drink." He made a face, and she had to laugh.

"Oh, honey, that's what I liked most about you. You weren't afraid to show your feminine side."

Both brows disappeared under his shaggy mop of luxurious dark hair. "Trust me, I don't have a feminine side. I'm all male."

"Prove it." A dumb challenge, but hey, she was all-in, regardless of the consequences.

A smile tugged on the corner of his so-kissable mouth. He dipped his head and claimed her lips and took a slow, sensuous stroll from one corner of her mouth to the other. She threaded her fingers in his hair. His lips pressed hers, demanding yet oddly gentle. She opened to him, closing her eyes and savoring the sensations of his tongue tangling with her tongue in a dance as powerful as the one their bodies were engaged in.

She inhaled the pure male scent of him mingled with a trace of aftershave, a heady combination of civilized and uncivilized man. Opening her eyes, she found him watching her with interest, those blue eyes shining with desire. He broke the kiss to nibble on her neck. She sighed a sigh of raw pleasure. His lips rained feather-light kisses on her neck, around the shell of her ear.

"I'm going to fuck you before the night's over." His steady gaze drove home the promise.

She nodded, unable to speak or even comment.

"I'd like to take you up against that wall over there while everyone watches." The intensity in his eyes said he wasn't kidding, and right now she'd probably go along with anything he wanted. Anything. Including fucking her brains out in a crowded ballroom up against the wall.

Waltzing her into a dark corner away from most of the dancers, he slid his big hands under her skirt and gripped her ass, grinding her against him. She was ready, her common sense replaced by blind lust. Izzy wrapped a long leg around his thigh and wedged her hand between their bodies, rubbing his erection. He groaned and his eyes rolled back in his head.

"It's your turn next, handsome."

"I'm counting on it," he rasped as she continued to stroke his erection. "Oh, fuck, you are so hot."

"So are you." Izzy nipped his earlobe, and he groaned, sounding like an animal in pain.

"Let's get to fuck out of here."

"We're on a boat."

"We'll swim to shore if we have to." Grabbing her hand, he pulled her along with him.

She couldn't do this. Shouldn't do this. Well, crap, she was going to do this.

"I thought we were going to do it in the ballroom?" she teased breathlessly as he stopped at the dessert table.

His heavy-lidded eyes regarded her. "Ever done it in public?"

Izzy shook her head.

"I figured as much. Probably be better if the first time was private."

"We're on a boat with a couple hundred other people."

"We'll find a place." He loaded up a plate with delectable desserts.

"Are you hungry?"

"I will be after I'm done with you. Screwing a beautiful woman's brains out makes me hungry."

"You romantic devil. Talk sexy some more to me." She moved closer to him, drunk on his hard, muscled body and hypnotic blue eyes. She'd lost her mind, her common sense, and every other thing she'd held dear over the years. All Izzy wanted was him, and the consequences be damned. She glanced over her shoulder, but none of her sisters paid her any mind, busy as they were entertaining their own sexy hockey players.

So much for their moratorium on sleeping with the guests.

Balancing the plate on one hand, Cooper led Izzy back toward

40

the private dining areas and hoped like hell no one was using them.

"So we've tried both bathrooms. What do you suggest this time?"

"I think I know just the place."

Minutes later after a few large bills were laid in a waiter's palm, Cooper escorted her into a private dining suite suitable for a small group of six to eight. On the upper deck of the boat, the large windows afforded a great view of the city, not that they'd be looking at the view.

Cooper placed the plate on a spare serving cart and turned to her. "This could get messy."

"I like messy," she countered. Oh, God, what was she doing? This was so unprofessional, so incorrect, so bad of her.

"You'd better take that expensive dress off." He looked her up and down and licked his lips.

"Why don't you take it off for me?" she teased with a saucy smirk. He seemed to like that idea.

Cooper backed her against the wall and lowered the straps on her dress, freeing her breasts. He dipped his head for an encore performance and sucked on a nipple. She arched her back and moaned while she unzipped his pants, slid her fingers along his flat belly, and squeezed his cock. It was his turn to groan.

"Let's get—"

Footsteps and voices came closer and closer. They both froze, him with his lips on her nipple, her with her fingers wrapped around his penis.

"Oh, crap, someone's coming. Did you lock the door?" Izzy asked.

"I thought you did."

The doorknob turned, and they dived behind the small bar in the corner of the room.

"Hey, in here. Nice and private and no one's in here." Cedric's voice.

"Perfect, big boy, now let's see if your stamina extends beyond the ice." Betheni giggled.

"I assure you, it does." Cedric was breathing heavily, his voice muffled at times. Izzy didn't want to picture what might be muffling it, such as a part of her sister's anatomy.

A zipper was unzipped. Clothing rustled. Another zipper, more rustling, a hearty chuckle, followed by heavy breathing. Talk about a mood killer. This *was* her sister about to have sex with a virtual stranger and only a few feet away.

"They're going to do it right here," Izzy whispered.

"Like we weren't?" Leave it to a man to point out the obvious.

"Yeah, but we were here first."

"They don't know that."

More groaning, laughter, dirty sex talk. Izzy so did not want to hear this.

"I need to stop them."

"Why?" He nuzzled her neck, planting little kisses along her jaw.

"Listen to them." She held her hands up to her ears, but couldn't block her imagination. She had to stop them before they got naked.

So much for the Party Crasher pact. How odd, it wasn't like either of them had ever done anything like this before. Chalk it up to hockey players with hot bodies and hotter intentions.

* * * *

Cooper couldn't believe his bad luck, but as a closet optimist, he wasn't giving up yet. He could take her behind this bar while her sister and his buddy drowned out any noise Cooper and Izzy might make. Izzy's sister was pretty damn vocal.

Stupid, maybe. Desperate, hell, yes. Hard as a rock, abso-fucking-lutely.

Cooper slid his hand under the V of Izzy's dress, cupping her breast. She stiffened and shoved his hand away. "They'll hear us," she hissed.

"You're ruining the mood, honey." He sucked on her earlobe.

"It's already ruined. I can't hide here while they're doing it a few feet away. She's my sister."

Well, hell.

Cooper's brain worked overtime in an attempt to salvage the evening. His dick throbbed, almost painfully. God, he needed her. He couldn't explain it, but she'd burrowed under his skin, a place he hadn't allowed a woman in a long time, and she'd done it in a few short hours.

Besides he had an entire tray of desserts he'd wanted to

sample—on her body.

Oh, yeah, that's it. Right there. Betheni let out a rebel yell to equal all rebel yells.

Izzy leapt to her feet before Cooper could stop her. "That's enough."

Cooper sheepishly crawled to his feet to survey the scene before him. If he hadn't been so horny, the twin deer-in-the-headlight expressions on Betheni's and Cedric's faces would've doubled him over with laughter.

Betheni lay sprawled on the table—the exact table he'd planned to use to take Izzy. Dammit. The straps on Betheni's dress were pulled down, her skirt was pushed up, and her thighs were spread wide. Cedric lay across the top of her, one hand between her legs, one on her breast.

Betheni screeched, an ear-shattering screech, and twisted away from Cedric. The violence of the motion sent her rolling to the floor and Cedric slamming to the floor on the opposite side of the table.

Izzy ran to her sister's side, while Cooper walked more leisurely to Cedric's side and glared down at him.

Cedric sat up and rubbed his back. "Fuck, that hurt."

Cooper gave him a not-so-gentle nudge in the ass with his foot. "What the fuck are you doing in here?"

Cedric pushed himself to his feet, still rubbing his back. "I could ask the same of you." He stared pointedly at Cooper's crotch, calling attention to Cooper's unzipped fly. Cooper quickly zipped it up.

Together, they glanced at the women. Betheni was on her feet, smoothing out her dress, pulling up straps, pulling down her skirt. Both women looked as if they'd been out for a stroll in gale force winds.

Hands on her hips, Izzy turned to her sister. "You know we have a pact."

"And so do you." Betheni braced her hands on her hips too, making them look like a pair of sexy bookends.

"This—this—Swedish oaf had his hand between your legs, and you were screaming for more." Izzy pointed accusingly at Cedric.

"Hey, now, I'm not an oaf—"

Izzy and Betheni both shot Cedric a murderous look. The huge man, who'd faced down the toughest men in the league, backed up several steps, obviously not wanting any part of a possible bloody catfight, as he inched toward the door. Cooper was no fool; he skirted the two women himself, several feet from safety and freedom.

"What were you doing in here with that toothless Neanderthal?" Betheni shouted.

Cooper ran his tongue over his mouth. All his teeth were still there. "I'm not—"

Both women turned on him and Cooper froze. He tried a tentative smile and received two kiss-ass scowls in return. Cedric reached the door and bolted through it. In three long strides, Cooper followed.

Both men stood in the hallway staring at the closed door. Angry, muffled words echoed from the other side.

Cooper ran a hand through his unruly hair and smoothed it back. "Damn."

Cedric blew out a relieved breath. "That was close. I thought we might end up castrated."

"No shit."

"I haven't seen you so tied up over a woman in a long time."

"I'd like her to tie me up, or even better, I'd like to tie her up." Cooper grinned. Cedric didn't.

"Are you walking away or are you going for it?"

"I don't know." He really didn't know. She did stuff to him, not just physically, but emotionally, getting more than his dick involved in this insane attraction to a woman he barely knew. That made him vulnerable, and he avoided vulnerable more than he avoided sushi.

Cooper cast one last, longing look toward the closed door, imagining Izzy all messy and ready for sex. He wasn't done with that woman yet. The night was young and the boat would soon be docking. This party wasn't over until the fat lady skated home, and she wasn't skating off the rink until he said so.

Chapter 5—Drop Pass

Izzy threw back her head and started laughing when the guys ran out like the devil was on their tails. She couldn't help it. Those big, strong alpha males couldn't handle a little sisterly disagreement. How funny was that? Betheni joined in, both of them laughing until their sides hurt. Finally, Izzy managed to catch her breath.

"We scared the crap right out of them, didn't we?" Betheni smiled, even though her eyes were still a little dilated and her hands shaky.

Izzy turned toward her and went on the offensive before her sister had a chance to state the obvious. "What were you thinking, fooling around with a guest at a party? You know we don't do that." She spoke calmly in her matter-of-fact, older sister, lecturing mode. No one would guess what a screwed up mess she was inside with conflicting thoughts bouncing around inside her head like a duck in a whirlpool.

"Really? And what were you doing in here with him?" Betheni raised her eyebrows and tilted her head toward the door the men had escaped through.

"We were dressed," Izzy shot back, trying to muster up indignance over something she had very well planned to do if she hadn't been interrupted.

Betheni walked over to the dessert tray and made a show of clearing her throat. "I see you were in here for a little dessert." She popped a chocolate-covered strawberry in her mouth.

Izzy joined her and picked up the small bite-sized cheesecake. "That's right. Just dessert."

"Us, too."

"What the hell were we both thinking?"

Betheni looked longingly at the door. "He's really hot, sexy, and a great dancer."

"So's Cooper." Cooper attracted her to the point that she'd been willing to ruin her new business, destroy her reputation, and decimate her sisters' respect. No man was worth that.

Or was he? Obviously in the heat of the moment, she'd thought he was, and so had Betheni. Yet, she expected this behavior from the family wild child. No one expected it from the practical older sister.

"You're really hot for him, aren't you?" Betheni asked.

Izzy snorted and licked some chocolate off her fingers. To think she could've been licking chocolate out of Cooper's belly button or off his—

"Isabella!" Betheni snapped her fingers in front of Izzy's face.

Izzy jumped with a guilty start. "Sorry, he is hot, so frigging hot, I almost gave up everything we've worked for just to screw his brains out one time."

"Me, too." Betheni tried to look solemn, but she didn't do solemn well. In fact, her lips twitched until she gave into a full-blown bad girl grin. "Go after him. Even good girls need to be bad once in a while."

"I can't. Not here."

"Then go home with him. I'm sure you'd be invited."

"I don't do one-night stands."

"By the look in his eyes, it wouldn't be just one night. The man was completely smitten."

"You think?"

"I know. Trust me." Betheni turned on the lights, dug a compact out of her purse, and refreshed her makeup. "Let's go back out and join the world."

Izzy grabbed her sister's makeup kit and did her own emergency makeover, but no amount of makeup covered up lips swollen from Cooper's kisses, eyes shiny with desire, and hair so messy it looked like she did it that way on purpose.

Composing herself, she walked into the hallway and ran headfirst into Ethan Parker. He put his hands on her shoulders and set her back on her feet. "Isabella, I've been looking for you."

"Oh, I, uh, my sister and I were discussing strategy."

Ethan grinned. "As far as I'm concerned, you've done more than enough. You're off the clock. Enjoy the party. It's a rousing success and wouldn't have been without you and your sisters. The guys are dancing up a storm, talking to the coaches, making plans. You've broken the ice, literally, and I can't pay you enough for what you've managed to accomplish."

"Well, thank you." It was nothing that couldn't be solved without having the team captain's tongue down her throat, hands on her ass, and lips in places they shouldn't be.

"I don't know how you did it. The way those boys were scowling at the beginning of the night, I didn't think anyone would get through to them."

"Thank you, Mr. Parker." Izzy smiled her most gracious smile.

"It was our pleasure," Betheni added in total innocence.

"Call me Ethan. Great job. You'll be getting a bonus for this, and I'll be recommending you to our friends." He grinned as Lauren came up beside him. "Stop by the team office next week, and I'll have a check waiting at the front desk."

"I will, and thank you, Ethan."

Ethan grinned at his fiancée and headed outside to the deck. "We did it."

"We sure did." Izzy should have felt on top of her world, and she did to a point, but there was still the little problem of Cooper and wanting to see him again.

"Let's get back to the party." Izzy almost broke into a jog, but something solid stopped her progress as she rounded the corner.

Cooper's sold chest filled her line of vision. She lifted her face upward. Judging by the thin, angry line of his lips and his hard jaw, he'd heard every word of her conversation with Ethan.

And he wasn't happy.

* * * *

Cooper had made up his mind. He wasn't going to let this woman get away. Sure, he wanted to sleep with her, but it was more than that. Something he hadn't felt in a long time, and he wanted to explore that heady feeling of being with a woman who intrigued him beyond the bedroom.

So he'd gone in search of Izzy to do the right thing and ask her out like a proper guy would a classy lady. Surely, the bathroom incidents were aberrations. They'd never happened to her before, but it was this intense chemistry between them—the same crazy feelings he felt—that drove her to do something she would never normally do.

At least that was what he'd wanted to believe.

Until he'd overheard her talking to Ethan Parker.

Humiliated and feeling like all kinds of fool, he rounded the corner with both guns blazing. She'd used him and used him quite nicely. He'd let down his guard for one night, believed in a woman for the first time in years, and this was what happened.

Her eyes opened wide as she spotted him in all his indignant fury.

"Are you going to be okay?" Her sister gave her a pat on the arm.

Izzy gave Betheni a curt nod to dismiss her. "I'm fine. Cooper and I need to talk."

Without another word, Betheni scurried away, glancing over her shoulder one last time before she disappeared back into the party.

"How much did you hear?"

"All of it." Cooper ground his teeth together, expecting his jaw to shatter any moment or at least for his many implants to be ground to dust.

"I can explain." She moved toward him, but he held his hands up to keep her body out of his personal space.

"You were paid to do me." Beneath the anger, he sounded pathetic and betrayed, even to his own ears.

"That would make me a prostitute, wouldn't it?" Now her annoyance matched his. She propped her hands on her hips, stood straighter, and pulled her shoulders back, inadvertently drawing attention to those nice breasts of hers, the same ones he'd been enjoying several minutes earlier.

His mouth went dry, and he licked his lips. "Uh, that's not what I'm saying." No, he didn't believe she screwed for money. Not deep down inside. Maybe his instincts hadn't always been the best when it came to women, but something rang true in her words and her previous actions. Her out-of-control attraction couldn't have been an act, any more than it had been with him.

"Then what are you saying?" she asked.

He didn't know what he was saying, had no clue what he was accusing her of. His anger turned to confusion.

"Ethan paid us to make sure this party was successful."

"And to be successful, you had to have me on board."

She nodded, her own anger fizzling out. She clasped her hands together in front of her and wrung them. "That's true, but I never planned on it going as far as it did. I just wanted to get you to dance, have a good time. It was never supposed to be sexual."

"And I'm supposed to believe you didn't plan on using every means you had."

"Believe what you want. That's not what we're about." She stared at her feet, obviously embarrassed. "It got out of hand. Something about you just made me forget every rule we had."

48

"I'm supposed to believe that?" Cooper ran his hand through his hair, frustrated and confused. "I don't know what to believe."

Izzy sighed, looking as sad as the beagle he'd had as a child with those big brown eyes that could melt the hardest heart. Only Izzy wasn't his trusted, loyal childhood friend. She was a woman with a job to do, and that job had involved using him to reach her goal. Whether it included actual physical acts with him or not, he didn't know. His heart didn't want to believe it did, even though his head screamed "sucker."

Cooper shook his head. "Know what? I was looking for you to ask you out on a date like a gentleman asks out a lady. That's what an idiot I am."

"Cooper, I—I'm sorry." Her face crumpled, she looked ready to cry, and it took every ounce of determination he'd honed over years of scrabbling and fighting in the toughest of sports not to give in to those beautiful brown eyes.

"I'm not. I'm ashamed of you. I thought we had something, and you took advantage of my stupidity. Goodbye, Izzy." He turned and walked away, grateful the boat was docking, and he could get the hell off the damn thing before he lost his resolve and caved to his baser needs.

He could get that from any number of women, but he'd thought Izzy could give him more, thought she'd stave off the loneliness of a single man, give him a reason to like this new place that'd been forced upon him.

Now he'd get none of the above.

Chapter 6—Delayed Penalty

Izzy held it together until she'd dropped off her sisters and shut the door to her little apartment. When she snapped the deadbolt shut, something snapped inside her.

She threw herself down on the ratty living room couch and cried her eyes out, not caring if her makeup ran or her expensive dress wrinkled beyond repair. Her sobs drowned out the sounds from the freeway next to her apartment. Her heart cracked wider with each second that passed.

She should be thrilled. Ecstatic. On top of the world.

Her company had just pleased a very wealthy client and was on the verge of something big. Really big.

Right now, none of that mattered. It would tomorrow or the next day when the shock of all these crazy feelings wore off and eased the humiliation of being branded a prostitute.

Had she done everything she'd done just for the money? Because if she had, then she deserved that title. God, she'd been a fool over a man who didn't care one damn bit about her. He'd used her just like she'd used him.

Only it hadn't really been like that. Not for her. She'd felt more, a seed of something that could've blossomed and grown into a beautiful flower, but instead of nurturing it with mutual trust and affection, she'd fed it with lies and behaved irresponsibly.

Cooper was right about her. She should be ashamed of herself. She'd taken advantage of their initial attraction, even though she never planned on it going as far as it had, never dreamed she'd lose her mind looking into those deep blue eyes, and shed her scruples as quickly as she shed her clothes for him.

Shame on her.

He'd wanted to ask her out on a real date, show her the respect she didn't deserve after her inexcusable and unprofessional behavior.

She'd been an idiot on so many levels.

Sitting up, Izzy wiped her face with tissues, blew out several deep breaths, and blinked the tears away. This was stupid. She barely knew the man. He was gorgeous, ripped, and a great dancer. So what? She called forth her practical side, that side which poo-pooed such bullshit as falling hard for a guy she'd only known three hours.

She'd learn from this mistake. Never again would she enter into any kind of a physical relationship with a party guest, not that it'd been a problem before, but it would not be again.

Her mind flashed back to those laughing blue eyes blazing with desire during their bathroom trysts, sympathetic with concern over her childhood story, and brimming with irritation because she'd latched on to him as a pretend boyfriend.

She sighed. It was over. The party was a success. They'd be making good money along with a bonus.

That's all that should matter.

Only it wasn't.

She missed him, crazy as it was. She shouldn't, but she did.

* * * *

Cooper opened his eyes to find Joker sitting on his chest staring him straight in the eyes. His head hurt like hell, courtesy of the half bottle of whiskey he drank when he arrived home.

"Hey, buddy. Miss me?" He reached up to pet the scruffy cat.

Joker meowed, most likely bitching about the quality of his life and the crappy servant he'd been forced to tolerate for more years than he could count.

"Yeah, I know. Life's a bitch."

Joker rubbed his face across Cooper's stubble.

"I met a woman last night. I thought she was someone special."

The cat studied him, as if to say, *I know where this is going.*

"Yeah, I kinda fell for her. She was gorgeous, great body, great dancer, confident, intelligent."

Joker's purring almost drowned out Cooper's words. Oh, to be a cat and not to have a worry in the world.

"I was going to ask her out until I discovered she'd used me, so I dumped her ass."

Joker dug his claws into Cooper's chest, but he didn't flinch. The pain didn't come close to matching the pain he felt inside. This was stupid. He didn't fall for a woman, not like this. Yet he had, and now he didn't know what the hell to do about it.

"Hey, you'd have done the same thing."

Joker continued to stare at him as if to say *dumb shit.*

Yeah, he'd wanted to spend more time with her, explore those unfamiliar feelings she elicited in him. He'd always been a bit of a daredevil, and she'd tempted him to take a chance on a relationship.

Only she'd been paid to do it. How did a guy get past that? And how did a guy get past that hot body, expressive eyes, sassy mouth, and long fucking legs? Obviously, he hadn't. He'd dreamt about her all night long, doing the things to her he hadn't gotten a chance to do on the boat, and letting her do the same to him.

He was a fool. A damn fool. She'd used him. That was a fact.

Despite it all, the truth behind her words about the team had sunk in. Nothing he did would move them back to Florida. Did he really want to leave his guys, guys he'd built a rapport with, and start over somewhere else?

The answer was no, he didn't.

Cooper sat up, knocking the cat off his chest. Casting an annoyed look over his shoulder, Joker stalked off in a huff and disappeared out the bedroom door, probably to extract revenge on the leg of an expensive piece of leather furniture.

* * * *

Cooper walked past Ethan Parker's sergeant major of an assistant, and swung open the door to Parker's office. Ethan looked up from his computer, surprise crossing his face.

His admin pushed her way past Cooper. "I'm sorry, Mr. Black. He got past me."

"It's okay, Mina. He can stay."

Mina hesitated and Ethan gave her an encouraging smile. With one last, disgusted look at Cooper, she left the office, shutting the door after her broad butt got through it.

"She's scary, that one," Cooper joked, trying to break the ice.

"Mina's been with me for years. I appreciate all she does." Ethan sat back, put his feet on the desk, and adopted a casual pose that was anything but casual. "What can I help you with, Coop?"

Cooper studied Ethan for a long moment, Ethan looked right back, his direct gaze never wavering.

He took a deep breath and let it out, as if it would cleanse him of all his ill-conceived notions. "I'm here to talk about the team, and what I can do to make this transition smoother."

"Are you serious?" Ethan's feet dropped to the floor, and he sat up straight. A slow smile spread across his face.

"Dead serious. I've been an ass. I want to start over."

Ethan nodded slowly but didn't answer right away. He was letting Cooper squirm, and Cooper had to respect him for that. The guy had some major balls. Finally, just as Cooper was starting to fidget, Ethan nodded slowly. "All right. Let's brainstorm some ideas. Let me take you to lunch."

"Sounds good." Cooper hesitated. "One other thing. Isabella Maxwell. How well do you know her?"

"I don't. Not really. I learned about her company through a mutual friend."

"What exactly is her company?"

"They're called the Party Crashers. They have a website. Look them up. They guarantee they can turn a bad party into a good one. Knowing your attitude and your teammates' toward this move and me personally, I figured that party could use all the help it could get. She did a great job, and I'll be the first to admit, I didn't believe they'd be able to pull it off."

Yeah, she'd done a great job, especially on Cooper. "That's it? They're paid to crash parties?"

"Yeah. That's it. Did you think there was more?"

"Uh, no. Not at all." Cooper stared over Ethan's head out the window, his brain a confused mash of conflicting thoughts.

"Seems like you two hit it off that night." Ethan stood and grabbed his coat, shrugging into it as he headed for the door, and Cooper followed. "Any chance you'll see Izzy again?"

"I don't know."

"She seems like a good woman."

"Yeah, she does," Cooper said, and he meant it.

Chapter 7—Power Play

When the bell tinkled over the coffee shop door, Izzy looked up and did a double take. A tall, fit man walked in, a hoodie pulled down low over his face.

His body looked a lot like Cooper's. But lately, she'd been seeing Cooper in every man who walked in that door, as if he'd come looking for her. It'd been a week, and she needed to get over him, but instead she'd taken to Googling his name, staring at pictures, and reading everything she could get her hands on about him, such as the charity work he'd done in Florida, how he always took time to talk to fans, how he played the game with all-in passion.

A woman had to admire a man like that.

She'd developed a bit of a fan crush on him, become a puck bunny before she'd ever seen her first professional game in person. Nothing unusual with that. Right?

Izzy tugged on the bottom of her Seattle Sockeyes number fourteen jersey that Ethan had given to her when she'd picked up her very generous check. Number fourteen happened to be Cooper's number.

She glanced around the coffee shop and back to the hooded man lingering near the doorway across the room. Midmorning wasn't her busiest time, and he was her only customer. A little jolt of fear ran through her, and she prayed she wasn't about to be robbed.

Izzy put on her bravest smile and waited for the man to come to the counter. His long strides carried him closer as he pulled the hood off his head. Her heart leapt over the Olympic high bar and set a world record. Her mouth dropped open. Her hands gripped the edge of the counter.

"Cooper," she choked out the words, shocked to see him. Delight raced through her body, alerting dormant parts to the hot man's presence, and alerted they were.

Too much.

"Hey." He stopped in front of the counter, his eyes on the menu board on the wall. "I'll have a double caramel macchiato." His lopsided grin warmed her heart.

"Do you even know what's in one?"

"Drink them all the time, gets me in touch with my feminine side."

"You don't have a feminine side."

He met her gaze but not before his eyes travelled lower and back up. "Number fourteen, huh?"

"Ethan gave it to me. Let me get that drink started right away."

He nodded. She could feel his eyes on her as she made his drink, watching her every move. She slid the drink across the counter to him.

He took a sip and licked his lips. "Yummy."

"I make the most awesome macchiato anywhere." She couldn't help but smile.

"You do, take it from a connoisseur." He grinned right back. "Can you join me? You don't seem too busy."

"Okay." Izzy tried not to sound too excited and poured herself a strong cup of coffee—she'd need it to get through the next few minutes—and joined him at a small table near the window. Outside the skies were gray with drizzle. "It's raining again."

Another smile quirked the corners of his mouth. "You know, this incessant rain is actually somewhat romantic."

"It is?"

"Yeah, or it would be if I had a special someone to share walks in the rain with me." He reached across the table and took her hand in his.

"I'm sure you'll find that person." She was afraid to read anything into the emotions lighting up his eyes.

"Maybe I already have." Cooper looked down at their intertwined fingers then back up. He swallowed and ran his free hand through his dark hair. "Izzy, I'm sorry. I called you a prostitute, and that was inexcusable. I hope you'll forgive me."

"I forgive you, and you were right, too. I was using you—at first. But it went further than that. I *never* get physically involved with guests or clients, ever. You blew through all my convictions with one epic, sexy smile."

"Really? Only one." He preened like a male lion after seducing his lioness into the den.

"Only one." She watched him, waiting and hoping.

"How about we start over?"

"That would be awesome."

He removed his hand from hers and stood. Her heart sank. He was leaving? Was that how he started over?

Instead he bent down and took her hand in his again. "I'm Cooper Black."

She giggled, batted her eyelashes, and gazed up at him. "I'm Izzy Maxwell."

"Well, Izzy, I think you and I should get to know each other better. Would you like to go to dinner with me tonight?"

"I'd love that, Cooper."

"So would I."

Cooper pulled Izzy to her feet and kissed her soundly, a kiss full of new beginnings and future promises—not to mention, hot enough to melt ice.

~ THE END ~

CRASHING THE NET (SEATTLE SOCKEYES)

GAME ON IN SEATTLE SERIES #3

By Jami Davenport

Hockey star Cooper Black and professional party crasher Izzy Maxwell return in this sequel to Crashing the Boards.

Jealous boyfriends and glitzy parties can be a recipe for disaster. When the gorgeous yet controlling Cooper interrupts a party Izzy was paid to crash and almost ruins her career as a professional party crasher, Izzy kicks him to the curb. She learned early in life not to count on anyone, and she will not relinquish her independence, not even to a sexy-as-sin pro athlete who can melt her heart with one wink.

As the Sockeyes hockey team opens their inaugural season in Seattle, Cooper finds himself minus a girlfriend and plus a surly teenaged nephew. Cooper doesn't want to be a surrogate dad, he doesn't want to play in Seattle, and he doesn't want to be alone. He misses Izzy, but seeing her with other men at parties turns him every shade of green. Regardless, he wants her back, and he's willing to change, if only she'll give him a second chance. Aware of her precarious finances, Cooper makes an offer she can't refuse by hiring her to be responsible for his nephew when he's traveling with the team.

Fearing Cooper isn't capable of changing his control-freak ways, Izzy resists his efforts to turn their financial arrangement into a personal relationship. He needs a sweet, docile girlfriend, and Izzy cannot be that woman. Yet, when tragedy strikes, Izzy is there when Cooper needs her the most, and love has a way of getting what it wants, no matter the circumstances.

Chapter 1—Neanderthal on Skates

Izzy could not believe her eyes.

That Neanderthal.

What was Cooper Black doing here? Other than ruining her business one big foot at a time. She turned her back on him and smiled up at Tanner Wolfe, the charismatic and overly confident young quarterback of the Seattle Steelheads.

Tanner cocked his head and leaned close, possessively stroking her neck. Izzy smiled up at him, faking interest when there wasn't any. After all, it was her job. Tanner wasn't Cooper, not by a long shot. Sure, he was gorgeous in a drop-your-panties-and-get-naked way, but he wasn't her type. She seemed to prefer surly and brooding over charming and carefree.

Tanner pulled her close for a slow dance, too close, so she put her hand between them and pushed. Over Tanner's shoulder, she spotted Cooper pacing on the outskirts of the crowd. Despite her annoyance with him, he was damn sexy when he went all caveman on her, ready to protect her from any perceived threat and throw her over his shoulder, claiming her as his own. He was one-hundred-percent male and made her feel one-hundred-percent female.

Tanner's hands slipped to her butt, and Cooper pawed the ground like a bull ready to charge. His eyes narrowed, and he stomped toward her and Tanner, pushing guests out of the way in a single-minded effort to get to her. The look on his face didn't exactly give the impression he was here for fun and games. In fact, he'd obviously forgotten how to shave in the past few weeks, lost the phone number of his barber, and disregarded any and all dress codes. Black tie did not mean jeans and T-shirt.

He was hot as hell and just as mad.

Regardless, Izzy plastered a welcoming smile on her face, hoping to diffuse his obvious anger. Heads turned around the crowded room and jaws dropped open. Elderly matrons of the arts stared in disbelief at the intruder with the manners of a drunken grizzly bear, even as they gazed appreciatively at the man's fine body and rugged face. They'd be having some good dreams tonight, and so would Izzy.

But she digressed.

Cooper could not interfere in her business like this, despite the jealous streak he'd been displaying recently. He needed to get over it and get a life. Training camp for hockey started in a month; maybe he'd be less smothering once he went back to work.

Izzy stepped away from Tanner, offering the Seattle quarterback an apologetic smile. He opened his mouth to say something but she held up a hand. "Hold that thought. I'll be back in a few. I have some business to attend to."

Tanner frowned, as he wasn't used to women leaving him high and horny. Well, tough. He wouldn't be scoring with her tonight any more than he'd scored in the last game of the season.

Leaving the quarterback to find a new game, Izzy marched toward Cooper, meeting him halfway. She grabbed his arm and spun him around, her anger giving her strength, and dragged him out of the ballroom, down the hall, and into a small private alcove.

"What are you doing here?" she hissed, ever mindful their voices could carry down the hallway to anyone loitering about the ballroom entrance.

"Looking for you," he growled right back while his gaze raked up and down her body clad in a form-fitting little black dress which revealed a tasteful amount of cleavage and bare thighs.

"Cooper, I told you I had to work tonight."

He scowled and stepped toward her, backing her up until she hit the wall behind her. He put his big hands on either side of her face and leaned in. "I don't like you hanging out with all these wealthy businessmen and athletes who're salivating after you like tomcats on the prowl."

"You are a wealthy athlete," she reminded.

"Exactly," he responded with a grimace.

"It's just a job." She stared up into his stormy blue eyes, forcing herself to stay on task and not get lost in those passionate depths.

"I have more than enough money to support you while you go back to school. You don't need to do this job."

"I love my job." Izzy shook her head. She would *never* be dependent on anyone. After all, when you couldn't trust your own parents to provide the bare minimum basics of food and shelter, why would you set yourself up to depend on anyone else?

"I don't." He glared down at her, his strong jaw set and his kissable mouth drawn in a firm line. If she kissed him right now, he'd forget about everything and the situation would be defused.

Until next time. She gathered her strength and did what she had to do. For herself, her sanity, and her business.

"You, buster—" she jabbed her finger in his hard chest. "Do not get a vote."

He ground his jaw. She cringed at the thought of what that'd do to his implants if he kept it up. "Cooper, please—"

"This isn't working. I can't live like this, not knowing where you are and what you're doing."

"You know where I am. I tell you what parties we're crashing."

"Yeah, but I worry about you." Concern softened the anger in his eyes, but judging by his clenched fists, it still bubbled beneath the surface even as he fought to control it.

"There's nothing to worry about." Izzy sighed. She wouldn't quit this job. Number one, she loved it. Number two, it supported her three younger sisters and their college tuitions. Number three, Cooper would not take away her ability to control her present or future.

"You don't know these people."

"I don't have to know them. It's not like I'm going to establish a relationship with any of them."

"You did with me." He pointed out the fact that they'd met at a party her company, the Party Crashers, had been hired to crash over a month ago.

"That was the only time that happened." She lifted her head and glared at him. "Is that what this is all about? You don't trust me?"

A muscle ticked in Cooper's square, stubbled jaw, and his face hardened to stone. That was all the answer she needed.

"You don't trust me," she stated, no longer asking a question. Something died inside her, like a little shoot pushing up through the earth only to be frozen by unseasonably cold spring weather.

Again, nothing but a stone-faced response.

"Cooper Black, how dare you?" She jabbed her finger in his chest again, so hard this time that he winced and backed up a few steps. Good, she hoped she drew blood. She jabbed him again, not caring if she broke a fingernail.

"Well, we almost did it at a party you were paid to crash."

Now that *really* pissed her off. "But we didn't. In fact we haven't done it yet."

"Not for my lack of trying," he muttered.

"What are you insinuating?" Izzy's blood boiled. She'd refused to sleep with Cooper, even though they'd done everything but. Something held her back, and she guessed that something had to do with trust issues from both sides and his controlling He-Man ways.

For a moment, uncertainty flashed across his ruggedly handsome face, as if he'd stepped in a pile and had no idea how to clean it off his shoes.

Sensing his momentary retreat, Izzy advanced on him, both guns blazing, along with her temper. "You think just because I'm not putting out to you, I must be putting out to someone else?"

His silence said it all.

"I thought we had something special. Obviously we don't. You are a Neanderthalic brute of epic proportions. Get out of here and let me do my job." She vibrated with fury. How dare this man ever think that. Just because she dressed the part at these parties she crashed didn't mean she put out to any and every man she met. Or even any man she met. In fact, it'd been so long since she'd put out, she'd probably regained her virginity.

Obviously, Cooper couldn't let that one go. She could see him battling with some inner demon, and the demon won. She could tell by the gleam in his eyes. "You're an uptight prude with delusions of getting your hooks into a wealthy hockey star."

Oh, now that stung. Really stung.

She reared back, standing straighter, and fisted her hands at her sides. Those were fighting words, and she hadn't survived—even thrived—years of neglect by absentee parents to tolerate that bullshit. "Fuck you." It wasn't exactly classy or eloquent, but those simple words did the job.

Being a proud man, she knew Cooper wouldn't take her dismissal lightly. "If I leave now, we're done."

"We *are* done." She pointed toward the bank of elevators, noticing for the first time that all three of her sisters stood several feet away gaping at the two of them. She ignored the girls. They'd talk later.

Something flashed in Cooper's eyes, gone as quickly as it came. Sadness? Remorse? Or relief. Hell if she knew.

"Good. I was just about done with your bossiness anyway." Giving her his broad back, he strode to the elevator. A few seconds later he was gone.

"Get back to the party," she ordered her sisters, playing the big sister role to the hilt. The twins gratefully escaped, but Betheni hung back.

"Izzy, are you okay?"

"I'm fine; leave me alone for a few, please."

Betheni hesitated then left for the ballroom. Izzy slumped onto the couch, trying to gather her wits about her. She had a job to do. Later she'd make sense of what just happened. Digging in her purse, she found some lipstick and reapplied it, fluffed her brunette hair, and stood.

Returning to the ballroom, she behaved as if she hadn't a care in the world.

Inside, her heart splintered into so many pieces she'd never put it back together.

* * * *

You are a Neanderthalic brute of epic proportions.

Cooper stood on his back porch, staring out at the water and the Olympic Mountains rising in the distance as the sun rose behind him. Already it was sixty degrees outside and pretty warm for an August morning in Seattle.

He buried his fingers in his tangled hair and leaned his elbows on the railing, rerunning the events of last Saturday night over and over in his mind for the millionth time.

Was Neanderthalic even a word? He'd failed at spelling but even he didn't think it was a real word.

But hell, that woman could chew ass.

Now the epic proportions part he liked, and it fit. Not that they'd ever gotten far enough that she'd sampled those proportions, except with her mouth.

Oh, fuck. He groaned at the thought.

He liked the brute tag, too. He was a bad-ass hockey player after all and being a brute went with the territory. Yet she'd wielded that particular sword to cut him deeply, not stroke his ego.

And he was bleeding all right, and not just his supposedly fragile male ego.

What he didn't like was being dressed down in front of her sisters, as their mouths hung open in shock while she ripped him new ones in places he didn't think would rip.

They had.

To shreds.

And he'd done the only thing a stubborn, pride-filled brute would do. He lashed out like a wounded animal, called her an uptight prude with delusions of getting her hooks into a wealthy hockey star. Oh, crap, then all hell broke loose, and he retreated like a soldier knowing when the odds were against him. He'd regretted the words the minute he'd said them, but pride wouldn't let him take them back, and he doubted Izzy would either.

So for his next act as a pigheaded-to-the-point-of-stupidity man, he'd left and never looked back, never called, never apologized, never did anything. Instead he re-lived the moment in his head over and over until he wanted to find a secluded mountaintop and holler at the top of his lungs.

That'd been five days ago. Hey, he wasn't counting but math happened to be his strong suit, and he had a memory for dates. He also had a memory for Izzy, for her seductive perfume, her sweet smile laced with sexy wickedness, for her long legs that tantalized him in his dreams. For her everything.

He'd been an idiot. It wasn't like him to be so jealous and out of control. But Izzy did something to him, and he couldn't think straight when it came to her. He never should've gone there, but he'd done it anyway, because this damaged part of him buried deep inside couldn't fathom that she wasn't just like all of the other women he'd fallen in love with since junior high.

His mother always said that he knew how to pick 'em, and he guessed he did. It didn't matter how many times he tried to convince himself that Izzy was different, that old doubt had crept in, and his insecurities when it came to women crept up on him and hit him over the head with a baseball bat, leaving him bruised, beaten, and crazed, like a wounded tiger.

Shit.

Why couldn't he be more like his best buddy Cedric, who've loved them once and left them? Not Cooper, he pictured a long-term relationship with every one of his girlfriends, while they used him as a stepping stone and cheated on him the first chance they could get.

His last serious girlfriend had taken him for everything she could get monetarily, sold all the sordid deets of their affair to any gossip site that'd pay her money, and screwed around on him with a country music star. He'd thought he was in love with her, and she'd played him for a fool until he'd returned early from a game because of an injury and found her screaming her lungs while humping a stranger in Cooper's own bed. After he'd booted them out, he'd thrown the mattress off the second floor balcony into the pool below.

That'd been two years ago. He promised himself he'd never journey that road again, yet he'd started down it with Izzy.

Some guys never learned. Cooper didn't want to be some guys. He was better off without her, better off without a serious woman in his life, especially one who got under his skin like she did. Hell, he'd never been the jealous type, never been five kinds of possessive—not like he'd been with her.

Izzy brought out the worst in him. He didn't need that. He was bad enough without a woman's assistance.

He needed a nice woman like his mother, quiet and agreeable yet strong, able to hold down the fort and stay unwaveringly faithful while his dad was away for long tours of duty, and willing to relinquish control when he returned. His parents were the perfect match, and until he found it himself, he'd stay single. Izzy was so not that woman. She had opinions for her opinions, did her own thing, and had to have everything her way. A little like him.

Joker, his half black, half white cat, rubbed around his legs. Cooper absently petted his silky fur. "Be glad you don't have to worry about women, female cats, whatever they're called." He thought for a moment. "Pussies?" He almost laughed.

Joker stared at him and blinked, not finding his joke funny and giving him that look cats give an inferior being.

Joker might be right. At least, in this instance.

Chapter 2—Faking It

Cooper walked into the team owner's office later that morning, feeling like shit from lack of sleep and not in the mood to play nice with management, but he'd do it anyway.

Ethan Parker and Cooper had a truce of sorts. Cooper hadn't been happy about the new owner uprooting his team and moving it to Seattle, but Cooper was ultimately a team player when it came to hockey. He'd play in Antarctica if that was where his team was.

He still didn't one-hundred-percent trust Ethan, but he didn't trust easily, and Ethan had betrayed that trust by insisting the team was staying in Gainesville when he damn well knew it wasn't. Besides with one more year on his contract, Cooper had the option to take his game elsewhere next year and fully intended on exploring the possibilities. His agent was putting out feelers already.

"Sit down, Coop." Ethan pointed to a small set of leather chairs flanking a couch.

"You wanted to see me?" Cooper sat on the edge of a chair, feeling like he'd been called to the principal's office, a familiar place back in his school days.

"For the past several days, you've been avoiding me." Ethan pinned him with one of those glares that said the man was on to him, but Cooper refused to squirm.

"My mother tells me you made a bit of a scene at a charity function last Saturday."

"It wasn't exactly a scene. I just didn't like how that asshole quarterback was dancing with Izzy," Cooper defended himself.

"Izzy was just doing her job."

"I don't like her job," Cooper groused, hating being called on the carpet for something so stupid.

"I wasn't aware you got a vote regarding her career path."

"I don't," Cooper said quietly, staring down at his hands. He could feel Ethan's eyes on him, dissecting him, judging him, and he felt like an even bigger ass for it.

"Well, next time you decide to barge into a black-tie affair dressed in jeans, call me first. You haven't met my mother yet, but trust me when I tell you it's not wise to piss her off."

Cooper lifted his head. "It won't be a problem."

"It won't?" Ethan's eyes bored into Cooper's.

"Yeah, we're through." Cooper stared over Ethan's head at the Space Needle in the distance.

Ethan nodded slowly as if digesting this piece of information. "Then I expect this next task I'm assigning you won't be a problem at all, and you'll handle it like the professional you are."

"Next task?" Cooper snapped his attention back to Ethan and tugged on his collar, sensing some invisible noose tightening.

"You got it." Ethan stood and walked to the door, opening it. Seconds later, Cedric, the first-line right-winger for the Sockeyes and Cooper's best friend, walked in.

The tall, blonde Swede grinned his trademark shit-eating grin, like he always did when he'd been clued in and Cooper hadn't. He sat in the chair opposite Cooper's and propped his big feet on the glass coffee table.

"So, gentlemen, I called you, as team leaders, here for a purpose." Ethan got right to the point, one of the few things Cooper actually liked about the man.

"Obviously," Cooper said dryly, drawing a frown from Ethan.

"My family has a long history of giving back to our community. We expect nothing less from our team."

Cooper narrowed his eyes, not sure was what coming, but certain he wouldn't like it.

"Brad's been in contact with Seattle's other major sports teams, regarding a joint project called Kids at Play."

Cooper nodded and clasped his hands in front of him. He'd worked with kids in Gainesville, loved it actually. He could do this. He glanced at Cedric, who was nodding.

Ethan studied them, as if assessing their interest. "Cooper, you'll be leading the Sockeyes, lining up guys to talk to schools, hold skate nights at various rinks in the area, and whatever else occurs to you." He stopped for a moment, a smile tugging at the corner of his mouth. "And you, Cedric, will be his wingman."

Cedric barked out a laugh. "I always am, boss."

"Good, the two of you are scheduled to meet with representatives from the other major Seattle teams next Tuesday night. I'll be emailing you the details on the program." He stood, signaling the meeting was over.

Grateful to be done, Cooper headed for the door.

"Cooper."

Cooper's hand froze on the doorknob.

"This is my mother's pet project. She's kicking this off with a huge fundraising party. Don't mess this up."

Cooper rolled his eyes.

"He won't. Trust me." Cedric gave Cooper a push out the door.

"And you'll be working with the Party Crashers," Ethan got in his last parting shot.

Cedric shut the door before Cooper could reply, and Cooper really wanted to rip Ethan a new one. What the fuck? Setting him up to work with Izzy?

Mina, Ethan's ancient sergeant major of an assistant, glanced up and shot them a wicked smile. "Be good, boys."

Cedric grinned at her. "Ah, Mina, I'm always good."

"I'm sure you are," she shot back.

Cedric hustled Cooper out of there before he opened his big mouth and pissed off the most powerful person in the organization.

"Meet ya at the place?" Cedric said, not waiting for a response. He was halfway across the parking lot before Cooper could recover from the blow he'd been dealt.

* * * *

On Tuesday night, flanked by the redheaded family wild child, Betheni, Izzy strode into the private dining room at The Waterfront, a classy restaurant overlooking Elliot Bay. The large banquet table seated about twenty people, and they were the first ones to arrive.

Izzy placed a folder of information at each plate, forcing herself to concentrate on her business rather than on the infuriatingly stubborn man who had stormed in and out of her life more than once. The storm was over, and she'd be damned if she'd allow him to screw up her carefully controlled life a third time.

She was done.

Now if only she could convince her heart and her body what her head already accepted.

She looked up as Steelhead quarterback Tanner Wolfe strode in as if he owned the place and every woman in it. He'd made it clear he wanted to start something with her, and she'd tried to be interested but every time she looked into his rich brown eyes, all she could see were Cooper's deep blue ones.

68

Good God. She needed to get over the man. And she would, given time. It'd only been a week and a half.

Tanner spotted her immediately and made straight for her. She smiled at him, finding him amusingly charming, even if she didn't want a relationship with him.

"Hey, beautiful. Have you reconsidered my offer?" He took her hand and kissed it.

She raised one eyebrow, tugging her hand from his firm grasp. "What offer?"

"You. Me. Naked. In a bed. In a closet. In a car. Elevator. Hell, anywhere you want."

Betheni giggled and stepped forward, ever ready when it came to a gorgeous man. "I'm Betheni, and you are?"

Tanner's wandering eye wandered right to Betheni with her enticing curves, silky red hair, and seductive smile. His eyes sparkled with mischief as he grinned. "I'm Tanner Wolfe, quarterback for the Seattle Steelheads, fondly known in these parts as The Fish."

"Well, Tanner, it's a pleasure to meet a Big Fish."

"In a big pond," he added. "The pleasure's all mine." He took her hand and kissed it, and Betheni batted her long eyelashes, leaning in closer to him. Izzy rolled her eyes. Betheni glared at her but took the hint, stepping away from Tanner.

Cooper took this moment to walk into the room along with Cedric. Izzy's heart skipped right up to the recalcitrant hockey player, which annoyed her to no end. Instead, she slid over to Tanner and linked her arm with his. Tanner winked at her, totally getting it. Devilment sparkled in his eyes.

"Let's have a little fun with the bastard, shall we?" Tanner whispered.

Izzy nodded. Tanner was no dummy. Obviously, he knew the score with Izzy wasn't in his favor, but that wouldn't stop him from toying with Cooper, who'd stopped and did a double-take when he spotted Tanner and Izzy. His eyes narrowed, he reluctantly followed Cedric who crossed the room to join them.

Betheni frowned, her scarlet lips in full pout, not used to being the odd girl out, but Cedric solved the little problem of her wounded pride, immediately looping his arm around her waist and engaging her in a private conversation.

Meanwhile, Cooper glared at Tanner. "Not you."

"Yup me, you lucky bastard." Tanner held out his hand. "Tanner Wolfe, but you can just call me Wolfe."

Cooper ignored him. "I'm not calling you anything other than an asshole."

"You wound me, Coop." Tanner held his hands to his heart and blinked back imaginary tears. "My brother has nothing but great things to say about you."

Tanner's brother played hockey and had a reputation of making the baddest of bad boys look tame. Cooper grunted, obviously not a fan of Tanner's brother—or Tanner.

Tanner didn't seem the least bit fazed. "We'll be working side by side on this project."

"Fucking wonderful." Cooper rolled his eyes.

Tanner didn't even blink. Instead he grinned as if Cooper had given him the biggest compliment ever. "So I hear you're the biggest stud in the NHL, next to my brother."

Cooper didn't respond.

"Well, I'm the biggest stud in the NFL, so we'll either get along great or kill each other."

"We'll kill each other," Cooper said with absolute certainty.

Betheni threw back her head and laughed. Izzy joined in. She couldn't help it. Very rarely did Cooper get his comeuppance but the Seattle quarterback appeared to know every button to push to get under Cooper's thick skin and into his thick skull.

Just like Cooper knew every button to push when it came to Izzy. She glanced away from his intense glare, the heat of it melting her from the inside out. God, she should've slept with the man when she'd had the chance, instead of holding out until they got to know each other. At least, she wouldn't be plagued with fantasies about how he'd feel inside her—instead she'd be plagued by memories of how incredible he'd been.

"Okay, gentlemen." Izzy extracted herself from Tanner's faux possessiveness. "We have a few more athletes on their way. I expect everyone to play nice for the greater good. And Ethan's mother will be here. Trust me, you don't want to cross her."

Cooper nodded as if he'd heard that story before.

Tanner shrugged good-naturedly. "Coop and I are old buddies. We go way back."

"We don't go back anywhere," Cooper muttered then slipped into silence as Ethan's mother entered the room.

Izzy watched as Mrs. Parker handled these huge men as if she were toting an arsenal of guns, only her arsenal was her steely gaze and take-no-prisoners smile, all the while looking like a sweet but classy grandma.

Even Cooper behaved, listening to her intently. Not that Izzy had noticed. Well, maybe a little bit.

Considering the personalities involved, this kickoff party might be Izzy's biggest challenge yet. She'd be wrangling and placating all these fragile male egos, while battling this insane attraction to a man she'd started a relationship with twice.

And she didn't plan on three times being a charm.

* * * *

Cooper clenched his jaw so hard his head hurt. Tanner Wolfe's cocky attitude and possessiveness toward Izzy boiled his blood.

What an obnoxious prick, and the kid's on-field performances didn't come close to matching his off-the-field antics. Cooper had no respect for a guy who didn't respect the game, even if football wasn't Coop's game.

He had even less respect for a guy who so blatantly hustled a woman like Tanner did. It was disgusting. Cooper would never behave like that when it came to a woman. He had more respect for women than that creep.

He put the brakes on that line of thinking. Maybe he had come on strong a time or two or three, but never with a smart woman like Izzy. She'd see right through that bullshit.

He watched her as she made a show of looking everywhere but at him.

That meant something, didn't it? Meant she cared, right?

Not that it should matter.

She was through. He was through. He didn't need her, didn't need a willful woman because he was a controlling man and that combination would be lethal. Better to find a nice, compliant, sweet woman who catered to his every whim in and out of bed.

He brought up a hand to stifle a yawn and received a sharp look from Mrs. Parker.

Jesus. He sat up straighter, and he'd thought his mother could deliver a deadly blow with one glance. She had nothing over Ethan's mom. He almost felt sorry for the guy.

But not quite.

His gaze slid back to Izzy like iron to a magnet. He couldn't stop himself. That damn woman starred in every dream he'd had since he met her, every woman he looked at was measured against her, and he couldn't drive her sensuous lips, gorgeous eyes, and hot body out of his head.

This was crazy—he needed to get over Izzy.

His parents' relationship worked because his mother was sweet and agreeable and his career soldier dad ruled the house with firmness and love. Yet it was his mom who held the family together during his father's long absences with her quiet strength, her unwavering loyalty, and her positive attitude, even as she battled through complications caused by Crohn's disease.

When it came to women, Cooper didn't trust his instincts, and he'd avoided a relationship since that last fiasco. Only Izzy made him want to stick around and figure her out, but she'd dumped him, too. At least she'd kept their relationship out of the media, proving more to him than the actual time they'd been together ever had.

Izzy was nothing like his mother on the surface, but she possessed that same inner strength. She'd proven loyal to her sisters, sacrificing her own education for theirs, and taking care of them when their flaky parents failed to do so.

Still…

Izzy's job required her to come in contact with powerful men, men used to getting what they wanted, men who took one look at Izzy and wanted her. Cooper couldn't deal with his own trust issues, couldn't tolerate her flirting even if it was part of her job, just flat out couldn't come to terms with his over-active imagination. He'd been burned one too many times, and he didn't trust his judgment when it came to women.

Yeah, it was better they'd moved on because right now he wanted to show Wolfe just how much better hockey players were at fighting. The prick wouldn't stand a chance if Cooper took off the figurative gloves.

Yet, he wouldn't. He'd play nice no matter how much it killed him because this cause happened to be something he believed in.

Kids were getting too soft, spending too much time playing video games, instead of outside playing ball or hide and seek. And for that reason alone, he'd put up with a million Tanners.

Mrs. Parker finished her spiel, drafted volunteers, and reiterated their next steps. Cooper volunteered to spend his days off visiting local elementary schools and family shelters, coordinating play days with kids and explaining their program.

Tanner volunteered to help Izzy with the kickoff fundraiser, which grated on Cooper to no end that those two would be spending more time together.

Cooper elbowed Cedric and shot him a look. Cedric raised his hand to help with the fundraiser.

"Let's get a beer." Cedric clapped him on the back as they walked out of the restaurant. Cooper stared straight ahead as Izzy and Tanner laughed and talked in front of them, but they went to their separate cars and left in separate directions.

"Coop, you couldn't be any more obvious," Cedric said, jerking Cooper from his jealous stupor.

"No shit." Cooper didn't bother to argue. He was being an idiot over a woman.

"Wolfe will play your weaknesses just because he enjoys needling you."

Cooper nodded. He understood; after all, he was an expert of the very same thing on the ice, getting under a guy's skin, making him doubt his abilities.

"So either beg her forgiveness because you're an idiot and acted like an ass or move on." No sugar-coated sympathy from Cedric; his buddy told it like it was. Usually Cooper appreciated that about him; tonight not so much.

"I'm moving on." Cooper squared his jaw and followed his friend into a nearby pub, wondering if moving on really was the solution.

Or if he could even manage to do it.

Chapter 3—Neutral Zone

August turned to September, and Izzy worked her butt off, trying to be everything to everyone, even when they didn't ask her to do so. She avoided Cooper the few times she'd been forced to be around him. Yet all the distance in the world didn't stop her insane longing for him or her late-night fantasies. Time flew by, and it was already the second week of September. Her sisters got ready for another quarter of college, and Izzy forced herself not to be jealous of them. She'd go to college later, once they'd had the chance to graduate.

On this particular night, Izzy applied finishing touches to her makeup, while Betheni lounged against the doorjamb of the small bathroom in the apartment they shared.

"So you have a date with Tanner Wolfe?"

"Not a date. We're meeting about the fundraiser."

Betheni frowned. "Why are we getting into party planning? That's not what we're about."

Izzy studied her pretty sister in the mirror. "We're about building our business, making money, and having a better life. Ethan and Lauren recommended us to Mrs. Parker. Besides, I like party planning. We've attended so many over the years and talked about what we would've done to make each party better if we'd planned it, why not try our hand at it?"

Betheni shrugged. "You have a point." She pushed her long red hair off her face and grinned a wicked smile, meaning she was up to something. "Tanner is hot, really hot. I wouldn't mind taking a run at him."

"Go for it."

"You're not interested?"

"Not in any way, shape, or form." Izzy turned back to the mirror.

"Why not?"

Izzy didn't want to answer that loaded question. Betheni knew her too well. She'd take her answer and run with it, imagining all sorts of things which weren't there, such as Izzy still having a thing for Cooper. Utterly ridiculous. Why would Izzy attach herself to a man who behaved all caveman and embarrassed the hell out of her?

Cooper did not fit into Izzy's life, and she didn't fit into his.

They were like fire and ice, fire one second and ice the next.

Betheni laughed, already reading her expression. "Don't answer that. You want Cooper."

Izzy opened her mouth to argue then snapped it shut. "How stupid is that? Really? Why would I want a guy like that?"

"Why? Because he's gorgeous and has a great body. He's very driven like you and underneath it all, a nice guy. Oh, not to mention, he's *riiiich*." Betheni's eyes glowed at the thought of all that money, and from what Izzy read, the team paid Cooper well.

"I don't care about the rich part. His money doesn't matter to me." And it didn't. Despite their constant struggles to make ends meet, Izzy never cared about Cooper's money. "But he's controlling and jealous. I can't deal with that."

"Because you have to be in control, too." Betheni picked up Izzy's red passion lipstick and tried it on.

"I'm the oldest. Of course I do." Izzy snatched her favorite lipstick out of her sister's hands.

Betheni just smiled. "Have fun with the Wolfe Man."

Izzy rolled her eyes, grabbed her raincoat, and head out the door. A few minutes later, she walked into a dark, neighborhood bar. Tanner was already there, entertaining a group of fans, mostly female, who gathered around the booth.

Izzy sighed. The guy had an ego as big as Mount Rainier and then some. He looked up as she approached and said something to the group of women who giggled and scattered, leaving them alone.

Izzy slid into the seat across from him. "Wow, what'd you say to them?"

Tanner grinned. "Jealous?"

"Not hardly, but a little surprised your adoring fans gave up so easily."

Tanner blew on his knuckles and scraped them across his chest a few times. "It's the ol' Wolfe charm. Gets 'em every time. I promised them my full attention later tonight." He leaned forward, staring into her eyes. Izzy stared back, wishing the man's gaze did things to her like Cooper's intense gaze did, but Tanner's seductive look only made her laugh. The man was so transparent.

"What's so funny?" Hurt flashed across his handsome features, gone as quickly as it came, revealing deeper emotions than she expected from him, or maybe it was just his bruised ego talking.

"You are, Tanner. You might as well quit before you start because this girl isn't buying front row tickets to your performance. I'm here to work."

He leaned back, crossed his arms over his broad chest, and grinned—a totally unexpected reaction. "Not buying it, huh?" His perfect, Greek-God sculpted face would sink a million women's ships, but not Izzy's. He couldn't sink a rubber ducky in her bathtub.

"Not one penny."

"Well, damn." He shook his shaggy head of gold-streaked blond hair.

"Tanner, I'm here for business not pleasure. My parents were rock stars, made a ton of money, and lost a ton of money. I grew up with a who's-who list of people going in and out of our house night and day. Know what? They're just people. Money doesn't impress me. Good looks don't impress me. Fame doesn't impress me. The only way you'll impress me is with hard work and dedication to our cause."

"Then you'll go out with me?"

"No, but I'll be your friend, one who only cares about who you are inside, not your outside image."

Tanner sat silently for a long while, as if digesting her words. "I don't have many real friends."

"Well, now you have one more. Let's get to work."

"One more question." He managed a small smile, all earlier cockiness had faded.

"What?"

"It's Coop, isn't it?"

"What is?" Izzy's heart stalled in her chest. God, was she so transparent everyone and their posse could see her strong attraction to Cooper?

"You look at him like you can't wait to see him naked." He ran his hands through his unruly hair. "You sure you won't ever want to see me like that?"

"Positive."

"That won't stop me from needling Black every chance I get. He has a thing for you, and it's a great sport to watch his ass squirm." He sighed, and as if accepting his fate, he opened up his iPad, tapped a few times on the screen, and showed her notes he'd made on ideas for the fundraiser.

She leaned forward, but her brain had fixated on seeing Cooper naked. She'd never seen him completely naked. Not once.

And she really wanted to see Cooper Black stark-assed naked.

Chapter 4—In a Bind

Cooper drove up the driveway to his secluded home in an exclusive area of Seattle overlooking Puget Sound and the Olympics. He'd leased the place at the end of August and moved in Labor Day weekend. The place was a little stark with minimal furniture and no pictures on the walls, but Cooper wasn't much for stuff unless it improved his hockey game, such as his state-of-the-art media system. Not that he used it much. He'd rather watch film at the Sockeyes Hockey Athletic Center, or the SHAC as the team called their shiny new Sockeye headquarters near the Space Needle.

Ethan had hooked him up with the home's owner looking to rent this place only minutes from Ethan's hundred-year-old mansion.

The house suited Cooper; retro to the max, it'd missed all the remodeling done by most inhabitants, and retained that weird early sixties' contemporary charm, with floor-to-ceiling windows, high, slanted ceilings, and one wall of cedar planking.

Most people would've bulldozed it and put up a McMansion. Not the owners. And not Cooper—if he owned it. He liked it just as it was, funky, old, and reminiscent of a simpler time.

The sun was setting in a late summer sky. Not a remarkable sunset, but Cooper appreciated it just the same. He'd get a beer and sit out on his patio, enjoy the evening, all the while wishing Izzy were here. What a lonely wuss he was. He tried to get her out of his mind, even dated a time or two, but none of the women he dated interested him.

Cooper frowned as his sharp eyes homed in on a lone figure sitting on his front porch. As he drove closer, the tall, lanky kid rose to his feet and stood on the top step to stare at Cooper.

Instead of pulling into his garage, Cooper parked in front of it and got out. He studied the kid for a moment, at first annoyed then curious. The kid wore a faded Raiders T-shirt and well-worn jeans. He'd guess him to be about fourteen or fifteen, a good looking kid, with unruly dark hair, long limbs, and big hands and feet, a lot like Cooper had been at that age.

The boy watched him approach, neither retreating, nor advancing. In fact, his blank expression struck Cooper as odd for a fan who'd cared enough to track him down at his new home.

As young boy, Cooper and his brother had stood outside in

frigid weather to get their idol's autograph, but the star hockey player pushed right past them, shoving Cooper's little brother into a wall and making him cry. That night Cooper tore down all his posters of the guy and burned them in the fireplace. He'd never destroy a kid like that. Despite the fact that this teenager was trespassing, he'd give him an autograph and send him on his way with a strong suggestion that he respect Cooper's privacy from this point on. Hopefully he'd get his point across without resorting to stronger tactics.

"Hey, buddy, you lost?" Cooper grinned. The kid didn't. In fact, he didn't blink. He stood statue still and said nothing. Not a damn thing, but the sweat beading on his forehead betrayed his nerves.

"I'm Cooper." Cooper held out his hand.

The boy ignored it. "I'm Riley."

Riley? Cooper's maternal grandparents' last name happened to be Riley. Cooper scratched his head and tried again. "Are you looking for someone?"

The kid blinked a few times. "You," he answered simply.

Cooper nodded, "You'd like an autograph?"

"Not exactly." Again that emotionless blank stare, only this time a muscle jerked in the kid's jaw, giving him away.

"Then what *exactly* do you need?"

"I didn't have anywhere else to go."

Cooper almost choked. He ran his hand through his too long hair and did a double take. Fuck, he did a triple take.

"Are you a runaway?"

The kid shook his head. "No." The plaintive, almost desperate way he said *no* wrapped a web of pity around Cooper's heart. Cooper took in the worn clothes and shoes and ratty backpack.

"Are you homeless?"

The kid swallowed and shifted his stance. He ran a hand over his face and sighed. "Yes, sir."

Well, hell, what was he going to do with a homeless kid? There must be shelters, places a kid like him could go.

He wished Izzy were here. She always knew how to handle stuff and say the right things.

Only Izzy wasn't speaking to him because he was an overbearing idiot of immense proportions. In fact, she hadn't spoken to him since that fateful night, except when it applied to their mutual project, and his pride refused to beg her to take him back.

"Look, kid, I can't have you stay here. It's—it's not legal." Cooper patted himself on the back for coming up with such a logical reason.

"I don't need a place to stay. I need your help." Frustration laced his voice as if Cooper was missing the point, and he was.

"I'll find you a place for the night. Let me make a few calls. That's the most I can do."

"She was right." The kid's shoulders slumped. His brave front crumbled, and his blue eyes filled with defeat and despair. Turning, he hoisted his bulging, beat-up backpack over one shoulder and started down Cooper's front walk.

Cooper stood there, uncertain if he should let a juvenile leave without insisting he go to the proper authorities. Besides, it was getting dark, and they were a long way from any kind of shelter. The kid probably hadn't eaten in hours. Come to think of it, neither had Cooper. He started after the boy.

The boy kept walking.

"Hey, wait. Who was right about me?"

"My mom. She said I couldn't depend on you, any more than she could." His eyes were filled with disappointment and accusation, the most emotion Cooper had seen from him all night.

"Mom? Do I know your mom?" Cooper quickly did the math. Surely, this couldn't be his kid? "How old are you?"

"Fourteen." Riley stood up straighter, his jaw jutting out, and his shoulders squared.

He'd had to have been eighteen when Riley was conceived. No, not possible. The one girlfriend he'd had at that age had never been pregnant as long as he'd known her. He blew out a relieved breath.

Riley stared at him, as if the answer to the question should be obvious, and Cooper had to be stupid not to see it. Cooper hated feeling stupid. Really hated it. He narrowed his eyes and wracked his brain, but couldn't come up with one hint of how he might know this kid or his mother.

"You don't get it, do you?"

Cooper shook his head, causing the shaggy mess to fall in his eyes. He swore to God the next free hour he had, he'd get his head shaved. He shoved it back from his face and waited.

"You think I'm your son?" The kid rolled his eyes, exasperated.

"No, but do you think you are?" Cooper asked. Yet, Riley looked like a younger version of Cooper, and that made his stomach hurt.

Riley shook his head, regarding Cooper as if he were too dense for words. "My mom is your sister."

"My sister?"

"Yeah? Remember her?" Sarcasm-laced sadness filled his quiet voice.

Cooper remembered all too well, even though it'd been over a decade.

* * * *

Riley watched the almighty Cooper Black with the growing dread he'd made a dumb mistake. He was all kinds of idiot to come here, but he'd been all kinds of desperate. Fuck, he still was.

Cooper didn't want to help them, just like his mother had warned. The same mother who'd walked out the door of their ratty hotel room fourteen days ago and never come back. The fear and desperation almost strangled him.

His mom had been gone before, a few days at a time, but she'd always come back, full of bullshit apologies that meant nothing because her addiction meant everything, but Riley forgave her. She was his mother, and she was all he had. He didn't know who his father was, and he didn't think she did either.

Yet, there'd been moments when she'd gone clean, gotten a real job that didn't involve selling herself, and they'd almost lived like real people, but those times didn't last long.

Now Riley was scared, really scared, about what had happened to the only person in his life who cared about him and about what would happen to him. Shit, he'd have been better off continuing his search on his own. His uncle would probably have him locked up in some foster care place or God knows what. He'd never be able to find her if that happened.

Cooper watched him warily, standing on the balls of his feet, as if he expected Riley to bolt any minute, and he'd have to give chase. Riley fully intended on bolting, but his feet wouldn't cooperate.

Finally Cooper seemed to find his voice. "Have you eaten?"

Riley's stomach growled in response. "I'm fine," he lied, and not very convincingly.

Cooper closed the few steps between them and wrapped strong fingers around his arm, reminding Riley that his uncle was supposed to be the fastest man on skates, at least in professional hockey. "Come in the house. My housekeeper made a stew in the crockpot."

Riley resisted, but Cooper didn't seem to give a shit. He hauled him into the house. Riley blinked a few times as he stood near the spacious, open kitchen that looked like it had survived from the set of a really old sitcom, the kind he and his mom used to watch on Nick at Night on the rare nights she hung out with him.

"Sit." Cooper pointed at one of the bar stools that weren't quite blue or green. Despite how the place appeared to be caught in some weird-assed time warp, Riley liked it, liked the open spaces, huge windows, and funky furniture. He especially liked the awesome view. Really awesome view. It beat the alleyway view of the dump he'd lived in until he'd found it padlocked this morning with an eviction notice on the door.

"Does Julie know you're here?" Cooper placed two bowls on the counter and filled them with thick, savory stew. Riley's stomach growled louder as he inhaled the incredible smell.

Riley licked his lips and shrugged as his stomach continued rumbling like a thunderstorm on the horizon. Cooper almost smiled. He pushed one bowl and a spoon across to Riley, who was pretty much drooling by now. After cutting up some thick bread and pouring Riley a glass of milk, Cooper opened a bottle of beer and sat next to him.

Riley dug into the meaty stew and was in pure heaven. He'd never tasted anything so good in his life. He didn't come up for air until the bowl was practically licked clean.

"Help yourself. There's plenty." Cooper pointed with his chin.

Riley wasn't used to plenty of anything in his life unless it involved bad things. He didn't wait for a second invitation but served himself another large bowl. He forced himself to eat slower this time, pride overcoming hunger. He didn't want his uncle to see how pathetic his life was, well, at least not any more than he already had.

Finally Cooper pushed his bowl away and studied him. "When I was your age, there wasn't enough food in the house to keep me satisfied," Cooper chuckled.

Riley didn't smile. Cooper wasn't his friend, and he needed to remember that. He bet Cooper never had to dig in dumpsters or beg for scraps from the back doors of restaurants just to get his next meal.

Cooper took a pull on his beer and sat back, watching Riley but keeping quiet until Riley finished. Riley knew what was coming, and his mind raced ahead as he tried to figure out how much to tell his uncle. Riley didn't have to wait long.

"Where's your mom, Riley?"

Riley swallowed as a lump formed in his throat and chose to tell the truth. "I don't know."

Cooper's eyes narrowed. "You don't know?"

Riley shook his head, unable to speak, and held his stomach, as if that would stop it from pitching and rolling like the deck of a ship in a storm—not that he'd ever been on a ship but he'd seen movies.

"Would you care to elaborate?" Cooper leaned forward, his gaze dark and disapproving.

"Not really."

"We need to call your mom, let her know you're here."

"You can't call her."

"Why not?" His uncle sounded exasperated at Riley's short answers, but Riley learned years ago never to give more information than absolutely necessary.

"I told you. I don't know where she is." Riley choked out the last few words and ducked his head in shame. He hated showing weakness, especially to a tough guy like Cooper Black, a guy who'd never cared enough about his sister to check on her. It sucked that desperation drove him to seek out Cooper now, but he'd swallowed his pride like he'd done too many times to count and soldiered onward.

"You don't know where she is?" Cooper's voice was low and measured, simmering with disgust.

Riley shook his head, feeling hot tears fill his eyes. The cat, who'd ignored him so far, stood and stretched. He leapt onto Riley's lap, purring, turned a few circles, and made himself at home. Riley loved animals. Though he'd never had a pet before, he'd often shared his meager meals with stray dogs or cats in the alleys near their many dumpy apartments. He stroked the cat's soft fur, feeling a little bit better.

"That's Joker. He owns the place, just lets me live here and pay the bills."

Riley frowned, not understanding.

Cooper almost laughed. "You've never had a cat before, have you?"

Riley shook his head.

"How long has your mom been gone?" Cooper got back to the subject.

"Two weeks."

"Two weeks?" The alarm in Cooper's voice caught Riley by surprise. "You've been on your own for two weeks?"

"Yes, sir."

Cooper blew out a breath and ran his hands through his messy hair. "Damn. How did you get to Seattle?"

"We moved here a few months ago from Portland. She thought there'd be better opportunities, a new start, and Mom knew you were here."

"She never tried to contact me—" Cooper's face paled, as if something came to him. "Crap," he whispered under his breath.

"I didn't know where else to go. I need help finding her. I'm scared something has happened." His mother might not be the world's best mother, but she was his mom. His stomach clenched at the thought of losing her.

"How the hell did you find me?" Cooper studied him, and Riley squirmed.

"My mom left your address sitting on the bed."

"Your mother had my current address? I just moved here a month ago."

Riley nodded, hating to admit that his mom kept tabs on her family, even though they didn't give a shit about her. "She stays in touch with her aunt. I guess she got it from her." He recalled a conversation between the aunt he'd never met and his mother almost three weeks ago.

"Yeah, I know Aunt Nancy keeps my mom up to date," Cooper admitted.

"I thought maybe Mom put your address there on purpose, knew she wouldn't be back. There was twenty dollars there, too."

"No note? Nothing like that?"

He shook his head. "She's not much for notes."

Anger laced with irritation flashed across his uncle's face, but he didn't say whatever he was thinking and changed the subject. "I'm guessing it wasn't difficult to get past the gate either?"

"Not really," Riley shrugged, suddenly tired, and yawned.

"Let me show you the guest room. You can take a shower and get some sleep. We'll figure out what to do next in the morning. In the meantime, I'll make some calls, get some balls rolling. Do you have a current picture of your mother?"

Riley pulled out a pay-as-you-go phone and found a selfie of him and his mother. They'd taken it over a month ago from the Space Needle. Cooper glanced at it, his jaw tightening. He nodded tensely, as if he'd swallowed some crappy medicine.

Without another word, he motioned for Riley to follow him up the stairs to a guest room that consisted of a big bed and a couple pieces of old furniture.

"There's an adjoining bathroom right through that door. Let me know if you need anything else. Good night," his uncle said and hesitated briefly, as if he wanted to say more but didn't. Instead he turned and left the room.

After tossing and turning in the big bed for an hour, Riley crept down the stairs for a glass of water. He stopped at the sound of Cooper's irritated voice coming from the kitchen. Riley stepped back behind the corner and listened. Cooper was talking about him.

Well, what the hell am I supposed to do with a teenage boy? I'm gone all the time. He can't stay here. A pause. Riley could hear Cooper pacing. *I can't. It's Mom and Dad's trip of a lifetime. You were my only option. Yeah, yeah, I understand.* More silence and a heavy sigh. *I can't put the kid in a foster home, not when he has relatives. Yeah, crap. I'll just have to find his mother so I can get him the hell out of here. Our sister is a damn flake.*

Cooper cleared his throat. Riley heard the frig open and the top popped off a bottle, probably a beer. His appearance had driven his uncle to drink. More pacing.

It can't be that hard to find her. The sooner, the better. I start camp in a few days. Besides, I'm not father material, hell, I'm not uncle material.

Riley slipped back upstairs, feeling sick to his stomach. He'd known the truth but hearing it made him even sicker. His mom's family didn't want anything to do with him or with her. The sooner he got out of here the better, but tonight he just wanted to sleep one night in a warm, dry place without the sound of rats scurrying through the vents.

The cat followed him to the room. Riley stared at the bed. Instead of getting in it, he sank to the floor between the bed and the wall. Unshed tears filled his eyes, and he swiped angrily at them. He would not cry. Crying was for sissies, and he wasn't a sissy. Hell, he'd taken care of his mother for years. He could certainly take care of himself.

Cooper didn't want him. That much was obvious. He'd tried to pawn him off on someone else. If the jerk put him in foster care, Riley would bolt. He'd rather live on the streets. But for now, he just wanted to sleep and weariness took over.

Riley curled into a ball on the floor and hugged the cat to him.

Tomorrow he'd plot his next move.

* * * *

Cooper had had an older sister once, but that was a lifetime ago.

Not that she was dead—except to him. Hell, as far as he knew she might well be dead—now. A chill ran down his spine.

No one in his immediate family had been in contact with her in years with the exception of an aunt, who heard from her once or twice a year. Julie's choice, not theirs. Though the drama factor in their lives decreased exponentially after she'd walked away and never looked back.

Cooper walked upstairs and opened the bedroom door a crack to check on the boy. The bed hadn't been slept in. He swung his gaze around the room, zeroing in on a lump on the floor. Curled in a fetal position, Riley lay on the floor between the bed and wall. He clutched a pillow and one arm was wrapped around Joker who purred happily. Frowning and feeling completely out of his comfort zone, Cooper crossed the room. When his nephew didn't wake up, he pulled a blanket off the bed and covered him.

With one last glance at Riley, Cooper left, closing the door quietly behind him.

He leaned his forehead against the wall in the hallway and closed his eyes, the weight of his world on his shoulders.

He was an uncle. A fucking uncle to a kid whose mother hated

Cooper and blamed him for everything bad in her life. Even worse, Cooper blamed himself.

His secret shame.

He'd never said a word; even when he could've saved his sister, he'd stayed quiet to save himself.

You were only ten years old.

Still, he'd been a coward.

He owed Julie that much. He'd take care of Riley, do right by him, until his parents returned.

Raw emotions swirled inside him, especially guilt. Guilt for a ton of reasons, guilt that he hadn't even cared enough to find out he had a nephew, guilt that he'd deserted his sister, guilt that he had every intention to pass this kid off to the next available family member.

He was a shitty brother and an even shittier uncle.

And now his sister's hot mess of a life had come to roost on his doorstep in the form of a pathetic kid with nowhere else to go.

Shaking his head, Cooper pushed himself away from the wall, his mind running one more time through his limited options.

Earlier he'd made a few phone calls, first to Cyrus, the team's attorney, waking him up and explaining the weird circumstances. After grumbling about the ungodly hour, Cyrus agreed to contact a private investigator he worked with on occasion and start the ball rolling. If anyone could find Cooper's sister, Cyrus claimed this guy could.

Then he'd woken up his younger brother, Dan, who wasn't any happier than Cyrus had been. The sooner he found a temporary home for Riley, the better. Training camp and preseason games started in a few days. Cooper couldn't have a kid living here, not when he was gone fifty percent of the time. Unfortunately, neither could Dan. With a rambunctious five year old, a baby on the way, and both him and his wife working, he declined to take on another person in their tiny New York flat. Of course, he sympathized and worried about their sister, but that was the best Cooper got out of him.

He knew better than to call his parents. They were travelling all over Europe for the next few months, finally retired and able to take their dream vacation, the one they'd saved up for years. Sure, they'd fly back in a heartbeat, but Cooper couldn't do that to them. Nor could he cause them any more worry over their missing daughter, not until he knew something concrete about what happened to her.

For now Cooper happened to be a substitute single father, something he'd never dreamed of being. He had no idea what to do with a thirteen-year-old boy, especially when he went on road trips.

Maybe Izzy could help. She mother-henned three younger sisters, while Cooper struggled to take care of just himself.

Besides, he was new to town, and she'd lived here all her life. She'd help him if he asked.

He started to call her and stopped. It was really late. Tomorrow would be soon enough.

Tonight he was tired. Bone-dead tired. He stripped off his clothes and crawled between the cool, soft sheets, feeling very alone and out of his element. He liked kids, but he'd never dealt with a kid he couldn't send home at the end of the day. He'd never been solely responsible for a kid, even temporarily. He swooped in, made kids happy for an hour or so, and swooped back out, like Superman saving the day.

He didn't think it'd be that easy to save his nephew's day, and he doubted he was up to the task. He'd let Riley's mother down all those years ago, and he didn't trust himself to know what was best for her son.

His life revolved around hockey. He lived, breathed, and slept hockey. He didn't have time for a kid.

His eyes snapped open and refused to close. Cooper stared at the ceiling. He flipped through all his concerns, looping back to Izzy over and over again.

Riley needed clothes; Izzy could help with that, and Cyrus would need to work on a temporary custody arrangement. Izzy could likely advise him on that. And he needed someone to care for Riley until he worked out other arrangements. Izzy could find someone.

There was one problem with this picture. Izzy didn't want anything to do with him, and Cooper wanted everything to do with her.

Beautiful Izzy. Sassy Izzy. Classy Izzy.

He wasn't beyond using a missing sister and a sad teenage boy to help him get Izzy back.

He'd messed up, and now he needed her more than ever, and he wasn't sure how to approach her other than to tell her the truth.

He missed her.

Chapter 5—Opportunity Knocks

Izzy worked days as a barista, since her business didn't make enough to pay the bills. It was midmorning, the early crowd long gone, and the place deserted.

She frowned at her phone as it played a ringtone she hadn't heard in almost a month and one she should've deleted—both the ringtone and the phone number. The ringtone was one of To the Max's hits—her parents' band—titled "Heart and Soul", and so not a song she should be tagging as Cooper's ringtone, or any man's for that matter.

She silenced the phone and ignored it, laying it on the counter. A second later it pinged, informing her of a voicemail. A few seconds after that, a text message came through.

Izzy rubbed her hands over her face and groaned. Don't look, she warned herself. *Just don't look.* She walked away from the phone and wiped down tables. The damn thing chirped again announcing another text message.

Dammit.

Izzy crossed the room, picked up the phone, and punched the Message button:

Izzy, call me please. It's important.

Izzy, I need your help. Please call me.

Cooper needed her help? Hard to imagine Cooper needing anyone but himself.

A glutton for punishment, she played the voicemail: *Izzy, please call me. I'm in a bind, and you're the only person I can think of who can help me.*

She sincerely doubted that. Money bought a lot of things, and Cooper had plenty of money. Whatever he needed, he could pay for it.

She hesitated.

Money.

Her twin sisters' tuition was due in a few days, and funds were low. Too low. Dropping out wasn't an option. She'd made that mistake, she'd be damned if they would. She'd hoped the Party Crashers would be bringing in more income by now, but the summer wedding business had ground to a halt and the fall parties hadn't quite kicked in yet. Even worse, the big job they'd done last week hadn't gone as planned, and the client, a big-time asshole attorney refused to pay. She'd put out a lot of money for that job banking on a big payout and gambled wrong.

If Cooper really needed her help, it'd cost him. These days nothing came for free, not when they were barely surviving day to day, and tuition was due.

With an annoyingly shaky hand, she called Cooper's number. He answered on the first ring, breathing hard and sounding anxious.

"Where are you?" she said.

"On the ice." Izzy stifled a laugh at the thought of Cooper Black racing around the ice while talking on his cell.

"I can only assume your coach isn't there."

"You assume right. Our player agreement doesn't allow us to use the team facility until training camp starts. I'm at a private rink."

"I'm at work, too, so let's dispense with small talk. What's so important you had to spam me with voicemails and texts?"

"One voicemail and two texts are hardly spamming."

"Cooper," she said in that voice which said way too much. *Remember? We're through. You and me. No more. Why are you bothering me?*

"Izzy, please, hear me out."

She blew out an exasperated sigh. "Fine, what is it?"

"Just a minute."

She heard clattering and doors closing.

"Okay, I had to go somewhere private." He paused and cleared his throat. "I have a nephew."

"I'm happy for you, but what does that have to do with me?"

"He's fourteen, showed up on my doorstep last night. He doesn't say much other than he's looking for his mother, my sister, who I haven't seen since before he was born. I didn't even know about him. He came to me because his mother is missing."

She hardened her heart to Cooper's sad story. No way would she let him suck her back into his life. Izzy kept her silence, waiting for him to continue.

"I need your help. Training camp starts tomorrow, and suddenly I have a fourteen year old in my house. I'm gone more than I'm here. I can't leave him alone. None of my family members are able to take him. I will not put family in a foster home. It's just until I find his mother, or my parents return from Europe, whichever comes first."

"You'd give him back to a mother who's left him alone?" Izzy's anger boiled to the surface. She knew exactly how it felt to be abandoned by unconcerned parents over and over again.

"I'll give her some money, help her get a better start, put her in rehab, whatever she needs."

"That's your solution to everything. Just throw some money at it. What she needs is a family who cares."

"You really don't understand."

"No, you're right, I don't. Cooper, I won't bail you out. That boy is your responsibility, like it or not."

"I wasn't asking you to take him in. I was hoping you might have a solution for me." He sounded so needy, so discombobulated, so helpless. There was something incredibly sexy about a strong man showing his vulnerability. But this wasn't about him or her, and she wouldn't cave to his brand of alpha-male charm.

"A solution? I'm a party crasher, not a babysitter."

"How's that working for you? The party crashing, that is."

"Wonderful. Never been better. Making scads of money." Which was exactly why she didn't know where she'd come up with the rent money, let alone tuition.

"I just thought you might know of someone trustworthy I could hire when I'm on road trips."

"Not that I can think of."

"I'll pay a finder's fee." He sweetened the pot.

Her ears perked up. "How much?"

"A thousand dollars if you guarantee they'll work out."

"I'll need the money upfront." Her mind raced ahead to what she should pay first with the money.

"I can do that, but you're ultimately responsible if something goes haywire when I'm out of town."

"Not a problem. I'll find someone."

She heard his relieved breath. "One more thing. The kid refuses to go shopping with me, but his clothes are too small for him and threadbare. Maybe you could persuade him to go shopping."

"Cooper, I'm not your personal assistant."

"I'll pay you to take him shopping."

Izzy was starting to feel like an opportunist. She sighed. The things she did for her sisters so they'd have a better life. "Okay. I get off in another hour."

"Good. I'll pick you up at your place in an hour and a half."

* * * *

Izzy paced the small apartment, pausing on each pass to pick up an item of clothing, a plate, or a glass. Her younger twin sisters didn't understand the concept of tidiness. Izzy sighed and shook her head. Four females in one two-bedroom apartment with one bathroom bordered on insane, but at least she could watch out for them, whether they liked it or not.

Old habits were hard to break, and she'd been her sisters' rock for as long as she could remember while their parents shirked their responsibilities and chased after the next big recording opportunity or played a slew of gigs up and down the Pacific coast, leaving their then teenage and younger daughters to fend for themselves.

Rock and Fawn Maxwell weren't exactly bad people, just free spirits who couldn't be tied down. Why they'd ever had four children was anyone's guess. Izzy had been in charge since her early teens when a family friend was supposed to care for them and never showed up—seems Fawn's friends were as flaky as Fawn. Izzy did such a great job caring for her sisters, Fawn and Rock never bothered with a sitter again.

At least Cooper wasn't leaving his nephew on his own, which gave the man bonus points in her mind, not that any amount of points would earn him back into her good graces. *Depend only on yourself then you're never disappointed.* Cooper had disappointed her one too many times. In her book, he'd used up his chances, even if he was mouth-watering delectable, even though her panties melted just thinking of his intense blue eyes, even if his deep voice vibrated right down to her core. Yes, even then.

Hearing his big SUV pull up, she looked out the window, grabbed her light jacket, and ran downstairs. She hopped in the front seat and turned to extend a hand to the boy sitting in the back.

"Hi, I'm Izzy."

The kid looked up at her and blinked a few times. What a good looking kid, a younger version of his uncle with the same black hair, handsome face, and deep blue eyes. With a tentative smile, he took her hand and shook it with a firm grip. "I'm Riley."

"Well, Riley, Coop tells me you need some clothes." She

glanced at Cooper who stared straight ahead and didn't say a word. Obviously he and his nephew weren't exactly on the best of terms.

"I don't need any clothes. I don't want anything from him except help finding my mother." Riley met her gaze, and the sadness in his eyes cracked open her heart.

"Honey, everyone can use clothes now and then. You like girls, don't you?"

He nodded, puzzled but looking as if he was well aware he might be walking into a trap.

"Girls are impressed by a sharp-dressed man."

Riley continued staring at her and saying nothing.

"Cooper can afford it. Let's have a little fun with his money. You'll be starting school soon, and you want to dress to impress."

She caught Cooper's quick glance. "You did enroll him in school, didn't you?"

"I—uh—hadn't thought of it."

"He's already a few weeks behind." She turned back to Riley. "Were you attending elsewhere before you found Cooper?"

"No." He looked away, as if embarrassed.

"Well, we'll get you taken care of. Clothes first, school next. Do you play sports?"

Cooper's gaze flicked to hers, and she realized he didn't know the answer to that question either.

"I love football and baseball. There was never any money to play, but I played when I could."

"With the Black genes, you'll be a natural," Izzy assured him.

Cooper swallowed and glanced in the rearview mirror. "Do you skate, Riley?"

"No." Riley shot Cooper a glare and focused his full attention on Izzy. "I guess I can go shopping with *you*." He emphasized the 'you' as if he didn't want to include Cooper.

Izzy caught the hardening in Cooper's eyes, the flash of guilt combined with pain and wondered what the story was. Cooper had talked about his family to her with pride in his voice on more than one occasion, but he'd failed to mention a sister.

If they'd still been going out, she'd be getting to the bottom of this particular mystery, but they weren't, and his family troubles were none of her business.

* * * *

Wow, Izzy was hot. Really awesomely hot. Riley had to consciously remind himself to shut his mouth because he was pretty sure his tongue was hanging out.

He was in love. He'd never met a classier, more beautiful woman in his life, and she smiled at him as if he mattered. Not like his mother's trashy friends or her boyfriends who weren't really boyfriends but paying customers. Some of her boyfriends looked at him in a way that gave him the creeps. His mom tried to shield him from men and women like that, but he'd been exposed to a lot in his fourteen years, and knew there were women and men who liked younger boys. His skin crawled thinking of it.

He liked Izzy. He wished he could say the same for Uncle Cooper.

Izzy grilled him in ways Uncle Cooper hadn't cared enough to bother. She'd asked him if he played sports. He'd skirted the question somewhat. Two years ago, he'd lived in a great foster home for six months until his mom got out of rehab. They'd let him play football, and he'd loved it. In fact, he'd been damn good at it. He'd made friends for the first time in his life, buddies in the locker room, even dated a junior high cheerleader. Then his mother ripped him out of that suburban home and school and back they'd gone to the rat-infested one-bedroom apartment in urban LA. He'd hated it, but he had to take care of his mom. She depended on him.

Unfortunately, the drugs sucked her back into their web months later.

She'd been up and down ever since. Straight for a few days and back on whatever drug she could get her hands on for a few more. Riley washed dishes in the greasy spoon on the first floor of their building for meals and a few under-the-table dollars, which he used for rent money.

Now she was gone. He didn't know if she was dead or hurt or what. But he'd swallowed his pride and come to his uncle for help. He didn't have anywhere else to turn.

Yet, Uncle Cooper didn't want him, had tried to pawn him off on other people. When that hadn't worked, he paid people to take Riley off his hands. Riley didn't care, wouldn't care. Once his mom was found he'd be out of his uncle's life and never have to see him

94

again.

Finding his mom was all that mattered. If he had to put up with his uncle for a while, it was a small price to pay, especially when his uncle had friends like Izzy.

* * * *

Later that night Cooper walked Izzy to her apartment door while Riley snored in the back seat, exhausted from their shopping spree and dinner out. They'd worn the kid out. Hell, he'd worn himself out. Izzy shopped like a crazed terrier, zipping from one shiny thing to the next, and making him dizzy as she tore clothes off the racks and piled them in Riley's arms. The kid followed her around with a stunned expression on his face the entire time.

"Thank you." Cooper paused in front of her door. "He's crazy about you." Cooper was too. In fact, he couldn't stop staring at her and was pretty certain he was as lovesick over her as his teenage nephew.

Izzy shrugged. A soft smile crossed her face causing his breath to catch. "He reminds me a little of me. He's had to be the adult for most—maybe all—of his childhood, and that's sad." Her gaze grew wistful as she looked over Cooper's shoulder toward the SUV.

Cooper nodded. "Since he won't talk to me, I don't know what he's been through. I think he blames me for what happened to his mother."

"Blames you? Why?" She gazed up and him, and he fought the urge to take her in his arms and inhale her sweet scent.

"Because I wasn't there for her, and I'm pretty sure she blames me." Guilt twisted his insides. "He doesn't know the half of it."

"What do you mean, Cooper?" She touched his arm, giving him hope, even though he knew the gesture didn't mean what he wanted it to mean.

"Someone tried to call me several times the week before she went missing."

"And you didn't answer." Her accusing tone made him cringe.

"I never answer unknown numbers. The caller never left a message." He shook his head, compelled to explain further. "My sister ripped my family apart with her addiction issues which started in high school. My parents did everything they could to help her, going deeply in debt for attorney fees and rehab costs. She put us on a roller coaster ride for years. My mom has health issues, and the stress was dragging her down. We had to cut my sister off in order to save ourselves. She called a few times after that until the calls dwindled to nothing."

Izzy's expression softened. "Sometimes what your family did is the only thing you can do." She rubbed his arm and gazed up at him.

Cooper nodded, a lump forming in his throat. "I can still remember what a great sister she was before the drugs. Julie was four years older than me, and she used to take me everywhere with her. She never missed a hockey game of mine in those early years, and she'd evaluate every performance. She was a figure skater, and we did a routine together once for a charity skating exhibition. She taught me to skate, instilled the love of skating in me. I'd never be what I was if it wasn't for her. Mom wasn't into sports, and Dad was gone a lot. Julie was my best friend, despite our ages."

"I'm sorry. You must mourn the loss of her—the life she had with your family, the loss of the person you knew."

Cooper nodded, almost choking on the huge lump in his throat. "I miss her. I didn't know she had a son, but I want to do right by him, make sure he doesn't fall to the same fate as his mother. I owe the real Julie that much."

"Get him involved in sports. You saw how his face lit up when he talked football." Hers shone as she talked, and he fell a little deeper in love with her, not that he was in love with her, just falling, but falling didn't mean he was there, or so he figured. Cooper moved back a step, trying to free himself from the spell she cast over him.

He'd prefer Riley loved skating and hockey but he'd settle for football, a team sport like hockey with great team camaraderie, even if he didn't like some of the players on the local team—specifically Tanner.

"What if she shows up and wants him back?" Izzy studied him as if she could see right into his very soul.

He shifted his stance. "She is his mother. I don't plan on being a surrogate parent."

"What do you plan on being, Cooper, to a boy who needs a little stability in his life?"

"Like I'd give him that," he answered defensively.

"Of course you would. You're not a partier, you're a straight-arrow guy who plays by the rules and expects everyone else do to the same. You're a hard worker and a great role model for kids."

Cooper's face grew hot, and he looked away for a moment. "I'm never home."

"Maybe it's the quality, not the quantity."

He rubbed his hands across his face and heaved a huge sigh. "I don't know what I'll do when I find Julie, or she finds me."

"Cross that bridge when you come to it. Have you had an attorney look into temporary custody? It'll make it that much more difficult for her to rip him out of your home."

"Yeah, I have. I don't foresee any problems with it. And you? Have you made any progress on a combination live-in housekeeper and teen-sitter?"

"I have—Aunt Barb, my mother's sister, just lost her job and is thrilled to get the work. She's a great cook and very neat and tidy. I'll text her contact info so you can meet her."

"Your endorsement is good enough for me. I'm out of time." He pulled out his wallet and counted out ten one-hundred-dollar bills. Izzy snatched the money out of his hand, almost too eagerly, cluing him into her current financial situation.

"Thank you." Her sincerity struck a chord deep inside him.

"Izzy?" His voice cracked a little when he said her name.

"Yes?" She cocked her head and looked up at him, sexy as hell with those glossy, so kissable lips, and eyes such a deep brown they pulled him in and held onto him.

"Do you need more?"

She hesitated and shook her head. "No, thanks." With an nervous smile, Izzy turned to unlock her door, swinging it open to the sounds of the twins fighting over who'd worn whose clothes and put a stain on an expensive dress. She sighed. "Family."

"They might be pains in the ass, but they're our pains in the ass."

Impulsively, Izzy leaned forward and kissed his cheek. "Good night, Cooper. Take care of our boy."

Cooper stared at the door long after she shut it. He could hear her voice rising above her sisters' shouting. The corner of his mouth twitched in a smile.

Our boy.

She was a good friend to him, better than he deserved.

97

And he wanted to be her man. Again.

A lump of regret settled in his gut for what could've been if he hadn't behaved like a jealous jerk.

Chapter 6—Blocked Shot

Being out of his element didn't come close to describing Cooper's situation. He liked kids, hell, he worked with kids on a regular basis, but spending a few hours at children's hospital or a school didn't exactly equal living with a teenager, especially one with a stubborn streak to rival Cooper's, not to mention all the other shit the kid must be dealing with, stuff Cooper couldn't begin to understand.

Walking into the high school to enroll Riley as a freshman didn't rank up there as one of Cooper's shining moments, especially when he couldn't furnish most of the information required to register Riley. The old crone handling the paperwork glared at him in disgust, making him feel like the worst uncle in the entire world.

"Birthdate?" she demanded, sniffing as if she smelled dog shit on his shoes.

Cooper wrung his hands under the table. Sweat beaded on his forehead. He glanced at Riley who stared straight ahead and said nothing.

"I, uh—"

She glared up at him, bony fingers poised over the keyboard and tapped one toe of her sensible shoes on the floor. "Mr. Black, surely you know your nephew's birthday?"

Cooper hated looking like an idiot. He definitely looked like an idiot. He shot a quick glance at his nephew and caught the kid's disinterested expression. No help there. The woman's frown couldn't possibly get any deeper; disapproval added more lines to her face than he'd seen on his ninety-year-old grandmother's face. Despite his embarrassment, Cooper didn't air his family's dirty laundry in public, so he let the woman think the worst of him.

"Riley, would you please answer the lady?" Cooper publicly conceded defeat.

Riley's smile was triumphant, yet laced with sadness, making Cooper feel like a real shit.

A half hour later, they finished the paperwork, and Cooper stood, fully intending to get the hell out of the place. He nodded at Riley. "You have a key and can catch the bus home?"

"Yeah." The kid looked completely lost.

"I'll be home by dinner." Cooper didn't know what else to say so he awkwardly patted his nephew's shoulder.

Riley stiffened and stared straight ahead, swallowing hard. "Whatever." He glanced at the door as if he wished either he could disappear out of it, or even better, that Cooper would.

Cooper gladly obliged. He escaped to the comfort of his car, glad to be long gone. Crap, he was a big, brave hockey player known for his toughness, and he'd just been taken out of the game by a little old lady and a fourteen-year-old boy. He was beyond pathetic.

He needed to talk to someone who'd understand or at least commiserate, which ruled out any of his teammates, especially Cedric. Without thinking, he dialed Izzy. He wasn't really sure why, and he knew he should just leave her alone, but he needed to talk to someone who might make some sense of all this.

But she didn't answer.

So he called the PI he hired, hoping like hell the man had news for him.

He didn't.

And the rest of his day pretty much followed the beginning.

He should've stayed in bed.

He couldn't even handle a fourteen year old. Hell, he was good with kids. Why wasn't he good with his nephew? Maybe because his sister stood between them, a ghost who accused him of countless sins.

At least, that appeared to be how Riley saw it.

* * * *

Tonight had been Izzy's idea, and it was a damn stupid one if she did say so herself.

Izzy was just concerned about Riley; that was the reason she suggested the Kids at Play team meet at Cooper's tonight. Cooper hadn't been overly thrilled to have Tanner in his house, but he'd grudgingly agreed.

She'd ignored Cooper's phone calls last week, refusing to get sucked back into his life. Riley started school a week ago and two weeks behind the rest of his class. Cooper most likely needed to talk about it. Regardless, she didn't call him back.

Each time fate threw them together, it was harder and harder to resist the man, not that he did anything she needed to resist. Swear to

God, she wanted him to do something. Anything. Instead he stared at her almost warily, and she didn't quite know how to take that. She'd dumped him, sent him packing, ripped him up one side and down the other. A proud man didn't get over that kind of humiliation easily, if ever.

But damn, she wanted him, wanted what she couldn't have. This insane longing to run her hands over his hard muscles and through his thick hair drove her crazy. Of course, her fantasies didn't stop there. Not by a long shot. Instead they stopped with both of them naked and him pumping into her until they both had epic orgasms and lay spent in each other's arms.

That was so not happening. Fantasies would be the only piece of him she'd allow herself to have.

Unfortunately, he had to be the sexiest man on earth.

If Izzy had been a sculptor she'd have sculpted his well-defined muscles. If she'd been a painter, she'd have painted his handsome face with those sexy lips, intense blue eyes, and unruly mane of dark hair. But she was just a woman, a party crasher by night and a barista by day, and Izzy couldn't do his body or his face justice, wouldn't have the first idea how to capture this strong, proud man on canvas or paper or even in a photo, but she'd definitely sign up for the task of preparing him for posing—in the nude.

She swallowed and licked her lips. She'd strip him naked and oil those rippling muscles, brush his hair away from his face, and kiss away the worried wrinkles in his brow.

Seriously? She had it bad, and she'd been the one to break it off with him.

Part of her was sorry she'd done it.

Izzy bit her lower lip as she raised her hand to ring the doorbell. She was early.

Her Aunt Barb's car wasn't in the driveway so she'd left for the day. Barb hadn't said much other than Riley was quiet and non-communicative. He'd communicated just fine with Izzy the day they'd gone shopping. In fact, he'd been animated.

Enough stalling.

Izzy rang the doorbell. A few seconds later, Cooper opened the door and her breath caught in her throat. Cooper's Sockeyes T-shirt molded to every muscle in his well-defined chest. Despite Izzy's five-foot-ten height, the man towered over her, making her feel delicate and feminine. She gazed up at him, sucked in by his clear blue eyes, which darkened with desire at the sight of her on his doorstep.

"You're early," he stated the obvious.

"I know. I thought I'd spend a little time with Riley."

"He'd like that." Cooper stood aside to allow her in, but close enough her body brushed his as she squeezed past him. She followed him into the large kitchen and breakfast nook area, staring at his strong back the entire time, admiring those broad shoulders and the muscles at play as he walked with pure male, athletic grace.

Cooper stopped in the doorway, and she was so busy drooling, she ran into his back. Chuckling, he turned and winked at her, holding her arms to steady her weaving body. "Having issues with gravity today?"

"No, I'm fine." Her face burned from her neck up to her forehead. Even the roots of her hair prickled with embarrassment.

"Sure, you are," he said way too smugly, as if he knew the effect he had on her. *The bastard.*

She stepped around him and approached Riley who appeared to be doing his homework at the breakfast table. Riley glanced up and did a double-take. A welcoming smile spread across his face.

"Izzy." He grinned with absolute joy at seeing her and made her feel like a bit of a bitch for avoiding him.

Izzy slid onto the bench across from him and smiled. "How are you, Riley?"

"Great, now that you're here." Riley shot a quick glance at his uncle and frowned.

"I'll be in the living room. I have a few things to finish up before everyone gets here." Cooper took the hint, but not before Izzy saw a flash of hurt in his blue eyes.

Riley visibly relaxed as soon as Cooper left. "Wow, it's really good to see you."

"How's school going?" Izzy nodded at the books, laptop, and miscellaneous papers scattered on the table.

He shrugged one shoulder. "It's going. I'm behind, but I have a tutor a couple days a week." He brightened, showing all that youthful enthusiasm Izzy admired. "I'm playing on the freshman football team. Would you come to one of my games?" He bit his lower lip, and his hopeful expression was so adorable, Izzy couldn't possibly say no.

"I'd love to. When's the first one?"

"Thursday night." He literally squirmed with excitement, giving Izzy the distinct impression no one had ever bothered to attend any of his activities in the past. Sadly, she could relate.

"Two nights from now?"

"Yeah. Maybe you could go with Uncle Cooper. He has that night off," Riley added hopefully.

"I don't think that'd be a good idea."

Riley's face fell. "Don't you like him? I wouldn't blame you if you didn't. He's a hard ass."

"I do like him, and he's a great guy." Izzy found herself defending Cooper. "You should cut him some slack. He's not used living with anyone or having the responsibilities that come with a teenager in the house."

"He doesn't want me here," Riley's jaw jutted out stubbornly, reminding her of Cooper.

"Of course, he does," she lied, and Riley saw right through it.

"I didn't ask to live here. I just wanted help finding my mother." Riley crossed his arms over his chest. "I can take care of myself."

"I'm sure you can, but you shouldn't have to. Now's the time to enjoy being a kid without adult responsibilities." Izzy spoke softly. She understood, more than he'd ever know.

"I'm not complaining. My mom needs me."

"I'm certain you're a good son." She patted his arm and he managed an embarrassed smile. "I had absentee parents, Riley. They were gone a lot. While they sometimes left us with food and money, it was never enough. That's how Party Crashers got started. At first, my three sisters and I crashed parties to have a meal, especially weddings because everyone doesn't know everyone else. My parents taught us to play instruments, sing, and dance at young ages, so we entertained in exchange for our supper. If they had karaoke, we sang. If they had dancing, we danced up a storm. If there was a piano, we'd play it. No one ever complained. In fact, those that realized we were party crashers thanked us for making the most epic parties ever. That's when we realized we could make money crashing parties."

"That's so cool. Can I crash a party with you sometime?"

Izzy smiled indulgently. "We'll see." She glanced up to see Cooper leaning in the doorway, arms crossed over his chest, and an unreadable expression on his handsome face. A muscle ticked in his jaw, giving away how upset he was.

The doorbell interrupted any further conversation. A few seconds later, Tanner appeared with his buddy and wide receiver Hunter McCoy, followed by Cedric. Cooper stood behind them, scowling and looking as if he'd like to use his stick to smack that arrogant grin off Tanner's pretty face.

Tanner immediately headed for Izzy and gave her a kiss on the cheek, while Cooper literally steamed. Tanner obviously loved every minute of it. He straightened and focused his laser-sharp quarterback gaze on the teenager who was gaping at him with an open mouth.

"Hey, buddy." Tanner grinned and reached out to shake hands. Riley fell all over himself in his haste to stand.

"Oh my God, you're Tanner Wolfe." Riley looked ready to pee his pants, while Cooper looked ready to strangle Tanner with his bare hands. Izzy stood, poised to run interference or break up a fight, whichever came first.

"One and the same. And you're—"

"—my nephew." Cooper stepped between the two. "You have homework to finish, Riley, and we have a meeting."

Riley's face fell, and he shot Cooper a look of pure dislike. Cooper caught it, judging by the jerkiness of his movements and the hardening of his jaw. Izzy's heart went out to him even when it shouldn't.

"Get that homework done, Riley, and we'll talk later." Tanner squeezed his shoulder and offered a friendly smile.

"Would you come to my game Thursday night? Izzy and Uncle Cooper are going." Riley couldn't seem to contain himself, but when he caught the annoyance on Cooper's face, he stared at his feet. "I'm sorry. I shouldn't have asked that."

"Hey, just so happens I'm free Thursday night. I'd love to." Tanner winked at Riley, who immediately brightened again, despite the murderous glare on his uncle's face.

"That'd be awesome," Riley gushed like only a kid could. "You're my favorite athlete."

Cooper stiffened as if he'd been slapped across the face, but only Izzy appeared to notice. She moved closer to him and touched his arm. He stared down at her, the pain stark on his face. For a moment they were the only two in the room, as they gazed into each other's eyes.

Cooper bent his head and spoke only for her ears as they followed the rest of the group into the living room with Cedric leading the way as if it were his house. "That's fucking awesome," he said sarcastically. "He never treats me like that. Most of the time I think he hates me. The rest of the time, he barely tolerates me."

"Cut him some slack, Cooper. You don't know what kinds of ideas his mother put into his head."

"I have a good idea they weren't complimentary toward me."

"Of course not. She's an addict, and her life is everyone else's fault but hers. You're doing right by him. That needs to be enough for now. Let him hero worship Tanner. Your role isn't to be his buddy, but his parent."

Cooper ran his hand through his hair, pushing it off his face. "I never wanted to be anyone's parent, let alone a teenage boy's."

"Sometimes we don't get a vote when it comes to the challenges life throws at us."

"You're right, Izzy. As always."

"And don't you forget it." She nudged a smile out of him with those words.

He opened his mouth to say something, but Tanner interrupted, hating it when he wasn't the center of attention.

Izzy settled them all down and tried to run a meeting. It would've been easier to herd cats than to channel the testosterone in that room tonight.

At least she kept Tanner and Cooper from duking it out, even as they argued over every little thing. It was going to be a long evening. And forcing herself to stay out of Cooper's magnetic pull made it exponentially more difficult.

* * * *

Cooper shut the door behind the last of his guests, except for Izzy, who volunteered to help clean up. Riley ran upstairs to call his teammates and brag about meeting the great Tanner Wolfe. Cooper wanted to gag. The guy was no role model for an impressionable teenager. His reputation as a partier and womanizer wasn't even the half of it. His big mouth and outrageous behavior completed the overall picture of a jerk.

Cooper already had a negative opinion of the guy before he ever laid eyes on him based on Tanner's hockey-playing brother, Isaac. Yeah, the three Wolfe brothers, dubbed by the press as the Wolfe Pack, all played professional sports. One hockey, one baseball, one football. Each one as arrogant and obnoxious as the others.

With a sigh that the torture had ended for another night, Cooper turned back toward the kitchen. Izzy bustled around, putting dishes in the dishwasher and wiping the counter.

Cooper paused to watch her zipping around like a mini tornado in his kitchen. Instead of wreaking havoc though, she transformed the chaos into neat, tidy order. Cooper liked things orderly, and he liked Izzy in his kitchen. Hell, he just plain liked her.

It'd been a weird night for him. He couldn't stand Tanner Wolfe. To watch the asshole flirt with Izzy all night was just about more than he could stomach. Yet, the ultimate betrayal came from his nephew who clearly worshipped the jerk. Now that hurt. Not that Tanner's obvious interest in Izzy didn't hurt, too, because it did, but Izzy didn't return the man's interest, which gave Cooper some satisfaction. Maybe he really could trust her. Maybe she wasn't like all those other women.

He missed her, and he wanted her back. He wasn't sure whether the gaping hole in his heart could get any bigger. He missed the way she smiled at him and lit up his day. He missed how her eyes sparkled as she sang along to "Hotel California," her favorite classic rock song. Hell, he even missed the frown on her face when he wore faded jeans for a night out on the town. Oh, yeah, he was a sap, and he fucking missed her.

Izzy finally glanced up and saw him standing there. Her expression softened, and he knew he must be wearing his heart on his sleeve.

Dropping the towel on the counter, she moved toward him. He stood his ground, waiting for her, his entire body buzzing with anticipation.

She stopped a foot from him and gazed into his eyes. God, he loved her brown eyes with those little gold flecks in them. He could lose himself in those eyes all day long.

"Are you okay?" Izzy brought up her hand and stroked his rough cheek.

"Yeah." As long as she kept touching him like that, he'd be

more than okay. Cooper swallowed and fisted his hands to stop himself from pulling her into his arms. He breathed in her sweet perfume. Like spring flowers on a sunny day, her scent surrounded him, enveloped him, wrapped him in a warm cocoon of contentment.

"He does look up to you, Coop," she said, mistaking his distress as being upset over Riley, which might be partially true, but Izzy was a big piece of that puzzle, too. She rested her hands on his shoulders, and he resisted trembling at her touch. Only a weak man did that, and she'd witnessed too many vulnerable moments lately when it came to him.

"He has a funny way of showing it," he said tersely, even as his brain fogged up. He fought to clear it, not sure he was capable of that feat.

"Cooper, give him time. He's struggling. Tanner is a safe choice."

"And I'm not?"

"No, because you matter. In the greater scheme of things, Tanner doesn't. Not to Riley."

"You think?" Cooper didn't understand her logic, not really. From where he was standing, Riley hero-worshipped Tanner and considered Cooper the latest incarnation of the devil. Cooper didn't know what the hell to do about it or even if he should.

"I *know*." She stroked his cheek, her eyes bright with emotion that drew him in while terrifying the shit out of him.

"I miss you." Unable to resist any longer, he leaned into her, his hands on her shoulders, while he searched her face for any sign that she missed him just as much.

She looked away for a moment, then looked back. "I miss you, too, but we're not a good match."

His heart sank just a little. "We never made it past third base, so how do you know that?"

Izzy rolled her eyes and backed away from him, putting physical and emotional space between them. "I'm talking about more than sex. You're the jealous, controlling type, and I'm the free-spirit, I'll-do-what-I-want type. Not exactly a good combination."

"I could change. Give me another chance." He was begging, he heard it in his voice. "I want you back." There he'd said it, laid it out there, opened himself up for her to either put a bandage on his partially healed wounds or rip them wide open.

Uncertainty wrinkled her cute little nose and gave him hope. He moved in, knowing her body had the hots for him. Even though she'd managed to hold back from doing the deed when they'd been dating, in a few more dates he'd have gotten her naked and in his bed.

She shook her head, her dark hair falling across her shoulders. He wanted to bury his face in those silky strands and inhale the scent of her.

"Izzy—" He took another step toward her, but she sidestepped and put the counter between them.

"No, Coop. No." She held up her hands to ward him off—as if she could stop him.

"Give me another chance." He circled the counter and cornered her in the kitchen.

She sucked her lower lip into her mouth, a sure sign she was considering her options. In his playbook, that was a helluva lot better than an outright refusal. She gazed up at him, her eyes bright with a challenge. "Show me."

"Show you?" He grinned and started to unzip his jeans.

She smacked his hand. "I mean, show me you can change. Show me you can release control and let me be my own person. Show me you can trust me. Show me you can tolerate my job and all the men I'm required to hang out with and schmooze. Show me, and I'll reconsider."

Damn, that was a tall order, considering how he craved every aspect of his life to be in perfect control. Yet, he'd never been one to back down from any challenge, and Izzy was worth it. Yeah, he could do this or he'd fucking die trying.

He clicked his heels together and saluted her. "You're on. I'll be the perfect gentlemen who trusts you implicitly."

"We'll see." He heard the skepticism in her voice, but rather than taking offense, he grinned all the more.

"How about we kiss on it to seal the deal?"

* * * *

Izzy's good sense, or what was left of it in Cooper's presence, floated out the window like an unleashed bundle of balloons into the stormy Seattle sky. His smile was an odd combination of wolfish and hopeful.

She leaned forward and looked up at him. His uncertain grin shifted to predatory, while her body hummed with giddy anticipation. She should just jump the man's bones and get it over with.

Like that would satisfy her longing for him. Yeah, right.

It'd only whet her appetite for more. She knew that as sure as she knew her parents hadn't had a hit song in twenty years, but that hadn't stopped them from wanting one either.

"Izzy," Cooper whispered, his deep voice a husky growl.

She leaned back and grabbed the edge of the counter to stop her knees from buckling. Sliding to the floor in a pile of overheated female mush wasn't the way to end this evening.

Neither was jumping in bed with this hot man who pushes every one of your buttons like he's been fully trained on how to drive your body crazy.

Besides, no one said anything about bed. Just one little kiss. That was all.

He advanced on her, ready to claim what she knew was his, even if she didn't want him to know it.

"Riley's upstairs," she pointed out, but he didn't seem to hear her.

"I want you back, and I'll prove it," he murmured as he cupped her face in his big, rough hands. She stared into eyes as deep and blue as a wind-tossed sea, while waves of desire rolled over her, cresting like twenty-foot waves.

She opened her mouth to point out that he'd never really had her. Their on-again, off-again relationship had spanned little more than a month. The first two hours they'd met she'd gone down on him, and he'd gone down on her. Then they'd gone their separate ways. When they'd gotten back together days later, she'd insisted they take it slow, rather than jumping right back into the deep end.

Izzy didn't trust easily, and while she'd never been a prude, her instincts told her that sex with Cooper would be more than sex. It'd be downright dangerous to the most vulnerable part of her—her heart. And she guarded that heart as jealously as she guarded her sisters, and Cooper hadn't earned her trust. In fact, he'd turned it inside out with his caveman behavior.

Sex with Cooper Black would ruin her for any other man. Did

she dare chance it?

If Cooper didn't want to keep his own nephew around, why would he keep her around once he got what he wanted?

Despite it all, she was going to kiss him.

His distinctly male scent of soap and man filled her nostrils. She reached up and laced her fingers behind his neck. He pressed his hips against hers, his hands splayed on the counter on either side of her body. His erection pressed against her crotch, and she fought to catch her breath.

"Oh, God, Izzy," he rasped against her neck. "I need you."

This big, strong man needed *her*?

Well, dammit, she needed him, too. Or his body, at the least. God, she was a weak woman when it came to this particular sexy hockey player.

Cooper's lips touched hers, and her eyes fluttered shut. He was gentle, careful, as if he were afraid he'd break her, or even worse, that she'd run. She didn't push him, just enjoyed the moment, enjoyed his warm, moist lips covering hers, as his tongue traced a circle around her mouth. He tasted so good. So very, very good. And so very, very right.

His strong hands cupped her butt, and he lifted her onto the counter. He settled his hips between her thighs with a groan and rubbed his erection against her. She buried her fingers in his shaggy, overly long hair, savoring how it felt sliding through her fingers.

He licked at the seam of her lips, enticing her to open for him. She didn't need a second invitation. She let him inside and twined her tongue with his in that age-old dance. Wrapping her long legs around his waist, she lost herself in the taste, smell, and feel of him.

Cooper affected her like no other man she'd ever been with, and she hadn't actually been with him—yet. At least not completely. But she wanted to be. And against every bit of better judgment she possessed, she wanted it to be tonight. She didn't want to wait.

She had to be the most fickle woman on earth. She'd ended it. Now she wanted to start it again.

Well, okay, so maybe with a little help from Cooper.

His warm hands slid under her T-shirt and caressed her bare back. He dragged his mouth from hers and kissed a trail down her neck, pausing for a nip here and there. Izzy tilted her head back to give him better access. Her body was shameless in its response to him. She fisted his shirt in her hands, ready to rip it off him at a moment's notice.

Cooper pushed her shirt upward until her lacy bra was visible. He cupped her breasts in each of his big hands and squeezed them. His face softened as he stared at them reverently. He bent his head as he slipped her bra cups below her nipples. Taking one in his mouth, he gently sucked and swirled his tongue around her sensitive nub, while his thumb rubbed the other nipple.

"Cooper," she hissed. "You're killing me."

"Not yet. But I'm getting there." He chuckled, but sounded strained, as if holding back were killing him, too.

"Take me to bed." She begged without thinking. And once she'd spoken those words, she honestly couldn't recall her reasons for not sleeping with him. Whatever her concerns had been, she didn't care about them tonight.

"Fuck, yes," he croaked, his voice breaking.

He picked her up, his mouth hungrily on hers as he carried her toward the entryway, which featured two sets of stairs, typical of a split-level. The master suite in this home was on the ground floor.

Izzy wrapped her arms around his strong neck and kissed him right back.

Just before the stairs, he pushed her against the wall, his breathing coming in short, desperate gasps. "I don't think I'll make it to the bedroom."

"This wall seems like a good place." She unwrapped her legs and slid her feet slowly along his thighs and calves until they were resting on the floor. Cooper's eyes glowed in the dark light of a nearby lamp.

"Any place is a good place as long as you're there." He panted and ran his hands down her sides, stopping at her zipper. She milked his erection through his jeans.

With a tortured growl Cooper sank to the tiled entryway floor, taking her with him. Izzy didn't care that it was hard and cold because Cooper's body against hers blocked out any other sensations. He rolled her onto her back and tugged on her zipper, yanking her jeans and underwear down to her knees. A second later, he pulled down his own jeans and his big cock sprang free. Izzy licked her lips and smiled up at him.

"You are beautiful," she said.

"That's my line." He winked at her, as he positioned himself between her spread legs. The head of his cock rubbed her wet pussy, and she whimpered, arching her back to take him inside.

One minutely sane part of her managed to speak. "Condom?"

"Oh, crap."

He scrambled to his feet, tripped over his jeans, and sprawled on the floor. Izzy couldn't help giggling. Muttering several creative obscenities, Cooper struggled to his feet, pulling his pants up and started downstairs.

"Is everything okay? I heard a crash," Riley said from the top flight of stairs.

Izzy froze as did Cooper in mid-step. Holy crap. In their horny frenzy, they'd forgotten all about Riley. Izzy quickly crawled out of sight into an alcove under the stairwell and pulled up her jeans. She crouched on the floor and straightened her clothes in case Riley ventured down the stairs to see for himself.

"I'm fine. Just slipped on the tile. Someone must have spilt something. It's a little wet," she heard Cooper say.

That wasn't all that was wet.

Despite being horrified that Riley almost caught them humping like animals on the entryway tile, she covered her hand with her mouth to muffle her giggle.

"Are you sure?" Riley said.

"I'm positive," Cooper answered, his tone tense and distracted. "Is Izzy gone?"

"Yes. Go back to bed." Cooper's voice sounded like a drill sergeant giving orders.

"Why can't Izzy stay with me when you're on road trips? I don't like Mrs. McCullum."

Cooper cleared his throat. "Izzy has her own career. *Now*. Go. To. Bed."

Izzy heard footsteps then a door slamming. A few seconds later, a disheveled Cooper peeked around the corner.

"Izzy?"

"Over here," she whispered, as she crawled to her feet. She held a finger to his lips and led him away from the stairs. "Do you know how close we came to—"

His look said it all. "Another good reason why I need to find that kid's mother. I'm a single guy. Having a kid here isn't working out for me." He studied her pointedly. "Or you."

Izzy didn't want to be the reason Cooper kicked Riley out. She turned and grabbed her zip-up sweatshirt. "I need to go."

"Are you sure?" Equal parts of frustration and disappointment were reflected in those blue eyes.

"You told him I was gone. Do you want him catching you in a lie? What kind of role model would that make you?" She headed for the door with Cooper hot on her heels.

"I'm a crappy role model anyway."

Izzy turned and put her hands on his shoulders. "No, you're not, but you could go a little easier on him. He has it pretty tough. His mother is missing. You're making it clear you don't want him here. He's in a new school and trying to fit in."

"Izzy, I—"

She cut off his protest, standing on tiptoes and brushing her lips across his, while resisting the urge to do a lot more than taste him. That'd almost gotten them into a load of trouble.

"I have to go." She hesitated as Cooper's intense gaze held hers.

"This isn't finished. Not yet."

She nodded. "I know."

"I can do this. I can meet your challenge. I can change. Preseason starts tomorrow. How about a late dinner? I'll have tickets waiting for you and the kid at will call tomorrow night."

She should've said no but obviously she wasn't that strong or that smart. With a nod, she ran out the door like a cat escaping a dog kennel. Cooper stood on the porch, watching as she drove down the driveway.

Chapter 7—Blindsided

One night later, Cooper stood before his team in the locker room of Seattle Arena, the Sockeyes temporary home. Not the best place to play hockey, but it'd do for now. The place had seen better days, despite the money Ethan had put into it earlier this summer. The building had been erected for the Seattle World's Fair back in the early sixties, and it looked every bit that old.

Yet, Cooper didn't care. Playing in Seattle didn't dampen his enthusiasm one bit for the game itself. Ice was ice, and skating was his passion.

Anticipation fueled by adrenaline thrummed through his veins like it always did. Only this time, he sensed a difference. This was a new town, a new team, a new era for him and his teammates. As much as he wanted to hate Seattle, and despite his every intention to leave when his contract was up, he couldn't deny that Ethan Parker ran a class act from the coaches to the support staff.

He looked around the room at each man, every face lifted toward him expectantly waiting for words of wisdom or inspiration from their team captain. Cooper didn't feel particularly inspirational or clever with words tonight.

The Seattle Sockeyes' first preseason game—a game which meant nothing and everything—sold out within a few hours of the tickets going on sale. Cooper, who'd spent his entire NHL career playing for Gainesville didn't know how to handle the pressure of instant popularity. In Florida, they'd faded into obscurity except for the few faithful, battling for sports fan attention with the local college football and basketball teams.

Seattle's football team, the Steelheads, had sucked for a long time. Seattle's beloved basketball team left town years ago amid a scandal that still pissed off Seattleites. The baseball team finished with a whimper, not a bang.

Suddenly all eyes rested on the Sockeyes, the new kids on the block.

Cooper was used to playing for himself, for his coaches, and for his teammates. He wasn't used to playing for a city with expectations and high hopes, and it was damn weird.

The team's best defensemen, Matt LeRue and Jason "Wildman" Wilder, watched him like they watched the puck when they were on

114

ice. Alert and ready to do battle, the guys vibrated with pent-up energy.

Martin "Brick" Bricker, their third-year goalie with a propensity to overheat, as usual was the only guy not suited up. In fact, he was stark-ass naked as he diligently taped his stick with the same precision he guarded the net. Brick liked women, minimal clothes, parties, and he loved hockey. In fact, Cooper forgave the kid's sins because of their mutual passion for the ice.

Next to Brick, sat Alex "Rush" Markov, a second-year guy, from Russia who loved everything American, especially the women, which made Brick and him the perfect duo off the ice. Rush loved to fight, which landed him in the penalty box more than any other player.

Cedric sat to the right of Cooper, giving a rookie shit to the point the kid was groveling at his feet. Cooper tried not to laugh. Ced already had the poor guy bringing donuts to every practice.

Coach had already given the traditional pre-game speech then he'd stepped back to allow Cooper to have his say.

As the captain, Cooper always said a few words before his team took the ice. He cleared his throat and focused his steeliest gaze on rookie Jasper Flint whose dark head was bent as he tapped a text message on his phone. Jasper had talent to spare but no discipline. The room grew quiet until the tapping was all you could hear. Jasper's finger froze mid-tap. Slowly, he looked up to see every head turned toward him. At least he had the decency to turn redder than an ugly Christmas sweater.

"I don't have to tell you guys that we have a packed house for a preseason game."

"No shit. When's the last time that ever happened in Florida?" Cedric grinned, ignoring Coop's murderous glare.

"Ced's right. Hell, we could barely sell out playoff games," Matt LeRue, the defensive captain, added, not the least intimidated by Cooper's irritation. Cooper didn't like them dissing their old team—it was like speaking ill of the dead.

"Okay, okay." Cooper held up his hands to silence them. "Ladies, listen up. This is the League's debut in Seattle, and a local TV station is interrupting prime-time programming to broadcast this game. The league is setting this game up as the birth of a new rivalry with Vancouver. We're going to give the fans something to talk about while waiting in line at Starbucks tomorrow morning."

Every head in the room nodded enthusiastically, even Brick, who was busy yanking on his uniform and lacing his skates in a last-minute flurry. Cooper never messed with a guy's pre-game rituals, no matter how weird. Guarding the goal was hot, hard work, and he didn't blame Brick for keeping cool until the last minute.

Cooper motioned to the door. "Let's get out there and kick some Canuck ass."

Everyone stood and cheered, filing out of the locker room with the eagerness of a new season ahead of them. Cooper took up the back of the line, preferring to be the last on the ice. Well aware of his captain's one little quirk, Brick hurried to the door, pulling on his sweater as he disappeared down the hall.

Cooper paused in the long tunnel under the bleachers, shocked at the noise. The entire place rocked from the sounds of stomping feet and one continuous cheer. Somewhere in those stands sat Izzy with his nephew. The thought gave him extra incentive, not that he needed it, but Izzy's presence filled him with this weird, warm feeling which nestled somewhere beneath his breastbone. He wasn't sure he liked it, and he should fight it, but for now he let it be, and enjoyed this moment—a moment he was sharing with her even if they weren't physically together. He could feel her nearby, knew she'd be watching.

Cooper stepped into the opening of the arena. Despite his dislike of his new home, he had to smile. He couldn't help it.

Spotlights waved across the ice in the Sockeye colors of blue and green. His teammates stood in a circle at center ice, waiting for him, while the fans in the packed stands rocked the place.

"Cooper Black, your Sockeye team captain," the announcer literally yelled to be heard over the crowd.

"Welcome to Seattle," Cooper whispered under his breath as he took the ice to a deafening roar.

* * * *

Riley sat in the seats Cooper had provided on the glass near the bench. He wasn't up on hockey like he was football, but he'd

116

followed Uncle Cooper enough to pick up the basics of the game.

He was starving so he bit into his hot dog and crammed a few fries in his mouth. Izzy shot him a disapproving look, and he smiled sheepishly. She probably thought he had the manners of a starving stray dog.

"Did you get your homework done like Cooper asked?" Izzy said, but she never took her eyes off his uncle skating around on the ice with more coordination than most people had on dry land. He made it look easy, but Riley knew enough about skating to know it wasn't.

"Yeah, the old hag made me," he said between bites.

"That's my aunt you're talking about." Izzy levelled him a chastising glare.

"Sorry." Damn, he'd screwed up twice in less than five minutes, and he really wanted Izzy to like him.

"Riley, give her a chance."

"She's mean."

"She's not mean. She's firm."

Izzy didn't know what she was talking about. Every day he inspected his food for glass and made sure the old witch hadn't poisoned his milk. Okay, so maybe he was exaggerating a little. But not much.

He flipped the subject to something that'd been nagging at him since last night. "Did I hear you with Uncle Cooper last night after I went to bed?"

Izzy's mouth pressed together in a way that reminded him of her aunt. He guessed they were related after all. "I finished cleaning up then I left."

"I heard something else." Riley was pretty good at reading people. He'd needed that special skill for survival on the streets, and she wasn't being straight with him.

Izzy stared straight at him, as if daring him to say any more.

He wasn't an idiot, and he knew shit when he stepped in it. He also knew when he should let stuff go and mind his own business. Uncle Cooper didn't want him, and he'd better do everything he could to not give the man a reason to send him to foster care. He'd never find his mother then.

"Sorry." Riley shrugged one shoulder and turned his attention back to the ice. Loneliness swallowed up all the good feelings inside him.

Nobody wanted him. At least his mother needed him, and that was kind of like wanting, wasn't it? He felt hot tears welling up in his eyes and swiped at them with his napkin. He hated crying, but he did it a lot lately when no one was around but Joker to hear him.

"It's okay," Izzy patted his arm and smiled at him. Her voice softened like his mother's did when she was clean and being a mother instead of an addict.

Riley swallowed hard, remembering the rare good times, but at least his mother loved him. That was more than he could say for Cooper. "I just want Uncle Cooper to find my mom so life can go back to the way it was for everyone."

Izzy studied him, pity in her kick-ass eyes. He hated pity more than he hated crying. He lifted his chin and gave her his best nothing-bothers-me look. She wasn't buying it.

"What was your life like, Riley?"

"Okay, I guess. I mean, I don't have anything else to compare it with, but my mom needs me. We have to find her." His voice broke, and he stuffed the last of his hot dog in his mouth so he wouldn't be expected to talk anymore.

* * * *

Izzy decided to back off on questioning Riley before he started crying and embarrassed them both. He concentrated on his junk food, and she concentrated on Cooper. God, he was beautiful, all raw power and athletic grace. He skated around the ice as if he owned it, body and soul. If it hadn't been for Junior here, they'd have done it in the entryway.

Damn.

Izzy wanted to do it in every room of Cooper's house, well, except Riley's room because that would be just plain weird.

When Cooper skated close to her, he tapped his stick on the glass and winked. She grinned at him.

Despite the bulky hockey uniform, the man's fluidity on the ice made her panties wet and her breath hitch. Imagining the bare skin and muscles under the layers of clothing made her even hotter.

"It's okay if you sleep with him. I don't care."

Izzy snapped her head around to stare at Riley, mortified that he'd witnessed her drooling over his uncle like a pussycat in heat. "We're just friends."

Riley narrowed his eyes and studied her. "Yeah, right."

"We are." Not that she wanted it to stay that way lately, or at the least, she wanted to progress to the *with benefits* type of friendship.

"Then are you with Tanner?"

"Tanner?" Izzy had to laugh. She supposed it was a logical question from Riley's point of view but not Izzy's. Tanner did nothing for her, while Cooper did everything.

"I'd understand if you liked him better. He's nicer than my uncle."

"No. No, not at all. Tanner and I are definitely just friends." Izzy ignored the "nice" remark.

"So you want to be more than friends with my uncle," Riley observed. It was a statement, not a question. "He sure has the hots for you."

Izzy wracked her brain for a way to steer this conversation to safer ground. "How's school?"

Riley clammed up. "You asked me that last night. Nothing's changed." He brightened. "Are you coming to my game this Thursday?"

"Wouldn't miss it for the world."

He smiled, a very rare happy smile, and Izzy smiled back.

The crowd chanted as Cooper skated to center ice for the face off. It was too loud to talk anymore, Izzy and Riley stood and clapped and cheered with the rest of the rabid Seattle fans.

Izzy had never seen NHL hockey before. It was fast, at times brutal, at other times a poetic symphony of skaters all in tune with each other. And it was sexy as hell, even though she held her breath and clutched the armrests when a big brute slammed Cooper into the boards. How he managed to skate away as if nothing happened she'd never understand. The offending defenseman took a turn in the penalty box, and Izzy rose with the crowd to heckle the jerk.

Cooper would need a nice, long soak in a warm tub and a massage after this was over. He'd sink down into a luxurious bubble bath, close his blue eyes, and she'd work her magic on those bruised and sore muscles of his. Then she'd let him work a little magic of his own on her starving body.

She rubbed her eyes in an attempt to clear that image from her mind.

Cooper promised he'd change if she gave him a chance. Deep down in her heart, she doubted a jealous, possessive, controlling man could ever change into a trusting and laid-back guy. She knew he'd try, really try, and while he was trying why not run the man through his paces? She'd never held off on having sex with a man who attracted her. Why was Cooper any different? It sure as hell wasn't because they wouldn't be damn good in bed together. In fact, she'd bet her party-crashing business that they'd dance the night away in the sheets.

Her reasons for not sleeping with him seemed ridiculous now. Especially since she'd resigned herself to only having a right-now relationship with the sexy hockey star. He'd leave Seattle at the end of the season with a fat new contract elsewhere, and she'd never leave. She loved Seattle. He hated everything about it. The trees and mountains made him claustrophobic, so he'd told her. He hated the rain. Hell, he probably thought it was too green.

A woman couldn't reason with a pig-headed man like that, so why try? Why not use him for what his body had to offer and have fun doing it? She wouldn't get any complaints from Cooper about that. Sure, she'd probably fall for him over the next few months, but she'd survive. If she was good at one thing, it was surviving. She'd been doing it for years.

He'd move on, and she'd move on. No harm, no foul, at least not permanently. Izzy had been in love before, and she'd fallen out of love just as quickly. Cooper wouldn't be any different. Sure, it'd hurt, but what doesn't kill you makes you stronger.

Izzy wasn't a romantic like her sister Emma, who believed everyone had one forever love. What a load of crap. She wasn't a party girl like middle child Betheni, though she did love her men. And she didn't avoid men altogether like Emma's twin, Avery, who preferred the company of horses.

The crowd around Izzy roared. Cooper had scored a goal, and she'd missed it, she'd been so deep into her own world. Belatedly, Izzy leapt to her feet and cheered as she watched the replay on the big screen. Cooper skated by, tapping the glass with his stick first in front of Riley then in front of her. He grinned. She grinned back. So did Riley.

She stayed in the present for the remainder of the game, which the Sockeyes won by one goal. Afterward, Riley begged Izzy to wait with him outside the locker room.

Cooper was the last one to come out. He stopped and looked around, all sexy with his hair still wet from his shower, and dressed in his street clothes. When he saw them, a slow grin spread across his face and made her want to spread her legs for him. Right here. Right now. How crazy was that?

Oh, God. This had to stop.

Cooper fought his way past several reporters until he finally got to them. He fist bumped Riley and picked Izzy up and spun her around, kissing her soundly. When he finally put her down, he draped his arm around her shoulders.

"Told you so," Riley whispered in her ear.

"Let's get out of here and grab a pizza. A bunch of the guys and their families are heading to that place down the block." Cooper didn't wait for an answer but pulled her along with him as he cleared a path through the crowds and turned down a hall leading to the team's private parking area.

He opened the passenger door for Izzy when her phone rang. She backed up a step and gave him an apologetic smile. "I need answer this. It's Betheni."

Cooper nodded, his impatience clear, while Riley said nothing and waited nearby.

"Izzy, you have to come home. Fawn and Rock are here, and they're insisting on borrowing some money. I don't what to do. The only money we have saved is for the power bill and our tuition." Rock and Fawn Maxwell were their parents. None of the sisters called them Mom and Dad because they'd never fulfilled the role of parents. Part of a washed up rock band, To the Max, they chased every impossible opportunity, convinced they'd hit it big again with a zealousness they'd never shown toward parenting.

"God, fucking dammit," Izzy muttered under her breath. She'd give anything for normal parents who supported their kids instead of the opposite.

Both Cooper and Riley stared at her, and she realized she'd spoken out loud. With a disgusted sigh, she said, "Sorry, something's come up at home. I can't join you for pizza after all." Or that soak in the tub she'd been fantasizing about all night.

"Anything I could help with?" Cooper offered with a boyish

121

eagerness.

"Yeah, me, too," Riley added, not to be outdone by his uncle. He shot Cooper a glare as if to say *she's my girl, hands off.*

Izzy would've found them both amusing and sweet if it wasn't for her panic that Fawn and Rock would manipulate and guilt her sisters into handing over all their cash before she could get home to stop them. Without further explanation, because Izzy didn't get outsiders involved in her screwed-up family dynamics, she pecked both Cooper and Riley on the cheeks, ran back down the hallway, and out of the arena, sprinting across the parking lot to her car.

Traffic clogged every street and alley, forcing Izzy to wait impatiently for her turn. She tapped her fingers on the steering wheel, muttered obscenities under her breath, and constantly glanced at the small dash clock.

The usual ten-minute drive home turned into a thirty-minute drive. Finally she screeched to a halt in front of their apartment and took the stairs two at a time.

She threw the door open and three shocked pairs of eyes glanced up at her from where they sat at the small dining table.

"No—" she almost wailed.

Betheni as the second-oldest, even though she was the most irresponsible, spoke first. "They took all our cash. I tried to tell them no but they were insistent."

Avery sighed, leaned her elbows on the table, chin on her hands. "They started in on that same-old, same-old story, blaming us for their career going down the tubes and saying we owed it to them."

"They promised to pay it back," Emma added, always trying to believe the best in everyone.

Izzy sank into the one empty chair, beating herself up for not taking the time to deposit the money into their bank account. Their last party-crashing client paid in cash, and she'd had Cooper's thousand, too. Now she had none of it. Stupid move on her part, but she'd been hoarding it for tuition and been worried if she deposited it too soon, it'd be used to pay other bills.

Betheni smacked her sister on the arm. "They've never paid back a penny they've *borrowed* from us."

"When they hit it big, they will," Emma insisted.

"Oh, seriously. You can't believe that bullshit." Betheni rolled her eyes. "They will never hit it big again. They're has-beens. The best they'll ever do is get a gig at a local casino."

"That money was to pay the twins' tuition. It's already past due." Izzy rubbed her temples, feeling a headache coming on.

"Will they kick us out of class?" Emma worried, as she exchanged a secretive glace with her twin sister.

Avery sat up straight and looked Izzy directly in the eyes, then she dropped a bombshell. "I'm going to quit anyway. I just didn't know how to tell you guys. This is the perfect time."

"Quit? You're not quitting. I've worked my ass off to keep you guys in school." Izzy's voice rose to a screech, but she couldn't help it. She'd given up her own college education to work two jobs so her sisters would be able to get degrees.

"I'm going to train horses and give riding lessons. Sam needs an assistant, and she offered me the job. I start next Monday," Avery declared looking every bit as stubborn as Izzy had ever seen her.

Betheni and Emma leaned back as if getting ready for an explosion.

"*What?* You are not quitting college to work with horses. What kind of a career is that?" Izzy was livid. She stood up and paced the room before she did bodily harm to her sister. No one spoke or even moved.

Avery cleared her throat. "I love horses. It's all I've ever wanted to do. You're the one who pushed me toward college. I don't want to go, and you're not forcing me anymore." Avery looked around the table at her other sister. "None of you are."

"What if you get hurt? Then what? How will you support yourself?" Izzy stopped a few feet from her sister's chair, hands on her hips, her body vibrating with anger.

"I'll be fine."

"You won't be fine. You'll be a barn bum the rest of your life." Izzy couldn't stop the disgust from creeping into her voice.

Avery shot to her feet, fighting mad. "You're just afraid that I'll forever be a burden just like Rock and Fawn are. Well, guess what? As of right now, you no longer have to worry about me. I'm leaving." She stormed to the hall coat tree and grabbed a jacket. Ignoring Izzy, she turned to her other sisters. "I'll come back later for my stuff when the controlling she-bitch sister isn't here."

On that note, Avery stomped out the door. A second later Izzy heard her piece-of-crap truck, badly in need of a new muffler, roar out of the parking lot.

Her remaining two sisters quickly made themselves scarce, while Izzy sank down into the chair, feeling shell-shocked and confused. She'd dedicated her entire adult life and a good portion of her childhood to taking care of her sisters. She'd known the moment would come when they'd no longer need her like they once had, but she never thought it would erupt like it had tonight. Never once had it occurred to her that her sisters didn't actually appreciate her meddling or her involvement in every facet of their lives, down to their career choices and their boyfriends.

Several minutes later, Izzy still sat there, staring at the wall.

"Hey," Betheni said as she peered around the corner.

"Yeah?' Izzy said quietly.

Encouraged by her calm response, Betheni slipped into the room and sat in a chair.

"I only want what's best for you guys."

"We know that."

"A career with horses isn't a career at all. I don't want to see her make such a big mistake. She'll be mucking stalls for the rest of her life."

"Lots of people would say party crashing isn't much of a career either," Betheni pointed out in her usual blunt manner.

Betheni had a point, as much as Izzy hated to admit it. "It pays the bills," she said defensively.

"Avery will get over it, Izz. She's a big girl. She needs to make her own decisions and make her own mistakes. You have to stop running interference for us and start living your own life."

"I've been the parent for so long, it's not like I can turn it off."

"You need to try. Why don't you get horizontal with that sexy hockey star? Then you'll quit obsessing about us and start obsessing about different ways to fuck him." Betheni grinned; never one to hold back, she said what she thought and to hell with the consequences. Which explained why she went through men and jobs like a mother of quadruplets went through diapers.

"Really, Bets." Izzy used a childhood nickname of Betheni's. Not only was it a shortened version of her name but all bets were off when it came to Betheni's potty mouth and outrageous behavior.

"Izzy, you know you wanna."

"Maybe," Izzy admitted, feeling her face heat up.

"When's the last time you screwed a guy's brains out or had one fuck you senseless?"

Izzy refused to answer that question because it was too much of a statement about her sorry life.

Betheni's eyes grew wide as the truth dawned on her. "You've never slept with Cooper?"

Izzy shook her head. "Crazy, I know, especially considering how we started out hot for each other like rabbits. I guess I just wanted us to slow down and date first. I had a hard deadline of one month before I would jump in bed with him."

"And you guys didn't make it one month."

"No, he turned into a jealous, controlling ass and jeopardized our business in the process. No one will ever control my future. Ever. Especially not a stubborn man."

"That doesn't mean you can't hook up with him in the naked sense of the word."

Izzy sat up straighter and grinned her most wicked grin. "That's what I'm thinking. No relationship to mess things up. Just plain and simple sex."

"You?" Betheni sounded shocked.

"Why does that surprise you?" Contrary to what Cooper said, Izzy was not a prude. She enjoyed sex as much as the next woman.

Betheni shrugged and studied her bright-red fingernails. "Because there's something different about Cooper. That's why you didn't show any interest in Tanner even though he was all over you."

"In that case, why wouldn't I jump Cooper's bones?"

"You tell me. Why haven't you?"

"I would've tonight if it hadn't been for all this drama." Izzy mouth pulled down into a frown and her stomach dived as she remembered what started all this. "Rock and Fawn took all of our money stash?"

"All of it. Every last penny. Of course, they promised they'd pay us back as soon as they got paid for the next gig."

"Yeah, right." As if their parents' promises meant a damn thing. "How am I going to pay the bills and tuition?"

"How are *we* going to pay the bills and tuition? We're in this together. Remember? Stop taking this all on yourself. At least we don't have to worry about Avery's tuition," Betheni said wryly.

"Please don't remind me."

"Izz, we'll work it out. Maybe we can get an advance from Ethan's mother for the Kids for Play thing we're doing."

"She's already advanced money to us twice. I can't ask again." Izzy stood, her mind made up. "Dammit, I'm going over there and getting our money back right now."

"They were heading to the Overtime Tavern. They're playing there tonight."

"Fine, I'll go there." Determination coursed through Izzy. Dammit, she would not let them take this money, not when her sisters so desperately needed it, including Avery. She had every intention of convincing Avery to stay in college, once she gave her a day or two to calm down.

"I'll go with you. You'll need moral support to face Rock's skewed logic and Fawn's extreme guilt trips."

Izzy nodded, grabbed her coat, purse, and car keys, and threw open the door, ready to do battle, only to collide with something solid and warm.

Cooper's broad chest.

Chapter 8—Scoring Drive

"Whoa, going somewhere?" Cooper said, gripping Izzy's shoulders. Not that he minded her sweet face buried in his neck, but the woman had obviously been on a mission to parts unknown, and he hoped like hell he was that mission.

Izzy stared up at him and blinked those big, gorgeous brown eyes of hers several times as if trying to get her bearings.

"What are you doing here?" She clutched his upper arms and stared into his eyes. For a moment they were the only two people in the world. He was a fucking goner when she stared at him like that. He'd slay any dragon, climb any castle wall, or swim any moat for her. Anything. Everything. Whatever she asked for, even what she didn't, he'd do it. Hell, he'd even sit through two hours of a sappy chick flick. Now that was pretty far gone.

Betheni cleared her throat and Riley coughed, bringing Izzy and Cooper back from wherever it was they'd both gone and breaking the spell between them.

Izzy backed away slowly, her eyes still locked with his. Cooper ran his fingers through his hair.

Riley pushed past Cooper. After shooting him a withering glare, he focused his full attention on Izzy. "We were worried about you."

Riley's words prodded Cooper out of his trance. "Yeah, we wanted to make sure everything was all right."

"It's not, but we'll manage." Izzy looked like she was going to cry, and Betheni stared at her feet at a rare loss for words.

"Could we help?" Cooper said a little too eagerly for a guy still trying to figure out where he fit in her life outside of the bedroom.

Izzy shook her head. "It's just family drama."

Cooper noted the coat Izzy was wearing and the purse slung over her arm. "You were just leaving."

Izzy glanced at Betheni. "Yes, we were. Thanks for stopping by, but we have an errand to run."

"This late?"

"Speaking of late, shouldn't Riley be in bed? Tomorrow's a school day." Izzy's observation properly dressed him down and drove home the point once again that he was a crappy uncle.

"Uh, yeah."

"Well, then, that settles it. We'll catch up with you later." Izzy gave Cooper a gentle shove out of her way.

His pride already wounded, Cooper forced a smile. "Good night, ladies," he said as if being pushed aside wasn't any big deal.

Riley hung back until Cooper tersely spoke to him. "Let's go, Riley. You need to be in bed."

Riley's eyes narrowed with animosity and resentment toward his uncle. He turned his back on Cooper. "Bye, Izzy. I'm here if you need me."

Cooper sighed. Being an uncle to a teenager definitely sucked hind tit, especially when the teenager blamed Cooper to some extent for his mother's problems. Cooper knew at a basic level he wasn't to blame, the drugs were, but he still felt guilt, felt he hadn't done enough to save her. Even worse, he carried around a good dose of guilt for being oblivious to Riley's existence. Maybe he could've done a few things to make the kid's childhood a little better. For now, he was doing the best he could by providing Riley with material things he'd never had before and by giving his PI a blank check to pull out all the stops to find his sister Julie. Once he did, he'd get her some help and set her up in a nice apartment, and he'd make sure Riley was taken care of properly.

Izzy patted Riley's shoulder, her expression softening to one of fondness. "I know, honey."

Unwelcome jealousy surged through Cooper, which irritated him. Jealous of a fourteen year old? What bullshit. He needed to get a hand on his jealousy. After all, that's what got him into this mess in the first place. If he'd behaved like a man who trusted his woman, they'd be enjoying each other's company in and out of bed right now.

But no, he had to behave like the Neanderthal he was.

If the insult fits, own it.

Then do something about it, Coop.

Even though it might take a while for stuff to sink into his thick head, he'd finally figured out he wanted Izzy around. He just had to prove to her he could change.

And admitting he'd been wrong was easier said than done for a stubborn, arrogant ass like him.

* * * *

With Betheni in tow, Izzy stomped down the apartment stairs and walked to her car. Looking way too much alike, Cooper and Riley stood several feet away next to his monstrous SUV. She knew what Cooper was doing. He was protecting her, waiting until she sat safely in the driver's seat. How could such a simple act of kindness both irritate and give her a warm fuzzy?

Izzy snapped on her seatbelt. "Betheni," she chastised her sister. With a sigh and a roll of her eyes, Betheni buckled her own seatbelt. Her wild-child sister hated being forced to do anything, especially when it was for her own good.

Izzy turned the key in the ignition. Her temperamental old car spit and sputtered. A puff of black smoke escaped the muffler. The car gasped and shrieked then went ominously quiet. No amount of coaxing, cussing, and pounding her fists on the steering brought the car back to life.

She'd known the poor little car lived on borrowed time but hoped to borrow a lot more time because she sure as hell didn't have the money to buy a new used car.

Izzy stared straight ahead, beyond frustrated and close to tears. Someone tapped on the driver's window, and she jumped. It was Cooper, of course.

Izzy rolled down her window. "Yes?" she said calmly as if her current world wasn't crumbling before her very eyes.

"Trouble?" Cooper stared down at her, his blue eyes full of concern. Riley stood a little behind him.

"No, not at all. Right, Betheni?" She looked to Betheni for confirmation, expecting her sister to have her back. She didn't.

Betheni snorted. "Where do you want me to start?"

Izzy shot her one of those shut-your-mouth glares, but since when did her rebellious sister ever listen to anyone, not even whatever voice of reason she might possess?

Cooper leaned down so he could see Betheni. "What's going on? Could I give you a ride somewhere?"

"No, we're fine," Izzy said.

"Yes, you can give her a ride," Betheni countered. "But brace yourself, this isn't going to be pretty." Betheni jerked open the door and got out. She gestured to Izzy to follow her. "Coop, you can drop me off at your house first, and I'll watch Riley to make sure he gets to bed."

"I don't need a babysitter," Riley groused.

Cooper ignored him and directed his answer to Betheni. "Sounds like a plan to me."

Several minutes later, Izzy stared out the passenger window as they drove to Cooper's in silence. Riley and Betheni hopped out before the SUV came to a halt in his driveway. Izzy didn't blame them. The tension between her and Cooper was thicker than a pea soup fog on Puget Sound.

Cooper pulled back onto the street and glanced at her. "So, where to?"

Izzy sighed. The last thing she wanted was Cooper involved in this mess with her parents. No one but her sisters knew what lousy parents they were, and she'd intended on keeping it that way. "Turn left at the next light and stay on that street for a few miles."

"Okay." He nodded and met her gaze briefly. Her heart thumped happily in her chest. The man might be sex on skates when he was on the ice, but even walking around like a mere mortal, he was so much more than that. If circumstances tonight were different— She briefly toyed with suggesting they pull into a deserted parking garage and finally get the deed done.

But she couldn't. Her sisters came first, paying the bills came second, and screwing Cooper's brains out had to be farther down that list. At least it was tonight. If they didn't hustle, Fawn and Rock would have every penny spent before she could get there.

Cooper reached over and took her hand in his big, calloused one. "You okay, Isabelle?" The sexy, gentle way he said her full name wet her panties with desire and need and something even stronger, yet elusive. Yet, she wouldn't go there.

He traced little circles on her palm with his thumb. Oh, dear Lord, that felt so crazy good. And that's what she wished they were doing right now—getting crazy. But she couldn't. Not until she completed her mission like the older, more responsible sister that she was. She'd embraced her role for so long, she didn't know how to be anything else. Yet for one night, she just wanted to be Izzy, a woman needing a man to hold her, support her, protect her, and make her feel like a desirable female and convince her that just once everything would be okay.

Cooper was that man.

But she was a woman on a mission, and until that mission was finished, she'd control her most basic urges. There was always later.

"Are you sure you have to do this tonight?" Cooper asked, hope and lust brightening his deep blue eyes.

"I'm certain." She ran a finger along his strong jaw. "But afterward, I might be able to squeeze you into my busy schedule."

"Honey, you can squeeze me all you want, anywhere, anytime, anyhow." He stared straight ahead, but his one hand held the steering wheel in a death-grip, and his other hand tightened around hers.

Izzy swallowed, as images of a partially clothed Cooper with his incomparable abs, broad shoulders, and powerful thighs crowded out worries over confronting her parents.

"I'll bet you're wet for me right now." If she hadn't already been—which she was—the sound of his deep, husky voice would've done the deed. She squirmed as her panties graduated from wet to plain drenched.

"I am, big boy." Izzy lowered her voice to a sultry, seductive tone she reserved to get her point across when she wanted to get dirty and naked with a guy.

Cooper picked up on it right away. "I've been waiting for this ever since we met at the party."

"So have I," Izzy said breathlessly. "Turn here. It's the bar on the right. To the Max plays here on Tuesday nights and weekends."

Cooper nodded and raised an eyebrow as he took in the somewhat sleazy bar in a not-so-great neighborhood. She might not admit it, but she was grateful for his support. The Overtime happened to be one of her parents' hangouts. They often played there in exchange for drinks and dinner.

Izzy removed her hand from his, closed her eyes, and tried to pull herself together, no easy task considering the proximity of Mr. Sex on Skates, soon to be sex on his back because she planned to have him every way she could, including a few ways she hadn't tried yet.

Cooper stared at her but kept his thoughts to himself.

Izzy took a deep breath and opened the car door. Cooper immediately got out, rushed to her side, and fell into step with her. She paused in the doorway, taking stock of the situation.

Fawn and Rock stood at the bar, talking with the bartender, while the other three members of their band set up the sound system and drank beer. None of them seemed to be in a hurry to do much of anything.

Steve, the bartender and a long-time friend of her parents, waved her over. Walking ramrod straight, Izzy avoided eye contact with her parents and slid onto a barstool a few feet from where they were standing.

Her father, Rock, grinned at her. "Hey, honey, we bought the bar a round. What would you like?" Rock loved to be the big man, portraying himself as a guy with deep pockets. He was still a handsome man, tall and lean, with long, thick black hair tied in a ponytail and handsome face lined with the ravages of age and drug abuse.

Cooper stiffened beside her, his hands on her shoulders in a show of support she found comforting.

"You bought the bar a round?" Izzy spoke through gritted teeth. Close to sixty patrons sat at tables throughout the large bar.

"Sure did." Rock seemed oblivious as usual. Fawn glanced at her, looking her up and down. Her mother's eyes settled on Cooper and widened. Izzy always knew her parents practiced an open marriage. It worked for them. It didn't work so well for Izzy, especially years ago when Izzy had caught her mom sleeping with her high school boyfriend. It hadn't been a good moment in their mother-daughter relationship, and things had gone downhill from there.

Her parents embraced that rock-star party mentality even though their star had long fizzled out and burned up in the atmosphere of drinking, drugs, and a once-lavish lifestyle. She'd seen enough of their tumultuous relationship over the years to swear off marriage and committed relationships, especially if said relationship gave her partner any power over her.

She glanced at Cooper, who was taking it all in. His keen gaze dissected the situation the same way he evaluated the opposing team as he raced down the ice with the puck.

Izzy leaned back against him, drawing courage from his quiet strength. Izzy drew in a long breath and let if out slowly. Bracing herself for the debacle to come, she jumped in with both feet.

"You bought the bar a round?" she repeated.

Her father winked at her. "Sure did. What would you like?"

"I'd like the money back you manipulated my sisters into giving to you."

Rock's smile slipped a bit, and his gaze flicked to Fawn, who wore the pants in the family.

Fawn feigned deafness, which she often did when her oldest daughter said stuff she didn't want to hear. Instead she focused her full attention on Cooper. His hands tightened on Izzy's shoulders.

"And who are you?" Fawn purred. Izzy's mother had done some modeling back in the day, along with partially nude shots for magazine covers and one very famous skin shot that graced their second album cover. No longer a young, super sexy bombshell, her hard-partying lifestyle had taken its toll, but Fawn still turned heads and attracted mostly older men.

"I'm Cooper Black." Cooper's chest vibrated against her back as he spoke with steely, don't-mess-with-me-or-her tone laced with just enough attitude to say he meant business.

"Ah, you're that sexy hockey player." Izzy could almost hear her mother's wheels turning.

"Cooper's not interested." Izzy kept a tight lid on her control. She needed that money and angering her mother wouldn't help her get it. She turned in the barstool and wrapped her arm around Cooper's waist. He grinned down at her and draped an arm across her shoulders, his pose deceptively casual and blatantly possessive.

Fawn continued her leisurely appraisal of Cooper, not seeming to care that her daughter watched her every move.

"The money, Fawn," Izzy repeated.

Fawn waved her off, completely unconcerned. "You'll get it back once our gamble pays off. Don't be so hung up on money, Izz. Just enjoy life."

"I want the money now, and I'm not leaving until I get it." Izzy's control stretched to the point of breaking. She wanted to yell at her mother, shake some sense into her, force her to act like a parent for once, instead of a badly-behaving teenager.

Fawn frowned, and her hackles raised. "I don't have it. It's gone."

"Gone? Already? How could it possibly be gone?" Izzy's voice rose to a high-pitched squeak. Heads turned in the room to watch the altercation like bystanders staring at a crime scene.

Fawn just smiled, as if the missing money were of no importance to her. "Yes, Lou met us here. We used it to pay for a recording studio for our next album. Money well invested, if you ask me."

"And the remainder you're spending here, buying a round for everyone." Izzy ground her teeth together until her jaw hurt. Trying to reason with her mother was more difficult than reasoning with all of her sisters combined.

Fawn shrugged, already bored with the conversation.

"I need that money to pay for my sisters' tuition. Remember them? Your daughters?"

"Really, Izzy. You don't need an education. If the four of you would use your musical talent like I've counselled you to do multiple times, you wouldn't be concerned with wasting your time on a piece of paper that costs tens of thousands of dollars and takes at least four years."

"Neither of you have an education, so you're reduced to stealing money from your daughters. How's that working for you, *Mom*?" Izzy said the last word with as much distaste as she could. Her body shook with anger and frustration, as she recalled the times she'd been left with three younger sisters to care for when she was only a kid herself, little money, no food in the pantry, while Rock and Fawn chased the next big break, treating their responsibilities as if they didn't exist.

Fawn's laid-back attitude disappeared, as she morphed into the ruthless bitch who'd been a rock star diva at one time. "You're delusional. You need to go before I have Steve call the police, which would be so unfortunate, considering you're my ungrateful daughter." Fawn's eyes glittered as if she'd just realized the publicity her has-been band would receive. After all, there was no bad publicity in her mother's eyes. Take a drama-filled altercation with her daughter and throw in an NHL player, and she'd have a recipe for some front-page coverage and prime-time viral attention.

Cooper leaned in close to Fawn, and Izzy froze, not certain what he was up to but suspecting her mother may have met her match. Misinterpreting Cooper's move, Fawn batted her eyes at him and fingered his collar.

"We're leaving," Cooper growled in a low voice only Fawn and Izzy could hear. "And if you so much as *borrow* one more penny from Izzy or any of her sisters, I will personally see to it that you never make it again in the music business. If you don't believe I have that kind of clout, just try me."

On that note, he tucked Izzy's arm in his and together they ambled out of the hushed bar into the rainy Seattle evening. Once outside, they ran for the car as the rained drenched them. Cooper opened the passenger door for Izzy and sprinted for the other side, jumping in the SUV, and revving the engine. He cranked the heat and sat back against the seat, his head angled toward the ceiling.

"I'm sorry, I didn't mean to drag you into the mess that is my family."

"You don't need to apologize to me. After all, I dragged you into my own family mess."

"Thank you," Izzy said simply.

"You're most welcome. You can call on me any time, and I mean that. I truly do."

"That means a lot to me." And she meant that, she truly did. "I don't want to talk about them anymore."

"Okay." He darted a glance in her direction and blew out a long breath. "So do you think a Neanderthal like me stands a third chance with a classy female like you?"

"If you're referring to between the sheets, then yes, you stand a good chance. A damn good chance." Grateful for the distraction from her family and financial woes, she slid her gaze down his fine, if somewhat soaked body, and back up to his face. The light of the dashboard cast shadows across his hard male angles, making him look dangerous and formidable.

Just her type of guy.

"How mad will Betheni be if we don't show up for a few hours?" he asked.

"She won't give a shit. By now she's drank half your good whiskey and is watching some pay-for-view movie." She needed his touch tonight, his assurance everything would be okay, at least for a short time. She'd forget all her troubles and lose herself in a hot man with a very large bulge in his pants begging to be set free.

He nodded and licked his lips. "I think we can find a private place for a few hours."

"And where would that be?"

"Fuck if I know, but I'd better think of something fast." Cooper rubbed his chin and stared straight ahead, his dark brows furrowed. Putting his car in gear, he pulled out of the parking lot onto the rain-slicked city street.

"Ever done it in a pool?"

She smiled and ran a hand over the corded muscles of his thigh. "No, but I'm ready."

"So the fuck am I." His gaze burned down her body and should've turned her clothes to ashes.

Several minutes later, he pulled down a familiar tree-lined street.

"Isn't this the way to your house?"

"Yeah, but we're not going home. My neighbors left on a cruise and asked that I keep an eye on their house."

"What if they have cameras installed?"

"What if they do?" He grinned like a naughty boy willing to take a risk stealing cookies from the cookie jar. He could steal her cookies any damn day.

"I like the way your naughty mind works."

Cooper pulled down a long driveway a few doors from his own house. He jumped out and lifted Izzy out of the SUV, leading her toward a fence gate. Izzy ran to keep up with him.

"Aren't we going in the house?"

"Afraid of a little rain?"

"Not in the least."

They snuck around the back of the house across the wet lawn. In the backyard was a pool with an attached hot tub. The rain pitter-pattered on the patio.

"I'm wet," Izzy slid up to Cooper, burying her hands in his hair.

"I hope to hell you are." He stared down at her, his dark eyes even darker. Rain water slid down his nose, and she leaned up to lick it off. He pulled her to him, his mouth rough and demanding. She parted her lips and welcomed him inside. He attacked like a starving man, and she clung to his hard body. The heat between them should've caused steam to rise from their wet clothes.

With a groan, Cooper pulled away and held her at arm's length. "Get those wet clothes off. Now," he ordered.

"Aren't we bossy?" She teased even as she tossed her coat and T-shirt over a nearby patio chair. Water trickled down her neck and between her breasts. Her nipples stood erect in the lace cups of her bra, and Cooper's gaze went straight to them.

"You are so fucking beautiful." He stared at her for several long

136

seconds.

"So are you. Now let's see some skin," she bossed him right back. His determined expression didn't bode well for her remaining the one in control.

He added his shirt to the growing pile of wet clothes. "Satisfied?" he smirked.

"Not even close." Izzy tugged and yanked until she was free of her jeans. "Your turn, handsome." Before he could respond, she dived into the heated pool, which was about to become more heated.

When she surfaced, he stood on the edge of the pool, completely naked. Rivulets of water ran down his chest to his erect penis.

"What are you waiting for? The water's warm, and my body's hot."

His purely wicked grin made her heart pound inside her chest. He dove in, his body all male grace and fluid motion, surfacing near where she treaded water. A second later, he was all over her with his hands and mouth, entwining his legs with hers, as they stood in chest high water.

"I've been waiting for you my entire life," he said against her ear. He left a trail of kisses down her jaw and bit her shoulder.

She groaned and nipped at his stubbled chin. "I doubt it's been that long," she teased.

"It feels like no one else counted until you came along. Like you're the missing piece of my heart and soul." The truth of his words shone in his eyes.

Normally Izzy would've run hard and fast away from any man who ever said words like that, but she dismissed them as the words of a sexually drunken man wanting to get in the pants of a woman who'd made him wait several weeks. A guy would say anything to bury himself in a woman after she held out on him, especially a man who loved challenges as much as Cooper.

"I want you." She literally climbed up his body, wrapping her legs around his waist, and sucking his tongue into her mouth. "I really want you, Cooper. Show me how badly you want me."

Wading through the warm water, Cooper plunked her ass on the edge of the pool. "How do you want me?"

"I want you wet, wild, and willing. Don't hold back." She pressed her crotch against his erection, taunting him, and he growled.

Cooper yanked the lacy bra under her breasts and took a taste of each one before sucking a nipple into his mouth, tormenting it with his tongue, and biting down gently. A sliver of pleasure-soaked pain jolted through her, and she clawed at his back. He moved to the other nipple, repeating the process. Izzy's vision blurred as she almost came.

Not yet. Not until she took Cooper with her. She grabbed fistfuls of his hair and pulled his face back to hers. "Condom?" she almost snarled.

He stared at her with unfocused eyes, as if his brain had lost the power to process words.

"Condom?" Izzy repeated, her voice taking on a desperate tone to match the throbbing between her thighs.

Cooper gave a quick shake of his head and nodded slowly. "Yeah, don't move. Not one muscle."

"Get the condom now," she ordered, not caring how bossy she sounded.

Cooper took no offense. His mouth kicked up at the corners. He swam across the pool, crawled out, and dug a packet out of his jeans pocket. Izzy watched as he rolled it onto his magnificent dick. A second later, he ran around the pool and lowered himself into the shallow end near her.

"I need you inside me *now*. We can worry about foreplay later."

"Honey, I'm your man." He bowed low in the water and rose to run his tongue across her bare stomach. "But these have to go." He tugged on her panties, and Izzy raised her legs. He yanked them off and chucked them over his shoulder.

"Now," he growled in her ear, "where the hell were we?"

"We were about to have mind-blowing sex in the middle of a rain shower on the edge of your neighbors' swimming pool. Get your ass over here and satisfy me."

"It's not my ass you want." His dark eyes glowed as he parted her thighs and positioned himself between her legs. He guided his thick, heavy cock to her entrance.

"Get ready for the ride of your life, mister."

"We'll see who's riding who." He pushed inside, stretching her, and Izzy leaned into him, taking him deeper as he filled every empty spot inside her with his dick and his overwhelming presence. She'd been with a fair amount of men since her high school days when a former drummer in her parents' band took it upon himself to teach her about sex. She'd been an able pupil, finding she enjoyed sex as much as any woman.

Focused on caring for her sisters, she'd had a modest sex life throughout the years up until this recent drought and her current obsession with Cooper, but none of those other men had a body that came close to Cooper's athletic body. The hard muscles of his pecs and his tight nipples rubbed against her breasts as he held her wet body to his. She could feel them flexing, tensing as he sought to control himself, and she loved the pure strength of his unleashed power.

With a final push and a satisfied grunt, he fully seated himself inside her. For a long, torturous moment he held still, his face buried in her hair. He trembled.

"I want you so fucking bad I'm in pain." He licked her neck and found her mouth again, silencing any spoken comment she might have made, so she spoke with her body. And damn did her body talk.

Panting, Cooper looked into her eyes. He wrapped his big hands around her ass and pulled her closer against him, going deeper inside her than any man ever had before.

Dragging her mouth from his, she gasped for breath. She could stay this way forever, yet as heavenly as it felt, she needed— wanted—more, needed him moving inside her, needed him claiming her in a way as old as mankind itself.

"Take me," she whispered in his ear. Izzy squeezed her eyes shut and bit down on his neck, marking him, and begging him to let loose.

"Not yet." He didn't move. The bastard was toying with her, sacrificing himself to torment her fevered body. Two could play at that game. She'd make him lose control.

Izzy slid her hands up his chest, running her fingers through his chest hair. She rubbed his nipples, eliciting a moan from deep in his throat. Taking each nipple between her thumbs and forefingers, she pinched them. Pinched them again. Hard. Cooper let out a sharp gasp. Izzy smiled against his neck and pulled on his nipples, twisting them.

"Oh, fucking hell." Cooper roared and leaned back, grinding his dick hard into her. "You're going to be sorry you did that."

"Make me sorry, gorgeous. Let that caveman out and pound into me. Take. Me. Now. Don't hold back."

"I will." His strained voice betrayed how hard this was for him, too, but he didn't give in. When he still didn't move, she wrapped her legs around his waist and leaned back against the cold tile of the pool deck, arching her back, and shoving hard against him.

"Awww, damn, honey. Damn."

Her eyes half-lidded, she smiled her best sultry smile. "Come on, you know you want it."

"Oh, yeah, I want it." His gaze raked over her body as rain peppered her skin with droplets of water. He leaned over her, holding her chest against his. Their slick bodies slid easily against each other.

Slowly Cooper pulled out halfway and slid back inside her. She purred like a kitten and savored the luxury of this man's extraordinary body training hers to crave only him. She didn't care if he ruined her for any other man. Didn't care if no one else would ever satisfy after she'd had her fill of Cooper.

How could she care? Tonight, her body belonged to him as much as it belonged to her, and there was no turning back. Not that she wanted to turn back or even take a slight step back. She gladly followed this path whether it led to paradise or an eventual dead end.

Cooper continued his slow assault on her pussy and her heart. With deliberate, forced patience, which took a toll on his body judging by how hard his arms and legs shook, he slid in and out of her. She didn't want deliberate and controlled. She wanted wild, unrestrained sex, wanted him to be as crazy for her as he'd made her for him, needed proof that this man couldn't do without her any more than she could do without him—it was her best kept secret, even from herself. Up until the moment Cooper's cock filled her, she might have been able to turn back and salvage some measure of sanity.

Not now. Not ever again.

She pulled Cooper down on top of her, their tangled legs dangling in the warm pool, and mounted a frontal assault on his mouth by sucking his tongue then biting down gently.

"God fucking dammit," he swore, his eyes stormy with swirling desire. She blinked up at him, squeezing his passion past his control point by gripping his ass and arching into him

"Give me the best you've got, hockey star," she taunted him.

His guttural growl didn't sound quite human. The next thing she knew, he was slamming into her over and over, lifting her hips off the slippery tiles with each inward thrust.

Waves of pleasure cycled through her, signaling an imminent orgasm and making her forget her name, but she wasn't about to forget his. She called it out over and over again. Just before passion exploded behind her eyes, Cooper dragged her into the water, still deep inside her and maneuvered her into deeper water. Her feet barely touched the pool bottom and made her body maneuverable and buoyant. He bounced her up and down on his submerged penis, their slippery bodies adding to the erotic feel of wet skin on wet skin.

She shuddered, and he drove harder, wringing every last drop of passion out of her until she flew into millions of tiny pinpoints of light, like a sun exploding with mighty force. He came right after her, spasming in the water as Izzy clung to his hard-muscled chest.

She'd just had the best debut sex with a man who took no prisoners. Or maybe she was wrong about that. Maybe he had taken her prisoner, leaving her with no hope of ever escaping his magnetic pull.

Cooper leaned against the side of the pool, holding Izzy tight, their bodies mirror images of each other as they sought to get their blood pressure and pulse rates under control.

Time seemed to stand still as they held each other. It could've been seconds or hours. Hell if she knew or cared. Izzy buried her face in his wet hair, smelling chlorine and Cooper. She'd never see a pool the same way. But then she'd never see Cooper the same way either.

"That was fucking awesome," Cooper said breathlessly.

"It was."

"I want us—"

"We will be doing this again. Trust me. Once will not do it for me."

"Or me. You're the perfect puck for my stick." He grinned at her, and she laughed.

"Did you say *puck* or *fuck*?"

"Does it matter?" he asked.

Izzy shook her head, spraying droplets of water around them. "We'd better go. Betheni will be wondering what happened to us."

Mutely, he nodded.

It wasn't until they were somewhat dressed and driving the few blocks to his home that it hit her.

They'd left her lace panties floating in his neighbors' pool.

Chapter 9—On Ice

Riley sprinted to the sidelines when he saw Izzy and Tanner standing near the edge of the field behind the home bench. They'd come to watch him play.

No one had ever bothered to watch him play sports. All the other kids had family at every game, but Riley had never had anyone. Now he had the quarterback for the Seattle Steelheads and Izzy. His teammates and coaches noticed, too, and Riley puffed up with pride.

He'd be big man on campus tomorrow.

Which should have made him feel really good about himself and his current situation.

And it did. Except—

He glanced around as he jogged up to Izzy and Tanner.

"Hey, you made it." He grinned as he shook Tanner's hand. Izzy gave him a big hug. Man, would the guys all be jealous that this hot older woman just hugged him. He didn't know which would impress them more, Tanner or Izzy.

They were guys—so he'd vote for Izzy.

"I wouldn't miss seeing my best guy play for anything," Izzy said, as she straightened his shoulder pads. "You look tough in that uniform."

"Thanks." He shuffled his feet, suddenly embarrassed.

"I'm always game to watch young talent." Tanner winked at him, as several of Riley's teammates crowded around Tanner, all talking at once.

With Tanner occupied with the guys, Riley turned toward Izzy. "Where's Uncle Coop?" His voice sounded too hopeful. He didn't want anyone to catch on that he cared.

Izzy narrowed her eyes and her mouth drew into a thin line. "I'm not sure he's going to be able to make it. He's working late at the training facility tonight."

All the good feelings from earlier drained out of Riley. Like sister, like brother. His mother never made it a priority to attend any of his school events or games. Not even one time. But his mother didn't like team sports much, and Cooper did.

Izzy must have read the disappointment on his face. She reached out and squeezed his arm. "I know he'd be here if he could."

"I don't care. He's a selfish jerk anyway. He doesn't matter to me. I just want to find my mother and get out of his house." Riley felt hot tears well up in his eyes, which fucking pissed him off. Uncle Cooper didn't deserve his tears or anything else.

Riley expected Izzy to chew his butt for calling his uncle a jerk, but she didn't. In fact, he got the impression she agreed with him.

"He's not a football guy anyway," Riley added, as if that made Cooper's absence okay. They both knew it didn't.

"Guys, get back over here. We have a game to play," Coach yelled at them.

Riley pulled on his helmet and smiled at Izzy and Tanner. "Later."

Tanner grinned at him. "Have a good game."

"I will." Riley ran to the bench near the sidelines. He'd wanted to play quarterback, but years of off-and-on participation in sports didn't help. For a quarterback, he was too far behind the other guys. So Coach put him at tight end because he was big, strong, and athletic. Surprisingly, he had good hands, too, with a great vertical leap and better than average speed. Must be those Black genes. From what his mom told him, they'd all been good at sports.

So despite his lack of playing time, Riley was starting in his first freshman football game. Winning a spot gave him a rare sense of accomplishment. He'd spent so much of his life watching out for his mother that it felt weird to do something completely for himself. For once, he didn't let the guilt ruin his day.

Riley caught three passes, one that he ran in for a touchdown. He could hear Izzy and Tanner cheering from the sidelines.

Afterward, Izzy drove Riley home in Cooper's second car, a Lexus sedan that seeming boring and old like his uncle. She helped Riley with his homework, and reminded him his bedtime was at ten. His uncle still wasn't home. He was probably out banging some chick or partying with the rest of the Sockeye team 'cuz those things were more important to his uncle than Riley would ever be. He might as well get it through his thick skull. Cooper didn't want him, and he'd unload him the first chance he got.

Izzy joined Riley for a big glass of milk before he headed to bed. Riley wished his mother could be like Izzy or that he had a big sister like her. Or an aunt. Instead he had Uncle Poop, the shithead.

* * * *

Cooper loved training camp, the locker room smells and the guys jawing with each other, the sound of skates on ice and sticks connecting with pucks, and the coaches shouting encouragement and suggestions. He loved it all and absorbed it like a sponge built exactly for this and nothing else.

And for those few hours on the ice, nothing mattered, not even Izzy, but the second he stepped off the ice, her sparkling brown eyes and luscious lips invaded his thoughts. God, had it only been less than two days since they'd done it in the pool? Seemed like a few minutes ago and yet a lifetime too long since he'd seen her.

Once training camp ended for the day, Cooper attempted to bury himself in game tape, while schooling a couple promising rookies. Brick and Rush slummed with them, harassing the rookies and bullshitting with Coop. Obviously, they'd struck out with the sisters they'd been bragging about earlier and figured talking hockey beat going home alone. Besides, the two idiots were like sponges when it came to hockey even if they perpetuated a devil-may-care attitude. They didn't fool Coop one bit. They hung on his every word, asked all the right questions, and contributed their own insights.

Now that training camp had started, Coop paid Barb to come in about three, cook dinner, and stay until he got home. Tonight he planned on making his night a late one, though he couldn't shake that nagging feeling he was forgetting something. It'd come to him eventually. For now, Cooper had to get Izzy out of his mind and absorbing himself in hockey, his first and only true love, had worked on the ice earlier though not so much now.

Cooper's phone rang, and he glanced at it. His PI was calling. With a nod to the guys, he took the call out of the room.

"Hey, Russ. What do you have for me?"

"Not much, Cooper. I'm busting my ass following leads that go nowhere. Most people in her profession don't trust outsiders, and they aren't exactly forthcoming with information."

"No indication if she's still alive?" Cooper choked on that last word, somewhat surprised that it hurt so much to say it. Regardless of what Julie had become, she was still that big sister who watched over him, baked his favorite cookies, and took him skating when his father was overseas.

Yeah, he wanted to remember Julie that way, not as a drug-addicted prostitute. She'd made her choices, but he still felt guilt over not finding her sooner and attempting to rescue her, or at least take care of Riley, and most of all about the summer that changed everything all those years ago.

He was pretty certain Riley had seen too much for his young age. He just hoped Julie managed to protect her son from some of the worst life had to offer. His stomach clenched at the possibilities, and more guilt sat heavy in his heart.

"I choose to believe she's out there somewhere. I had a tip she'd followed a biker to Portland. That's one of the reasons I called. Do you want me to travel out of Seattle?"

"Absolutely. Hell, if you hear she might be in Antarctica, I want it checked out."

"Okay, boss. Later," Russ said and promptly ended the call.

By the time Cooper returned to the film room, Brick had sent the rookies on a mission to buy pizzas—with their own money, of course. Cooper rolled his eyes and sat on the edge of a desk staring out the window, lost deep in his own troubles. Brick and Rush debated on who was the greatest goalie ever. Cooper pushed Brick's bare feet off the table and shook his head. Neither guy noticed him.

Cedric walked in, looking around the room. He avoided Brick and Rush and sank into a chair next to Cooper. "I figured I'd find you here. Where the fuck did you go last night after the game?"

Cooper frowned. "I, uh, had Riley with me."

"So you're going to let a snot-nosed teenager with attitude stop you from hanging with the guys after the game?"

"He won't be with me for long. Either I find his mother or I send him to my parents when they get back from their Europe trip in another month; then I'll hang with the team."

"As captain, you need to hang with us now, especially the new guys who don't know you."

"Like I don't know that?" Cooper blew out a long sigh. He took his team captain duties seriously, and he knew relationships built off the ice extended to the ice. The young guys needed to bond with him, and the veterans new to the team needed to understand this was first and foremost his team.

Then there was Izzy. Where did she fit in? Where did he want her to fit in? Where did she want to fit in?

Riley might be an added complication, but that situation was

146

temporary. It couldn't be anything but. He didn't have time for a kid, and Riley deserved more than he could give. He should see Izzy that way, too. Only he couldn't. Not really.

He wondered where Izzy was tonight. He'd texted her a few times but no response.

His stomach clenched at the thought she might be with Tanner or on a party-crashing assignment. He ran a hand through his hair, frustrated by the unfounded jealousy coloring his thoughts. A woman like Izzy didn't have that kind of mind-altering sex with a man one night and go after another guy the next night. That was not Izzy.

Cedric snapped his fingers in front of Cooper's face. Shit, he hated when Ced did that. He shot him a glare even though he knew it would never work. The only things that affected Cedric were loose pucks, the opposing team's goalie guarding the net, and scantily clad, hot women.

Cedric leaned back and laced his fingers behind his head, one of his patented and deceptively casual poses that were anything but. "What's the straight story with you and Izzy?"

"Nothing," Cooper spoke too fast and immediately Cedric's bullshit radar went on high alert.

"You fucked her." Cedric grinned at him. "About damn time. I was beginning to wonder about you, my man."

"I—" Cooper started to deny the facts. Ah, hell, why bother. Cedric was already onto him. "It's nothing serious." He shrugged and snagged a handful of peanuts from the bowl on the table.

"Yeah? Is she doing Tanner, too?"

"No. She is not." Cooper shot forward, getting into Cedric's face.

"Hey, Coop, calm down." Cedric held his hands out, palms up. "Jesus, don't get so riled about her. Makes people think she means more than a quick lay to you." He jerked his head toward Brick. "If dumbshit there gets wind of your interest, there'll be no shutting him up."

"I'm not afraid of Brick." Cooper forced himself to relax back against the cushion, though his body was anything but relaxed. He was drawn tight and ready for a fight. Too bad they didn't have a game tonight, except the way he was feeling, he'd spend more time in penalty box than on the ice.

"Of course, you aren't, but you need every guy on this team to believe you're all-in, rather than distracted by a woman who has your balls in a vise grip."

"She doesn't have my balls in any kind of grip."

Cedric laughed. "Cooper, that woman knocked you on your ass the first time you laid eyes on her. Remember? I was there?"

Cooper wished like hell he could forget. Izzy had been crashing the team party and had followed him into the men's room. She was about to go down on him when Cedric interrupted. So Cooper followed her into the ladies' room to return the favor. She'd driven him bat-shit crazy ever since. He'd never done anything so blatant at a team function, always behaved like a team captain should behave. Yet with Izzy, all common sense was jettisoned out the nearest window.

Case in point: last night. They'd done it in the neighbors' pool, and he'd never given much thought to security cameras or being caught by another neighbor. In fact, the danger of being discovered had only added to his sex-crazed insanity.

Even worse, he'd do it again in a heartbeat. Already his mind spun with ways to get her naked this next time.

He should be absorbed in training camp which ran concurrently with preseason games, not lusting after a woman who tied his dick in a knot so tight, he swore he'd explode if he didn't feel her soft skin writhing under him soon. Very soon.

He wondered what she was doing later.

He had a big house. If they were in the den with the double doors shut, Riley wouldn't hear a thing. And the master suite was downstairs while Riley slept upstairs.

"Cooper," Cedric almost yelled at him.

"Huh?"

"You didn't hear a fucking thing I said. Jesus. You are a pathetic idiot. Get your head out of that pussy and back to hockey." Cedric shook his head, clearly disgusted. Usually Cooper did the chastising of teammates when it came to women versus hockey. Everyone on the team understood hockey came first during the season. Always. No exceptions.

Now Cooper's head wasn't in the game. It was buried tongue-deep in Izzy's tight, moist pussy. His dick hardened instantly, straining against his zipper.

Cedric glanced at his crotch and rolled his eyes. "Shit, I never thought this would happen to you, and I'm not talking about the hard-on, I'm talking about your obsession with Izzy."

"I'm not obsessed with her."

The rookies picked that moment to burst in with steaming boxes of pizza. Grateful for the reprieve, Cooper grabbed the first piece and sat between Brick and Rush, effectively blocking Cedric out.

Only Cedric wasn't easily discouraged, not when it came to the game he loved.

Worst of all, Cooper knew his buddy was right.

Izzy was a distraction he couldn't afford.

* * * *

Izzy itched to wrap her hands around a certain thickheaded, selfish bastard's neck.

Riley put on a brave show, but he didn't fool her one damn bit. The poor kid was devastated that Cooper hadn't bothered to show up for his game.

She sent Riley to bed and waited up for Cooper, pacing the floor as her temper soared. She was going to ream his ass and rip into him like he'd never been ripped into. She'd pound some compassion into that thick skull of his if it was the last thing she did.

She heard his SUV pull in the garage after ten PM. Izzy waited at the door for him. He walked in and tossed his jacket on the small table in the entryway. Stress and fatigue drew lines on his handsome face but didn't detract from his rugged good looks.

Her body immediately reacted to him, and she fought the attraction. Dammit, this was about Riley, and Cooper's indifferent treatment of the kid. It was not about her body's attraction to him.

He must have caught movement out of the corner his eye. He turned his head and a slow smile replaced the preoccupied frown on his face. Of course, he was smiling at her. He probably assumed she'd returned for an encore after their hot sex in a warm pool two early mornings ago. And her double-crossing body wanted that encore.

"Baby," he said quietly in his deep, sexy voice. He pulled her into his arms and kissed her soundly. He appeared to be so wrapped up in her body, he didn't seem to notice at first how stiff she was or how she wasn't kissing him back.

Izzy put her hands on his chest and shoved him away. He staggered back a few steps, caught off guard by her anger.

"I texted you. You never responded."

"I was with Tanner," she baited him.

"Oh."

She had to give him points for not going all possessive He-Man on her when she mentioned Tanner.

"Is something wrong?" The idiot didn't seem to have a frigging clue.

"You're what's wrong," she hissed, her claws unsheathed as she prepared to pounce on him like a tigress guarding her cub.

Cooper's eyes opened wide. He took on the look of a man looking for an escape route from a crazy woman. "I'm sorry. Could you at least explain what I did?"

"You really don't remember?" Somehow that set her off more than if he'd been apologetic for not making it or come up with a lame excuse.

He shook his head and pushed his hair off his forehead.

"Tanner and I went to Riley's game this evening. You didn't show." She shot each word at him like sharp arrows meant to pierce through his self-absorbed armor.

Cooper pinched the bridge of his nose and let out a long sigh. "I forgot."

"You forgot? You *forgot?*" Her voice rose to a screech, making her sound like the wicked witch. "What was so important that you couldn't remember your nephew's first football game?" She glared up at him, anger shaking her body, along with pity for the boy who didn't have one family member who gave a damn about him.

Cooper scrubbed his hands over his face, looking distressed and out of his comfort zone. "I—I couldn't stop thinking about us in the pool so I stayed late to help some rookies and get my head back in the game."

Whatever answer she'd been expecting, this wasn't it. Thoughts of her distracted him to the point where he'd forgotten Riley's game? Flattering, but no excuse. Not in her book and definitely not in Riley's.

"Tanner remembered, and Riley isn't his *nephew*." She squared her shoulders and drew up herself up straighter, toe to toe with

Cooper.

"Tanner should've been watching game film. He's had a crappy season so far," Cooper countered. By the expression on his face, he realized he'd stepped in it too late.

Izzy almost smiled. "And still, Tanner made Riley his priority, while you, the man who should've done the same, didn't even bother. You're a selfish ass."

"Okay, you're right. I'm sorry."

"Don't tell me you're sorry. Tell Riley. Your callous disregard for him broke his heart."

Cooper had the audacity to roll his eyes. "That's bullshit, and you know it. Riley doesn't like me. He's using me just like his mother always did. He wants something out of me and once he gets it, he'll be gone and won't look back."

The truth hit Izzy right between the eyes. The mighty Cooper Black was scared shitless he'd get attached, and Riley would reject him and walk away. Cooper was afraid of getting hurt. Imagine that.

It made total sense to her considering how Cooper dealt with the personal relationships in his life. Or in fact, didn't deal with them. Ignored them, skirted around them, ran from them, attempted to control them, but didn't face them head on.

The only thing Cooper was capable of facing head on was hockey.

And she was certain she knew why.

Cooper didn't believe he could do anything well but hockey. Not even love.

Izzy almost choked on that thought. She'd never considered Cooper a love match, definitely a rough-and-ready sex match— another area he excelled in.

She gazed into those deep blue eyes of his, those same eyes that'd been dark with lust last night, and backed a few steps away from him. Anger brought out passions, and while she'd love a repeat of two mornings ago, she'd be damned if she'd reward the man for his bad behavior.

"Cooper, did you ever pull your head out of your selfish ass to really think about Riley and what he's been through? He thinks he's a throw-away, and you're one in a long line of people who'll toss him out with the trash the first chance you get. He played a really good game. He has his uncle's athletic talent."

"He does?" Cooper seemed genuinely surprised.

"Of course, he does. Haven't you paid any attention? He moves like an athlete. I can see it even though he's at that awkward teenage boy stage." Izzy was exasperated with this man. Could he really be that dense?

Probably so. In her experience, it was a common male trait.

"Riley needs you. He needs stability in his life. He needs to know someone has his back."

"I give him everything he needs. He lacks for nothing." Cooper's jaw tightened and he stared over her head at some distant point.

"Everything? You call throwing money at him, everything? What about giving him yourself? Your time? Your attention? Your compassion?"

"I can't." Cooper shook his head. "I don't want him to get attached to me. He'll be moving on as soon as I find his mother."

"You're going to let this poor kid go back to a rat-infested, drug-riddled apartment with a mother who turns tricks and does drugs?" God, she wanted to shake some sense into him.

"I doubt it's all that bad." He shifted from one foot to the other. This conversation obviously was making him uncomfortable. Well, he deserved to be uncomfortable because allowing him to stay in the sheltered world he chose to live in wasn't working for her—or Riley. She doubted it was even working for Cooper.

"Have you ever taken the time to talk to him about what it was like?"

"Uh, no, but I doubt he'd tell me anyway."

"You are impossible." Izzy grabbed her purse from the floor, and the car keys from the entry table.

"Where are you going?" He followed her into the garage.

"I'm going home. *Understand?*"

A muscle jumped in his jaw. "But—" He tried to open the driver's door but she was faster with the lock. She waved at him and blew him a kiss, backing out of his garage and driving down the street. Her last view of Cooper was of him standing in the driveway, mouth open, arms spread out wide.

Izzy started to laugh, hysterically, then her laughter turned to tears.

* * * *

A road trip had never looked so good. By the weekend, Cooper was oh-so-ready to get out of town. They flew into San Jose early Saturday for a three-game California and Arizona road trip. Then they'd finish the pre-season with two home games. They'd lost tonight, and Cooper had played a crappy game, which matched his mood. His personal life had him too distracted, and his head wasn't in the game, which pissed him off. He was a professional, damn it, and he'd played long enough to leave his personal issues off the ice.

Only he was struggling with doing just that.

Riley hadn't said one word to him since Thursday. And Izzy, how did he even handle Izzy? He'd assumed one great night of pool sex would lead to sex in every room of his house, in his car, pretty much in anything they pleased, as long as it ended with him inside her.

Only Izzy wasn't speaking to him either, or calling him, or texting him. Nothing.

Izzy's silence hurt him, but Riley's cold shoulder hurt, too, and that surprised him. The kid didn't like him anyway. So what if Riley ate his breakfast in silence and preferred Joker's company to his uncle's? So what if Cooper caught Riley making plans to hang with that arrogant asshole and crappy excuse for a quarterback?

Yet, it irritated the hell out of Cooper when he overheard Riley on the phone with Tanner on more than one occasion joking and laughing and talking sports. He never talked with Cooper like that. Hearing the two of them made his stomach twist and his heart ache for something he couldn't begin to explain or even want to explain. Riley was his road not taken, and regardless of what others might think, he couldn't go down that road because Riley needed stuff Cooper couldn't give him, like a home, like a stable family life, like love. Cooper couldn't be that guy.

Then there was Izzy. Sure, she was hot as hell and flipped his shit right back at him like no one else ever did. Yeah, so what? He attracted tons of beautiful women. Izzy was replaceable. But, fuck, it didn't work for him that she'd completely forgotten about their night together like it never happened, while Coop lay awake each night and replayed every detail in his mind, and later in his dreams.

He was fucked up. Bad. By both of them.

The sooner he found Riley's mother and banished Izzy from his mind, the better.

An hour later, Cedric found him lying on his hotel bed, staring at the ceiling. His buddy shot him a curious glance as he headed for the bathroom, coming out minutes later in a pair of briefs. Cedric crawled into the other bed and shut off the light.

Cooper faked sleep, but he didn't fool Cedric. Ced knew him too well.

"I hope I have the energy to play tomorrow night. Since you wouldn't help me out, I had to satisfy all four of the ladies, and Cedric the Great never disappoints."

"Sorry. Not in the mood. Too many things on my mind."

"And one of those things happens to be Izzy."

No use denying the truth to Cedric so Cooper laced his hands behind his head and stared at that same ceiling he'd been studying all night, casually noticing how different it looked in the dark.

"She's the reason your boxers are in a twist."

"Yeah, she's pissed at me."

"What did you do this time?"

Cooper sighed. Not one for dumping his troubles on someone else, he gave Cedric the short version about how he missed the game.

"Man, you really are a bigger douche than I ever imagined." Cedric's disapproving snort bounced off the walls of the hotel room.

"I don't understand what they're both pissed about. After all, Tanner was there." Cooper spat out the words with venom that surprised even him.

"I detect a little jealousy, my friend. And not just of Izzy and Tanner but Riley and Tanner."

"Bullshit," Cooper muttered. "Doesn't matter to me if Riley worships the dumb shit like he's the second coming, or Izzy treats him like a lifelong friend."

"You're a lame ass liar." Cedric roared with laughter.

Cooper hated being laughed at, especially when there might be a good reason for it. He sputtered with unspoken words of denial that would only incriminate him more.

Cedric, true to form, couldn't let it go. "Hey, if wallowing in denial works for you, I don't give a shit. Just don't let it affect your game again."

"I won't. Nothing comes between me and my game. You know that. We've been together since the minors."

"It did tonight," Cedric drove him the dagger.

"It's preseason."

"You've never played any differently in preseason compared to regular season."

Cooper didn't have a response for that. A few seconds later Cedric's phone rang, and he answered it. After a short conversation, he hung up with a grin on his face.

"Seems I left something at the ladies' apartment. Don't wait up for me." Cedric threw on his clothes and slid out the door.

Sometimes Cooper really hated that asshole. Nothing weighed heavily on the Swede, not guilt, or regret, or jealousy. He breezed through life completely unscathed by the crap everyone else dealt with on a daily basis.

Cooper often wondered who would be the man or woman to finally bring his friend down.

Just like a surly nephew and a beautiful party crasher might finally bring Cooper down.

Chapter 10—Smarter Than That

It wasn't the biggest party the Party Crashers had been paid to crash, but it was one of the toughest. Izzy and her sisters worked overtime to beg, cajole, and seduce the guests into loosening up and having a bit of fun. Even the free-flowing alcohol wasn't doing it.

Izzy regretted agreeing to crash the wedding of two senior citizen transplants from London. The party was as stuffy as the British royal family. She didn't get British humor, and they sure as hell didn't get her and her sisters. Betheni alternated between British and Southern accents which left the guests frowning at her and whispering behind their white napkins. Emma stuffed her face and looked totally at a loss. Avery hadn't shown and didn't call. Her sister hadn't spoken to her since their big fight. At the least, she should honor her commitments.

Izzy couldn't afford to refund their money, but she feared she might be forced to do just that. Izzy was at a loss on how to get this dullest of dull parties started.

Finally it came to her. She motioned to her sisters to follow her into the hallway.

"I think we're going about this all wrong. This is a different crowd. They like the symphony, opera, and classical music. Let's give them some classical entertainment." She pointed at Emma. "You're the best singer. I want you to go over to the piano player and start singing. Keep it to slow and classy. Betheni and I will work the crowd, try to get a few of the old men dancing."

The girls nodded and made for the grand piano in a corner of the oddly quiet room.

A half hour later, the dance floor was filled with dancers and the conversation in the room rose to a polite din. All in all, while it'd been touch and go, they'd pulled off another successful party and their client discreetly passed Izzy a five-hundred-dollar bonus check.

Izzy checked her messages for the first time that evening. Her cell phone had been blowing up while she'd been taking care of business. The flurry started with Aunt Barb.

I'm leaving. You take care of this kid.

Then several texts from Riley doing damage control.

Barb left. She's mad at me.

Izzy, are you there? Barb's gone, and Uncle Poop is on a road

156

trip. He's going to kill me.

Izzy, I need you to call.

Izzy, please, don't tell Uncle Cooper. He'll be really pissed.

And so it went. Thank God this "wild" crowd had just about wrapped it up for the night at nine PM. Izzy grabbed her coat and turned to her sisters, filling them in on the disaster.

"You're going to babysit?" Betheni's eyes grew big as she stared horrified at Izzy.

"I have to until I can convince Barb to come back."

A short phone call to Barb on the way to Cooper's didn't do much for Izzy's confidence. "Barb, please, at least stay until I can get someone else."

"Not a chance, Izzy. This was supposed to be a part-time job, not a seven-day-a-week job. I'm there every night because the almighty Mr. Black is in denial that his young nephew is living in his house. He ignores the kid in the worst of moments, and grunts at him in the best of moments. Then Riley takes out his anger and frustration on me. I'm done." Barb hung up on her after a few more choice words about Riley and how there wasn't enough money in the world to make her go back.

When Izzy pulled Cooper's Lexus into his driveway and opened the garage door, Riley came running out. His panicked expression reminded her that while for the most part he pretended to be grown up, he was still a kid.

She stepped out of the car, and Riley skidded to a stop in front of her. Suddenly all the spunk drained from him and he stared at his feet, kicking the tires of the car.

"Riley, what have you done?" Exasperation crept into Izzy's voice. He'd screwed up bigtime and needed to know that his selfish actions affected a lot of people.

"I don't like her. I wanted her gone. I don't need a babysitter. I've been taking care of myself for years." He peeked up at her then looked away quickly.

Izzy let out a long sigh as she pushed past Riley into the house. "Wait for me in the kitchen. I'll be right back."

A few minutes later she returned in one of Cooper's old T-shirts and a pair of his sweats to find Riley pacing the kitchen.

Izzy plopped into a chair and rubbed her tired feet. She'd stood too long in those heels. "You are in deep shit, young man."

Riley had the decency to cringe. "I can't lie and say I'm sorry."

"You're not going to get your way either. I'll find someone else, maybe a nice retired drill sergeant who won't tolerate your crap."

"I don't need anyone." Riley's mouth pulled into the stubborn line that reminded her way too much of Cooper.

Crap, Cooper.

What was she going to say to him? He'd be beyond pissed. He'd paid her handsomely to take care of his kid problem, and her aunt hadn't lasted more than a few weeks.

Izzy didn't have any choice but to fill in until another solution came along. They had a few small parties to crash, but the sisters could handle them. Izzy needed to handle this teenage boy and stop from throttling him in the process.

"Are you going to call Uncle Cooper and tell him?"

"He's going to find out soon enough. I'll wait until he gets back from the road."

Riley breathed a sigh of relief and plopped into a big overstuffed leather chair. "Good. I'm fine by myself."

"Not so fast, buster. You're in trouble and I'm not letting you—" She stared down at the phone vibrating in her hand. It was Cooper. She jabbed a finger in Riley's face. "It's past your bedtime. Get to bed."

Riley ran upstairs as if grateful to get away from her.

"Hi," she said, trying her damnedest not to sound breathless.

"Hey, still mad at me?"

"Yes, but I'll get over it if you make it up to me. And Riley." Though right now, Riley didn't deserve anything from Cooper or her. "How was your game?"

"Crappy." He sounded tired and almost defeated. Now wasn't the time to tell him about Riley.

"I'm sorry. Where are you now?"

"I'm lying in bed, thinking of you. Wishing you were here to cheer me up." Cooper's deep voice did all sorts of things to her, and she forgot about anything else but him.

"What are you doing?" she whispered, as she went downstairs to Cooper's room and shut the door. She plopped onto his big bed, not bothering to turn on any lights.

"Rubbing my dick and wishing it were you, not me, doing the rubbing." His deep, sexy voice wet her panties even from halfway across the country. "What are you doing? Or even better, what are you wearing?"

"Nothing. Not a thing," she lied knowing she'd get a rise out of him.

He groaned a deep guttural sound from the back of his throat. "Tell me what you'd like to do to me right now."

Izzy hesitated. Did she dare? Was it wise?

Oh, what the hell.

"If I were there, I'd be running the tip of my finger up your impressive cock. On the trip back down, I'd draw slow circles around it, slide my hands down and around and cup your balls so very gently. I'd squeeze them, lift them, test their weight. I'd bend my head and lick the precum off the tip of that impressive dick, take you in my mouth, while holding the shaft. I'd work the head deeper, past my throat until I'd taken in all of you. Even single luscious inch." Izzy grinned with satisfaction as his heavy breathing rasped in her ear. She relished the power she wielded over this big, strong man.

His breathing came faster and more desperate. He wasn't actually pleasuring himself, was he?

Of course he was.

He moaned and called out her name, going strangely quiet afterward.

"Did you just jack off?" As if she didn't want to join him and get her own satisfaction.

"Damn right," he panted, sounding every bit like a man on his death bed and happy to be there.

"Is Cedric there?"

"Seriously?" He snorted. "Nah, he's not here."

Izzy didn't comment.

"Your turn, honey."

She could listen to his sexy, deep voice in her ear all night long, but she'd rather be in the same room with that voice, rather than merely the same continent. She grinned into the phone as she stretched out on the bed like a satisfied, or about to be satisfied, feline.

"Are you really naked?" Cooper's breathing sounded close to normal. She imagined him sprawled on his bed, his hand still toying with his spent cock, the other hand resting on his taut belly. That incredible chest of his would be rising and falling and his hair would be pushed off his forehead except for one unruly lock.

"I'm in sweats." She purred, lowering her voice so he'd have to strain to hear her or turn up the volume on his phone. Teasing Cooper might be the best fun she'd had in ages, excluding the swimming pool incident.

"Fuck," he whispered, and she had to smile. "Put your hand down those sweats between your legs and tell me how wet the sound of my voice makes you on a scale of one to ten, ten being the highest."

"Twenty," she answered.

"Good answer. Now slip a finger inside yourself, pretend it's me pumping my finger in and out of you." He paused. "Pull out and add another finger and fuck the hell out of yourself."

It didn't take much. Not much at all. Good thing the master bedroom was separated from the upstairs bedrooms. Riley wouldn't be able to hear a thing. Izzy could be noisy at times.

She closed her eyes, braced her legs apart, and shoved three fingers deep into her sopping pussy. "Oh, God. Oh, God. Cooper."

"Yeah, that's it. That's my baby. Feel good?"

"Yes," she gasped. "Really good, but not as good as you'd feel sliding in and out of me. Pounding me into oblivion."

"Holy shit," he muttered, and she imagined his fingers wrapped again around his once-more erect dick while he pleasured her with his voice and himself with his hand.

"Are. You. Getting. Off. On. This?" Izzy arched into her hand and gripped the phone tighter as she listened for instruction.

"Hell yeah. Now—harder. Harder. Faster. Rub your clit. Make yourself come."

He stopped talking and so did she. The phone fell from her hand as she concentrated on her task. Cooper's own moans and shouts seeped into her lust-ridden brain, driving her crazier. She pumped harder, rubbing her clit, and feeling the first tremors rack her body, building up to a full-blown explosion.

She heard his strangled shouts and knew he'd reached his climax a second time.

Izzy lay still, limp, spent, and almost fully satisfied. The only thing better would've been Cooper's buff body sliding over hers, riding her harder than an outlaw outrunning a sheriff's posse.

"Izzy?"

She groped for the phone and held it to her ear. "Yeah?"

"Do one more thing for me. Take a selfie on your phone."

"Of what?" She put him on speaker as she fumbled for the camera.

"Is the camera ready?"

"Yeah."

"Put your wet fingers in your mouth and suck off the juices. Now take a pic and send it to me." She did as told, hardly able to contain herself as she texted the picture to him.

He was silent, except for a few choice groans.

"You like?"

"I love it. Next time I want a video of you fucking yourself with your fingers."

"I can manage that, but can you?"

"It might kill me, but I'm willing to make the sacrifice." She could hear the smile in his voice and the anticipation.

"I want something in return," she teased with a naughty giggle. "I want a video of you jacking off as you listen to my voice."

"I promise. Next time."

"Next time, I'd rather have the real man in the flesh, every gorgeous inch of him."

"You won't get any argument out of—"

She heard muffled noises, cursing, and laughter followed by a bang.

"Sorry," he said sheepishly. "I dropped the phone."

"Cedric's back," she guessed.

"Yeah, complete with the team idiots." Cooper's harsh breathing almost drowned out his lowered voice.

"That would be Brick and Rush?"

"You got it." Cooper sighed, his breathing slowly returning to normal. "Any word from your aunt? Is my nephew behaving himself?"

The one question she wasn't prepared to answer. She hated lying to him. "Uh, yes, uh, everything is fine."

"Is there something you aren't telling me?"

"Only that one night with you wasn't nearly enough, and I need more. Purely for research purposes, of course, just to see if the first time was an anomaly." She sidestepped his question, patting herself on the back for her clever fakeout.

He chuckled. "I can guarantee you that it wasn't."

"When are you back?"

"Tuesday late." She heard more noises and a long string of obscenities from Cooper. "Hey, sorry about that. I need to knock a couple heads together."

"Sure. Good night."

"Yeah, sweet dreams."

"They will be."

She listened to the sound of dead silence and lay back on the bed with a sigh. She was getting in too deep with Cooper and his nephew.

This was so not supposed to happen. Each time she pulled away from him, life pulled her right back. He was too alpha, too controlling, too much of everything. His strong will butted heads with her need for independence. She couldn't have that, no matter how much he attracted her. He'd smother her, she'd turn into a raging bitch, and they'd end up hating each other.

Only staying away from him wasn't an option either—as stupid as it was.

* * * *

Something was off despite how hot the phone sex had been, but Cooper hadn't been able to get to the bottom of it before the guys showed up. Izzy wasn't telling him something, something important, and most likely something that would piss him off.

He'd pulled up his sweats at the first sound of the electronic key in the lock and thanked his good luck Cedric and the boys hadn't arrived ten minutes earlier.

Cooper had been suspiciously panting when Cedric walked in with the dufus brothers in tow, which earned him a raised eyebrow from Cedric. Brick and Rush didn't notice. They'd been too caught up in their latest scheme to pull a prank on one of the team's top defensemen. Didn't those two ever do anything without attempting to drag Cedric or Cooper or one of the other veteran guys into their schemes?

Brick balanced a box of pizza over his head and grinned at Cooper. Cedric just grinned as if he knew exactly what Coop had been doing and with who.

Cooper narrowed his eyes at Brick who was dressed in Hawaiian shorts and a bright orange tank that showed off his Playboy tattoo on one arm. On the other arm was a new tat of a goldfish or something equally lame.

Rush snatched the pizza out of Brick's hands, dropped it on the desk, and dug in. Grabbing one piece in each hand.

Suffering from phone sex hunger, Cooper snagged a piece before it was all gone. Not bothering to chew first, talk later, he poked Brick's tattoo. "What the hell is that?"

"Awesome, isn't it." Brick grinned proudly and flexed his biceps, making the fish grow bigger, like a bloated goldfish floating dead in a fish tank.

"It's stupid as hell." Cooper leaned in closer. The Space Needle was hooked in the fish's mouth and a mountain suspiciously resembling Mount Rainier served as the background.

Rush pulled up his sleeve and revealed a matching tattoo.

"What the fuck?" Cooper scowled. The fish was a God damn Sockeye.

"All the guys got them to show our support for hockey in Seattle," Brick said.

"And next year when they trade you, then what?" Cooper scowled. That was stupidest damn thing he'd ever heard.

"Doesn't matter. Ve're making history here. This is special. Ve are the first Sockeye team, and no matter where ve go or who ve play for, ve'll always be Sockeyes," Rush answered with his Russian accent thicker than usual.

Cooper rolled his eyes and tried not to gag. He stared harder. "What's that empty space for next to the fish's tail?"

Brick's eyes lit up. "That's for a picture of the Cup."

"You guys are delusional."

"Great confidence in your team, Cap." Rush spit out some pizza accidentally and scooped it off the bed into his mouth.

"You're disgusting." He turned to Cedric who'd been oddly quiet. "Can you believe these idiots had Sockeyes tattooed on their arms, and we haven't played our first regular season game?"

Cedric shrugged, not joining in on the razzing like Cooper expected. Cooper narrowed his eyes, suddenly suspicious. "No. Not you? You didn't."

The two idiots started laughing. Cedric shrugged and pulled up his sleeve.

"Ah, hell, you did."

"Seemed like a good idea at the time."

"I'll play my heart out on the ice, but I'm not putting any team's logo on my arm until I win the Cup."

"Everyone on the team did it but you," Rush said, then backed up a few steps at Cooper's murderous glare.

The guys gobbled up the pizza and rumbled out the door, leaving an empty box and the smell of cheese, tomato sauce, and pepperoni floating in the room.

Cooper threw himself back down on the bed. "How'd you end up with them?"

"My encore performance with the girls came to a crashing halt when I had to drag those two jokers out of bar before they busted some big mouth's nose."

Cooper nodded, fighting off a twinge of guilt. As team captain he should've been keeping those morons in line instead of having phone sex with Izzy. "Thanks for that."

Cedric gave a small nod and stripped off his clothes, leaving them in a pile on the floor, he crawled into bed and turned off the light.

"I can't believe you went along with the rest of the guys," Cooper muttered, disgusted by his best friend's betrayal.

"I like Seattle. It's a beautiful city, the fans welcomed us with open arms, and I plan on being here a long time."

"You do?" Cooper sat up and stared into the darkness at the lump on the next bed which was his former best buddy. They'd planned on staying together as long as possible because they had such great chemistry on the ice.

"Yeah. Ethan promised he'd make it worth my while."

"So now he's sucked you in?"

"No, he's won me over. There's a huge difference, and if you'd get beyond your stubborn ignorance and admit you're wrong, you'd see what the rest of us see. I'm staying, Coop. With you or without you."

Cooper grunted and rolled over in the bed, his back to Cedric. A few seconds later, Ced's snores drowned out the traffic sounds on the street.

What started out as good night ended as a crappy one. Cedric betrayed him. He couldn't fucking believe it. Ethan got to him, leaving Cooper the last man standing.

Well, he didn't give a fuck. He'd be gone to sunnier pastures. These dumbshits could fight off the gray gloom all winter while he sported a tan year round.

Part of him recognized how unreasonable he was being, while the other, louder part didn't give a shit. Disloyal bunch of ingrates. But disloyal to whom? Him? Definitely. The team? Not at all.

The part that bothered him was his own disloyalty to his current team. The old team didn't need his loyalty. They didn't exist anymore. His old city had moved on, and the handful of fans who mourned the loss of their team seemed few and far between.

Only Cooper couldn't stay in Seattle, and no one could know why. It was his secret shame, *his* bad memories. He knew how unreasonable his behavior appeared. Hell, the fans had packed the stands for their first and only preseason game. They'd been noisy and rabid beyond what he'd seen in most arenas around the country unless that particular team happened to be a frontrunner for the Cup.

God. Those tattoos. Every member of his team sported those tattoos, while he, as the captain, hadn't even known a damn thing about it. They'd done it behind his back. His team's deception really stuck in his craw and twisted his gut. His fingers weren't on the pulse of this team. For years, he'd been their heart and soul, the center of the team's spirit. Now they were shutting him out.

He wasn't sure how to take that.

But he sure as hell didn't like it.

He was the team captain, dammit, and his team was keeping secrets from him.

The sooner he left Seattle, the better. This place held nothing but bad memories, except for Izzy.

Maybe he'd demand a trade during the season instead of waiting.

He knew they thought he was being a dick for hating Seattle as much as he did, that last summer he'd spent here haunted him. No one knew what happened to him and his brother and sister as children. He'd never told his parents out of fear and later out of concern for his mother's precarious health. That past lived in a tightly locked compartment, but living here ripped off that lock and brought back the pain, confusion, and guilt of a small boy. If only he'd confessed when it first happened, told his parents, done something, instead of shutting his mouth. Yet, his dad had been oversees, and his mom had been dealing with a flare up of Crohn's disease. Not to mention the perceived threat hovering over him and his siblings. He'd only been ten years old.

Seattle was the one place on earth he swore he'd never live, and here he was in the shadow of the Space Needle, Puget Sound, and the Olympic Mountains, not to mention Mount Rainier.

Cooper squeezed his eyes shut in an attempt to block out the memories, but his mind replayed those scenes over and over like a bad horror movie. He did the only thing he could do to distract himself from his past. He thought of Izzy.

Where *did* Izzy fit in his life? He wanted her. She wanted him. She'd never leave Seattle, and she wasn't the type of forever woman he was looking for. She didn't have the qualities his mother had, content to be in the background and concede control to his father. Izzy was so not a background person, and she needed to be in control as much as he did.

Despite the stupidity of it all, he wanted a temporary relationship with her, not just sex but also friendship because right now he could use a friend. He felt alone, separated from his team and disliked by his nephew—not that he blamed the kid. Regardless, he'd keep his distance, not wanting the kid to get attached to him and expect Cooper to be there for him. Cooper wasn't that guy, and Riley needed to understand that.

Cooper's life was hockey. He didn't have room for any other number ones in his life, not Riley, not Izzy.

Maybe it sucked in some ways, but it was what it was.

He'd given his heart and soul to women too many times and been screwed. This Cooper was more mature, savvier, better at protecting his heart. This Cooper didn't fall hard and fast for the wrong woman. He'd be damned if Izzy and Riley would suck him into a situation where he put himself out there only to have his heart chopped up in little pieces and fed to the circling sharks.

Nope, not him. He was smarter than that.

So why was he fighting so hard to get Izzy back?

Chapter 11—Off the Ice

Izzy stopped pacing long enough to check the clock on the dining room wall. It was past two AM on Wednesday morning. The team plane should've landed by now. Cooper would be walking through that door within the hour.

And then all hell would break loose.

She'd already paced a path around the dining room table, the kitchen island, and the big deck. At least she was getting some exercise. Izzy took her responsibilities seriously, all the more so when she was being paid good money to perform the task. At first she'd thought Cooper had overpaid her to find a "nanny" for Riley, but now that she'd been searching for an acceptable replacement for her aunt, she wasn't so sure. Most nannies didn't want to deal with a teenager or work around Cooper's crazy schedule. Cooper would not be happy.

Izzy paced some more until she saw headlights from Cooper's SUV coming up the driveway. A few minutes later she heard the door to the garage open and close.

She waited in the split-level's retro foyer, wringing her hands and rehearsing one final time what she'd say.

Cooper opened the door connecting the garage to the rest of the house. He stopped in his tracks, his duffle swung over one broad shoulder, and that errant lock of dark hair brushing his eyebrow. He wore his travelling suit of black pants with a knife-blade crease and a black blazer. A light green dress shirt unbuttoned a couple buttons teased her with a view of that sprinkling of chest hair.

Maybe they could just hop in bed and forget about reality for a while.

"Izzy?" A slow, sexy smile crossed his face. Obviously, he thought he was going to get some tonight. The bad news she was about to deliver would wipe that smile right off his handsome face and most likely ruin any chance of an encore performance between the sheets.

"Cooper. I—uh—we have something to discuss." It was best to get it over with now. Her carefully rehearsed speech retreated to the dark recesses of her mind and stayed there.

"Oh, yeah?" He grinned, misinterpreting her statement. "You want the real thing instead of phone sex?"

They'd had phone sex the last couple nights, and she did want the real thing. But first she needed to explain the "nanny" problem.

He shrugged his bag off his shoulder and let it drop with dull thud on the floor, followed by his jacket. With a confident smirk, he stalked her like a predator stalking its prey. She froze, a deer in his headlights so wanting to be his prey because the rewards would be oh-so awesome, but first her bad news.

He stopped six inches from her. Even though their bodies didn't touch, heat radiated off him in waves, warming her body and wetting her panties. God, he was so gorgeous and so very male.

"I have it on good authority that in-person sex far surpasses virtual sex." He didn't touch her, just captured her gaze with his and wouldn't let it go. His blue eyes darkened with promises of a carnal night of pleasure.

"I don't know who that good authority is, but I love him." She ran her tongue over her bottom lip, and he groaned.

"Dick. Dick is my authority." He grinned at her, while his eyes smoldered.

"Ah, yes, I adore your friend Dick."

"He's led me astray a few times, but not on this occasion," he chuckled.

"Dicks do that." Izzy laughed, loving how his eyes lit up when he was teasing her. For just one night she could lose herself deep in those eyes and forget the rest of the world.

"Where's Riley?" Cooper asked almost as an afterthought.

"He's spending the night with his football coach's son. They've become good friends."

His grin grew wider, and she didn't have to read his mind to know what he was thinking. "It's just you and me." He cocked his head in the direction of the stairs.

"And Dick," she reminded him with a pointed look at the bulge in his pants.

"I love threesomes when Dick is the third party."

"Dick's always a party." She wrapped her arms around his neck and leaned into him, deciding the nanny thing could wait. Oh, yeah, could it wait. "You're a goofball."

"So are you."

"Takes one—"

"—to know one," he finished for her.

The fondness in his eyes scared her while warming her insides as much as the lust, but lust she could handle just fine. All the emotional crap that came with caring about someone, trusting them, depending on them to do the right thing—that crap was what scared her. In Izzy's world, the people who should care the most were the ones who hurt you the most, except for her sisters. Sure, they had their moments, but they'd take a bullet for her—even Avery despite her current unhappiness with Izzy.

Cooper, on the other hand, wanted out of the city she loved, the city that had been her home for her entire life, and he treated his nephew like an inconvenience at best. Sure, he was damn good in the sex department, but nothing else about him worked for her.

So why had she told him she'd give him a chance if he changed his controlling, jealous ways? Part of her didn't think he could change; the other part wanted him to change. And what if he did? Then what? Where would they go with this? How long could it last considering their conflicting goals?

Before she could further analyze every detail of their relationship, his sinfully sexy mouth touched hers. He kissed her lips, starting in one corner and working his way to the other corner. The man could tease, and the man could kiss. Oh, Lord, could he kiss.

Nanny? What nanny? Right now she needed to get to know Dick a little better—maybe a lot better.

Izzy gripped Cooper's shoulders and lost herself in his smoldering eyes. Burning a deep blue, they peeled away layer after protective layer until she swore she'd bared her very soul to him or so it felt.

She didn't bare her soul to anyone, not even her sisters, and definitely not a man. She was the child of free-spirit artists, and she'd learned a thing or two from them. She didn't like to be tied down or held to anyone's standards but her own. She did not need a man to make her complete, just to give her pleasure.

And if she just kept telling herself that, eventually the words might sink in.

Cooper was an uptight, play-by-the-rules guy who liked everything lined up neatly and planned out. He craved control, lived for it. As the eldest of the sisters, Izzy cherished her independence. Two people unwilling to relinquish control and trust each another were a recipe for failure. They were too much alike in a lot of ways.

Still, that didn't mean they couldn't have fun, and a lot of fun.

Cooper's tongue slid along her upper lip, and she gasped. He took advantage, slipping his tongue inside, exploring her mouth with his lips and tongue. He paused long enough to suck on her lower lip and nip playfully.

Izzy clung to him, lost in his incredibly sensual kisses, and ready to do his bidding, at least in the bedroom. Elsewhere, not so much.

He picked her up as if she weighed nothing and carried her to the master bedroom, placing her on the bed. His handsome face split into a grin when he noticed some of her clothes draped across a chair and her suitcase near the door. One dark eyebrow spiked with smug amusement.

"Planning on staying the night?"

Now would be the time to tell him the truth, but Izzy didn't want to ruin the mood. Tomorrow morning would be early enough.

She made a show of batting her eyes at him. "What do you think, big boy?" she asked in a sultry, forties' starlet voice.

"I think this big boy likes you staying the night." He lay next to her, brushing her hair off her face. His mouth turned up in a half-smile. "Good thing I slept on the plane."

"Good thing I don't work at the coffee shop in the morning." Really good thing because if they both got their way, neither one of them would be sleeping tonight.

For a woman who hated to depend on others, she didn't mind depending on him in the sack. His kisses drugged her with lust and desire. He alternated between gentle and slow and passionate and rough. She'd never been with a man who mixed it up like this and managed to maintain control. Most men would have lost it by now and simply screwed her senseless.

She was damn sure the senseless part would come later for both of them.

Izzy entwined her legs around his thighs and rubbed his erection through his pants. The hard, long length of him welcomed her. She smiled and lifted her gaze to his.

"Have I ever told you how much I love Dick?" She unbuttoned the top button of his pants to show him how much. He sucked in a breath and held it, as if afraid expelling it would change her mind about touching him. Nothing would change that. She lowered his zipper, slid her hand under his briefs, and wrapped her fingers around his penis.

"For once I'm not jealous. Not at all. You can love Dick all you want."

"I will. I promise."

"I'll hold you to it."

Cooper unzipped her jeans and pulled them down her thighs and calves to her ankles. Izzy slid down the bed and licked the velvety tip. His taut stomach tightened.

He maneuvered them into the classic sixty-nine position with him on the bottom. He held her splayed thighs apart as he licked his way up to her pussy. Izzy prodded herself back to work, trying to concentrate on giving head while he sucked and licked her cunt.

"Gawd. Gawd. Oh, my Gawd," she muttered, as she licked her way down to his base, cupping his balls, licking up the other side.

It was his turn to beg and plead, and he did himself justice. Cooper grasped her butt cheeks in his big hands and pulled her down onto his face. His groan of satisfaction pulsated through her pussy. His tongue pushed between her wet folds and up inside her. It was her turn to groan around the cock in her mouth. How was a woman supposed to concentrate on giving a man pleasure when the man's tongue was doing magical things to her pussy and clit?

She gripped his thighs when he sucked on her clit, certain her body would shoot to the ceiling and take him with her. Cooper lapped at her juices, swiping his wet tongue up her folds and back down; then he pushed his tongue back inside, mounting an all-out assault on her pussy, while thrusting his cock in her mouth back to her throat. She took him deeper with each thrust, loving how his partially clothed body ground against hers but wishing it was bare skin instead.

Time for that later.

Lots of time, and she planned to use every minute of it exploring his delectable hard body, while he explored hers.

She went down on him, or would that be up, considering their position. Whatever. She took him as deep as she could, his pubic hair tickling the tip of her nose, and the head of his penis deep down her throat. Pulling back, she gasped a breath, and sucked hard on his head, taking him back inside. Cupping his balls in one hand, she felt them tighten and knew he was about to come.

Not one to be left behind, her body reacted to his talented tongue. When he took her clit between his teeth and sucked, it was all over. Her body bucked as waves of pleasure swept her out to sea. She managed to maintain enough sanity to pump him in and out of her mouth a few times before she felt him jerk inside her mouth. Soon his warm cum filled her mouth, and she swallowed before she collapsed in a boneless heap on the mattress. Cooper's grunts and shudders subsided and his body relaxed under hers.

She hugged him tightly to her, not wanting to ever let him go.

She'd had tons of sex, probably more than she wanted to admit, some ho-hum, some mind-blowing. But a sixty-nine with Cooper blew her mind more than that best sex with any other man ever had.

She hadn't even recovered yet but being a greedy bitch, she wanted him inside her, both of them naked, while she rode him into oblivion. She wanted him to do her doggy style, do her against the wall, do her on the couch.

Yeah, she wanted to do him, all right, and nothing was off limits, except anything involving her heart.

But that was a given.

She knew better than to give her heart to a man who admitted he was a temporary fixture and moving on at the end of the season, but giving her body, yes, she was all in.

* * * *

Cooper disentangled himself from Izzy's hold and dragged his spent body around so that Izzy and him were facing each other. He kissed her deeply and passionately, the taste of her mingling with him as their tongues mated.

He wanted to tell her how fucking incredible she was, but he couldn't find the words, didn't know how to say what he was feeling. So he kissed her, saying what words couldn't and savoring the feel of her plush lips on his. Her hands pushed up his shirt and stroked his back. He loved it when she touched him, loved how she knew all the right places.

"We're wearing too many clothes," she spoke against his mouth.

He hadn't even noticed. He'd been so wrapped up in her body. "Yeah," he grunted.

She pushed at his chest, and he rose up on his elbows, smiling as she unbuttoned his dress shirt. He helped her pull it off and cast it aside. Cooper removed her sweatshirt with a flourish and paused, doing a double take.

"That's my sweatshirt."

"It was. Now it's mine. I like it." She tossed him a sassy grin.

"I like you wearing my stuff." Reaching behind her back, he unhooked her bra with ease. It joined the growing pile of clothes on the bed.

Cooper hugged her close again, as they lay side by side on the bed, not talking much, just enjoying the closeness, the bare skin against skin, and stealing kisses here and there.

He wasn't done with her, not tonight and probably not for a lot of nights to come.

His cock completely agreed and recovered quickly, already hard and ready for action.

"I need to be inside you," he said through gritted teeth.

"I thought you'd never ask."

"I didn't. I ordered."

She laughed and slapped his ass. Hard. He liked that. A lot. He slapped her ass back. Twice because he always gave better than he got.

"Ouch, you're going to pay for that." She giggled and squirmed against his erection, taunting him with her wet pussy and a long, toned leg wrapped around his hip.

He flipped her onto her back and straddled her, staring into her desire-laden brown eyes. Crap, he needed a condom. Without moving off her, he managed to grope for a condom in his nightstand and rip the package open with his teeth.

"Let me help you with that." She took it from him and slowly and deliberately rolled it on his dick. Fuck, he just about came right then and there, but he managed to hold it together.

"Give me all you've got, Cooper. Right now," she demanded. He should've taken exception regarding her bossiness, but he was way beyond that.

"Are you sure?" He hesitated.

"I'm absolutely certain. If you wait any longer, I'm going to spank you."

He raised both eyebrows and grinned. "That a promise?"

"Inside. Me. Now."

"Bossy wench. I give orders, not take them." He toyed with her despite how hard it was to hold back.

"Then you don't know me," she challenged.

Oh, he knew her all right. She waved her independence around like a big red flag, refusing to rely on anyone for anything, but he was Cooper Black, the stubbornest man on the planet who went after what he wanted, and he wanted Izzy. Not only did he want her, but he wanted to ruin her for anyone else, wanted to show her that relying on him—at least for sex—wasn't a bad thing.

He put on his best arrogant smirk and postured. "You need me, and you'll be glad to take orders from me." He watched as her face hardened in denial even while her brown eyes glowed gold with lust.

"In what fantasy world do you live in?" She drew in a sharp gasp as his cock pushed past her wet entrance. He had her where he wanted her, and they both knew it.

He took it slow, torturously so, despite her urging for him to pick up the tempo. He'd show her who controlled this situation and give her incredible pleasure in the process.

She tossed her head back and forth on the pillow as he ignored her attempts to hurry him. When she arched her hips to take him deeper, he withdrew and grinned at her. "Not so fast, sweetheart."

"Asshole," she cussed at him under her breath.

"You'll be thanking me for being an asshole." God, while he was torturing her, he was torturing himself. He wanted nothing more than to be buried deep inside her with her wet warmth surrounding his dick, sheathing him in her hot heat.

He slid back inside, biting his lower lip as he pushed deeper. She surrounded him, enveloped him, completely took over his senses. He kissed her mouth, and she tangled her fingers in his hair. Her heels dug into the small of his back. Her nipples rubbed across his pecs.

She was fucking hot. Third-degree burn hot. And he didn't care if those burns left scars on his heart forever because he was that far gone. He squeezed his eyes shut and locked his jaw, attempting to maintain control while this writhing, panting little hussy underneath him did everything she could to rip his tightly maintained control from his grasp.

That control faltered like a car slipping a gear, and he shoved himself deep inside her. Panting for oxygen, he pressed his face against her neck. His dick twitched with anticipation of the main event, while the opening act of being buried deep inside her pussy just about ended the show. He couldn't lose control now, not without leaving her sated first. No, he absolutely could not.

With more effort and control than he'd ever expended on the ice—and that was saying a lot—he withdrew partially from her.

"Oh, Cooper. Baby, deeper. Deeper," she begged, and he did love a woman who begged.

His control slipped a couple notches, and he slammed into her, lifting her hips off the bed. She arched into him, taking all of him, her body pleading for more.

Damn. What a woman.

Izzy bit down on his shoulder, and the last of his steely control melted to red hot metal.

His mouth found hers as he withdrew and rammed into her again. She didn't flinch, didn't back off, but gave it right back to him, meeting his deep thrusts with her own brand of wild need. Harder and harder he thrust as she moved with him in perfect harmony. Her walls tightened around him, pulsing with life and giving him life. His cock jerked once, twice, a third time, and he was crying out her name over and over. He heard his name on her lips as she came beneath him.

Cooper detonated into millions of pieces never to be put back together into the same man he was before her.

She'd destroyed him—in the very best way possible.

* * * *

The moment of truth had come.

Izzy lay with her head on Cooper's chest listening to his easy breathing and wondering if he was awake or asleep.

After a night of epic sex with an athletic man in the best shape of his life, Izzy could barely move, not even her little finger. He'd taken her so many times she'd lost count. Four? Five?

Her body ached in a good way. She touched her swollen lips and smiled, remembering his passionate kisses and the sweet words he'd murmured against her mouth or in her ear.

"Cooper," she whispered, not wanting to wake him on the off

chance he might be sleeping, since they'd done very little sleeping until the sun had peeked through the dark gray clouds.

"Yeah?" A slow sexy smile crossed his face but he didn't open his eyes. His big hands rubbed her back and slid downward to cup her bare ass in his hands. "You have such an amazing ass."

"So do you." She cleared her throat, hating to ruin the moment, but it had to be said. "Cooper, I—"

"Oh, crap, let's not go there. No morning-after guilt. No expectations. Just you. Me. Good company. Good sex. And the promise of more in the future." He opened his eyes to watch her. Putting a hand under her chin, he lifted her face to his and gave her a tender kiss, a kiss that promised so much more than sex.

She slapped those stupid emotions down and reminded herself not to ruin a good thing by making more out of it than it was.

"Thanks for that, but this is about Riley."

"Damn," he muttered, the mood gone. He rolled to the side of the bed and rubbed his eyes. "What did the little shit do now?"

"He's not a little shit. He's a scared, insecure boy who could use your compassion." Her feathers were ruffled, and she resisted the urge to smack some sense into Cooper because he'd like it too much.

"Izz, for his sake, I can't let him get attached. It'll give him false hope. This is a temporary situation. I failed his mother, and I'll fail him if he starts counting on me." He almost sounded sad, even regretful. "So what's so important?"

Izzy closed her eyes for a moment and rallied her courage. She lifted her head to find him studying her with that inscrutable expression he used when he was guarding his heart. "There's no easy way to say this. My aunt quit on Saturday night. I've been staying here with Riley ever since." She braced herself for the storm, knowing it'd hit any moment.

"God fucking dammit. I knew he was giving her a hard time. I told her to let me know, and I'd take care of it." Cooper raked his hands down his face and sighed. He muttered something she couldn't hear and was glad she didn't.

"I don't know what finally happened, but it wasn't all his fault. She wanted a part-time job. You had her working twenty-four-seven."

"I did not. Only when I was on this road trip. Prior to that, I sent her home as soon as I got here."

"Cooper. She's retired. She wants to travel with her husband. This wasn't what she signed up for."

"I pay her handsomely." He watched her from his perch on the side of the bed, his gaze hooded, his expression unreadable. Cooper the formidable was back.

"That's your solution to everything. Throw money at it. Guess what, Mr. Star Hockey Player, money doesn't fix everything. In fact, I'm not sure it fixes anything." Izzy fought to control her temper as she wrapped a sheet around her and got out of his big bed.

"I'm doing the best I can. I'm hardly father material. Hell, I'm not even uncle material." His gaze met hers, and she read a glimmer of defeat in those blue eyes. Cooper heaved a heavy sigh, as if the burden of the world rested on his broad shoulders.

"I know you're trying, but you could pay a little more attention to him. Show him some compassion. He's lost his mother. No one knows if she's dead or alive. In his mind, she's all he has. Being alone at such a young age has to be devastating."

Cooper nodded slowly, propped his elbows on his thighs, and rested his chin in his hands. "Any ideas for replacements?" He offered her a lopsided grin that stole her heart.

Still wrapped in the sheet, she sat down next him and lay her hand on his arm. "Since you paid me to find someone, and that someone left you high and dry, I'll handle this until I can find the right fit."

"I know I've found the right fit. I fit perfectly inside you," he chuckled and she punched him in the bicep. Drawing back she rubbed her knuckles.

"Like hitting steel, isn't it?"

"Conceited ass."

He raised both brows, still grinning. "You'll do the cooking, cleaning, and babysitting?"

"No. Let's get this straight. You can hire a cook and housekeeper. I'm the temporary nanny, and that's the extent of it."

"Demanding."

"Just like you."

"I'm confident and in charge," he countered.

Izzy snorted. "You're arrogant and full of yourself."

He didn't seem to mind either label. "We start regular season a week from today at home. Then we play at home Saturday, then I'm off on a long road trip."

"How long?"

He ticked the dates off on his fingers. "A week."

"Oh." She frowned, already missing his warm body in this big bed. "I'll try to find someone before then. I can be here when he gets off practice this week."

"I'll leave money for takeout since I can't get a cook that soon, and you're not cooking."

She nodded.

"Izzy, I'll also pay you handsomely. I know I'm intruding on your personal life."

What personal life? Besides her sisters and her struggling career, she didn't have a personal life or even a life. She'd dedicated her life to her sisters, and one sister had already moved out. Even worse, it was now October first and her rent was due.

Her life was pathetic.

"Did your parents pay back the money?" Cooper asked in that uncanny way he had of reading her mind.

She shook her head.

"How much do you need?" he asked as he pulled out his wallet.

"I can't take handouts from you," she balked, already in debt to him more than she'd ever planned on being.

"Don't consider it a handout. Consider it an advance for the nanny duties, including combat pay."

"I don't need combat pay to take care of Riley. We get along just fine."

Cooper shook his head and smiled. "You did, but now you're an authority figure and the roles have changed. Good luck with that." He chuckled and kissed the tip of her nose. "You're damn cute when you're all indignant."

She huffed and stood, turning her back on him as she pulled up her panties.

"You don't need to hide that fine body from me, sweetheart. I'm pretty sure I explored every square inch of it last night and then some."

He came up behind her and nibbled on her neck, sliding his hands up her hips, waist, and rib cage. Izzy sucked in a breath and waited. Those big, amazingly gentle hands grazed her hard nipples, still sore from his persistent hands and mouth. "I love your nipples.

They're quick to harden at my touch."

Touch, hell. They hardened when she just thought about him, but he didn't need to know that. His head wouldn't fit through the tunnel into the stadium as it was.

Cooper sucked on her ear lobe as his erection rubbed against her ass. "Why are you in such a hurry to leave?" He rubbed her nipples, tweaking them with his fingers and waking up her libido, even though it should've been in a state of exhaustion.

"I have some errands to run if I'm going to be back here by this evening. It's almost noon."

"We're lazy asses. I have to be at the SHAC for meetings at two. That gives us enough time to shower and have a quickie." He bit her earlobe. The minor pain sent a shock of sexual energy through her veins.

"You're definitely into water sports."

"I'm partial to ice, which is frozen water. We should try it on the ice sometime, all that cold and heat mixed together."

She moaned and nodded. "You're on."

He pulled her into his big tiled shower with all the jets and shower heads. She shucked off her panties. Putting her hands on his shoulders, she stood on tiptoes to kiss his proud mouth.

Cooper turned her around so her back was to him. "Bend over, beautiful. I want to take you from behind and watch my cock pump in and out of that gorgeous pussy of yours."

Izzy opened her mouth to protest on principle, but he smacked her ass hard. In fact it fucking hurt, but she liked it. Really, really liked it. Her pussy swelled with renewed interest.

"Bend over," he growled. "Or I'll have to punish you."

"No," she refused, partly to be contrary and partly because his man-in-charge attitude turned her on in a big way.

He put his hand on her shoulders and bent her over. She struggled against him just to make it more of a challenge for him. He captured her hands behind her back and held them in his strong grip, keeping one big hand free to smack her ass.

She'd usually been the one in charge in the bedroom, but much to her surprise, she liked him taking charge and exerting his male dominance and superior strength over her. She'd never enjoyed being dominated by another man.

She wiggled her butt at him. Despite how sore it was, she could feel her juices flowing. Her pussy tingled and begged for something large and hard inside it. He must have spanked her a dozen times before he stopped, and it hurt so good.

"Are you going to behave?"

She was tempted to argue but decided to zip her mouth shut. Her ass stung like hell, and she needed him to do the nasty. "Yes, sir," she said, faking a meek, subservient voice, so unlike her.

"Good." He almost sounded disappointed, and she laughed.

Instead of smacking her again, Cooper slammed his full, hard length balls deep inside her. "Oh. My. Gawd," she screamed out as he retreated and pounded into her again. And again. And again. He adjusted his angle, hitting her higher on the next several thrusts. Letting go of her hands, he gripped her hips and ramped up his rough thrusts, plunging his dick deep inside her with the force and speed of a well-oiled piston. Pleasure mixed with the pain of an already sore body, and Izzy came fast and hard, leaning her hands against the wall for support.

"Awwww, shit," Cooper shouted. He pulled out at the last minute, emptying his seed on her ass and thighs. She felt its warmth as it slid down her legs mixed with the shower water.

He leaned over her back, holding her tight, his breathing harsh and irregular.

Finally he straightened and washed the cum from her legs and tender ass.

They stepped out of the shower together, and Cooper wrapped her in a big towel. He kissed her forehead and rested his cheek against hers.

When he lifted his head, his eyes were troubled, which surprised her. That was the last thing she expected. What the hell had gone wrong?

"I've never done that before," he said.

"Done it doggy style in a shower?"

"No, I forgot all about a condom. I pulled out just in time."

"Oh." She thought about it for a moment. "I've never forgotten to make sure the man was wearing a condom. I don't have unprotected sex."

"Neither do I." His eyes lit up with desire. "But it's one hell of a fantasy. I'd love to feel my cock inside you without anything between us, fill your body with my cum. I guess I wanted it so badly,

I got carried away."

"That's okay. Really. I did, too." Because she wanted the same thing, which horrified her. Unprotected sex was the worst idea in the world, and it represented a relationship hurdle she didn't want to think about.

"Sorry, it won't happen again."

"No, it won't."

He nodded, but she could see the disappointment in his eyes.

They dressed, spent some time holding each other and kissing. Finally Izzy forced herself to leave. As much as her body wanted Cooper, she didn't think she could take more without some recovery time.

She waved goodbye and drove down his driveway onto the street, glancing in the rear view mirror. He stood on his porch, shirtless, and watching her. Her chest tightened at the oddly domestic sight. Cooper Black did things to her, scary, wonderful things. Things she wasn't sure she could handle because being in a relationship with a domineering man like him required her to relinquish some of her independence.

She'd fought too long and hard to be in charge of her own destiny. She'd be damned if she'd give it up to anyone. Even a sexy hockey player with unruly hair and blazing blue eyes.

The problem was it appeared they were already in a relationship.

Chapter 12—Hat Trick

"Where the hell have you been?" Betheni met Izzy at the door, her hands perched on her hips.

"I'm sorry, I was taking care of Riley."

"That's bullshit, and you know it. Riley would've left for school hours ago." Betheni leaned in and studied her sister. Izzy looked away. "You've been fucking Cooper."

"Sort of," Izzy admitted, then laughed at how ludicrous that sounded.

"With that man, I'll bet my booty there's no *sort of*. I bet he's all in." Betheni threw back her head and laughed.

Izzy rolled her eyes.

"Besides, it's about time. I hope being thoroughly fucked improves your bitchy attitude."

"How do you know I was thoroughly fucked?"

"Several reasons. One, you have that dazed, thoroughly fucked look. Two, you're relaxed instead of wound tight. Three, you've been AWOL since last night, and Cooper should've gotten home sometime this morning. The way I see it, at least eight hours are unaccounted for. Therefore, you've been screwing the man's brains out and vice versa."

Izzy saw no reason to continue an argument she'd lose. "Guilty as charged. Now I need to sleep for the next twenty-four hours." Did she ever. Her entire body ached in a good way. She still felt his presence between her legs, on her cheeks, and on her sore ass. A girl didn't easily forget a night like that or a man like that, especially when every movement she made brought back memories of a particular sex act. She couldn't believe she was able to walk upright instead of crawling.

"He rode you hard, did he?" Betheni narrowed her eyes and looked her up and down, smirking that knowing smirk that drove Izzy mad.

"Like a Triple-Crown winner." Izzy managed a tired smile. This filly needed to go back to the barn and crash. Only she was ravenous. It'd been hours since she'd eaten. Betheni followed her to the kitchen as Izzy pillaged the cupboards and refrigerator in search of food.

"Good luck. We don't have a thing in this house to eat, unless you want a piece of moldy cheese with ketchup on it."

Right now even that sounded good. Izzy found a can of chicken noodle soup and poured it into a pan. She leaned against the counter waiting for it to boil. "Have you heard from Avery?"

Betheni looked away, chewing on her lower lip and picking at her fingernail polish. Not a good sign.

"Betheni, have you?"

"Uh, yes, she came by this morning. That's why I've been trying to call. She's living in an apartment over the barn."

"At least she has that." Izzy felt a small measure of relief her sister had shelter.

"Uh, there's one more thing. Emma packed up her stuff and moved out. She's moving in with Avery."

"What?" Izzy's hands shook with anger at the ultimate betrayal. Sweet, compliant Emma never gave her an ounce of trouble. Of all the sisters, she'd always been the dependable, level-headed one. "Why? Why did she do that?"

"I don't know." Betheni lied the best of any of the sisters, but right now her talent for fabricating appeared to elude her. "She did say she was worried you'd be pissed, and she still wanted to be a party crasher."

"Can you talk to Brad? Find out what the situation is? His sister-in-law runs the barn."

"Okay, I can, but we're not much for talking. We'll just end up in bed together."

"You two are such sluts."

Betheni grinned. "Isn't it fun?"

Izzy rolled her eyes. Like she should be lecturing anyone on sleeping with a guy for fun rather than with an eye to a future with the man. "I have bigger problems than the twins."

"Oh, yeah? Cooper getting to you, is he?"

Well, there was that. "No, it's just fun with Cooper. Just sex, sex, and more sex. My problem is Riley. Aunt Barb is gone for good. She isn't coming back, and until I find a replacement, I'm now a nanny."

Betheni laughed so hard, she bent over, holding her sides, as her entire body shook.

"I don't think it's that funny," Izzy huffed, not in a mood to see the humor of the situation.

"Sorry." Betheni straightened and rubbed her eyes.

Izzy opened her purse and pulled out some cash. "At least I have money now for the rent."

"Oh, that. I, uh, have one other thing to tell you."

"What?" Izzy rubbed her hands over her face. She wasn't going to like this, she just knew it.

"Well, speaking of Brad, he's offered to let me stay in the studio apartment over his garage. I told the landlord we're moving. Since we were such good renters, he's giving us until tomorrow to be out, and he won't charge us."

It was a conspiracy. Izzy dropped down onto the old sagging couch and put her head in her hands. "You're deserting me too?"

"No, not really. You can move there with me. It's free, and it'll allow me to get back on my feet."

"The two of us in a studio? One bed, right? One bathroom?"

"It has a hide-a-bed."

Izzy shook her head. "No, if something happens between you and Brad, we'd be out on our asses. Not to mention we'd kill each other being in that close proximity without even walls between us."

"Okay. Then stay with Cooper for now. Everything is falling into place as it should." Betheni perked up, as if she had it all figured out.

"I can't stay with Cooper." Izzy rubbed her eyes, feeling a headache coming on. Moving in with Cooper was the last thing she would do. Talk about giving up her independence—that'd be the final nail in that coffin.

"Sure you can. Most nannies live in the house with the children." Betheni covered her mouth with her hand in an obvious attempt to stifle her amusement.

"I am not a nanny." Izzy glared at her, beyond irritated.

Betheni shrugged. "Don't be such a stubborn bitch. If you don't want to stay with Cooper, pay the rent or move in with me."

"I can't afford this place on my own." Izzy couldn't believe this was happening to her. She couldn't live with Betheni in a one-room studio. One of them would have to die.

And Izzy didn't want it to be her.

She'd already become too indebted to Cooper, as it was. She would not move into his house, even if he was okay with it. At least, she'd be staying at Cooper's when he went on road trips.

Betheni glanced at her watch and threw on a jacket. "Hey, I have to go. I'm meeting Brad for lunch. Get packed. Brad's helping us move stuff out tonight." Betheni breezed out the door.

Izzy didn't know whether to laugh or cry, but she did know that her control over the situation teetered on a dangerous precipice. Not only had her sisters mutinied, but they'd left her homeless for all intents and purposes. She'd never have done this to them. They were growing up and away from her, while she still wanted to be the big sister who took care of everything for them. Only they didn't want that. They'd changed. She hadn't.

Izzy sat down to eat her soup, but finally poured it down the garbage disposal without eating a bit of it.

Her choices dwindled with every breath she took. Despite the money Cooper had advanced her, she couldn't afford this apartment on her own.

All those old feelings of helplessness from her teen years flooded back. Her life was spiraling out of control, and nothing she did worked to bring it back into her tight clutches. And what started the spiral happened to be the same thing that started it every damn time.

Her parents. The people who were supposed to love her, protect her, nurture her. Yeah, right. Not her parents.

She put her head in her hands and did something she rarely did. She cried. She cried until snot ran out her nose, her sobs turned to hiccups, and her makeup made her look like a member of KISS.

Such an incredible night had turned to shit in a matter of minutes.

Gathering her wits, Izzy wiped her eyes and nose and started packing. Not sure where the hell she was going but knowing she had to go somewhere.

Her body voted for Cooper's house. Her head told her to put up with Betheni, and her heart held its tongue.

Several hours and a loaded car later, she pulled into Cooper's driveway.

* * * *

Saturday night after the game Cooper toweled off his body as he walked out of the showers into the locker room.

As tired as he was, his game should've been off. But he kicked major ass in this last preseason game and took no prisoners. He was one of the league's top players, still at the top of his game, not that he gave a shit about statistics, and he'd proven that tonight.

He only had one thing left to prove. He wanted the Cup. That elusive silver cup which had eluded him while he suffered through the purgatory of his former team and their destructive ownership. The Sockeyes' organization was everything the Giants hadn't been. They were committed to winning. In any other city, he'd have been committed to staying, but not Seattle. Never Seattle. He couldn't stay in this city for reasons that had nothing to with the weather and everything to do with being haunted by the past.

Cooper shook his head to clear those memories and re-focus on the great game he'd just played. He'd pay for the lack of sleep later, but these last few nights of incredible sex with Izzy had energized him.

Cedric leaned against the counter as Cooper walked over to get a drink. He held the sports drink to his lips and took several long, hard swallows, just like Izzy had when she'd gone down on him.

Cedric's knowing smile brought him back to the locker room. "Who is she?"

"Izzy," he answered without thinking.

"Ya, that would've been my guess. I've never seen sex put that kind of smile on your face or escalate your game like that."

"Yeah, well, most women aren't Izzy."

"Imagine not. I scored a couple puck bunnies. I'd invite you to join me, but I already know the answer." Cedric combed back his blond hair in the mirror in his locker and grinned at himself. "Damn, but I'm a good looking guy."

Cooper put his finger in his mouth and made a gagging sound.

"What can I say? The ladies love me." And they did. They adored Cedric with his charming ways and electric personality. Cooper, on the other hand, was the quiet, brooding type, though he could turn on the charm when necessary. But he'd called bullshit on all that stuff long ago, especially when he could get in a woman's pants without charming them off her. The dark, brooding persona worked as well for him as charming and charismatic worked for Ced.

"So it didn't work out between you and Betheni?" Cooper asked.

A moment of hurt flashed in his friend's eyes. "Nah, she was just a bootie call, just like I was for her. I hear she's banging Brad Reynolds." Again, that hurt in his eyes.

"No shit?"

"No shit," Ced answered.

"Don't you ever get tired of it all, Ced?" He leaned against the back of his locker and watched Cedric.

Cedric's brows knit together, and he slanted Cooper a wary glance. "Of what?"

"A different woman every night, a revolving door. Never getting to know one long enough to become comfortable, to make her your best friend." Cooper had tired of it long before the team had moved to Seattle. Once he'd met Izzy, no other woman held even the slightest interest for him. Hell, they'd burned up the sheets all week since that marathon Wednesday morning.

Riley hadn't say anything, but Cooper suspected he'd figured it out. Cooper's love life was none of the kid's business anyway.

"No, never get tired of it, but obviously you are." Cedric plopped down on the padded bench next to Cooper. "Take it easy, man. You know you're a sucker for a certain type of woman, and Izzy is that type."

"I'll keep that under consideration."

"Seriously. She's playing with you, and I hate to see you get burned."

"Have I been burned once since Carrie?" Cooper pointed out. "I finally learned my lesson after that one."

"No, but Izzy's different. I can tell. Watch your step."

Cooper shrugged. Watch his step? Fuck, he'd been doing anything but watching his step. In fact, he'd tripped over her luscious lips, killer body, and dazzling smile and couldn't get back up.

"She could ruin you, Coop."

"Not a chance. We're having epic sex so, yeah, I'm seeing a lot of her, but what guy wouldn't take that to the net?"

Cedric didn't say anything.

"Besides, we're too much alike. We both have to be in control. We'd kill each other over the long haul, that's all there is to it." Cooper was explaining too much, but he couldn't stop himself. Yet, he sounded like a girl.

"Whatever." Cedric rose to his feet, gave Cooper a mock salute, and hurried out of the room to meet up with his hotties.

Izzy was working a party tonight, and Riley had stayed at his buddy's again. He'd barely grunted at Cooper, who'd missed another one of Riley's games yesterday—even though he felt like a total ass for doing it. He didn't want his nephew to start depending on him. Giving the kid false hope would hurt him more in the long run.

He realized such thinking made him a selfish jerk in most people's eyes, but Cooper tried to tell himself it was for Riley's own good. Cooper cringed a bit, as guilt washed over him. His sister had depended on him to do the right thing, to rescue her, but he hadn't. She'd been ill-equipped to handle that childhood summer in Seattle, too, the one that had changed everything for all of them.

Izzy hadn't said anything about him missing Riley's game, but her icy glare had said it all. Regardless, he'd thawed her pretty quickly once they hit the mattress.

Cooper smiled at the visual in his head.

Standing, he glanced at his phone, hoping for a text from Izzy. Nothing. Must be one hot party. His insides ground together at a vision of Izzy chatting up some fifty-something CEO, and the guy sliding his hand down her butt in a possessive manner.

Now that pissed Cooper the fuck off.

He sighed and combed his wet hair with his fingers. If he couldn't get beyond this insane jealousy toward every man who looked at her and all those in his imagination, they'd never last the season. He had serious trust issues when it came to women and for good reason. He just didn't know how the hell to deal with his problems, but he was trying. That should count for something.

Izzy wouldn't tell him where the party was, and he could imagine why. She didn't want a repeat of a couple months ago. Cooper didn't either because he doubted she'd give him another shot. He'd play it cool and loose, like it didn't matter to him what she did as long as she spent quality time in his bed every night.

Only she was starting to matter. Just a tiny bit. And she couldn't, but she did. He couldn't control what grew inside him every time he thought of her or spent time with her any more than he could control the physical chemistry between them.

Izzy hated depending on anyone, and he hated not being the go-to guy, the guy a woman would depend on. Add the fact that he'd be gone as soon as the season ended. No reason to start anything serious when they'd be living on opposite sides of the country.

He couldn't make his permanent home in Seattle, and he couldn't explain why to her. He wasn't certain he understood it all himself, but what happened to him as a child in Seattle exposed a weakness he'd forever keep hidden.

His phone chimed and interrupted his almost journey down a bad memory lane.

How was the game?

He grinned like an idiot at his phone. *Fucking awesome. I had a hat trick. Know what that is?*

You scored three goals? Congrats!!! I'll have something special for you tonight.

Cooper's grin spread to his ears. *Promise?*

Have I let you down yet?

No, I'm up the second I think of you.

Naughty boy.

Naughtier girl.

I thought you liked me naughty.

Oh, yeah, he loved her naughty, naked, and willing. In a few days he'd be on a week-long road trip, and he was missing her already.

Chapter 13—Trick Play

Izzy couldn't stop smiling when she saw Cooper's tall, muscular frame silhouetted in the light of the open doorway. Next to him sat Joker, tail swishing, as if he'd kept tabs on how late she was.

And it was late—really, really late. She should be dog tired, and she had been until she laid eyes on him in all his alpha-male glory.

Relief relaxed his face when he saw her, and a grin softened the hard lines of his cheeks and jaw. He'd been worried about her. Even a few weeks ago, she'd have felt smothered by such concern, because worry led to control and control led to loss of independence.

Yeah, she had issues but didn't everyone?

Despite her paranoia about depending on anyone in her life, she'd been unofficially living with Cooper since Betheni and she moved out of the apartment four days ago. Sure, she'd moved her clothes and personal items to the small studio at Brad's, but she hadn't spent one night there. In the meantime, little by little she hung clothes in Cooper's closet, stacked shoes on the floor, and put underwear in a dresser drawer next to his socks. If he noticed, he didn't say anything. Nor did he mention her makeup scattered on the bathroom counter.

Taking his front porch steps two at a time, she barreled into his arms. He easily held her, barely moving a fraction as she threw her arms around his neck and kissed the hell out of him. He kissed the hell out of her right back.

Finally she pulled free and leaned away from him. "Where's Riley?" she whispered.

"Staying the night with a friend. Besides, even if he was here, a freight train rumbling through his bedroom wouldn't wake him." He kissed the tip of her nose and ran a finger across her thoroughly kissed lips.

"Do you think he knows about us?" Izzy looked up into his blue eyes; his expression turned guarded like it did whenever she approached the subject of Riley.

Shrugging one shoulder as if it didn't matter to him, he grabbed her hand and led her into the kitchen.

"Wine?" he asked, not waiting for an answer but pouring her favorite Washington chardonnay into a wine glass. He twisted the top off a beer and sat next to her on a barstool.

190

"Cooper?" She couldn't drop the subject. She had to do this for Riley.

"Yeah?" he answered warily, instantly suspicious as well he should be. If she had to be his conscience where Riley was concerned, then so be it.

"What would it hurt you to attend one of Riley's games? Your mere presence would mean the world to him."

Cooper grunted, his face etched in stone, his eyes dark with repressed anger and irritation. Izzy didn't care. She pushed on. "Riley looks up to you, and you treat him like he's a burden."

Cooper's dark brows drew a hard, uncompromising line.

"Cooper," she prodded, refusing to let him blow her off about Riley this time.

"What?"

"Why are you being such a shit about this? Riley needs you. You're all he has."

Cooper looked right through her. "I'm not that guy. Don't make the mistake of thinking I am. Once I locate his mother or my parents return, whichever comes first, he'll be gone. I see no reason to give him false hope of this being a permanent arrangement."

Izzy crossed her arms over her chest and glowered at him. "Of course, he's no different than me; we're only temporary in your life."

"Do you want to be more?" His gaze met hers, and something flickered in his eyes, gone as quickly as it came. Regret? Fear? Hope? Denial? She couldn't put a finger on it.

"No, I'm not saying that. You know we'd kill each other eventually. We're not compatible."

"Except in the bedroom," he pointed out as he slid off his barstool and moved to her, pulling her legs apart so he could step between them. Her short little cocktail dress rode up higher on her hips, displaying a generous amount of thigh and ass, which wasn't lost on Cooper judging by how his pupils dilated, and he ground his erection against her crotch.

Damn, but he was hot. She wanted to be mad at him for Riley's sake but her wayward body refused to comply. When it came to Cooper, her body overruled her good sense and her self-preservation. Cooper always melted her frostiest resolve.

He slipped his hands under her skirt and cupped her bare ass, pulling her against him. He ran his tongue along her throat, and she leaned her head back. He nipped and kissed her neck until he found her mouth again and almost made her come solely with his talented tongue.

Izzy moaned and clung to his broad shoulders, such a weak-willed woman when it came to this man. She didn't have the strength to resist him, and the bastard knew it.

"I like the g-string," he whispered against her mouth.

"I'd like your cock inside me," Izzy shot back.

He stared deep into her brown-gold eyes. "I can accommodate that."

She protested when he backed away until she realized he was shucking his clothes with the same breakneck speed he displayed on the ice. Seconds later, a naked Cooper except for a condom resumed his spot between her legs. He hooked a finger in the scrap of lace covering her pussy, and pushed the head of his penis inside her, stretching her, filling her. Izzy dug her fingernails into his shoulders and wrapped her legs around his waist.

"Take me. Take me and have your way with me, big boy."

"As you wish," he answered, his generous mouth quirking up at the corner. His lips came down on hers, as demanding as his cock which now pounded into her with increasing intensity. She clenched around, as if she could hold him inside her forever. Not a bad thought, though not the least bit practical.

Cooper thrust three more times before burying himself inside her and holding himself there. The tension in his body betrayed the iron will it took him not to let go. Instead he slid his hand between their legs, finding her clit, and pressed against it with his finger, coaxing her to come first. It didn't take much. She clenched her eyes shut. Seconds later stars exploded behind her eyelids. Her body defied gravity and catapulted her above the clouds.

Cooper's climax followed. His body shuddered, and he hugged her tightly to him. Izzy buried her face in his sweaty shoulder and relished the bone-melting aftermath of one of the best orgasms ever. But then Cooper always gave the most awesome orgasms.

She'd never know how he did it, but Cooper managed to carry her to the couch and deposit her on it. He plopped next to her, tucking her under his arm. His cheek rested against hers. She heard his contented sigh as they sat in comfortable silence.

Several minutes passed before he cleared his throat. "Izzy?"

"Hmmm." She nuzzled his stubbled cheek and rested her hand on his strong thigh.

"I wanted to come to your party tonight in the worst way," he confessed, sounding as contrite as a small child who'd broken Mom's best vase.

"But you didn't know where it was."

"That wasn't what stopped me. I could've found you."

She believed that. He'd done it before. "Then what stopped you?" She turned slightly to look into his eyes, his expression earnest, even concerned.

"Don't give me that look. I'm working on it, but I have trust issues."

"I've noticed." She studied him, wanting to know what made Cooper Black the man he was. Someone had broken his heart and betrayed his trust, and she needed to know the facts. "Tell me why. Who hurt you so much you mistrust the people in your life? Was it a woman?"

"Maybe." His dark eyes shone with amusement, which was odd. "Are you the woman in my life now, Izzy?"

'You tell me." She shrugged. She didn't honestly know what she was other than his friend, his babysitter, his part-time conscience, and definitely his lover.

"You don't see anyone else sharing my bed, do you?" He almost grinned. He'd try to turn this into something else so he could avoid the real question. She'd been around him long enough to know Cooper approached most problems head-on and full-steam, except personal relationships. Those he avoided like most people avoided liver and onions.

"Who was she, Cooper?" she prodded, not letting him off that easy.

He stared at her, his mouth in a tense, stubborn line. He removed his arm from around her shoulders and buried his head in his hands. Izzy waited him out.

Finally he looked up. "My uncle, my sister, and then my former fiancée, and several women before her."

"Tell me about them, Cooper. I want to know."

She shouldn't want to know, shouldn't care that much because this thing between them couldn't go much further without entering the real relationship stage.

Yet, it didn't matter what was wise. Izzy couldn't repress this driving need to know everything about this man and what made him the man he was.

So she waited and hoped he'd answer.

* * * *

Cooper couldn't talk about this stuff when he was naked. He wasn't sure why, other than it made him too easily distracted by sex or too naked and exposed. He pulled on his boxers and sat back down, handing Izzy his big sweatshirt so she could cover up that delectable little dress. She seemed to understand and pulled it on, except she looked even sexier in his shirt which left everything to his imagination. He liked that almost as much as he liked her naked or in that mouth-watering little black dress she wore tonight.

He caught Izzy's hand and held it, staring down at their entwined hands, as if he'd find the answers to his questions there. He never talked about his sister, Julie, or Carrie, the former love of his life. And he sure as hell never talked about his uncle.

He could easily distract Izzy with his kisses and more, but he didn't want to do that. He wanted to tell her, wanted to share a portion of the ache inside of him that wouldn't go away. Maybe sharing his pain with someone else would lessen it. Maybe it didn't matter if it did or not, he wanted Izzy to understand him, to understand the struggles he'd been through with his sister and the women in his life.

Pushing his hair off his forehead with his free hand, he started talking, and once he started, he couldn't stop as his words transported him back to one of the most painful periods of his life. "I guess my sister came first. Julie was beautiful. Four years older than me. Straight-A student. Star athlete. She loved me and our younger brother, Dan. She protected us, watched over us." Only the one time she'd needed her brothers, they hadn't been there for her. It was his secret shame. He'd played a part in making her what she was today.

He paused, inhaled a deep, calming breath, and closed his eyes for a moment. Izzy squeezed his hand, giving him strength. When he opened his eyes, she was smiling at him, a warm, encouraging smile, a smile that said she supported him no matter what.

Cooper took another breath and continued as he held tight to Izzy's warm hand. He couldn't tell her about that Seattle summer, couldn't stand to see the censure in her eyes so he skipped that part of the story. "Julie met this guy when she was fifteen. He was bad news, but nothing anyone did could stop her from seeing him. Dad eventually kicked her out a year later. He didn't want her influencing her two younger brothers, but he was too late. Her behavior did influence us. I need absolute control over my life and any people in my life so I can make sure they're going to do the right thing. My brother, he did the opposite. He married a woman who controls his every move."

"I can understand the need to feel in control of your life."

She didn't know the half of it because the worst thing of all he kept to himself. Cooper shot Izzy a look that said *no kidding,* before continuing. "Julie's drug addiction tore my family apart. My parents did everything they could, spent tons of money on therapists. My mom suffers from Crohn's disease, and the stress of dealing with Julie caused it to flare up multiple times, putting her in the hospital more than once. The last time she almost died from complications after surgery, which scared the shit out of my dad. He put his foot down and gave Julie an ultimatum, get clean or get out. She didn't. He cut her off, refused to give her money. He banned her from family gatherings unless she was one-hundred-percent clean. Dad decided it was her or us, and he couldn't have her dragging the rest of the family down with her any longer."

"Addiction is a tough thing for families to handle. Cooper, I'm so sorry you dealt with that."

Usually sympathy irritated him, but from her it filled some of the empty places inside him. He could've left it at that, but he didn't, he kept talking. "I was Riley's age the last time I saw her, and Julie was about eighteen. She came to my parents' house, all freaked out on meth, threatened us with a gun. She waved it in our faces and shot into the walls. A neighbor heard the gunshots and called the police. It took a SWAT team to free us from her craziness. They hauled her off to jail. The entire family took out restraining orders against her. Other than a few drunken phone calls begging for money over the years, that was the last we heard of her directly, though she kept in minimal contact with an aunt." Cooper buried his face in his hands and took slow, deep breaths. Izzy rubbed his back and leaned into his body.

"Cooper. I'm so sorry."

"I should've done something to save her." He removed his hands from his face, but he didn't meet her gaze. She put her hand under his chin and lifted his face to hers. Guilt she wouldn't understand choked him. He'd done this to his sister. He'd kept his mouth shut when she'd needed him the most. He should've said something about what happened all those years ago in Seattle. Julie changed that summer of her fourteenth year, and nothing was the same after that.

"Cooper, you can't blame yourself, but you can help Riley." Izzy leaned forward and brushed her lips across his, a sweet gentle kiss that said more than all the rough passionate kisses from earlier. It warmed him from the inside out, gave him hope that maybe, just maybe, a normal life might be in the cards for him.

"I knew that was coming," he muttered. He did blame himself for his sister. He'd kept Julie's secret all these years. How many others suffered because he'd been a coward?

"Cooper. Put your misplaced guilt to good use. Be a father figure to Riley." She pulled away from him, glaring down at him.

Cooper snorted at such a ludicrous idea. Him? A father figure? Now that was laughable. Only Izzy wasn't laughing. She'd pulled her hand from his and leapt to her feet, glaring down at him.

"It's not funny," she said, hands on her hips, eyes blazing. He loved that about her, how she could go all sweet and loving one minute then be ready to rip him a new one the next minute. It was sexy as hell and turned him on big time.

"If you say so. Tell that to the guys."

"You're great with kids. I've seen you work with them in Kids at Play and you have a reputation as a good guy who goes to the Children's Hospital and always makes time for kids. Why don't you make time for your own flesh and blood?"

Cooper's head pounded. She'd never understand, and he doubted he'd be able to explain it well enough not to make it worse.

"Cooper."

He sighed. She wouldn't give this up until she got some kind of answer. "I don't want him to get attached to me."

"Oh, for God's sake. That is the stupidest reason I've ever

heard. You're a coward, Cooper Black. A pansy-assed coward." She shook her head, clearly disgusted. "You aren't protecting Riley. Admit it. You're protecting your sorry ass."

He stood, walked casually to the kitchen, and found a beer in fridge. After popping the top, he took a long swallow. Izzy watched him from across the room, still glaring, hands still on hips.

"You're not going to let me off that easy, are you?"

She shook her head, walking in that sexy, graceful way only she had which made his mouth water. She sat down on the very barstool that he'd fucked her brains out on earlier and leaned on her elbows. Stalling, he poured her another glass of her favorite sweet white wine, even though she hadn't asked for it, grabbing himself a bottle of beer.

"Any word on Riley's mom?" Instead of pushing him about Riley, she'd surprised him with that question, though he knew she'd work it back around to the previous subject.

"My PI thought he'd spotted her a few times, but when he moved in, she disappeared. I think she's still alive."

"If she's still alive, why doesn't she contact Riley?" Izzy seemed as incredulous about that fact as Cooper.

"Fuck if I know." Cooper fisted his hands in frustration born from years of dealing with his sister. He'd like to punch something, but knew he couldn't. "As soon as Russ finds her, he has strict instructions to tail her until I can get there."

"Then what?"

Cooper was pretty certain this would circle back around to Riley any moment, but he stepped into her carefully laid trap anyway. "I'm going to find out what the hell she's been doing and why she walked away from her son almost six weeks ago without a word."

Izzy nodded. "He's a good kid. He doesn't deserve a mother like her. From what I understand, he raised himself and watched over her. He needs security, Cooper. He needs to know that someone is always going to be there for him, no matter what. He needs you."

"Oh, fuck, I knew you were going to flip this around on me. I can't be that person, Izzy. Don't you understand? I'm not that guy, but I promise you I'll make sure he's well taken care of either by a sane and sober mother or my parents. I won't dump him back out on the street."

"If that's the best you've got?" Her disappointed scowl made him feel like a shit, as if he were failing Riley.

"It is," he said, wondering if he was believing his own words any more.

"At least do me one favor. One little favor."

"It'll cost you," he slipped into his teasing mode, hoping to be free of the uncomfortable and confusing subject of what to do with his nephew.

"Name your price, sweetie." She stood and sashayed around the counter to stand before him. He grinned down at her and tucked a strand of hair behind her ear. He should've sensed another trap, but he ignored the warning bells blaring in his head.

"Let's start with me, you, a shower, and lots of steamy, hot water. Your mouth on my dick as the water runs down your face." He couldn't stop smiling at the thought, and his dick hardened appreciatively. He put his hands loosely on her hips and kissed the tip of her nose.

"Deal." She smiled, as if moving in for the kill. "Now for your part of it. Come to Riley's next game."

The smile slipped off his face. He sighed in resignation. "When is it?"

"Next Thursday. They play every Thursday."

"I'm on a road trip."

"Then the following week."

"Okay, I'll do it." By then he should know more about Riley's mother. Russ was confident he was on her trail and just a day or two behind her.

"Thank you." Izzy's smile lit up the room. He'd attend a hundred freshman football games to see her smile like that.

He pulled her against him in a gentle hug, burying his face in her soft hair and inhaling the scent of her shampoo. Emotions swelled inside him, emotions which scared the living hell out of him. He was falling for her, and there wasn't a damn thing he could do to stop it, even if he'd wanted to. Only he didn't want to stop caring for her, adoring her, didn't want to lose her. Not today. And not when he finally left Seattle.

Chapter 14—Slap Shot

A slight gust of crisp fall air lifted the collar of Cooper's coat as he walked to the edge of the field and scanned the smattering of people sitting in the bleachers. Weather wise, he'd missed the seasons living in Florida where every day seemed like the one before it, but he'd be the last to admit that he enjoyed any aspect of Seattle, especially its weather. Cooper couldn't believe it was already the second week of October, and Riley had been living with him for a month.

Last night the Sockeyes played their very first regular season game in Seattle. The place had been electric, packed to the rafters with rabid fans. Cooper played lights out with a goal, a couple assists, and a penalty. He was especially proud of the penalty, because it'd been against Tanner Wolfe's asshole brother, Isaac, and the jerk deserved it.

Yet, something was missing from the game, and Cooper didn't have to delve too deep into the psychology of his feelings to know what it was. Neither Izzy nor Riley attended. Izzy couldn't. She had a senior citizen wedding to attend. Riley begged off when Cooper invited him, claiming he had to study for a test. What kid studies for a test when he's offered seats on the glass to watch the first regular season NHL game ever played in Seattle? Hell, he'd even offered a ticket for Riley's buddy and his coach.

So maybe that was why he was here today. It hurt like hell that the two people in his life hadn't attended his game. He'd never given a shit about stuff like that before, but he'd never been in this weird situation either. It shouldn't matter if they attended or not. Yet, it did. His feelings didn't make a damn bit of sense to him, but they were what they were.

There were times when the three of them almost felt like a family, and those feelings made Cooper vulnerable and scared as hell.

Regardless, here he was at Riley's game to show Izzy and Riley that he supported them both. He didn't want Riley to feel abandoned like he had last night.

Cooper caught sight of Izzy waving at him from the stands. He walked toward her before he noticed that asshole Wolfe sat next to her. He couldn't stand Wolfe's arrogant hockey-playing brother, who he grudgingly admitted might be the best defenseman in the league, and Tanner was cut from the same douche-bag cloth.

Did that fucking jerk attend all of Riley's games? Now that really pissed him off for reasons he rather keep to himself. Yeah, he hated Tanner sitting next to Izzy, sharing popcorn with her, and making her laugh. But he didn't like the douche watching his nephew as if the kid were his blood, not Cooper's.

How stupid was that?

Cooper walked toward Izzy and Tanner. He'd play nice for Izzy, but he didn't give a shit about the jerk sitting next to her.

Izzy's face lit up with approval when she saw him and his heart kicked it up a notch. Seeing her smile made putting up with Wolfe that much easier.

"You came?" she said as he slid onto the bleacher seat next to her.

"I promised," he said simply, lacing her hand in his as if it were the most natural thing in the world.

Tanner reached across her and held out his hand. "Hey, man, glad you could make it for Riley's sake." Cooper ignored the censure in Tanner's voice. He shook the cocky quarterback's hand and faked a friendly grin, giving a command performance that would make his mother proud.

Not bad for a jealous Neanderthal like him.

Forcing his gaze from Izzy, Cooper spotted Riley immediately. Big for his age, Riley stood taller than most of his teammates, except for Brian, his best buddy and the head coach's son. Riley's back was to him in his number eighty-five jersey. Cooper recalled that the kid played tight end on offense and defensive end on defense.

Cooper hadn't actually planned on paying much attention to the game. He'd rather imagine Izzy naked underneath him or in his hot tub. Izzy concentrated on the game instead of him. With resignation and to keep his butt from being kicked by a pissed off woman, Cooper watched, too, and he enjoyed every minute of it—except for those minutes which required he talk to Wolfe.

Riley surprised him, but he shouldn't have. Those Black genes shone through, and the Black family was a talented bunch when it came to athletics

Toward the end of the 2nd half, Riley intercepted a pass and ran it eighty yards for a touchdown. Izzy leapt to her feet screaming with unabashed enthusiasm as did Tanner. Frowning and not to be outdone by the douche, Cooper stood, too, and clapped loudly.

Riley jogged back to the sidelines and glanced up in their direction, a triumphant smile on his face. For a second their eyes met and something shifted inside Cooper's chest. Riley looked away first to cock his head at whatever his teammate was saying, acting as if nothing had happened. But it had. Cooper couldn't deny it. That damn kid had burrowed under his skin, despite Cooper's best efforts to keep him at arm's length.

In the last two minutes of the game, Riley caught another pass ten yards from the end zone to set up their fullback to run it in for six. They won the game, and Riley grinned from ear to ear as he jogged with his team into the locker room. Cooper caught himself smiling, too. He'd enjoyed the game, enjoyed Izzy's hand in his the whole time, and he was damn proud of Riley, even if he hadn't earned the right.

A group of parents stood near the locker room door waiting for their sons. Cooper stood off to the side, still holding Izzy's hand, while a group formed around Tanner, who ate it up like the attention slut he was.

One of the mothers broke off from Tanner's adoring crowd and approached Cooper.

"You must be Riley's dad. He looks just like you," she said as she looked pointedly at his ring finger.

"I'm his uncle." Cooper shifted his stance, tucking Izzy closer to him, while that asshole Tanner, who'd also joined them, let out a snort.

"Wow, really? Strong resemblance. You look like an athlete yourself."

Tanner snorted again, inserting himself into their conversation. "He is, if you think skating for a living qualifies."

Izzy squeezed his hand, more as warning to keep his mouth shut than as support.

The woman's perfectly made-up eyes widened. "Oh, you're a figure skater?"

Tanner roared with laughter, and Cooper wanted to shove Tanner's head into his ass. "I'm a hockey player," he answered through gritted teeth.

One of the other fathers spoke up. "You play for the Sockeyes, don't you?"

Cooper nodded, and for the next few minutes, his popularity outshone Tanner's as Cooper fielded questions and signed autographs.

"Your nephew has your ability, all right," one of the dads noted. "He's the best player on the team. You must be really proud of him."

Cooper opened his mouth to make some non-committal statement, but what he did say surprised him. "I'm very proud of him. He's an amazing kid."

And he meant it.

Izzy leaned into him, squeezing his hand and rewarding him with a sweet smile, warming him inside and making him wonder why he'd been such an ass and held out so long.

He'd used Riley's well-being for an excuse, but it wasn't Riley's heart he was protecting.

It was his own.

* * * *

Riley toweled off after his shower, feeling as if his feet couldn't possibly touch the ground. Today had been one of those rare perfect days in his life that he'd cherish and pull out whenever he needed a boost.

Like he did before every game, Riley had scanned the stands for Izzy and Tanner. They never disappointed him. Only today he'd done a double take. His uncle had sat next to Izzy holding her hand and grinning at her like a lovesick idiot.

For a second, hope swelled in Riley's heart, a feeble hope for a real family or even a half-assed family. Hell, anything would be better than what he'd had for all of his sorry life.

Yet, when he saw the way Cooper stared at Izzy, as if they were the only two people on earth and nothing else existed but them, the truth stabbed him like a sharp knife in the heart. His uncle came for Izzy 'cuz he wanted to get in her pants.

Regardless, Riley would take what he could get. Maybe Cooper wasn't there for Riley, but he was there. Riley swore he'd play the game of his life and make Cooper notice him.

Riley was good. His teammates said so, his coach said so. The high school coach told him he'd be starting varsity as a sophomore next year.

If there was a next year.

And just like that, all those good feelings were punched right out of him. Riley slumped onto the bench in front of his locker and his shoulders sagged. He felt as if all the wind had been knocked out him.

His mother couldn't afford to live in this school district. For the first time, Riley almost wished Cooper wouldn't find his mother, but a blitz of guilt tackled those traitorous feelings. His mother needed him, and he needed her. They were all each other had. Cooper didn't give a rat's ass about him, but his mother, with all her faults, did. She loved him. No one else in her family loved either of them.

It was only a matter of time before this storybook life he'd been living for the past couple months went south.

Every time things went his way, Riley held his breath waiting for stuff to go to hell. Just like he was now. He went to a school with a lot of wealthy and upper-middle class kids. They thought he was one of them because Uncle Cooper was a rich, pro hockey player. It gave Riley an undeserved status, one he'd never had before. Uncle Coop had furnished the money and thanks to Izzy he looked the part, but that was it. Inside, he was the same—the poor son of a prostitute who didn't have a clue who his father was, the same kid whose mother's family pretended she didn't exist and the same kid whose mom disappeared without a word, leaving him in the shitty situation of depending on an uncle who didn't want him around.

He felt like a fraud and wondered when his new friends and classmates would figure that out. They'd realize he was poor white trash with a mother who gave new meaning to the phrase "working mother." Riley cringed, his disloyal thoughts choking him with more guilt.

He'd shown Uncle Coop, shown him that he wasn't a loser. Having his uncle there had driven Riley to be that much better, and he had his best game ever just to prove a point. It was the game that'd get him out of poverty, not Uncle Coop or the rest of his mother's family. Riley was determined to make something of himself and prove everyone wrong, including his mom and her dreg friends.

Yeah, that's what he'd do. Prove them all wrong.

Riley finished dressing and walked out of the locker room. He stopped and blinked a few times. Izzy, Cooper, and Tanner waited for him among the group of parents.

Izzy rushed to him and threw her arms around him. Riley couldn't stop grinning. He caught the jealous stares of a few of his teammates and grinned all the more.

Next, Tanner approached him, gave him a manly half hug, and congratulated him on the game. "Good job, kid. You'll be playing for the Steelheads in no time."

"Thanks," Riley shuffled his feet and stared at the ground. His face grew hot, but he managed to play it cool.

"Hey, bud, I've gotta go. I'll catch up with ya next week. We'll hit the pizza place or something." Tanner saluted him and slipped through the crowd.

"He must have a hot date," Cooper muttered.

Riley didn't say anything. Cooper and Tanner didn't like each other much.

Izzy elbowed Cooper and he grunted. Riley bit back a laugh. Izzy and Cooper were hot for each other. They tried to hide it, but Riley wasn't stupid. Izzy never went home. She stayed in Uncle Cooper's room even when he was home, and she didn't need to stay.

Riley wasn't sure what she saw in his uncle. She could do better.

Izzy cleared her throat and gave Cooper another elbow to the ribs. He grunted again. His blue eyes lifted to meet Riley's. "Good game."

"Thanks." Riley wished he could run away and get out of this situation. He didn't like talking to his uncle. He knew it was out of obligation not love, and he didn't need the man's pity.

"So are you hungry?" Izzy, all smiles and cheerful sweetness, interrupted the silence. "Let's get pizza to celebrate your game."

"Okay," Riley said.

"Sure," Cooper said. He nodded to Riley and tugged on Izzy's hand, as if in a hurry to leave.

Coach pushed through the crowd of parents, holding his hand out to Uncle Cooper. Riley backed up a step. "Well, finally, we get to meet. I'm Bill Mars, Riley's coach."

Riley's best friend, Brian, was the coach's son. Brian gave Riley one of those looks that said *so your uncle finally decided to slum with us?*

"I'm Cooper Black." His uncle seemed uncomfortable, which was weird. Uncle Coop always had his act together.

"I know. I'm a big hockey fan, and I've always enjoyed watching you play. Like poetry on ice."

Cooper seemed surprised. Riley tried not to laugh. Poetry on ice? His uncle? Now that was funny. "I've been called many things, but I'm not sure that's one of them."

Izzy stepped forward. "We were just getting pizza. Would you like to join us? It's on Cooper."

"Well, in that case, absolutely." Coach looked to his son. "Sound good, son?"

"Yeah."

Fifteen minutes later, Riley found himself wedged between Cooper and Izzy at the pizza place with his coach and best friend across the table. It was damn weird. Almost like a normal family.

Riley couldn't recall ever having such an average moment before.

And he really liked it. A whole lot.

* * * *

Izzy would not let this moment go south, not for Cooper and not for Riley. They meant too much to her, an admission which scared the crap out of her and gave her warm fuzzies at the same time.

The boys kept up a steady stream of conversation, while the men seemed content to let them talk. Cooper put his arm across the back of the booth behind Riley's back and rubbed her shoulder. She suppressed a shiver. When Riley leaned forward, Cooper leaned back and winked at Izzy. His lecherous grin promising she'd be naked soon.

She scowled at him, causing him to frown in confusion. Izzy jerked her chin toward Riley. They could engage in foreplay later when they were alone.

Sure, she'd be a lying fool to deny that getting Cooper naked later didn't turn her on. Her brain raced after her body as both recalled the feel of Cooper's stubble on her face, his fingers in her hair, and his cock deep inside her.

Only this moment was not about her or Cooper. This moment was about Riley, and Riley bonding with Cooper.

Izzy didn't want Riley to go back to his mother if and when she was found. She'd force Cooper to see that he was the perfect choice as Riley's guardian even if she needed to beat that realization into him with his hockey stick.

She just wished he'd quit rubbing her shoulder in slow, sensuous circles, or she might become the first woman to orgasm from shoulder circles. Izzy scooted out of Cooper's reach. He glared at her, promising she'd pay for this later. She couldn't wait. She'd pay his price gladly.

Coach Mars leaned forward to speak to Cooper over the boys' animated conversations about the high school girls two booths away. "So Cooper, have you ever played football?"

Cooper shook his shaggy head of hair. "Never had time. It's been hockey twenty-four-seven since I was old enough to skate. In fact, my dad swears I was skating before I was walking."

"You'd have been a good football player," Bill Mars stated with absolute certainty. Izzy imagined Cooper would be good at anything he set his mind to, including capturing her heart.

Riley stopped making eyes at the girls and turned his head toward Bill and Cooper, watching intently.

"I'll let Riley be the football player in the family. Hockey is my life." Cooper winked at Riley and grinned. Riley appeared caught off guard; embarrassed by his uncle's rare display of affection, Riley ducked his head and concentrated on his pizza. Cooper seemed oblivious as to the effect of his praise.

"Riley's good, you know," Bill said.

"I could see that."

"He's athletic and smart."

Cooper nodded, his expression wary, as if he sensed a trap.

"I'll be moving up to coaching JV next year. I'd like Riley on my team unless varsity steals him away." Bill moved in for the kill.

A quick glance to Riley revealed that he was holding his breath, as if trying to discern whether or not Cooper would be pissed. Izzy read the hope in his eyes and suspected the teenager must have confessed his woes to his coach.

"Riley's a good player," Cooper said smoothly, not committing to anything, not emotionally and not in the way of Riley's future.

The hope drained from Riley's face, as if he'd been emotionally bludgeoned by his uncle's words. Izzy wanted to strangle the insensitive ass, but she couldn't. At least, not here.

Still, she'd chew his ass tonight. They'd fight, and he'd turn those blue eyes on her and melt her anger. She couldn't resist him as hard as she tried, but she could hold him off long enough to pummel some sense into his thick skull.

Chapter 15—Right Now

Silence echoed off the walls in Cooper's big old house as he wandered from room to room.

One minute he'd been eating pizza with Izzy and Riley and the next he'd been driving home alone. His evening plans had involved getting Izzy naked and keeping her occupied all night long. Instead, she was occupied by her business.

Betheni had called with a small emergency at a party the sisters were crashing. Izzy took off to do damage control. Cooper so wanted to check on her and make sure no asshole was hitting on her. Hell, of course, guys were hitting on her. She was fucking gorgeous with a body hot enough to inspire a million wet dreams.

Fine, he'd thought, he still had Riley and maybe they should spend a little uncle-nephew time together.

Then Riley went home with the Mars family, leaving Cooper to go it alone. In the oddest way, he felt betrayed, which didn't make one damn bit of sense. He liked it when Riley spent the night elsewhere. It allowed Izzy and him to make as much noise as they wanted. Yet tonight, he wasn't so thrilled. For reasons he couldn't explain, he'd assumed they'd go home and talk sports. Cooper might not be a football player, but he was a fan of the game. As a guy used to analyzing game film, he had a few tips for Riley. Little things, such as where his eyes went just before the play started, which provided clues to a savvy defender as to the route he'd be running.

Yeah, grudgingly, he admitted he was disappointed and lonely. He liked people, but he'd never minded being alone. He'd always been comfortable with both. Not so much tonight. He tried to watch an adventure movie, but the car chases and bombs only bored him.

Cooper stared around the family room, not sure what to do with himself.

Riley spent a lot of time at his coach's house, and it was starting to bother Cooper. Maybe because he loved to control every aspect of his life, and he couldn't control Izzy, so now his attention switched to Riley as a distraction. How come the boys never came to Cooper's house when Cooper was home, like they did when it was just Izzy here?

Maybe because you're an indifferent asshole who doesn't give any indication you'd enjoy having them around?

Even worse, on a few of those occasions when Cooper had been gone, Tanner came to the house. Cooper could just see it now, and he seethed with jealousy over Tanner hanging out at Cooper's house with Cooper's nephew and girlfriend.

Girlfriend?

Yeah, girlfriend.

That was exactly how he saw Izzy, and he might as well man-up and admit it. He wondered how she saw him. She'd been informally living in his house for over two weeks, not that he was complaining, not at all. They never talked about dating exclusively. He'd taken their exclusivity as a given, just like he had too many things in his life, but maybe she didn't see it that way. Cooper sure as hell did. He didn't want anyone else. When girls threw themselves at him after games, he didn't feel even a twinge of interest.

Izzy was different, and being with Izzy had never been just physical, not even the first night he met her.

She made him laugh, made him stretch his comfort zone, made him think, and she didn't take his shit. Instead she flipped it right back at him. Most people didn't do that, and strangely, he liked it. He liked her here with him, keeping him in line, and keeping him excited.

Only she wasn't here. No one was. God, he wanted to hop in his car and hunt her down. But he couldn't. He'd promised, and he kept his promises.

At loose ends and out of sorts, Cooper trudged upstairs. He wasn't sure why, but he went to Riley's room. He stood in the doorway and glanced around, a typical kid's room. The messiness drove him crazy, but he forced himself to look past it. Who was this kid who'd lived in his house for a month? He didn't know a damn thing about him, didn't know about his past, didn't know about his hopes or dreams. Nothing. And he hadn't wanted to know.

Until now.

Cooper walked around the room, stopping to stare at the signed poster of Tanner Wolfe on the wall. He snorted and rolled his eyes. Cooper picked up a worn five-by-seven on the nightstand of Riley and his mother. Cooper's sister didn't look good in the photo. Her eyes were unfocused, her smile a little forced. Riley's huge smile didn't quite hide the sadness in his eyes, old eyes, much older than they had a right to be.

Anger gripped Cooper, anger at his irresponsible sister and a more than a little anger at himself. Riley deserved so much better than he got from his mother or his uncle. Riley deserved stability.

In that moment, Cooper vowed he would do the right thing. Once his parents returned, he'd send Riley to live with them. They were good people, and Riley would be loved and well-cared for. He'd be better off there than with someone like Cooper who travelled a lot and didn't have time for a teenager.

Cooper put the photo down and accidentally brushed against a stack of papers. The papers scattered to the floor. What kid did anything with paper anymore? Cooper stooped to pick them up and stared in shock, his mouth dropping open. They weren't girlie pics or anything like Cooper might've expected to find in a teenage boy's room. They were printed photos of Cooper, lots of them, along with a Sockeyes program opened to Cooper's page. But there was more. There were pictures of Cooper as a Giant, his old team.

Cooper shook his head. The kid had collected photos and kept tabs on him?

Fuck.

What did that mean?

He thought Riley resented him, even blamed him for his mother's problems because to an extent Cooper blamed himself. But worshipped him? Cooper never would've guessed.

Now he felt like an even bigger shit and deservedly so.

* * * *

Izzy dragged her tired body into Cooper's house and glanced around. She expected him to be waiting up for her, but it was late, after midnight. Those senior citizens had partied down once Izzy and her sisters worked their magic. She thought they'd never leave.

"Cooper?" she called, glancing around the dimly lit entryway. "Cooper?"

"Hey." He stood at the top of the stairs grinning down at her, but his grin didn't reach his eyes. Something troubled him, and she sure as hell hoped it wasn't her being at a party. They'd broken up before over his jealousy, and Cooper had promised this time would be different.

Broken up before?

Did that mean they were a couple again? They sure as hell were sex partners, but only a fool would deny they didn't have chemistry that went beyond sex. Nor could she deny she only wanted Cooper, wanted to see his sexy smile, see his blue eyes darken with desire, and hear his hearty laugh. God, she just wanted him. His imperfections made him perfect.

"Hey," she called up to him as he walked down the stairs toward her. He skipped the last couple and swept her in his arms, kissing the hell out of her.

"I missed you," he whispered against her hair. "Take me with you next time. I can crash a party as well as anyone."

She leaned back and stared up into his deep blue eyes. "Are you kidding me? First of all, you're the jealous type. Second, people will recognize you."

"Yeah, I guess." He kissed her forehead. "But I did miss you."

She'd heard him the first time but chose to ignore his words. Missing someone meant you were getting attached, and attachments led to dependency on each other. Izzy did not depend on anyone, and she never would. Never. Not even sexy-as-melted-chocolate Cooper.

Izzy touched his rough cheek. He had that stubble thing going on lately, and it was hot. She opened her mouth to invite him to the bedroom, and stopped. There it was again. That flash of sadness. She doubted anyone else would have caught it, but she did.

"Cooper, what's wrong?" She cupped his strong jaw in her hands and kissed his chin.

His eyes darkened, and he smiled. "Nothing, now that you're here."

She almost believed him, but she'd seen something, and she'd never been one to let well enough alone. "What is it?"

She caught his quick glance up the stairs.

"Did you know Riley has a bunch of pictures of me in his bedroom?" Cooper said.

"Were you snooping in Riley's bedroom?" No wonder he'd been upstairs.

"It's—it's not what you think. I wasn't looking for anything bad. I just wanted to know him better. I haven't done a very good job of that," he said sheepishly, shifting his weight from one foot to another in a rare display of discomfort.

Izzy couldn't mask her surprise. "No, you haven't, Coop." She wouldn't cut him any slack where Riley was concerned.

He looked up at her, letting her see the sadness in his eyes this time. "Yeah, I've been an ass. I was disappointed he didn't come home with me tonight, and—and—caring like that shocked me."

"You were disappointed?" She honestly thought he didn't like Riley underfoot.

"I wanted to talk to him about his game. As a pro athlete, I'm pretty good at analyzing stuff. Even though I don't play football, it's very similar to hockey in a lot of ways, and I had some tips for him on his game."

"Really?" Her heart swelled with affection for this strong, proud man. "I think he would've liked that."

"Or told me to fuck off and die," Cooper said with a self-deprecating smile.

"That's always possible." She grinned and pressed her lips to his. She liked this side of him, a little uncertain, a little vulnerable, and a lot sexy and sweet. Sweet had been a word she'd never thought she could use for Cooper. "You know, I was going to come home tonight and lecture your ass about how you're treating Riley, but maybe a lecture isn't necessary."

"God, I hope not." He pretended to shudder.

"Yet." She grinned at him and backed him up against the wall. Those intense blue eyes of his burned with need and desire for her. Her heart pounded in her chest, and she threaded her fingers in his hair. His mouth came down on hers and she clung to him as they kissed long and hard.

God, she was crazy for this man, even with all his faults. Maybe his faults made him more attractive. He wasn't perfect, but he was perfect for her. True perfection would be boring.

Drawing back, she slid down his long, muscled frame until she knelt before him on her knees. He smiled down at her, his fingers massaging her scalp. "Hungry?"

"Absolutely. I've been hungry for you all night."

"So have I, honey. So have I." His gravelly growl reverberated through his body right down to the object of her attention, a rather large object and quickly becoming one of her favorite objects. Okay, maybe already her all-time favorite object.

He leaned against the wall, as she unzipped his faded jeans and lowered both jeans and underwear down past his hungry cock. Her mouth watered at the sight of it.

"You're so beautiful," she whispered, worshipping his gorgeous athlete's body with her eyes, loving the muscles on muscles, even loving the scars because each of them told a story from his life. Someday she'd know all those stories.

"Hey, that's my line."

She glanced up at him, a slow smile crossing her face. Lowering her head, she sent him to paradise.

* * * *

Cooper didn't have a game that next evening. Izzy cuddled on the couch with him, watching *The Sound of Music*. Cooper had admitted to liking classical musicals. They both had the night off. A hazy rain blanketed the landscape visible out the windows, making Izzy feel lazy and content.

Neither of them had gotten much sleep in the past twenty-four hours. It was Friday night, and Riley pouted in his room because Cooper insisted he stay home, which surprised Izzy. Usually Cooper jumped at any chance to pawn his nephew off on someone else.

Cooper stretched and yawned. "I suppose we should get off our lazy asses and do something about dinner. The kid has to eat, even if we can skip a meal."

"He is a growing boy," Izzy agreed.

Cooper arched his eyebrows. "Uh, yeah, he sure is. A horse eats less than he does."

"Do you have any chicken?" Izzy asked.

"I'm sure I do." Cooper kissed the tip of her nose and gazed down at her with a lopsided smile.

Izzy stood quickly, knowing if she didn't, they'd be doing it on the couch in seconds with Riley able to walk in on them at any time. "I'll make my signature fried chicken."

"Sounds great. I'll help."

Much to Izzy's surprise, Cooper was pretty handy in the kitchen. He chopped veggies for a salad and put potatoes in the steamer.

As Izzy manned the frying pan, Cooper moved behind her and put his arms around her waist, pulling her against him. His erection pressed against her butt, and she giggled. Cooper nuzzled her cheek and nipped at the skin on her neck. She tried to shoo him away, but he wasn't having any part of that.

"Cooper, I'm trying to cook." She elbowed him in his hard stomach. He didn't even flinch.

"You're doing a damn good job because I think I'm already way past well done." He bit her earlobe, and she couldn't stifle the groan.

"Oh, God, we can't do this right now."

"Who says?" He slid his hands under her sweatshirt and cupped her breasts through the thin material of her bra. He drew circles around her nipples until they were hard and aching for him.

Izzy arched her neck to look into his eyes and his mouth caught hers in a searing kiss that just about blew her Dearfoam slippers off her feet.

"Oh, God, get a room, would ya?"

Cooper jumped back at the sound of Riley's voice, while Izzy straightened her sweater. Her face burned with embarrassment as she wondered how long Riley had been standing there.

While Izzy gathered her composure, Cooper put on a good show for Riley, as if he hadn't just been caught coping a feel, leaving Izzy light-headed and weak in the knees.

Riley looked from one to the other, his eyes narrowing and a frown dominating his face. "I don't see why I couldn't go to the Mars' house; then you guys could mess around all you wanted."

"Because," Cooper said, sounding so much like a stern father that Izzy hid her smile, "we are going to eat dinner tonight as a family."

"Why? We aren't a fucking family." Riley's frown deepened and his chin jutted out in a display of stubbornness so much like Cooper's.

Cooper jerked as if Riley had physically hit him. "Watch your language," he growled.

Izzy bit her lip and watched the two. This confrontation had been brewing for a long time, and there was nothing she could do to stop it. Maybe it'd be better if they both aired their differences.

"Whatever." Riley rolled his eyes, which incensed Cooper all the more.

"Wash your hands and sit down at the table. It's time to eat." Izzy gave Cooper points for not nailing Riley on his attitude.

"I'm not some little kid you can order around. Legally, you

don't have any control over me." Riley, behaving as a typical teenager, didn't seem to know when to shut his mouth.

"I have *legal* temporary custody until we find your mother and sort out this mess." Cooper's own jaw jutted out, and Izzy covered her mouth with her hand to stop the laughter from bubbling out.

Riley seemed at a loss for words, as if he hadn't expected Cooper's response. "You do?"

"Yes, I do. Now, let's eat." Cooper started carrying food to the dining room table. Izzy couldn't recall ever eating in this large room with its formal table. She'd rather keep it casual and sit at the round oak table in the breakfast nook area. It'd be more comfortable for all three of them, especially Riley, but now wasn't the time to argue.

They ate in strained silence, but that didn't dampen Riley's appetite one bit, even though it did Izzy's. Cooper caught her staring at him and winked. He ran his foot up and down her leg, and she shoved a chicken leg in her mouth to muffle her moan.

Riley glanced up, finished chewing, and actually smiled at her. "This is awesome fried chicken."

"Oh, yeah, it is," Cooper grinned, knowing exactly why she was moaning. "I especially like the legs and breasts."

Izzy kicked him under the table, and Riley actually laughed. Cooper laughed, too, and a second later, Izzy joined in. It was juvenile, but it broke the ice.

"I have tickets for the game tomorrow night," Cooper announced. Both Izzy and Riley stopped laughing to look up at him. "We're all going together."

Now, wait a minute—Cooper was taking this family thing too far, and Izzy hadn't agreed to attend anything tomorrow night. She bristled slightly, as did Riley.

"Coach invited us over to watch the U-Dub-USC game tomorrow night." U-Dub was what Seattleites called the University of Washington.

A muscle ticked in Cooper's jaw, a sure sign he was upset, but instead of being mad, Izzy caught the sadness in his eyes, the same sadness she'd seen earlier.

Riley hesitated, as if debating whether to make Cooper pay for his neglect or to cut him some slack. "I really want to watch the Huskies," Riley finally said.

"Okay, that's fine." Cooper's voice was tight and his expression closed off.

"Thanks," Riley pushed his chair away from the table. When he saw Cooper's narrowed eyes, he paused. "Can I go now?"

"Yeah, sure."

Riley ran from the room as if he couldn't wait to get away from the adults.

Izzy reached across the table and held Cooper's hand. "Don't take it personally. He's a teenager."

"I do take it personally. I've been a shit to him, so he's paying me back. I deserve it."

"You're a good man, Cooper Black, even if you forget to be one sometimes." Izzy squeezed his hand, her heart going out to him.

Their eyes met and locked. Something shifted sideways inside her, throwing her emotions off their foundation and leaving her disoriented. Her heart pounded with knowledge, and her head spun, as her entire world whirled off its axis.

She loved this man.

She'd known for a long time Cooper was special, even though she fought it with everything she had. She loved him, and she'd probably loved him since the night they first met, and she'd pretended to be his girlfriend, despite his protests. He loved her, too. Even if he hadn't said the words, she saw it in his eyes.

Yet, with love came a certain dependency on the other half of the couple, and Izzy wasn't ready to be dependent on Cooper or anyone, if she ever would be. Independence, the freedom to make your own decisions, and living with those decisions was paramount to her. Loving Cooper would strip away her independence, and she couldn't allow it.

They could not have a forever love, just a right-now love.

Chapter 16—Goal Tending

The Sockeyes lost their home game that Saturday and left Monday on their road trip with a one and one record. Cooper played a decent game, but not enough to carry the team to victory, despite one last-minute goal.

In his early twenties, Cooper had lived for road trips. He loved the different cities and different women in each city. Since he'd be leaving town, he never worried about some crazy female stalking him later or expecting more than a one-night stand.

That was then.

Izzy had ruined him for any other woman. It was funny how she'd essentially moved into his house even though neither of them officially acknowledged it. Yet more and more of her stuff appeared in his walk-in closet. In fact, she had more clothes hanging in there than he did. He didn't say a word, for fear she'd get scared and bolt. Nor did she mention getting another nanny for Riley. She'd quit her barista job and taken on the role. Once a week, Cooper left cash for her wages in an envelope on the counter, and neither of them talked about that either.

Tomorrow night the Sockeyes played their first game of the road trip. They'd flown to New Jersey earlier today, had a skate and a team meeting, and eaten dinner as a group in the hotel. It was only eight-thirty, and Cooper was restless. He texted Izzy a few times and received no response. He'd even texted Riley, a first for him. No response there either.

He was worried. What if they'd been in a car wreck? What if one of them was in the hospital? What if they needed him? He'd never been much of fretter. He was a man of action. Just do it, don't worry about it.

Jesus. He was making himself crazy. Two hours later and nothing—not a word from either of them. They didn't have to account for every minute of their lives to him, and he knew he needed to get a grip on himself. Izzy wouldn't appreciate him hounding her, and Riley wouldn't either.

He finally grabbed his wallet and headed for the hotel bar. Since the hotel mostly catered to businessmen, he doubted he'd be bothered by fans or puck bunnies, but he hadn't counted on being bothered by his own team.

Cooper blew out a breath when he saw them. They'd pushed a few tables together in the back of the room and were sharing pitchers of beer. Brick, wearing a Hawaiian shirt, shorts, and flip-flops despite the chilly weather outside, entertained the troops with one of his many stories. The guy was certifiably nuts, but then all goalies were, at least the good ones.

Cooper could use a little craziness tonight so he headed toward the table. Halfway across the room, he noticed Coach Gorst sitting at the table with the guys.

As team captain, Cooper took his obligations seriously. Even though he wanted to turn on his heel and head the other way, he kept walking toward them. Brick snagged a chair from nearby and dragged it between him and Rush, effectively putting him across the table from Coach.

Cooper respected his coach. Who wouldn't? He was the youngest coach ever to win the Stanley Cup, had been a tough player himself until injury forced him out, and he coached the game like Cooper played it—with everything he had.

Any team would be lucky to have Mike Gorst. The Sockeyes lured him away from his former team by paying him more money than any coach in NHL history. Sure, Coach said it was about the challenge, but Cooper knew better. Money talked and so Mike had walked. If Cooper was being a little honest with himself, the situation with Mike's old team had gone south with new ownership who was cheap and interfered in every aspect of the team business. Gorst couldn't get out of there fast enough.

Cooper loved playing for Gorst; too bad it had to be in Seattle. The guy was tough, energetic, and a proven winner.

"Cap, ready to kick some ass on this road trip?" Brick grinned at him and saluted.

Cooper faked a cocky grin and saluted right back. "As ready as you are."

Brick grinned even wider and poured himself another beer. Cooper glanced at Coach who nodded at him. Coach stood and yawned, making a show of being tired. Cooper knew he was leaving because the team captain had shown up. Not that they didn't get along—they both had enormous respect for the other—but their relationship was slightly strained since Cooper had made it clear to his coach that he wasn't staying in Seattle.

"Now that Coop's here to babysit, children, I'm going to hit the hay. I'll have four hours of watching film and hashing out game plans before any of you gentlemen hit the ice for the morning skate."

The guys turned back to swapping tales, and Cooper sat back to listen, but his mind drifted to Izzy. He really missed her, and he'd never missed a woman like this before. He missed her so much that his stomach ached thinking about it, and they'd only said goodbye this morning. He was a sorry lovesick sap, and hell if he knew what to do about it. He fished his phone from his pocket, relieved to see a message from her.

Hi, what's up?

Wish you were here or even better, I was there, he texted back to her.

Me, too.

He grinned when he read that.

How's Riley? It occurred to him that he'd never asked about Riley before.

Fine, we just got out of a movie with Betheni.

Oh, so that's where they'd been. He was an idiot. *Did he do his homework?*

Of course, he did. He's a good kid, and you're turning into a good uncle.

Cooper blushed. Yeah, he actually blushed. *Thanks. What're you wearing?*

Nothing, wanna see?

Oh, crap. A smart man would say no, considering he sat at a table full of jocks who'd enjoy razzing him, but Cooper wanted to see.

Yeah.

Several seconds later a picture came through of Izzy completely naked in the bathtub. The suds covered strategic parts and made it even more erotic than if she'd been stark-ass naked.

You're fucking beautiful.

Your turn.

Shit, he couldn't exactly strip in front of the boys to take a photo of the goods. *In hotel bar with the guys.*

Go back to the room. I need text sex.

Cooper stood and pushed back his chair so quickly that it fell to the floor. Every guy at the table stared up at him in open-mouthed shock.

"Gotta go. Don't miss curfew," Cooper said as he hurried from the room.

He heard Brick say, "Must be a woman." The rest of the guys chuckled. Cooper didn't care. He punched the Up button on the elevator, punched it harder, punched it again. A beautiful leggy blond slid up next to him. Her over-powering perfume filled his nostrils.

"That won't make the elevator come any faster, but that kind of forcefulness might make me come faster," she whispered in his ear in a low, husky tone.

"Thanks, but no thanks." Cooper backed away from her and stepped into the elevator as the doors opened. She followed him in, not the least bit deterred and ran a hand down his arm. Cooper shot her a murderous glare.

"What part of 'I'm not interested' do you not understand?" He was being rude and didn't give a shit.

Her pretty face turned damn ugly as she frowned at him. "Fine." She turned away, hands across her chest and focused on another man who stepped into the elevator after Cooper.

When his floor was reached, Cooper shot out of the elevator and ran for the room, praying Cedric was still out with whatever woman he'd picked up earlier. Even if he was there, Cooper would lock himself in the bathroom.

I'm in my room, Cooper texted.

What are you wearing?

A smile. He grinned as he pulled off his clothes.

Show me.

Cooper hopped on the bed and took a picture of himself sprawled on it with his dick standing up proudly. He pressed Send and waited while he stroked himself and wished it was her.

God, I miss you. And Dick.

Ditto, he typed.

Call me and turn on the video.

Fuck, but Cooper loved technology.

* * * *

Cooper wouldn't appreciate Izzy dragging his nephew to the

220

party she was crashing, but she didn't have a choice. Besides it was Tanner's party, and she wouldn't let him down. She'd helped him plan every aspect, and he'd invited his teammates' families which guaranteed the event to be G-rated.

Riley was having the time of his life hanging out with some of the other kids, especially a cute little redhead who stared at him as if he were the hottest guy in the room. To a teenage girl, he probably was with those deep blue eyes and messy, almost black hair. Riley had a face that made teenage girls swoon along with being taller than most boys his age. Izzy saw Cooper in him especially in the way he smiled, how he walked, and in his profile. No wonder people thought Cooper was his dad.

Cooper was over halfway through his five-game road trip, and she missed him like crazy. Video sex was no substitute for the real man despite how much fun it was. The team had won their game tonight, winning two out of three so far, and she'd texted him a congratulations, but that was all she'd had time to do.

Party crashing was one thing, party planning was a whole different ball game. Despite the challenges, Tanner and the guests declared the party a resounding success. By the time the last guest left, it was too late to call Cooper. Izzy couldn't wait to soak her tired body and aching feet in a nice warm bubble bath, but Emma approached her as Izzy and Riley left the building.

"Izz?" Emma seemed nervous.

"Yes?" Izzy couldn't keep the weariness from her tone.

"Why don't you and Riley come to our studio? You haven't talked to Avery since—well, since…" Emma looked everywhere but at Izzy.

"I know how long it's been. She can call me, too, you know?" Izzy tapped her toe impatiently on the sidewalk, more than ready to go home. She glanced at Riley who stood beside her in silence, while his keen gaze watched the two sisters and Izzy interact.

"I know, but you're our big sister. It'd mean a lot if you went to her first." Emma looked up at her with luminous blue eyes full of unshed tears. She'd always been the peacemaker in the family and hated conflict among the sisters.

Izzy opened her mouth to say no, tired of being the one to make concessions and extend the olive branch, but she couldn't bring herself to break Emma's heart. Her sisters were her world, and she'd do anything to keep that world together, even come begging at Avery's door.

"Okay, I'll do it."

Emma's huge smile was reward enough for doing a little sisterly groveling.

A half-hour later, Izzy followed Emma into a gravel parking area in front of a large horse barn. Riley's eyes widened as he took in everything. Walking down the barn aisle, he stared at each horse, leaving Izzy to suspect he'd never seen a horse up close and personal before. He didn't touch any of them, just stared at each one as if in complete awe of the large animals.

Izzy didn't much care for horses or the smell. She couldn't fathom anyone quitting college to work in a barn. Even now, it angered her. Avery was throwing away her life, for what? Some broken bones and a job that didn't pay benefits or have any job security. Riding horses was a hobby, not a profession.

As they mounted the stairs to the apartment, Izzy trailed behind Emma and Riley, holding back in the hope Emma would warn Avery she was here.

Izzy walked through the doorway and stared at the surprisingly tidy little apartment with its worn furniture complete with a black barn cat lounging in a ratty easy chair. The flooring was a wood-type laminate. A short hallway led to at least one bedroom and a bathroom. Sliding glass doors opened onto a small balcony. It was actually nicer than many of the apartments Izzy had rented over the years.

Avery stood across the room, wringing her hands and ignoring Izzy. Emma introduced Riley, who smiled shyly and studied the shelves of horse trophies on the plywood and concrete block bookcase.

"Wow, did you win all these?" Riley said to Avery in wonder.

Avery nodded. "I love horses. I've been showing horses since I was your age. I worked at barns after school to earn the money for lessons."

"I've never seen a real horse until today," Riley admitted.

"City boy," Avery teased, and Riley blushed.

"I guess."

Avery turned to Izzy. "What do you think of the place?"

"It's nice. Especially for an apartment in a horse barn." Izzy cringed at her disparaging words and was about to apologize, but Avery interrupted.

"That's the problem, isn't it? It's in a horse barn." Avery rounded on her sister, eyes blazing, hands fisted. Anger reflected in the tight stance of her body.

"You are a straight-A student. You could be anything. A doctor. A researcher. An engineer. Anything at all."

"This is what I want to do. My grades are irrelevant."

"You have the brains to do so much more than this," Izzy countered.

Avery closed her eyes for a moment. When she spoke again, she was much calmer. "I don't expect you to understand, but I expect you to accept my choices instead of criticizing and belittling me."

"I'm not. I just don't want you to make mistakes you'll regret for the rest of your life."

"Seriously?" Avery rolled her eyes. "Guess what, Izz, this is my life. You do not get a vote. I'm done living the life everyone else expects of me. I'm living my life, my way. I love horses."

"Just like Mom and Dad love music? At the expense of everyone and everything else in their lives?" Izzy propped her hands on her hips and stared down her sister. Her glare usually intimidated the twins and caused them to back down. Only it wasn't working right now.

"Yes, just like that. Only I won't make the mistake of having kids. This is what I want to do, what I've always wanted to do, with or without your approval."

Izzy glanced over at Riley, knowing he was getting an earful. He kept his back to them as he studied the trophies, picking several up and reading the inscriptions. He paid more attention to her sister's prizes than Izzy ever had. In fact, with a twinge of guilt, Izzy tried to remember if she'd ever attended one of her sister's horse shows.

Not that she could recall.

She'd always prided herself on being there for her sisters because their parents weren't. She'd attended their high school choir concerts, their sports activities, yet she'd never attended any of Avery's horse shows. Mostly because she didn't approve of the horses. Considering how expensive horses were, she'd resented the time Avery spent with them, the money she'd spent on them, even though it'd been money Avery earned. Every penny Izzy earned went toward her sisters, and Izzy disliked Avery's selfishness. So she'd responded in the only way she could, by being absent at the one thing Avery held most dear.

Izzy swallowed hard and looked into the cold eyes of her sister. She'd never seen Avery so angry. Turning to Riley, Izzy pointed toward the door. "It's time we go."

Riley glanced from Izzy to Avery and back. "Yeah," he said, visibly relieved they were leaving.

Izzy hugged Emma, who was obviously distressed that her attempt to reconcile her two sisters failed miserably. She turned to Avery and nodded. "Good night, Ave, you know how to reach me if you need me."

"I won't need you," Avery responded stiffly.

That was exactly what Izzy was afraid of.

* * * *

Riley kept his mouth shut as they drove down the long driveway and onto the country road and wondered why the adults in his life always disappointed him. He'd considered Izzy as near perfect as a person could get until tonight. She'd been his champion, and he was pretty damn sure that Izzy was responsible for his uncle's change of heart toward him.

He'd adored her until this evening. Gone were the good feelings he'd had flirting with the daughters of one of the players at the party. Now he felt this big lump in his gut, as if he'd eaten concrete, and it'd hardened in his stomach.

"You're mad," Izzy finally said.

"No," Riley lied.

"Yes, you are. I can feel the disappointment and disapproval rolling off you in waves, and I want to set the record straight." She didn't look at him but kept her eyes on the road.

"Go ahead." Riley looked at her beautiful profile in the dashboard light. He'd always been a tiny bit jealous of Cooper for having such a gorgeous girlfriend. Tonight, not so much.

"Avery has always been a top student; she had her pick of colleges, earned scholarships, and only had a year and a half to go until graduation."

"What's her major?"

"Pre-med."

Riley was surprised. Avery didn't seem the doctor type, whatever type that was. "Was that her idea or yours?"

"She's always wanted to be a—" Izzy stopped in mid-sentence as if suddenly realizing something. "I mean the family always had such high hopes for her."

Riley blew out a breath. "Maybe they aren't her hopes."

Izzy glanced at him, a funny look on her face. As if she'd just realized something.

Riley figured he'd gotten this far, why stop now. "Why aren't you proud of your sister?"

"Proud of her?"

"Did you see all those trophies? She's good."

"I, uh, horses aren't a viable career path."

"Maybe they are to her. She's won all these championships. It can't be easy. I mean, piloting around huge animals like that." Riley watched her face, pretty sure he was actually getting through to her.

Izzy sighed and said nothing, but Riley could tell what he said bothered her. He stared out the window, deep in thought. He had his own troubles, most of which centered around his missing mom, his guilt over enjoying his new life, and the realization that he didn't want it to end. Sure, he wanted his mother found, but he wanted to live in a normal household rather than dumpster diving for his next dinner or getting teased by kids 'cuz his clothes were torn and dirty.

The weirdest thing had happened when Uncle Cooper left for this last road trip. Riley kinda missed his uncle. Strange, but true. They'd been getting along okay, and Uncle Coop had made it to Riley's game which shocked the shit out of Riley, but he loved having his uncle there. He'd even called and texted him a few times since he'd been gone.

Riley wanted to live with his uncle permanently, but his mother needed him, and as soon as Uncle Cooper found her, he'd have to move back in with her. Someone had to take care of her, try to keep her off the drugs and be there when she came down from a high.

What if she never came back? The thought made Riley's stomach hurt even worse so he tried not to think about it.

Uncle Coop would send him away to live with grandparents he'd never met. He didn't want to live with old people. He wanted to stay right where he was, play with the same guys on the same team all through high school, like normal kids did. Was that really too much to ask?

For him, it probably was because if anyone knew about living a tough life, Riley sure as heck did. He also knew that stuff never worked out for him. Just when things were going well, the bottom would drop out and everything would fall to pieces. But Izzy liked Riley. Izzy might convince Uncle Coop to let him stay.

"Do you love Uncle Coop?" Riley asked.

Izzy was quiet for so long, Riley assumed she wouldn't answer. "Why would you ask a thing like that?" she finally said.

"Because of the way you look at him, how you're always together or texting. Isn't that what people do when they're in love?"

Izzy choked and her face turned red. Really, really red. Riley almost laughed. And they said teenagers were flaky. "I like him. A lot," she admitted.

"Are you going to marry him?"

She coughed again. "I think it's a little early for that."

"Isn't that what normal people do? Fall in love and get married?"

Izzy glanced at him. In the light of a street lamp he saw pity in her eyes. "Riley," she hedged.

He'd come too far to stop now. "We could be a family if you guys got married."

She reached over and patted his shoulder as they pulled into Cooper's garage. "Riley, don't get your hopes up. Cooper's set on leaving Seattle, and I'm not."

Riley's heart sank. "I can't leave either. I can't leave my mother."

"Then I guess you'll need to get those crazy thoughts out of your head."

Riley got out of the car and trudged into Cooper's house, feeling more lost and alone than he had in weeks. If Uncle Cooper moved, then every hope and dream he'd had these past couple months moved with him.

Nothing ever worked out for Riley Black.

Nothing.

* * * *

Thank God for roommates who were man whores and partiers. Cooper could count on at least an hour or two alone in his room every night. Cedric was so hyped up after a game he'd either find a willing female or party with the boys. Cooper jacked off while having video phone sex with Izzy.

It didn't make up for the real thing, but it was close.

Yet, it wasn't just the sex. They talked. Actually talked. He couldn't recall when he'd spent as much time talking to a woman as he did having sex with her. He loved talking to Izzy, loved that she didn't cater to him, but was honest and straightforward. They talked about anything and everything. Her family. His family. Riley. Their dreams. Their hopes. She even gave him tips on his game.

Cooper talked to Riley a few times, too. The kid had a girlfriend and sounded so happy. Riley's happiness gave Cooper a warm feeling inside, like he'd done something truly good and meaningful for the kid.

The team won two out of three on the road with two more games to go on Sunday and Tuesday night. Cooper couldn't wait to get home.

It was Saturday night, and Izzy happened to be working. Cooper didn't feel like going to the room and sitting by himself so he headed for the hotel bar. Across the room sat a table full of his teammates, as usual. Near the door sat Ethan and Coach. Cooper fast-tracked it to his guys and was almost home free when Ethan called to him.

Reluctantly, he turned and walked back to their table. "Yeah?" he asked as he looked down at them.

Ethan nudged a chair with his foot. "Have a seat, Coop."

Cooper dropped his big body into the chair, while Ethan signaled for a waitress to bring Cooper a beer. They made small talk until she'd delivered another round of drinks and left.

"So," Cooper cut to the chase, "you didn't call me over here to chat. What's up?"

A smile tugged at the corner of Ethan's mouth. "Cooper, I know I should be talking with your agent, but I wanted to approach you directly first because that's how I do business."

Cooper shrugged non-committedly, but he had a good idea what was coming. Less than a month ago, he knew what his answer would be, now he wasn't so sure. There were so many variables. Riley and Izzy, to name a few.

Cooper raised a brow. "What do you want, Ethan?"

Ethan's slow smile seemed almost predatory; at the least it was calculating. "I want what's best for the team, and that happens to be you. You're the heart and soul of this team. The cornerstone. The piece that makes all the other pieces fit together."

Cooper glanced at Coach, who was rubbing his chin and saying nothing.

"We'd like to wrap you up before you enter unrestricted free agency, and we'll make you the richest man in the NHL."

"It's not about the money. It never has been."

"Okay, what is it about?" Ethan pushed.

"Stuff you can't change." Cooper stared at a point on the wall. A nerve ticked in his jaw and his head pounded.

"I can't change the weather, if that's your complaint," Ethan said quietly. "But anything I can change, I will. The Sockeyes' organization is committed to putting championship teams on the ice year after year. We need *you* to do that. You're irreplaceable."

"Cooper," Coach finally spoke. "This is one of the best organizations in the NHL, even though it's in its infancy."

Cooper nodded slowly. "I know. It's not that. Not anymore. It's Seattle. I can't stay there."

Both men stared at him like he was nuts. Maybe he was, but the gray clouds hanging over Seattle had nothing to do with the weather, and the only way to exorcise the demons from his past was to leave Seattle and never look back.

Cooper stood and shook both men's hands. "Thanks, but I'm not interested."

"That won't stop me from trying," Ethan promised.

Cooper shrugged and headed for his teammates, but his phone vibrated. It was Russ. Cooper took a detour to a quiet table and sat down. "Russ, you have news for me?"

"Yeah, I do. I found her."

"Is she in jail?" That was the only plausible explanation Cooper could imagine for his sister abandoning her son and not bothering to look for him.

"No. She's in Tacoma with a guy. Some biker dude who works as a bouncer at a strip joint. They're living in a trailer park."

"Seriously? Is he holding her against her will?"

"No, she's been coming and going."

228

Cooper sat back in his chair and absorbed this information. "Are they doing drugs?"

"Meth, at least."

Anger vibrated through Cooper. "I want to talk to her. Can you keep her in your sights until I get back next week?"

"Sure, as long as you keep those checks coming."

"You know I will. Thanks. I appreciate all your help."

"Just part of the job," Russ said. Being a man of few words, Russ ended the call. Cooper wrapped his hands around the cold glass of beer and stared at the painting on the wall of a tranquil farm with rolling green meadows. Only he didn't feel so tranquil right about now. He was pissed at his irresponsible sister. She'd walked away from Riley without a word, not even bothering to make sure he was okay or dropping him off somewhere so he'd be safe.

God, he wanted to throttle her. He didn't give a shit about what she did with her life, but Riley didn't deserve her neglect.

Shit. Cooper buried his face in his hands.

Riley didn't deserve his neglect either.

No longer feeling like joining the guys, Cooper took the elevator to his room and lay on the bed in the dark, staring at the ceiling and waiting for Izzy to call.

He needed to talk to her in the worst way, needed her sympathy and understanding and her sound advice. With her mama-bear attitude toward Riley, she'd be even more pissed than Cooper was.

He'd be home soon and in her arms once again.

He missed her, he needed her, and he *loved* her.

Jesus, he loved her. He did. He really did. And it changed everything. Maybe he'd made bad choices in the past when it came to women, but he'd protected his heart too long. Life was pretty boring without risk, and Cooper had always been the ultimate risk-taker.

Loving her was a risk he'd take, and he couldn't wait to tell her.

That was the last thought he had before he fell asleep.

Chapter 17—Out of the Game

Izzy woke up to warm lips on hers. She curled into Cooper and sighed happily. He held her close, drugging her with his urgent kisses.

"You're home," she said sleepily.

"Damn, I missed you," he said against her mouth.

"Me, too."

He cut her muffled response short as his mouth toyed with hers, while his big strong hands cupped her butt, pulling her tight against his erection.

"You feel so good," she whimpered and laid little kisses along his shoulder and collarbone.

"So do you, baby, so do you." He nipped and bit his way down her body, making short work of the oversized Sockeyes T-shirt she'd worn to bed. His hands slid up her body to her breasts, and she closed her eyes, enjoying his hard body pressed against her softer one.

In a matter of seconds, she was flat on her back, and he was moving inside her. She arched her back and took him deeper, her fingernails digging into his bare back. He set a strong rhythm. Despite the obvious difficulty he was having holding back, he slid in and out of her, refusing to let her hurry him along.

It didn't take them long to climax and collapse in a sweaty heap of tangled limbs and spent bodies.

Izzy lay in contented silence with her head resting on his broad chest. Cooper held her loosely to him, his now steady breathing causing his chest to rise and fall under her cheek. She wanted to talk to him about Riley, but somehow she didn't think this was a good time.

"Izzy?" His voice vibrated in her ear.

"Yes?"

A long pause. She could tell he was holding his breath. She waited, forcing herself to be patient. A girl couldn't hurry a man like Cooper.

"I'm in love with you," he said simply.

Izzy raised up and looked him in the eyes. "You are?" Her heart soared with joy, and a small smile sneaked onto her face. Even a few weeks ago, his declaration would've frightened the hell out of her, but not now because she'd fallen in love with him.

"Yeah. That doesn't surprise you, does it?" He watched her intently, as if her answers were as crucial to him as his breathing.

Izzy thought about his question for a split second, but she already knew the answer. "No, not really."

"I love you, Izzy," he said again, as if savoring the taste of the words on his tongue. She savored them, too, embraced them, and oddly enough they didn't scare her like she thought they would.

"I love you, too, Cooper." She said the words without thinking, without taking the time to protect her heart. She said them because she felt them from the tips of her raspberry plum toenails to the roots of her brunette hair. He'd been special from the moment she hooked her arm in his and pretended to be his girlfriend, despite his shock and annoyance at a total stranger accosting him at a party. Yes, she'd known, and now he knew.

"I know you do." His slow sexy smile warmed every empty place inside her. He kissed her forehead and laced his fingers behind her back.

"Conceited much?" She winked at him, feeling her own smile spread across her face.

He chuckled. "Confident. There's a difference." He studied her face, and his smile faltered a bit. "I sense a *but*."

"What kind of future could we possibly have? You want out of Seattle, and I won't leave."

"We'll work it out. We're in love." He planted little kisses on her checks.

"Sometimes love isn't enough," she said. "This isn't just about location. There's more to it than that."

"What is enough, Izzy? If location isn't a deal breaker, tell me what is, and I'll fix it."

"How about trust? Mutual respect. Letting go and not trying to control the outcome of every aspect of your life and the lives of the people around you."

"It's hard to trust when the people who are supposed to care about you let you down," he said.

"Hello. This is me you're talking to." Izzy managed a smile.

"True, but we don't have to solve the world's problems tonight. We have lots of time to figure this out. In the meantime, I have news."

"News?" She couldn't imagine news any bigger than the news he'd just given her.

"Russ found my sister."

Izzy sat up, wrapping the sheets around her and flipped on the nightstand light. "He found her? Is she okay?"

"I almost wish she wasn't. At least then I'd be able to understand why she deserted Riley."

"Where is she?" Izzy hugged herself, feeling cold after feeling so warm.

"She's in Tacoma shacking up with some guy. I'd like to make her pay for what she did to Riley." Cooper's gaze so full of love a moment before, turned hard and uncompromising.

"So would I."

"Will you go with me tomorrow night to talk to her? It'd mean a lot to me if you came along."

"Absolutely. We'll ask Coach Mars to take Riley for the night." Izzy ran a finger over the wrinkles in his brow. "You're worried, aren't you?"

"I haven't seen her in years. I know she blames me." Cooper stared at a point over her shoulder and clenched his jaw.

"That's not fair. She messed up her life, not you."

"I still worry I didn't do enough, that I didn't help her like I should have." He grabbed her hands and held them tightly.

Izzy kissed his lips, all the feelings she couldn't put into words, she put into that kiss. "I love you, Cooper Black. I love the man you are, I love how you're trying each day to be a better man. You've grown. You've changed."

"I still a work in progress," he admitted.

"Aren't we all?" Izzy sat up and grabbed both their phones off the nightstand, making a split-second decision. "I'm going to do something for you. Consider it a trust exercise."

He watched her with hooded eyes. "What?"

She messed with both their phones and handed his to him. "You now have access to my phone on the stalker app. You can see where I am any time of the day or night."

"Stalker app?" He stared at her, puzzled. The map on his phone showed a blue dot right in the precise location of his house.

"Find My Friends, but I call it the stalker app."

"Okay," he said slowly.

"Cooper, you can find me, know exactly where I am, know the location of the party I'm crashing. I'm going to trust you not to abuse the gift I just gave you."

He nodded, understanding in his blue eyes. "You don't want me embarrassing you at another party."

"That's correct, but the temptation is there."

"It's like putting a case of beer in front of an alcoholic and leaving the room."

"It sure is, and I'm trusting you to have the strength to resist because you love me and you trust me because without mutual trust, love means nothing."

Cooper grinned. "I won't betray your trust. I promise."

Izzy kissed his lips softly. "See that you don't. You won't get another chance, Cooper."

And she meant it.

* * * *

Cooper was nervous, which was absolute bullshit. This was his druggie sister for God's sake. Nothing to be afraid of. Not a damn thing. What was the worst she could do or say?

Go to hell?

I hate you?

You did this to me? You didn't save me when you could?

Yet, he'd done everything a ten-year-old boy could do, considering his mother's health concerns and his own fears.

Cooper pushed his hair off his forehead and glanced over at Izzy sitting in the passenger seat. Her presence gave him strength he wasn't sure he had on his own. "Russ says she works the late shift. I'd like to get the lay of the land before she shows up."

They were sitting outside a sleazy bar. Russ believed a public place would be safer than going to her house. After driving by the dump to check it out, Cooper couldn't agree more.

Cooper flexed his fingers on the steering wheel. Izzy reached across and stroked his cheek. "It'll be fine. I'll be right there with you."

He reached for her hand. "I'm glad. I need you here."

"I know," she said simply, and it hit him that being vulnerable like this didn't make him less of a man in her eyes. He wasn't an island anymore. He had her love to support him, and together they'd get through this.

Cooper heaved a big sigh and steeled himself for the drama that swirled around his sister everywhere she went. "Let's do this."

Izzy nodded. They got out and walked to the bar hand in hand. Cooper took strength from her as they opened the door and entered the dark room. Several heads turned to look at them. The men sized up Cooper and undressed Izzy with their eyes. The women did the same to Cooper while glaring jealously at Izzy.

Cooper ignored them all and walked to the bar with Izzy, ordering a couple beers from a surly bartender covered in tattoos and sporting an immense beer belly. They took a seat at a corner table, and Cooper sat in a chair with his back to the wall and a clear view of the door.

Izzy scooted her chair next to his, and he put an arm around her, wishing he could protect her from the hungry gazes of the men in the room. Izzy was beautiful enough to start a riot, and the last thing they needed would be a barroom brawl. Cooper was damn good with his fists, but he was outnumbered, and lots of these guys were probably packing.

Russ walked in, much to Cooper's surprise. His PI nodded at him and sat down at the table next to them. He leaned over and spoke, "I thought you could use a little backup."

Cooper nodded gratefully at the PI and bought him a beer.

They nursed their drinks for an hour. The patrons went back to what they were doing and ignored the strangers. Finally the door swung open, and a tall, thin woman with jet black hair walked in. Cooper sucked in a breath. He'd know his sister anywhere, despite how rough she looked. She wore a short skirt, tight T-shirt, and a leather jacket. Her chest was tattooed as were her thighs. Cooper didn't have a damn thing against tattoos, but they looked out of place on his once beautiful sister's body. Her long, dark hair hung in greasy strands around a gaunt face with too much makeup.

Izzy touched his arm. "Is that her?"

"Yeah." He nodded, not removing his eyes from Julie. He waited for her gaze to swing in his direction. She spoke to the regulars and chatted up the bartender, but didn't seem to notice him lurking in the darkest corner of the room.

Cooper's mouth went dry and his palms were sweaty. He

hugged Izzy closer, needing her now more than ever. He couldn't believe a woman who didn't weigh more than 110 pounds soaking wet scared him more than the meanest, toughest enforcer in the NHL.

Julie took some drink orders from the other side of the room and slowly worked her way toward Cooper, still oblivious to her brother.

Finally, she glanced his way and did a double take. Recognition crossed her face along with an entire range of emotions Cooper didn't dare interpret. Instead of a welcoming smile, a huge frown marred her once pretty face. Her eyes narrowed, and she walked toward him with purpose. She paused to say something to the bartender, who raised both brows and stared openly at them, contempt in his bloodshot eyes.

In a protective move, Cooper pulled Izzy closer to him. He shouldn't have brought her here. By the look on Julie's face and the bartender's belligerent stance, there could be trouble, and he didn't want Izzy in the middle of it. He glanced over at Russ, who appeared to be alert and watching for the first sign of a problem.

Thank God for Russ.

Julie dropped into the chair across the table and studied both of them. She addressed Izzy first in a hoarse voice ruined by too many cigarettes and drugs. "Slumming it, honey? This doesn't seem like your kind of place."

Izzy smiled sweetly, one of those scary smiles that would send a smart person running for cover. "Any place with Cooper is my kind of place."

Julie studied her, shrugged, and turned her full attention to Cooper. At least, she appeared straight and sober—for now.

"I have something of yours," Cooper said, forcing his voice to stay neutral.

"Riley found you, did he?" She leaned back and yawned. "He's a smart kid. I knew if I left your address where he could find it, he'd go to you."

"You walked out on your son, leaving him to fend for himself. What kind of a mother does that?" Cooper looked for a sign on her face that she regretted what she'd done to Riley, but all he saw was contempt. He hadn't come her to fight with her or piss her off. He'd come here hoping she was sorry for what she'd done to Riley and willing to clean up her act for her son.

He'd been wrong. So wrong. He was a damn fool to think she cared about anyone but herself.

"Riley can take care of himself. I raised him to be independent," she said insolently. "We don't need anybody but ourselves."

"That's bullshit, and you know it. He's a kid." Cooper's anger started a slow boil. Izzy rubbed his thigh, but her touch didn't calm him this time.

"What's the matter, little brother? Is Ry cutting into your party time?"

"This isn't about me. It's about Riley. It's about you abandoning your son." Cooper itched to reach across that table and shake some sense into her. "He's been worried sick."

"He doesn't need to be. I'm fine, but my boyfriend doesn't like kids." She toyed with a napkin, tearing it in small pieces, as if the conversation bored her. "If his presence is an issue, put him in foster care, and pretend you never met him. That's what you're good at anyway, pretending stuff never happened, and going on about your perfect life while the rest of us die a little inside every day."

Cooper bit down on his lip until the pain forced him to concentrate. "I was a kid." This was not the place to have this conversation, especially in front of Izzy.

"So was I. But I grew up pretty fast, and you didn't do anything but run and hide while I faced his wrath and took it for my two baby brothers." The resentment and hatred in her voice hit Cooper like a punch in the gut by a heavyweight boxing champion.

He glanced at Izzy. Her brow furrowed with puzzlement and worry.

"What did you expect us to do?"

"You were little cowards. When the neighbors called the police because they were suspicious, you guys denied anything was going on. They could've rescued us, gotten us out of there. It was my word against yours, and I paid for it once the cops left."

Cooper wanted to cover his ears with his hands, but the sounds of Julie's begging and crying were in his head, and nothing would shut them out.

"I'm sorry." Cooper shook his head. "He said he'd kill us if we ever talked, and I believed him."

"You were taking care of yourself. One thing you've always been good at. You're the reason I'm like this. The drugs are the only thing that dull the pain, help me forget, even for a little while."

"I knew what it would do to Mom. She wasn't well."

"What about what it did to me?" She jabbed her finger at him, close to his face. He refused to flinch.

"I'm sorry. I was scared, too." Cooper's stomach rolled, and he forced back the bile that caught in his throat. Not only had he been scared but he'd been suffering his own trauma at the hands of their new uncle. He'd barely been able to save himself, let alone her.

She rolled her eyes. "Get out of my life. You've been out of it for years, stay out."

"Then why did you come to Seattle, knowing they'd moved my team here?"

Julie looked away and swallowed, for a moment reminding him of the older sister he'd once adored. "I don't know." When she looked back at him, tears were in her eyes.

"Let me help you, Julie," Cooper pleaded. "I can help you get in the best rehab program—"

"No, I'm not interested. I like my life as it is." Her face hardened, and she shut down.

"But Riley—"

"Riley will be just fine. Tell him I'm okay, and I'll catch up with him later."

Cooper stood, disgusted with his sister and overwhelmed by guilt. His brain was a muddled mess of conflicting feelings. He'd never realized how much Julie blamed him. As unfair as it was, he blamed himself, too.

Dragging Izzy with him, Cooper hurried from the bar, not caring that the rain ran down his face. He paused to thank Russ then ran with Izzy for the SUV. Once inside, they didn't speak until they were on I-5 heading for Seattle. He knew Izzy was dying to ask questions about things he'd kept locked tight in a compartment all these years, just like his uncle had locked him in that trunk a couple hours a day while he molested Julie. Cooper could hear her screams and whimpers, and he didn't know which was worse, being locked up or listening to his sister plead while the old man grunted and groaned. The memories made him want to throw up.

"Cooper, slow down. You're scaring me." Izzy touched his arm, causing Cooper to pull himself back from the brink. He stared down at the speedometer, shocked to see it hovering near ninety. Cooper let off the gas, and the car slowed to sixty.

"Sorry," he muttered.

"What happened to you guys as kids?" She stroked his arm, but her touch didn't comfort him like it usually did.

"Nothing happened," he said tersely as he ground his jaw together and wished she'd just shut up and stop asking questions.

"Don't lie to me."

"I don't want to talk about it." Cooper gripped the steering wheel and stared straight ahead. He felt that tell-tale muscle jerking in his jaw.

"Cooper, this is about trust. You need to trust me, if we're going to have a future."

"That subject is off limits." He shot her an angry glare. "Don't bring it up again."

"That's why you hate Seattle, isn't it?"

"I fucking said, drop it, and I mean it," he raised his voice, almost yelling and immediately regretting his outburst of temper.

Izzy stared at him as if he were a stranger. She crossed her arms over her chest and looked out the side window. He heard her sniffle and knew he'd screwed up bigtime, but he couldn't talk about that summer.

He couldn't ever talk about that summer.

And why he couldn't stay in Seattle.

Chapter 18—Iced

Maybe Cooper wouldn't talk about his past, but Izzy sure as hell would get him to talk about Riley and what his plans were for the boy. She planned to do just that after the game Thursday night, but Cooper played like a wet-behind-the-ears rookie. He was in such a foul mood afterward that Izzy kept her mouth shut.

Still, they needed to tell Riley they'd met with his mother a couple nights ago, and neither of them were looking forward to that. Friday night, Izzy cooked lasagna, while Riley and Cooper played a video game together. The laughter coming from the family room made her smile. Despite Cooper's unwillingness to open up to her about whatever happened all those years ago, this evening almost made her believe the three of them could be a family.

Families weren't perfect. They were often messy and irritating, but she loved this odd little family they'd become, just as much as she loved her sisters.

Her sisters.

Avery.

Did you see all those trophies? She's good.

Out of the mouths of babes. Riley's words rang in her ears. Ashamed, Izzy realized that she didn't know how good Avery was when it came to horses. She'd always blown off her sister's love of horses as nothing serious. Yet, Avery had picked horses over Izzy.

Or had Izzy forced her into making a choice?

Izzy jumped when Cooper wrapped his strong arms around her waist.

"Sorry, didn't mean to scare you." He rubbed his stubbled cheek against her smooth one.

"I didn't know you were there."

"We're starving. How much longer?" Cooper asked then lowered his voice. "And I'm really hungry for your hot little body."

She elbowed him in the stomach. "Be nice. Riley's close by."

"Yeah, I know."

Izzy swung around and kissed Cooper on the lips. Before he could deepen the kiss and make her forget her name, she gave him a little push. "Put the salad on the table. We're ready to eat."

He grinned at her, desire shining in his eyes. "I'm definitely ready to eat. And the lasagna looks good, too."

She swatted his ass. "Put that bowl on the table, please."

"I'd like to put you on the table and eat off you."

Izzy didn't mind that idea at all, but now wasn't the time or place. Cooper watched her with those blue eyes of his, then did as he was told.

Izzy followed with lasagna and rolls. Cooper and Riley already sat in their spots waiting. Riley grinned at her. He'd done a lot of that lately, and she loved seeing him so happy. But to Izzy, happiness had always been fleeting, and she spent most of her life waiting for the next bad thing to happen. Riley had to feel the same way with the life he'd had. Maybe that was why she had a connection with the kid.

As they ate dinner, Riley didn't seem to notice Cooper and Izzy didn't say much. He was too busy talking about the football team, school, and his friends.

Cooper smiled and nodded, like an indulgent father, even though Izzy sensed his nervousness. Riley asked for tickets to Saturday's game for him and his buddies, and Cooper promised he'd get them if Izzy was the chaperone. Fall wasn't the best time for parties, so Izzy had Saturday night off.

During a lull in the conversation, Cooper cleared his throat. Riley glanced up from the lasagna he'd been shoveling in his mouth at an alarming rate. He seemed to read Cooper's expression and put down his fork, waiting with a worried frown.

"What is it?" The poor kid swallowed hard and looked from Cooper to Izzy and back to Cooper, his eyes full of dread.

Cooper glanced at Izzy. She gave him a small smile and squeezed his hand under the table. He took a deep breath.

"Riley, we found your mother." Cooper's voice came across as steady and calm, but Izzy watched that muscle jerk in his jaw.

Riley's face paled, and Cooper gripped Izzy's hand tighter.

"Is she okay?" Riley asked. His hands started shaking, so he hid them in his lap.

"Yes, she's living in Tacoma."

Hurt and betrayal put lines in Riley's forehead. "Why didn't she call me?"

"She thought you would be fine. She assumed you were with me." Cooper covered for his sister, and Izzy silently applauded him.

"But she didn't know that. She couldn't know that. She never bothered to find out." Riley pushed his plate away, and stared at a point on the wall. Izzy's heart broke for the poor kid.

"I'm sorry, Riley." Cooper shrugged as if he didn't know what else to say. Izzy squeezed his hand in encouragement.

"Is she coming for me?" Riley didn't sound as if he wanted that to happen.

"Uh, no." Cooper reached across the table and patted Riley's arm, but his nephew jerked away from him.

"She doesn't want me. No one wants me." Riley lashed out like a wounded animal, tears starting to form in his eyes.

Izzy longed to make it better, but she feared nothing could fix what Riley's mother had broken. "That's not true, Riley. You have us."

"For how long?" He looked from one to the other. When Cooper didn't reply, Riley shoved back his chair and shot to his feet. The chair crashed to the floor, and Riley ran from the room.

Joker sat in the doorway, looking at them in that judgmental manner only cats have, then he turned and followed Riley up the stairs.

Cooper pushed his hand through his hair. "That didn't go over so well."

"Did you really expect it would?"

"Hell, no." Cooper sighed. "I should go talk to him."

"Let him be for a while. He needs time to process all this."

"Process what? That his mother doesn't want him once again? And he thinks I don't either?" Cooper pulled his hand from hers and covered his face with both hands, groaning. "What a fucking mess."

Izzy nodded. "Yeah. What *are* you going to do about your nephew?"

"I'll be moving next year, and who knows—there are no guarantees in hockey—I could get traded during the season. That's no life for a kid."

"So says you." She rolled her eyes. He was making feeble excuses, and he knew it. "You're the man who moved all over the country as a military brat. Do you regret it?"

He looked like a trapped animal. "Uh, no, but Riley's not me. He needs stability."

"He needs the stability of people, not places. He needs to be able to count on one person in his life. Obviously, that person isn't you."

At least Cooper had the decency to look guilty, but she wasn't done with him yet.

"You're taking the easy way out. You love your life planned out. No disruptions. Exactly how you want it to be. That's why you're leaving at the end of the year. You want to control your destiny, and you're scared shitless you might not fit in Ethan's future plans so you're bailing first and using your past in Seattle as the excuse." She leaned forward and tapped his chest. "You, Cooper Black, are a spineless coward, afraid to take risks."

"Spineless coward?" He stood and straightened his shoulders, raising his chin. His eyes shone with defiance. Izzy resisted the urge to smile. Cooper wouldn't back down from a challenge, and she'd played him perfectly. Now what he chose to do with her challenge would be up to him.

"You're just going to throw him away," she said just to add a little more incentive behind her challenge.

"I'm not throwing him away. I'm sending him to live with my parents in a few weeks when they get back from their Europe trip."

"And when were you going to tell him that? And me?"

Cooper had the decency to look sheepish. "Soon. I just found out myself. I called them after we talked to Julie."

"At least let him stay through the football season. Don't uproot him now."

Cooper chewed on that for a moment. "I guess it wouldn't hurt."

Izzy glared at him, sad and pissed for Riley. Not only did he face rejection from his mother but from Cooper as well.

"You're an asshole," Riley yelled from the doorway, startling both Izzy and Cooper. A few seconds later, they heard Riley's footsteps pounding up the stairs.

"I wonder how long he's been standing there?" Cooper sighed and put his head in his hands, looking tired and defeated. Izzy almost felt sorry for him. *Almost.*

"Long enough."

"I should go talk to him." Cooper hedged, as if he were hoping she'd give him a reason not to.

"Yes, you should." Izzy refused to cut him any slack. Their eyes met, and Cooper nodded, his mouth drawn in a grim line.

Cooper went upstairs, while Izzy waited. She clenched her

hands together and prayed it'd work out for all of them.

A few minutes later, Cooper trudged back down the stairs, his shoulders slumped and his eyes troubled. "His door was locked. He wouldn't talk to me. Told me to go to hell. I guess I deserve that."

Izzy didn't deny the fact or sugar coat her answer. "Somewhat. You're just one more person who's abandoning him."

"My parents can do a better job than I can. This is for the best." Only Cooper didn't sound so convinced. In fact, he looked downright conflicted.

"Are you sure, Cooper? Are you really sure?"

"I'm not fucking sure of anything anymore." He shook his head and scrubbed his hands over his face. Izzy went to him and put her arms around him. She might be pissed as hell at him when it came to Riley, but she could see he was hurting. He wrapped her in his arms and held her close.

"I didn't think it would be this difficult," he whispered in her ear.

Izzy smiled against his cheek. He might pretend he didn't care, but he did, and she'd do everything in her power to show him how much Riley meant to him.

And how much he meant to her.

She grabbed his hand and led him to bedroom.

They needed time to sort this out, see where things went, but right now they needed time in each other's arms.

Yet it broke her heart to think of Riley alone in his room with nobody.

* * * *

Two weeks later, life went on, and November wasn't exactly starting out well. Cooper's convictions to send Riley to his parents wavered. He didn't have all the answers anymore. Instead he had questions, lots and lots of questions.

Cooper lay on his back, stroking Izzy's hair. She slept soundly next to him. He couldn't sleep. Too many things ran through his mind over and over.

His sister's blame.

His own guilt.

Riley's hurt.

243

Izzy's disappointment.

For a man who prided himself on controlling every aspect of his life, Cooper didn't have one ounce of control over the recent incidents in his life, except maybe his hockey game. Though lately, even that seemed to be spiraling out of control.

Coach had called him into his office before the last road trip and chewed his ass, giving him the *I don't give a shit what's happening in your personal life, but you're a professional, behave like one. This team expects nothing less from its captain.*

That three-game road trip had come and gone, and Cooper had actually looked forward to getting out of town and away from the tension in his house. The Sockeyes won two and lost one. Cooper played okay, but he wasn't on his game, and everyone knew it.

The team lost last night's home game and neither Riley nor Izzy attended. Cooper played like shit, which seemed to be the norm for him lately. The guys looked at him as if he were jinxed. He even caught Brick crossing himself when Cooper walked by, and Brick wasn't Catholic.

Riley barely spoke to him. Izzy only talked about superficial, meaningless things and hadn't said *I love you* once, not even in response to his declarations of love. Wasn't everything supposed to go better than this when two people told each other they loved each other? Instead everything had fallen apart.

Cooper had created this hot mess, and he just wanted things back the way they were, only he didn't know how to get back there.

"Cooper?" Izzy raised her head and met his gaze. Despite all the stuff between them, the sex couldn't be better.

"Yeah." He smiled at her as she crawled up his body until they were face to face.

"I've decided to stay at Betheni's when you're home from now on."

"What?" He sat up abruptly, causing her to slide off his body. She wrapped the sheets around her and sat up, too.

"I think we need some distance. We both know this isn't going anywhere. It's better to cut it off now than wait and make it that much harder." She wouldn't look him in the eyes.

"Like hell we aren't going anywhere. I love you." He stumbled over the last word as his throat constricted, and he choked up.

"I know, but as I once said, love isn't always enough." She

244

covered her face, and he was pretty sure she was crying.

"Izzy. Please. Don't do this." He was begging like a wuss, but he didn't care. He couldn't lose her. She'd become as big of a part of his life as hockey.

"I've stayed too long as it is, hoping you'd change, but nothing has changed, least of all you."

"But I have changed. You gave me access to your location via the stalker app, and I haven't shown up at one of your parties, have I?" God, he sounded like a pathetic weakling, but right now he didn't care about his male ego. He cared about convincing her to stay.

She nodded. "No, you haven't, but there's more to trust than that. Whatever demons you have locked inside you, won't let go so you can move on." Izzy sighed and turned her back to him. She buried her head in her hands. He could tell by her shaking shoulders she was crying, sobbing crying. He reached for her, but she pulled away, and he let her go.

"We can make this work. Give me a chance," he begged, not caring how pathetic he sounded.

"I'm not leaving Seattle. Not for all the wrong reasons." She looked up at him with red and swollen eyes. Even so, she was gorgeous, beyond beautiful.

"And you think I'm leaving for the wrong reasons?" God, this hurt. He hurt more inside than he had when he'd been slammed into the boards by Judson Phillips and broken three ribs.

Izzy nodded, as if unable to speak. Tears streamed down her cheeks, and he longed to kiss them away and make her smile again. Only he couldn't because she wouldn't let him.

Cooper watched in stunned silence as Izzy gathered her clothes and put them on. He swallowed back the lump clogging his throat and wondered how he'd survive without her.

Chapter 19—Comeback

Izzy sat on the leather couch in Cooper's family room and stuffed popcorn in her mouth. At this rate, she'd be fatter than a pig in no time. Her jeans were tighter, that's for sure. In a few weeks, it'd be Thanksgiving, but she wasn't feeling overly thankful.

It was Friday night, and Cooper had been gone for over a week on a two-week road trip, and dammit, she missed the big muscle-bound jock. And how flaky was that? She'd dumped him for the final time. She shouldn't miss him. She should be thrilled that she'd freed herself from a man with baggage he kept locked tight instead of trusting her enough to open up his heart and let her see him, bumps, bruises, and all.

Whatever happened during that Seattle summer, his sister blamed him, and he blamed himself—as a ten-year-old boy. How could he even begin to think he was responsible for what the adults in their lives did? But he did, and he seemed to hate Seattle for it. Cooper might be a private man, but even a private man should share his secret pain with the woman he professed to love. She shouldn't stay with a man like that, but she couldn't completely let him go either.

Obviously, he felt the same way because he called and texted her on a regular basis, as if nothing had happened, and Izzy couldn't bring herself to tell him they were supposed to be through. Maybe because she knew they weren't.

No one was perfect, and she had her faults just as he did. After all, she was estranged from the twins because she wouldn't accept Avery's career choices.

Then there was Riley. Izzy didn't quite understand why Riley was still here. Cooper's parents were back from Europe and had flown out last weekend to meet Riley, presumably to take Riley home with them. Yet they left without him. Izzy didn't ask Cooper why as it was none of her business. Or she pretended it wasn't.

Riley, in the meantime, seemed to be dealing with his world the best way he knew how, one day at a time. He didn't mention his mother once. The few times Izzy broached the subject, he steered the conversation to football or something equally less painful. He was like Cooper when it came to locking the bad stuff inside and going about his business. Izzy didn't consider it healthy behavior for either of them, but it was how they coped. Just like she coped when it came to Avery by refusing to admit she might be wrong.

She glanced over at Riley. He was curled up in Cooper's big recliner watching some adventure movie on TV. He didn't seem to notice her staring at him. Boys and car chases. She smiled as she shook her head.

Izzy opened up a book on her iPad and tried to get into it, but she couldn't. Finally she put it on the coffee table.

Riley glanced up and muted the TV. "You okay?"

"You were right, Riley," she admitted.

"I'm always right." He grinned. "But remind me what I'm right about this time."

She gave him a playful sock on the arm. "My sister. I need to accept her as she is."

Riley nodded, rubbing his shoulder as if she hurt him. "I did that with my mom a long time ago. As much as I'd love for her to be different, I have no control over what she does."

"No, you don't."

"At least what your sister does isn't self-destructive." Riley watched her with those old eyes of his.

Izzy almost argued that point. In her mind, Avery's pursuit of a career with horses was somewhat self-destructive, but Izzy understood what Riley was saying. Her sister could have a worse addiction than horses.

Making her decision, Izzy stood and gestured to Riley. "Are you up for a ride out to the country?"

"Yeah, sure." Riley hopped to his feet, ready to go. "I was bored with this movie anyway. Are you going to see your sister?"

Izzy smiled at him. "Yes. Yes, I am."

Izzy grabbed the keys as Riley tagged along behind her. The heaviness around her heart lifted slightly, and she smiled to herself. She may not like her sister's choices, but they were hers to make, and Izzy would support her anyway.

It was time to let go of something she couldn't control, no matter how hard she'd tried.

Somewhat like she should let Cooper go.

Only she couldn't.

* * * *

A half hour later, Izzy parked in front of the horse barn. Riley got out and followed her up the stairs, hanging back a little in case Izzy's sisters slammed the door in her face.

"Betheni's here, too," Izzy noted.

"Is that good or bad?"

"Good, I guess. All three of them should hear what I have to say." Izzy knocked on the door, and Riley noticed her hand was shaking.

Wow, that set him back on his heels. Izzy always seemed to have it together. She'd been a rock for Riley since he'd come here, along with Tanner, but he didn't see much of Tanner now that the football season was in full swing, and Tanner was busy.

The door opened, and Betheni motioned them inside.

Pizza sat on a small kitchen table, and Riley's mouth watered, even though he'd eaten a huge dinner a few hours ago. He couldn't seem to get enough to eat anymore. His uncle said he'd been just like that when he'd been Riley's age. Riley liked being like his uncle, even though he'd never tell him that.

Betheni must have caught him looking longingly at the pizza. "Riley, help yourself. We're all stuffed."

Riley glanced at Izzy, and she nodded her okay. He sat down and the table and dived in, pretty sure he could eat what was left all by himself. Besides, it kept him out of the line of fire. Nothing worse than a cat fight, and he avoided them at all costs. Females could be vicious.

Only no one seemed angry, more nervous, and worried, too.

Izzy motioned to her sisters to sit down, while she paced the floor in front of them. Riley ducked his head, pretending he wasn't paying attention.

He wanted Izzy to be happy because he really liked her. She'd become a big sister to him, and sometimes more of a mother than his mother could ever hope to be. At the thought of his mother, he got that sad, painful feeling inside, the one he'd been fighting for a while now. Mom didn't want him. She'd pushed him off on Uncle Coop so she could stay with her loser boyfriend.

And now Uncle Coop would be pushing Riley off on his parents because Cooper didn't want him either. Riley tried really hard to be good. He tried to stay out of Uncle Coop's way, and not make any trouble, but it didn't seem to matter. He didn't like Riley. No one did because Riley wasn't worthy of love. He wasn't sure why, but that was sure as hell the message he got from his family, if you could call them a family.

Riley's eyes grew hot with unshed tears. He hated that. He wiped his eyes with his sleeve and forced himself to focus on Izzy rather than his own problems.

"Avery," Izzy said, "I'm sorry."

Avery shook her head as if she couldn't believe what she was hearing. "Sorry?"

Izzy nodded slowly and cleared her throat. "I won't lie and say that I understand your passion for horses, but I will say that I was wrong. You have a right to do what you want with your life, and whatever it is, I'll support you." She looked to each of her sisters. "All of you. I've tried to be your parent and control your lives for too long, long after you were beyond the age to need me."

"Izzy, we'll always need you. We've appreciated everything you've ever done for us," Avery said. "It means a lot to know that we're okay."

The other sisters dabbed at their eyes.

"I love you guys," Izzy said.

All of sudden these women were hugging each other and crying. Riley stared at them, horrified that they might force him into this group hug, but they didn't.

He kept his head down and wolfed down the last of the pizza while they giggled and jabbered and talked about nonsense stuff like girls did. At least everything was okay now for Izzy, and she could be happy.

Riley frowned. Okay, partially happy because Uncle Coop was still being a shit to her. Riley wasn't sure what happened with them, but he was pretty sure it had something to do with him, and that made him sad.

Izzy and Cooper made a good pair. He liked them together. He didn't want to be the one who'd torn them apart.

Riley sighed. Just when stuff started going good for him, he managed to screw stuff up, no matter how hard he tried to make things work.

Somehow he'd screwed up things with Riley and Izzy, which made him feel like a first-class shit.

No wonder his uncle wanted to send him away.

* * * *

This road trip had been brutal. The Sockeyes won three out of five, but not without fighting for their lives in every one of those wins. Cooper had aches in places he didn't know a guy could ache. He had bruises on top of bruises, and he was bone-dead tired. Two more games, and they'd be flying home. Or to Seattle, because he'd never call Seattle home.

Even though he just had.

Jesus.

He must have moss on the brain already—or his brain cells had molded in the Seattle rain.

"Are you still a full-time dad?" Brick asked, interrupting Cooper's inner dialogue.

Cooper glanced up from taping his stick for the night's game. "Just for a short while longer."

"Yeah, he's been saying that for a few months now," Cedric interrupted.

"I'm not right for Riley. I'm never home, and I'm not good with him." Cooper concentrated on his stick and tried to block them out. He didn't need his teammates butting into his business.

"If I was a fourteen year old, I'd love living with you," Brick noted.

"Seriously?" Cooper snorted. "You don't know me very well then."

"Well enough." Brick shrugged and sat back against his locker space, stretching his long, bare legs out in front of him. "He gets along with Izzy, and you two are practically married. So what's the holdup?"

"Izzy and I are over." Cooper's stomach twisted when he said those words. Hell, he'd been denying it ever since she'd broken it off with him, but facts were facts, and pretending it didn't happen didn't alter the facts.

"What'd you do to screw that up?" Matt LeRue asked, turning this into some kind of team interview session, and Cooper had no intention of becoming fodder for these idiots.

"We both want different things." And why was he even

answering these questions?

"That means she gave him his walking papers," Drew Delacorte snorted.

"Whatever happened to that cute redhead who had you wound up so tight you couldn't find the puck on our last road trip?" Cooper shot back.

Drew colored bright red, while several of the guys chuckled.

"She dumped him," Mike Gibson happily answered for his buddy. Drew shot him a murderous glare, but Mike kept smiling. Not much bothered Mike. The guy had nerves of steel and ice in his veins. Sometimes the guys called him the Robot because he never got riled. Hell, even in the few fights he'd been involved in, he'd thrown his punches with mechanical precision and very little emotion.

"She did not," Drew argued, "and what about Candy? Huh?"

"We were never an item, just fooling around."

With a smirk, Cooper went back to his stick. He'd safely deflected their questions about Izzy and Riley by pitting them against each other. He was a great captain.

Cedric raised an eyebrow at him and grinned. Cooper just shrugged. Cedric knew, and Cooper didn't try to bullshit him.

Cedric leaned close to him. "You're in love, you dumbshit. Glad it's you and not me."

"Yeah, well, I didn't exactly plan on it."

"No guy ever does, but a lot sure fall prey to a pretty face and a hot body. I'll never be that guy, but you, buddy, are screwed. You might as well beg her forgiveness because your play isn't up to par when you're pining for her."

Cooper glanced up at Cedric. "My play has been pretty damn good lately."

"Yeah, but I know you, and something's off. You know it, too. Maybe you're still good enough to be better than most, but you aren't you."

"I'm fine," Cooper growled, denying Cedric's statements. He'd been scoring, and he'd been playing good hockey, even though he knew Cedric was right.

At least he had everyone else fooled.

* * * *

It wasn't supposed to happen this way. Cooper was supposed to come home early in the morning, and Izzy would go to Betheni's with nothing more than a hi and bye.

Only it didn't work that way.

Izzy had packed her bags, left them by the front door, and fallen asleep on the family room couch watching a sad movie with Joker on her chest, purring loudly.

She startled awake when Cooper bent over her, his blue eyes dark with a little concern and a lot of lust and affection. She knew that look. It was the same look that'd gotten her into trouble on too many occasions with this man. He was all sorts of trouble, and her body loved his brand of trouble.

"Izzy?" His big hands rested on her shoulders, and she could smell the soap he used after the game that night.

She opened and closed her mouth, unable to clear her hazy brain enough to form words. It wasn't sleep that fogged her brain, it was the nearness of Cooper and his incredibly hot body. Yet, her attraction to him went beyond that body and that sexy lopsided smile, and she'd be a fool to deny the chemistry between them.

She'd be a bigger fool to let that chemistry drag her back into a relationship with him a fourth time.

He knelt down next to her and cupped her cheeks in his hands, his stormy blue eyes searching her face for answers she couldn't give him. When his lips touched hers and ignited her body and soul, her ability to resist sizzled and burned with the rest of her body.

One more night couldn't hurt.

She slid her fingers into his hair and pulled his mouth harder against hers. Their kiss deepened and intensified, while Cooper's strong hands slid under her shirt and up to her bra. Izzy moaned as he rubbed little circles around her nipples.

She whimpered and tried to press her body closer to his, an action which rolled her off the couch. Laughing, she fell on top of him onto the floor. A second later, he'd swapped their positions and straddled her, all the while kissing the hell out of her.

Finally coming up for air, he propped himself up by his arms. His gaze roamed her upper body, resting on her breasts, which were heaving.

"You're killing me, baby," he panted. "I just want to bury

myself inside of you and forget the rest of the world for a while."

If he was asking for her permission, she gave it by sliding her hands down his ribcage and cupping his ass, squeezing hard.

"Oh, God," he groaned. "I've been dreaming about this for two weeks."

"I have too," she admitted, even if it made her an idiot to do so. They were supposed to be broken up, but right now she flipping did not care.

"Good." With a slow, satisfied smile, he pushed her shirt upward until he could see her lacy bra. He grinned, obviously liking what he saw. It was her sexiest bra, and she'd put it on today for reasons she refused to admit to herself.

"You like?" she asked, already knowing the answer.

"I bet the drool was your first clue." He chuckled. "You wore this for me."

"Maybe." She refused to admit the truth because it gave him power, and Izzy was all about power and keeping it, even though there were times like this one when she couldn't remember why it mattered.

Cooper pushed her bra upward and feasted on her breasts, kissing and licking, even nipping at them until Izzy cried and writhed beneath him. The man was a master at knowing her body and just the right way to drive her to sexual insanity.

Two could play that game. She unzipped his dress pants and pushed them down. His erection bulged against his underwear. She cupped his balls in her hand through his briefs.

"Izzy, I—"

"You want to be inside me. Now."

"How did you know?"

"I know you, and I want the same thing."

Cooper didn't wait for a second invitation; he shucked his clothes and the rest of hers in world-record time. He positioned himself between her legs and smiled down at her, like a kid who'd just opened the best Christmas present ever. His cock tickled her opening, and Izzy bit her lower lip to prevent herself from crying out.

Cooper's intense blue eyes held hers captive, along with her heart.

"Cooper," she gasped.

"Honey, I need you so badly. I swear I need you like I need breathing," he said.

She couldn't deny she felt the same way so she kept her mouth shut.

Just as Cooper was about to slide into her warm, happily willing body, he groaned and withdrew.

"Cooper," she whined pathetically.

"I need a condom," he said, sounding as if he were in physical pain.

"No, you don't." She tried to stop the slow smile from giving her away.

He stared down at her, open-mouthed. "I don't?"

"I'm on birth control."

"Birth control?"

"Yes."

"Why didn't you ever tell me this? Damn, honey, you have to know that I would love nothing better that feel us skin to skin with nothing between us, to empty myself into you. Do you have any idea how much that turns me on?"

"I was saving it. My little gift to you. Then we—well, it was over, and I never got the chance."

"But you're giving it to me now?"

"Yes, I am." Because it might be their last time? She didn't know. What she did know was that she might not be strong enough to make this their last time.

"I love you." He looked at her with such love on his face, the realization that no man could ever love her like him struck her hard in the chest.

"I love you, too, Coop," she said, meaning every word.

He slid inside her with a happy groan and began to take her to heaven and all places in between. When he came inside her, and she could feel his seed filling her, she came, too, with an orgasm so powerful it scared the crap out of her.

Cooper rolled onto his side and hugged her close to him, not speaking until his breathing returned to normal and so did hers.

"Where do we go from here?" he whispered in her ear.

"Your bedroom before Riley finds us like this," Izzy quipped, knowing full well that wasn't the answer he wanted.

"Izz, you should be punished for toying with me like that." He grinned as if the thought of punishing her really appealed to him. It should, because it appealed to her.

"Is that a promise?" she teased while running a finger along his jaw.

"Oh, yeah. So answer my question, naughty girl."

Izzy blew out a breath. "We take it one day at a time."

"Been there before."

"Yes, we have, but we have unresolved issues that we may not be able to resolve." Such as his hatred of Seattle, her refusal to leave her hometown and her family, and his stance on Riley. Especially Riley.

"Yeah, I know," he said grimly. He held her that much tighter, as if he couldn't let her go.

But the day might come that he would have to let her go, but Izzy didn't want to think about it.

She loved that damn man and believed if they were truly meant to be, they'd find a way to work it out. She loved him too much not to try.

Chapter 20—Gut Feelings

Cooper couldn't shake that dark, niggling feeling something bad was going to happen. This deep sense of foreboding lodged in his gut, and he couldn't get beyond it. It'd hung over him all morning like the stormy gray clouds on Seattle's horizon.

He called Izzy that morning, making up a stupid reason just to hear her voice, not that he needed one. She'd spent the night with her sisters, and God, he missed her. Missing her probably explained the dread coursing through him like some crazy-assed premonition. Cooper didn't believe in that BS, except on the ice. When he was in the zone, he could see where the puck was going before he hit it with his stick. He could feel a defenseman bearing down before he saw him. He knew when a shot was going in before it left his stick.

But this had nothing to do with the ice and was just his mind playing tricks on him, jerking him around because he'd let Izzy walk out of his life twice, and he was about to let Riley do the same. Only both of them were still there, and he could salvage this. He had time.

When he'd arrived back from his first long road trip yesterday morning and found Izzy fast asleep on his couch, he had to have her, had to find a way to keep her in his life. The next thing he knew, they were naked and all over each other, just like old times. Even better he'd made love to her without a condom, which was the purest form of heaven known to man, skin to skin, nothing separating them, and emptying his seed into her body had been the most sensual bonding experience he'd ever had.

Then she'd told him she was spending the evening with her sisters, and he'd spent the night alone in his bed, which probably explained why he was feeling a little out of sorts and full of dread.

Her sisters? She'd rather spend the night with her sisters when he'd just returned from a two-week road trip? That seemed so wrong. But in an effort to show her how supportive and laid-back he'd become, he told her to have fun and watched her go, hoping she'd come back to his house after a night with her sisters and change her mind about giving him another chance, but she didn't.

This morning he drove Riley to school, and the closer he got, the more his gut clenched. He couldn't explain his reluctance any more than he could explain why he hadn't sent Riley to live with his parents yet. When they came out to meet Riley, they'd assumed

Riley would be going back with them. Only Cooper hedged, claiming that he didn't want to uproot Riley in the middle of a semester and would wait until winter break.

The sooner Riley moved out, the sooner Cooper's life would get back to normal. Only he wasn't sure he wanted that normal anymore. He used to answer to no one, had no responsibilities except to his team, and had the house all to himself.

Only there was a big problem. The old normal didn't appeal to him anymore.

God, he was so messed up in the head right now.

"Uncle Coop, are you okay?"

Cooper jerked himself back to the present. "Yeah, I'm fine."

Riley's gaze dissected him as Cooper pulled up in the front of the school.

Shit.

Cooper broke out in a cold sweat. His hands fucking shook. His breath came in short gasps, as if he were on the verge of a panic attack. Disgusted with himself, Cooper shook it off, but it took every bit of control he'd learned from years of hockey to do so. He glanced at Riley, whose brow was furrowed with worry.

Just as his nephew was about to get out of the SUV, Cooper grabbed his arm.

"Riley." His voice broke in a rare display of emotion.

"Yeah?" Riley had his hand on the door as if ready to bolt.

"Why don't you play hooky, and we'll hang out?" The words rushed from Cooper's mouth before he could stop them.

Riley stared at him as if he were nuts. "I have a test today, and we have a big pep rally."

"Oh, okay. I just—I just want you to know that—" Cooper swallowed. The words stuck in his throat.

"What?" Riley said with typical teenage impatience.

"I—uh—I—" Cooper raked his fingers through his hair. "Have a good day."

Riley frowned at him, then glanced around quickly as if to make sure none of his friends noticed Cooper being clingy and weird. "Sure."

The kid literally leapt from the car.

Cooper sighed. He couldn't blame him. Cooper hadn't exactly been the doting uncle, or even much of an uncle at all. Somehow he'd make that up to Riley in the time they had left together.

Yeah, that's what he'd do first chance he got.

* * * *

Riley sat in the cafeteria surrounded by his buddies, wishing he could bottle this memory and save it forever. It was such a normal kid moment, but it wouldn't last because Uncle Cooper didn't want him. He was going to send him away. Even though he was acting all emotional and weird today, Riley refused to get his hopes up. Cooper and Izzy were on the skids, which explained his uncle's strange behavior more than it explained any feelings Uncle Cooper might have for him.

Riley wasn't sure why Cooper hadn't sent him away yet, especially when his grandma and grandpa came to visit. He'd been certain they'd come to get him. Only they left without him. They were nice people, but they weren't Cooper and Izzy.

If Riley were staying, he'd find a way to get those two back together. They'd been missing each other ever since they split up. It was stupid. They were meant for each other, but they were too stubborn to admit it. Riley had caused all this somehow. His mom had always told him that he was in the way, and everything bad was usually his fault.

Riley looked over at the next table. Gina caught his eye and smiled. Riley's heart thumped in his chest.

Gina was hot, like the hottest girl in his class and lately she'd been paying attention to him. At first, he'd been confused because girls like Gina never paid attention to him. Besides, he was still stinging from the rejection of his former girlfriend. Okay, so he'd only actually met her once at the party Izzy took him to, but they'd had a virtual relationship ever since. Until a few nights ago when she'd told him she liked another guy who went to her school.

Tonight the varsity team had a playoff game, and the cafeteria buzzed with excitement, especially at the jock table where Riley sat. Freshman jocks, that is. The older guys sat at a table nearby, joking and laughing, and being general dicks. When Riley got to be a senior, he'd never be a dick. He'd be a nice guy to everyone and not be mean to anyone.

Riley heard a pop like some joker was popping a plastic bag.

Next to him Gabe clutched his chest and fell to the floor, clowning around like he always did. Riley rolled his eyes and glanced around at his buddies. Wide-eyed, they were staring at the seat that Gabe had been sitting in. A couple of them looked at something over his shoulder, horror on their faces. Riley frowned, feeling like he was missing something.

Pop. Pop. Pop.

Across the table from Riley, Eric slumped over. Confused, Riley stared at the growing puddle of red oozing out from under Eric. The same kind of puddle now surrounding Gabe on the floor.

After that everything happened in slow motion.

All around him kids started running and screaming as the pops became more frequent. His classmates fell like they were in a video game.

Like they were being shot.

But this wasn't a video game. These were his friends, his classmates, his teachers. This carnage was real, so real his mind rejected it. Riley turned and raised his eyes to meet the cold, hard eyes of the shooter only a few feet from him.

Jacob, a former wide receiver on the varsity team, held a rifle in one hand, a gun in the other. Riley didn't know anything about guns, but these guns were big suckers. Next to Jacob stood Ely, Jacob's best friend, similarly armed. Both guys had been kicked off the varsity football team earlier in the week for violating the athletic code by drinking, which meant no playoffs for them.

Jacob levelled the gun at Riley's forehead.

Riley braced himself, surprised he hadn't wet his pants, pretty sure his short life would end in the next second or two. Instead Jacob swung the rifle around to fire several rounds at the varsity players running for the door and a couple girls huddled on the floor. One of the girls was Gina. Riley dived for her, covering her with his body.

Sharp, white hot pain burned through the muscles in his arm. He lay atop Gina and her friend, whispering to them not to move, to play dead.

And wondered if he wasn't dying himself.

* * * *

Cooper skated around the ice, trying to relax. He noticed Mina talking to Coach and then Coach gestured to him. Cooper skated over to where they stood.

"What's up?" He looked from one to the other.

Mina patted his arm and scurried down the hall, as if she couldn't wait to get away from him. Cooper stared after her, confused and slightly alarmed. When he swung his gaze back to Coach, Gorst was staring at the ice and wringing his hands.

"What's going on?"

"Coop, doesn't your nephew go to Yesler High School?"

That gnawing feeling gnawed a hole right through his stomach. "Yeah?"

Gorst's face had turned pale. "There's an—uh—uh—incident at Yesler."

"A *what*?" Cooper broke out into his second cold sweat of the day. Behind Gorst stood Ethan, looking equally nervous and pale. Cooper looked from Ethan to Coach. "What kind of incident?" Only he knew, deep inside he knew, it was the worst kind of incident.

Ethan shouldered his way past Coach, who took up most of the narrow passageway that ran from the ice to the lockers. "Cooper. Calm down."

"Calm down? Calm down? What the fuck is going on?" Cooper grabbed both of Ethan's arms, squeezing so tightly he most likely left bruises, but he didn't give a shit.

"Early reports are that there's a shooter in the building," Ethan said with a false calm.

Cooper heard him as if he were far away. He'd fallen into a dark pond and struggled to swim to the top with an anchor wrapped around his ankles, and his lungs screaming for oxygen.

"Cooper?" Ethan pulled free of Cooper's grip and shook him.

Cooper still couldn't breathe, couldn't think, couldn't function. He shouldn't have let Riley go to school today, should've trusted his instincts.

"Mina just heard it on the news. It's an on-going situation." Coach's words penetrated the foggy haze and prodded Cooper into action. He had to do something, had to save Riley, had to tell him that he mattered before it was too late.

"Fuck." Cooper raced for the locker room as fast as a guy on skates could race. He didn't bother to change, but he couldn't drive a car with skates. He fumbled with the laces and finally managed to loosen them enough to yank off his skates, just as his phone erupted with text messages.

He grabbed the phone and scanned the messages. One was from the school informing him there was an incident and to stay away from the school but directing parents to a nearby church.

Fuck that.

Fear slammed through him. Fear something might have happened to Riley. Fear that he'd never see the kid's scowl again when he thought Cooper was being a dork. Fear that he'd never watch him play another high school football game. Fear that he'd never get to tell him that he was proud of him, and he loved him.

Yeah, he loved his nephew.

As he ran to his car, ignoring the concerned faces of teammates and staff, he texted three simple words to Izzy:

I need you.

Followed by the three most important words in the English language:

I love you.

* * * *

Izzy heard the news when she came out of the shower that morning. It was everywhere. Social media was blowing up, and all the news stations carried the incident live and in all its horror.

Riley went to that school.

She picked up her phone to call Cooper and saw the texts. He needed her. She texted him back. No response. She tried calling him, the phone went straight to voicemail.

She told her sisters goodbye and ran to her car, promising to call as soon as she found out something.

Izzy knew Cooper. As unwise as it was, he'd go straight to the school, not to the nearby staging area for parents. At the least he'd get in the way, and the worst, he'd storm the building himself.

She couldn't lose him and Riley, too.

Izzy drove like a crazy person to the school, unable to reach Cooper. Ethan called her, concerned for Cooper and Riley, but visibly relieved when he heard Izzy was en route.

"If anyone can calm him, you can," he'd said.

Izzy pulled out her iPhone and fired up "Find My Friends."

261

Most of the routes were blocked off, so she parked and followed her phone until she spotted Cooper's vehicle parked haphazardly on a side street blocks from the school. He'd done exactly what he shouldn't have done—gone barging into an active crime scene.

Damn that stubborn man.

She ran down the sidewalk, grateful for her flats rather than her usual mile-high heels. Pushing past hysterical parents and concerned onlookers, she detoured toward a commotion right at the edge of the barricade of police cars.

Four officers attempted to hold a crazed Cooper, and they were losing the battle. Izzy stepped up, put on her calmest face, and moved into Cooper's line of sight.

He caught sight of her and instantly stopped struggling, as if all the air had whooshed out of his body. He sagged against the officers, his face grief-stricken.

"He's still in there. No one's seen him." Tears streamed down his face, and his breath came in wheezing gasps, as if he couldn't take in enough oxygen.

"I can handle him." Izzy nodded to the officers, who stared at her in amazement, as if they couldn't believe her appearance had managed to calm this savage beast.

"Cooper." She put a hand on his arm. "You aren't helping. They need to focus their attention on the students and the situation, not on you."

For a long, tense moment, no one seemed certain what Cooper would do next. He swallowed, his hands fisted, his face turned toward the school, watching as kids sprinted out accompanied by SWAT team members.

He nodded, suddenly looking sheepish and crumpled into her arms, a broken man badly in need of the right glue to put his pieces back together. Izzy was that glue, and Riley was one of the missing pieces. Izzy only hoped she could repair the damage.

She looked over Cooper's shoulder at the officer who appeared to be in charge. "I'm sorry. I'll take him off your hands. We'll wait at the church for word."

The officer blew out a relieved breath and gladly foisted responsibility for Cooper off to her.

Cooper held her so tightly, she couldn't breathe, but she didn't complain. Sobs wracked his big body and tears wet her neck where he pressed his face against her skin.

Lifting his head, he stared at her, his cheeks wet from his tears. "I knew. I knew something was wrong. I shouldn't have let him go to school today. I can't lose him any more than I can lose you," he moaned in pure agony.

"He has to be okay, honey. He does. He has to be." She set him back, holding his arms and looking into his eyes. "Let's go to the church. They might already have information for us."

She grabbed his arm and led him down the street. Their cars were now blocked by several news vehicles. No matter, he needed the walk to the church on this cold brisk fall day.

"He doesn't answer his phone or his text messages." Cooper's devastation struck deep inside her.

"He's probably holed up in a safe place and doesn't have his phone with him." She stroked the tight muscles in his back, trying to relax him, but for once her touch didn't seem to help.

"I don't know what I'll do if something happens to him."

"He'll be okay, Coop. He will." Izzy wasn't sure if she was trying to convince Cooper or herself.

"I heard on the police radio that they have at least a dozen kids down, and they can't find the shooter. He's in the building somewhere. Oh, God." Cooper's face distorted with agony and pain, while more tears slipped down his cheeks. He buried his face in his hands, his shoulders shuddered with sobs.

Izzy rubbed his shoulder, glancing toward the cop studying them with equal parts of suspicion and annoyance. "All the more reason for us to get out of their way and let them do their jobs." She pried his hands from his face and gently kissed his tear-stained cheeks. He managed a feeble smile.

"We need to go." Izzy tugged on his hand. He took a few staggering steps, then found his stride and allowed her to lead him down the street past crying parents and hysterical kids. His blind faith in her meant more than he could possibly imagine, especially in the wake of tragedy.

And she loved him all the more for relinquishing that control to her and trusting her to handle the situation better than he could.

Chapter 21—A Ray of Hope

Cooper was a hot mess of emotions. If it hadn't been for Izzy, he'd have completely lost it and probably ended up arrested. Instead he followed her to the church, more than happy to let her take charge. It felt good to relinquish control while he coped with the tragedy of the situation. He'd always assumed losing control would put him into a claustrophobic panic, but with Izzy, it felt right and comforting to know she had his back. And, God, he needed her to have his back today.

He paced the floor of the large conference area in the church. All around him he heard the quiet sobbing of some parents and the heart-wrenching wailing of others. A flat screen TV across the room showed SWAT teams and uniformed officers, guns drawn, running into the building.

At times, a group of students with hands above their heads would run out of the building, flanked by armed escorts, or a stretcher would be wheeled out, or a student would stagger out being held up by friends. Each time, he stopped his pacing and joined the countless other parents searching for their children. It'd been game day so the football team wore jerseys to school, even the non-varsity players, making it hard to identify individual team members. But Cooper knew Riley's walk, knew how he held his head, and how he stood taller than most of the boys his age.

Cooper didn't see Riley anywhere.

Parent after parent received word from their kids via cell or text or saw them on TV. Some rushed from the room to go to the hospital, others were reunited with their kids as they were brought into the church.

Watching tearful reunion after tearful reunion, Cooper's hope began to fade. Despair settled in his stomach, while a swirling storm of dread fogged his brain.

Cooper texted Riley a hundred times and called him just as many, but his phone went straight to voicemail. He'd heard enough to know that the shooting started in the cafeteria and spread out from there. The police captured one shooter and were looking for a second, which meant the kids still in the building were either barricaded in rooms or unable to leave for various reasons.

Izzy sat nearby attempting to comfort a distraught mother, who appeared to be all alone without a support group. Cooper stopped pacing and sank wearily into the empty seat next to Izzy. He pushed his fingers through his hair and buried his face in his hands.

The news reported that a second shooter had gotten into a shootout with the SWAT team and been killed. Cooper breathed a sigh of relief. The danger was over, now the damage could be assessed. The news cameras showed kids running from the building, others being taken out on stretchers.

But he still didn't see Riley.

His mouth filled with saliva and clogged his throat. He was pretty sure he was going to throw up. If it hadn't been for Izzy's quiet strength, he'd have lost it worse than any of the parents in the room.

She put her arm around him and pulled him close. "Cooper, he'll be fine. I know it."

He couldn't begin to count how many times she'd said those words in the past hour. "I don't know how I'd handle this without you," he admitted.

"You don't have to. You have me." She touched his cheek with her finger, a gentle, caring touch that meant as much to him as all their hot, steamy nights together.

He looked at her through blurry eyes burning with unshed tears. "For how long, Izzy?"

"Cooper, this isn't the place to discuss this."

"I want you back, honey. I want you with me forever—you and Riley."

She kissed his cheek, as if indulging him. She couldn't possibly know how true his words had become, how the two of them had managed to weasel their way into his heart and entwine themselves around his soul until he knew he couldn't survive without them.

Right now, he needed to deal with the present.

The future would come later.

* * * *

When the shooters left the cafeteria in search of more victims, several students barricaded the doors so the shooters couldn't come back in.

As soon as they were out of immediate danger, Riley pulled

Gina into his lap. A big hole in her chest pumped blood all over him, mingling with the blood from where the bullet had grazed his arm. Weird but he didn't feel a damn thing after the initial stab of pain.

He ripped off his jersey and held it over Gina's wound, putting pressure on it in an attempt to stop the bleeding. There was so much blood—sticky, thick blood—and the strong smell of iron and gunpowder filled the air. He didn't know if help would come in time. Each beat of her heart became more and more feeble.

All around him were groans and cries for help. A teacher bent down to assess Riley and Gina. "Are you okay?" he asked Riley.

"Yeah," Riley said, his voice a gravelly whisper.

"Good, keep pressure on her wound," the teacher said grimly. "That's all we can do right now, but helps coming." Despite his positive words, his voice gave away his desperation. The teacher hurried off to the next victim.

Riley talked to Gina, told her about anything and everything, willing her with his voice to hang in there. He didn't know if she could hear him, but he kept talking anyway. At least it made him feel like he was doing something.

Riley heard a crash and was certain the shooters had returned. He ducked, pulling Gina close and squeezed his eyes shut, bracing for the inevitable. He stayed absolutely still, hoping they wouldn't waste bullets on kids they thought were already dead.

"Son, can you walk?" A hand touched his arm. Riley startled and glanced up to see a fully uniformed SWAT officer kneeling beside him.

"Uh huh." Riley nodded. "But she can't."

The officer gestured to another man. "Take him out of here with the rest. We need medics over here stat."

Riley resisted, not wanting to leave Gina, but he was herded from the room with several other crying and wailing kids and hustled outside into the dreary Seattle day. A fine mist coated everything as Riley was helped into an ambulance with a few other non-critically injured classmates and driven away.

He stared out the window holding a towel over his arm. They passed several news vehicles, while sirens wailed. Then it hit him as the shock wore off. He started shaking, and one of paramedics draped a blanket over his shoulders. He was damn lucky to be breathing right now. Several of his classmates, possibly friends and teammates, weren't so fortunate.

Riley had to call Uncle Coop. He'd be worried sick. Wouldn't he? Well, Izzy would be for sure.

He reached in the breast pocket of his letterman's jacket for his phone and pulled out a mangled mess. Holy shit. The bullet that had grazed his arm must have hit his chest first, or he'd been shot twice. Either way, his phone had stopped the bullet. He stared at the phone and struggled to process the full extent of what'd happened to him.

One or two inches had stood between him and life or death.

His world spun around him as the shock of how close he'd come to dying sank in.

Riley gripped his head in his hands and lost his breakfast.

* * * *

Izzy held Cooper's hand, as they watched the one TV in the large room, waiting for word on the survivors or the victims—any kind of word—because knowing beat the shit out of this horrible dread that filled them both.

"Everything will work out," she spoke with absolute conviction. Riley had to be okay. Anything else was unthinkable. She swallowed as she glanced around the room and was hit with how many parents would be getting unthinkable news as reports came in fast and furious of multiple fatalities and injuries.

Riley wasn't responding, nor had he contacted them, which made her beyond sick to her stomach, more like near hysteria. Only she had to be the rock for Cooper, she had to be the person he could lean on. He needed her now, and she'd be what he needed. She could fall apart later.

"He has to be okay, honey. He has to be." Cooper squeezed her hand so tightly, it hurt, but she held on without one complaint.

"We'll all be okay, Cooper," she promised, kissing him lightly on the cheek.

"Cooper Black?" A reporter with her camera guy bore down on them. Cooper stiffened beside Izzy and glanced around frantically as if looking for an escape route.

Izzy narrowed her eyes and glared at the news team. Standing, she blocked their access to Cooper. "Mr. Black needs his privacy right now. This is a very trying time for him. I'm sure you can appreciate that."

The female reporter unsheathed her claws and sized up Izzy. "We only have a few questions for him."

"Mr. Black has no comment." Izzy spoke with absolute certainty, her own claws sharpened for a cat fight. "You need to leave now."

The woman looked down her aristocratic nose at Izzy. "And who are you?"

"I'm his girlfriend." Izzy propped hands on hips and stared down the woman.

The reporter didn't move.

"Either you leave, or I'll have Ethan Parker, the team owner, talk to your station manager. You are aware Mr. Parker is part owner of your broadcasting company, aren't you?"

For a long moment they stared each other down until the news reporter turned to her camera man and left in search of another unfortunate victim to exploit their grief and trauma for TV ratings.

"Wow, you're tough." Cooper managed a chuckle. "Remind me to never cross you."

"That would be wise." She smiled back and sat down next him. He grabbed her hand again, giving her as much strength and comfort as she gave him.

"So Ethan owns part of that TV station?" Cooper asked.

"Hell if I know." Izzy shrugged.

Cooper laughed a real laugh, and so did she. It felt good to laugh and relieve some of the overpowering tension. Several people shot chastising glares in their direction, while others actually smiled.

Cooper ran his hand through his hair and sobered as he glanced around at the room full of parents. "Thanks for running interference."

"You're welcome. I'm glad I was here to help. Reporters can be ruthless."

"So are you, but I have a question—you're my girlfriend?" He watched her with a guarded expression, almost as if fearing her answer and a possible rejection. Only Izzy had no intention of rejecting him. Being with him today and enduring this tragedy, seeing all these parents, some reunited with their children, others finding out they'd never see their children alive again, changed every truth she thought she held dear.

This was life stripped bare of all its fancy adornments until only the essentials that really mattered were left—love, family, and friends.

Being independent and never relying on anyone didn't hold the appeal it once did. Yet, being part of a couple who were a greater force together than they would be apart did appeal to her. They were a team. Yeah, there'd be bumps and bruises along the way. They'd lose a game or two, maybe get penalized, but they'd emerge champions because together there wasn't anything they couldn't conquer, including this tragedy. Riley would need their loving support more than he'd ever needed anything, even when he'd been scrounging for food or witnessing his mother's downward spiral.

They'd be a family, if only God and fate gifted them with that second chance.

Izzy would give anything to see Riley walking through that door.

Anything.

She gave Cooper a soft kiss on his lips and cupped his cheek in one hand. "You're damn right, I'm your girlfriend. Do you have a problem with that?"

"No, ma'am, you scare me when you get like this."

The teasing felt good, but she knew they were only trying to mask their nerves. "I love you, Cooper Black. I don't think until today I truly knew what that really meant."

"I love you, Izzy." He nodded, as if he too understood how this tragedy had changed them forever, regardless of the outcome.

"I want us to be together."

"What if I sign with a different team?"

Izzy stopped to think about that, but she'd known her answer for a while now, even if she hadn't acknowledged it to Cooper or herself. "You and me—we're a team. We're meant for each other. Wherever you go, I'll be there for you and for Riley."

He opened his mouth to say something but Izzy held up a hand and stopped him.

"Don't bother denying it. Riley has a permanent home with you, and anyone who dares to challenge our claim on him will have to come through you and me first."

"And that's not happening." Cooper managed a small, tense smile. "But what about you, Izzy? You love Seattle and your sisters are here. You say you're fine leaving with me now, but what about later, a year from now, or a few years from now? Will you resent me for taking you away from your business, your city, your family? Will you see me as a selfish bastard because I did that to you?"

"Of course not," Izzy said but doubt crept into her voice, and she could tell by Cooper's expression that he caught it. "You're not leaving here without me, mister. If you do, I'll follow you to the ends of the earth so don't even try it."

She stood on tiptoes and brushed her lips across his. "I can't bear to be without you or Riley. We'll make our home wherever we are."

"Home is where the heart is?" His smile was bigger this time. "Cliché, but true."

Cooper pulled her into his arms and held her tight. "All I know is that the three of us will be together as a family."

"And that's what matters, Cooper. The rest will work itself out." Izzy meant it. They'd form a family and give Riley the life he deserved.

Because Riley had to be alive. He had to be.

* * * *

Cooper's phone rang with a local phone number he didn't recognize. He stared at it as if it were the devil himself coming to take him to hell.

Izzy looked at the phone, seeing what he did. She gripped his hand tighter, and God, he needed her right now. It could be the hospital or the police or another nosy reporter who'd gotten word that hockey star Cooper Black's nephew had been involved in the school shooting. The press loved shit like that, especially if they could get him in a vulnerable moment showing some real emotion.

Bastards.

But it sure had been fun seeing Izzy put that woman in her place.

"Aren't you going to answer it?" Izzy nudged him.

"Yeah." Cooper hit the Talk button and held the phone up to his ear. "Hello."

"Uncle Coop, it's Riley."

Every bit of tension drained out of Cooper. He didn't know

270

whether to laugh, cry, or scream to the heavens that his nephew was okay. Izzy stared at him, reading his relief, and a tentative smile graced her beautiful face.

Riley? She mouthed the words.

He nodded and grinned at her. Izzy's smile lit up her face and tears fell down her cheeks. Hell, tears were falling down his cheeks. It was a strange bittersweet happiness while a woman wailed in the background, obviously receiving the worst news of all. Cooper's heart went out to her even as his own spirits soared.

"Uncle Cooper?" Riley's voice jerked him out of his stupor.

"Yeah, yeah, I'm here, buddy. Are you okay? Where are you?"

"Yeah, I'm okay. I'm at the hospital." Riley sounded strange, like he was sleepwalking and taking at the same time.

"The hospital? Are you hurt?"

"My arm was grazed. I'll be okay."

"Grazed? By a bullet?" Panic rose in Cooper. Sweat dripped down his face, and his hands shook. He swore he was going to throw up right here. Using every ounce of control he'd learned from playing hockey, Cooper fought the panic and nausea.

For Riley.

Riley didn't need his uncle in a panic. He needed him to be brave because Riley was facing some tough times ahead. Cooper could only imagine what he'd seen, what he experienced, and how many of his classmates and friends he might have witnessed being gunned down before his very eyes.

Cooper swallowed and pulled himself together. Izzy held his hand, watching his face, her own face hopeful yet concerned.

"Is he okay?" she asked anxiously.

Cooper nodded. "Ry, where are you? We'll be there as quickly as we can get there."

"I'm at Harborview. I—I need you guys."

"Izzy and I will be there in a few."

"Thanks, Uncle Coop." The phone went dead.

"Let's go." Cooper grabbed Izzy's hand and almost dragged her from the church. Together they sprinted to his car and once in, tore down the street.

Izzy patted his arm. "Cooper, slow down. Riley's okay. We need to get there in one piece."

Cooper nodded and slowed the car to the speed limit. "He's

okay. Thank God he's okay."

"I know, honey, I know."

"All those other people who weren't so lucky—"

"Cooper, I know, but Riley needs the two of us more than ever. Let's concentrate on what we can control." Izzy rested her head on his broad shoulder.

"I'm so glad I have you. Together, we can do this."

"Together, we can do anything," Izzy said, and she meant it.

* * * *

Riley sat up in the hospital bed with a bandaged arm. He didn't need to be hospitalized. He needed to go home. He stared at the open door, watching nurses and doctors hustle back and forth, and wondered about Gina.

He'd asked about her, but no one would give him any answers. He gripped the blanket, feeling so very lost and alone.

He lay back against the sheets and closed his eyes, but the images of his earlier nightmare ran through his head in vivid HD color. He snapped his eyes back open and wiped the sweat off his face.

His uncle's big frame filled the doorway, and their eyes locked. He'd never seen his uncle look like that, almost crazed with worry. Uncle Coop always seemed so in control, almost cold. He didn't look cold right now. He looked scared shitless.

Uncle Coop looked him up and down, as if assessing his injuries. Relief relaxed the tension on his face, and he grinned as he strode to Riley's side.

Riley reached out his arms in a totally spontaneous gesture, and his uncle smothered him in a hug, careful to avoid his bandaged arm.

Riley couldn't be strong anymore. Sobs wracked his body, and he buried his head in his uncle's shoulder. His uncle might think he was a wuss, but he couldn't stop. He'd looked death in the eyes and somehow survived. Why him—the kid who never had anything go his way? Why him?

Uncle Cooper finally let go, only to be replaced by Izzy. She hugged him tight and blubbered, her tears wetting his shoulder. She finally stopped hugging him, but she sat on the bed and held his hand, while she sniffled and wiped her nose and eyes with a tissue.

Riley hiccupped a bit and squeezed his eyes shut, but nothing stopped the tears from leaking out so he opened them.

"Are you okay?" Uncle Coop asked, wiping his own eyes. Shit, Uncle Coop had been crying? Riley couldn't believe it. His uncle was too strong to cry.

"Yeah," Riley managed.

"The doctor told us you saved a girl's life and put yours in danger."

Riley hadn't thought of it that way. "I just did what I had to do."

"I'm proud of you, Riley." Cooper smiled at him. "And damn glad you're okay." A tear ran down his uncle's face, and he didn't even bother to wipe it away. Riley watched it, mesmerized as it left a wet trail down his cheek and a wet spot on the leather jacket he wore.

"Is she going to be okay?" Riley glanced from one to the other. Their troubled expressions said it all.

Cooper took a deep breath, while Izzy managed a comforting smile. "Riley, she's in surgery. I won't lie to you—she's critical, but the doctors here are the best at what they do," Cooper said, staring at him so intently, it made Riley nervous.

"My letterman's jacket is ruined," Riley said. He'd gotten the jacket only a week ago, and it'd been his prized possession. He'd be getting the football letter for freshman football at the awards banquet at the end of the month. Only now he wouldn't have anything to put it on.

It was weird the kind of meaningless crap that filled a guy's mind at a time like this. He guessed that was how people coped at the worst of times.

"I'll buy you a dozen more, Riley," Cooper said, patting his shoulder. Izzy squeezed his hand.

They were acting like a—a family. Riley had never had a family before, and he was pretty sure he was going to embarrass himself and start crying again.

"Hey, buddy, we'll get through this. Little by little. You've got us."

Riley nodded, "How many—how many people died?" he choked out the words. Another one of those looks between Izzy and Uncle Coop.

"We don't know yet, Ry."

He nodded and gripped Izzy's hand. Cooper sat next to him and put his arm around Riley's shoulders, as if knowing somehow that Riley was going to lose it again. He did, only this time he didn't feel so embarrassed. He knew they didn't care if he cried.

"It's okay, buddy. Let it out. You'll feel better." Cooper spoke quietly as Riley cried until there just weren't any tears left to cry. He sniffled, while Izzy dabbed at his face with a hand towel, coddling him like he'd never been coddled even as a small boy. He liked it a lot, even though he was too old to be treated like that.

Uncle Cooper kept staring at him as if he had something to say. Riley met his gaze and waited, sniffling and hiccupping.

"We love you, Riley. We'll get through this together. The three of us."

Riley's heart swelled in his chest to a point it was painful. "I'm not going to live with your parents?"

"You're not going anywhere." Cooper's response was so definite that Riley almost smiled.

He glanced at Izzy who teared up again, but then so did Uncle Coop. "I love you, too, Uncle Coop. And you, Izzy."

"You can call me Aunt Izzy." She smiled at him, and her smile lit up an otherwise gloomy room.

Riley didn't feel so alone anymore. For the first time in his life, he had people who cared for him and wanted the best for him.

Despite how much his world had been irrevocably changed today, he knew he'd make it with their love and support.

And through tragedy a small ray of hope warmed him inside.

Chapter 22—In the Net

The hospital was overrun by reporters and family members to the point that it took Izzy forty-five minutes to get lunch and bring it back to the room.

Tanner was there, as were Cedric, Brick, Rush, Coach Gorst, Lauren, and Ethan, all crowding around Riley's bed. Riley managed to smile at some outrageous joke Brick was telling.

She glanced around the room. Cooper was conspicuously absent. Maybe he'd stepped out to use the bathroom. Yet fifteen minutes later, he hadn't returned.

"Where's Coop?" she asked, no one in particular.

"He said there was something important that he had to do. He'll be back as soon as he can," Riley answered.

Izzy couldn't imagine Cooper leaving Riley at a time like this unless it was something so important and necessary he had to do it now.

Or lose his nerve.

There was only one thing she could think of, only she didn't know where he'd go to confront the past which haunted him.

Thank God for the stalker app.

Izzy left the guys with Riley, promising to be back soon, and drove to the location indicated by the app. It was a run-down part of Seattle with old houses, many ready to be demolished by an urban reclamation project. Cooper's SUV was parked in the overgrown driveway of a condemned house. The front lawn was a tangle of blackberry vines and tall weeds. A small path led up to a leaning front porch.

The door stood ajar.

Izzy gingerly mounted the front steps and peered inside the dark, boarded-up house.

Cooper stood in one corner, hands over his face, his body heaving as if he took deep breaths.

"Coop?" She picked her away across the room littered with beer cans, garbage, and other stuff she didn't want to look too closely at.

He didn't move, either not hearing her or expecting her. She touched his arm, and he stiffened, taking his hands away from his face and not meeting her gaze, but he didn't tell her to leave either. If he hadn't wanted her to find him, he'd have left his phone in Riley's hospital room.

He needed her here, so he'd made himself easy to find.

Whatever had happened in this place was why he hated Seattle.

* * * *

Cooper had been expecting Izzy. In fact, he was relieved she'd found him. He needed her right now as much as he'd needed her hours ago.

"Cooper, what are you doing here?" she asked, even though he suspected she had a damn good idea.

"Exorcising the past." He stared at a corner in the room, but he wasn't seeing it the same way she was, but as it had been. The trunk had sat in that corner. To this day, he would never have a trunk in his house.

Izzy moved closer to him, as if sensing his distress until she was so close to him, he could feel her body heat in this cold, oppressive house.

"This was your aunt and uncle's house," she said, answering the question he couldn't bring himself to answer.

He nodded. "I'm glad it's being torn down." In fact, he'd personally pay to have it bulldozed if that was what it took.

"Why did you come here today of all days?"

"When I saw Riley today, heard how he tried to save that girl, and thought of all he's been through, I realized that kid is stronger than I am, and it humbled me." He needed to do this, to move on so he could help Riley move on. Izzy and Riley deserved his entire self, instead of only a portion because the other portion was imprisoned by a past he'd never come to terms with. And most of all, he needed to purge the guilt he'd felt all these years.

"He's stronger than both of us, Coop, because any tough times we've lived through, he's seen in spades."

Cooper nodded slowly as he turned to her. Nothing but concern and affection shone in her eyes. Her beautiful mouth was drawn in a tight line of worry. "It's time to look ahead, instead of behind, to heal the scars of the past, and move onto a better future."

"Yes, it's time." She rubbed his arm, and her touch comforted him, warming him a little in this cold, soulless place.

"That's why I came here. To say goodbye, once and for all."

And to stop being a coward, to be the brave man Riley and Izzy deserved.

"What happened here, Coop?" Izzy grabbed his hand. Hers was warm and dry, while his was cold and clammy.

He stayed silent for a long while, gathering the nerve to put into words a summer he'd locked away in his mind, just as he'd been locked away all those years ago.

"My siblings and I used to love this place. My aunt was childless and had us visit every summer. When Julie turned thirteen, and I was nine, our aunt married a guy we all adored. He was a city cop, an upstanding guy, and a good provider. Or so we thought. We were wrong. Eventually I came to hate Seattle because of him."

Izzy kept quiet, letting him talk at his own pace. He didn't need prompting. It was as if once he started, he couldn't stop, despite how hard it was for him. She leaned into his solid body, giving him the strength he didn't have on his own.

"The first summer we loved our new uncle. He was such a great guy, and he took us all sorts of places. The next summer, we knew as soon as we arrived that things had changed. Drastically. He'd turned into someone else, and my aunt tiptoed around him as if she were scared to death. He worked graveyard so he was home while she was at work. Instead of taking us fun places, he kept us inside with all the drapes shut. In fact, he hated us boys and liked my sister too much. He did weird things, like was really friendly with my sister. I didn't understand at the time. But it got worse. He started locking my brother and me into a large steamer trunk during the day, sometimes for so long that we'd end up peeing our pants in there, then he'd spank us for doing so. And I mean spank. While we were locked in the trunk, we could hear our sister begging him to leave her alone. He swore he'd kill us all if we told anyone."

Cooper sucked in a breath. "We just wanted to go home and never come back, but we loved our aunt and were afraid of what he'd do to her as well as us if we said anything. If she suspected what was going on, she never said. Not once. She didn't seem to know how to get out of the situation. He was a cop, and he had power she didn't have." Cooper paused and buried his face in Izzy's shoulder, drawing in deep, calming breaths while she rubbed his back.

"Oh, Cooper, I'm so sorry. So very sorry." She held him to her, and he never wanted to leave her calming presence. He felt the love flowing from her to him and knew as he knew how to put a puck on the top shelf that she would forever be the best thing that ever happened to him.

Finally, Cooper drew back and the words started again, as if he couldn't contain them. Cooper avoided looking in her eyes. If he looked now, he'd lose it, and he couldn't, not yet. Not until he'd told her everything.

"One night he threatened all of us with a gun, shot it into the ceiling, and the neighbors called the police. Of course, a couple of his buddies answered the call and asked us a few questions. My sister spilled her guts, crying and wailing. My brother and I were so afraid of all of them that we said everything was fine. So they left, assuming my sister was being a dramatic teenager. But my aunt, she knew, I know she did. She never said a word, but the next day, we were on the plane flying home. Within twenty-four hours, she was dead."

Izzy stared at him, horrified. "He killed her?"

"I'm positive he did, but it was ruled an accident. He claimed he'd been about to clean his gun and it misfired or some dumbshit excuse. We never said a word because we were so afraid he'd hunt us down and kill us and our parents."

"So your sister blames you for not speaking up that night?" Izzy wrapped her arms around his waist, holding him.

"My sister blames everyone in her life—me, my brother, our parents. Hell, she blames Riley for being born. I see that now. I feel as if the sister I knew died in this house that summer."

"It wasn't your fault. You were just a kid dealing with abuse and fear the best way you knew how."

"My sister never recovered from that summer. She'd been a happy, energetic teenager, loving, great student, and full of life. After that she turned sullen and angry, started hanging with the wrong crowd and went into self-destruct mode. Everything went downhill from there."

"I'm sorry, Cooper, so very sorry. Whatever happened to your uncle? Is he still around?"

"No, he was shot by an armed robber about ten years ago. I'm glad or I'd have tracked him down and killed him with my bare hands."

Izzy nodded grimly. "That bastard wasn't worth going to jail."

"No, he wasn't, which is the only thing that held me back."

"Do your parents know about all this?" Izzy asked.

"No, my mom has Crohn's, and she would suffer a relapse if she knew the truth. I don't know if she could handle it. Telling her won't make the past go away." Cooper glanced around the room one last time and turned to Izzy. "Let's get out of here."

"Let's do."

They headed back to the hospital and Riley.

"Cooper," Izzy said before they got out of the car, "I want you to know that it meant a lot to me that you shared your pain with me today."

"I'm glad I did, too." Cooper took the key out of the ignition and turned to her, hugging her to him as best he could with the console between them. Much to his surprise telling her made him feel better, as if he'd cut free this anchor that'd weighed him down all these years.

"We've come a long way," Izzy said. "I always thought I had to be independent because of my parents' irresponsible behavior and what it did to my sisters and me. I didn't want to depend on anyone because I knew I'd be hurt, and they'd disappoint me."

"And now?"

"I realize trusting someone enough to depend on them doesn't mean that I have to give up my independence. That trust is power in itself."

He understood her words. Sharing his secret had miraculously minimized the past's power over him. Yeah, he'd still be claustrophobic in tight spaces, and he'd jump when he heard a gun go off, but he'd finally started down the path to healing.

They all had.

"I love you, Izzy." He cupped her face between his big hands and kissed the hell out of her. It was a kiss like no other, a kiss full of passion and promises, a kiss that gave hope, a kiss that healed.

Chapter 23—Home Ice

Cooper loved his early morning skates, just him and the sound of his blades gliding across the ice. He turned on the speed, relishing the wind he'd created in his hair, and the ache in his muscles as he pushed himself faster and faster.

It was Christmastime, a month after the shooting, and Riley and Izzy's life had settled into a routine.

Cooper was so proud of his kid, and Riley was his kid, that his chest swelled with pride. Cooper had wanted to put Riley in a different school, but Riley refused his offer. He said he wanted to face what happened and be part of the healing process. Gina didn't make it, but Riley took the news like a trooper, jumping in to help her parents with a memorial to her and the other kids who lost their lives.

Riley and Cooper worked with the team and the Kids at Play organization to start the healing process for the school and the city. Tanner joined in, giving his time, along with generous donations. While Tanner still wasn't one of Cooper's favorite people, Cooper had to admit he was an all right guy. So was Ethan. Cooper and Ethan had started skating together again in the early morning hours a couple days a week.

He contacted his attorney to take steps to adopt Riley, offering to pay Julie money to sign the papers. She took the money and ran. In some ways, he wished she had cared enough to fight for Riley, but she hadn't. The court papers gave her visitation rights as long as she agreed to regular drug testing.

So far she hadn't bothered.

Izzy insisted Riley go to regular therapy. While he wasn't wild about it, he did it for her, which made Cooper smile. He called her Aunt Izzy now, and that made Izzy smile.

They weren't half bad at this parenting thing, and Cooper decided he wanted more kids and soon.

He wasn't sure what Izzy would think of that, but hey, he wanted them, just the same, and he'd convince her to see things his way. He was damn good at it, especially when they were in bed.

The Sockeyes were winning more than losing. The city embraced the team, selling out almost every single game.

Yeah, life was pretty good.

Cooper had a few more loose ends to tie up before he opened the next chapter in his life. He didn't like to leave anything hanging.

When Ethan stepped onto the ice for their morning skate, Cooper was already breathing hard. He waited for Ethan to catch up to him, and they skated side by side around the rink several times. Ethan's skating had improved considerably. Maybe he'd never be NHL caliber, but he was a damn good amateur skater.

As they slowed to cool down, Cooper glanced over at Ethan. "My arm's pretty sore."

Ethan gave him a sideways glance, "And you're telling me this why?"

Cooper pulled off his sweatshirt to reveal his bare chest.

Ethan stumbled on the ice and skidded to a halt. Cooper skated a sharp circle and did a perfect stop a few feet in front of his boss. Hands on hips, chests heaving, both men stared at each other.

"My agent will be calling Garrett next week, but I warn you, he's a ruthless bastard, and he drives a hard bargain," Cooper said.

"So do I," Ethan said with a slow smile.

"Yeah, I'm sure you do." Cooper smiled back.

"Welcome to the Sockeyes for the next ten years, Mr. Black." Ethan held out his hand.

Cooper shook it firmly. "You'd better be putting some Stanley-Cup caliber teams on the ice, Mr. Parker, or there'll be hell to pay. I expect nothing less."

"So do I." Ethan sobered for a minute. "What changed your mind? I thought you hated Seattle."

"I thought I did, too. Guess I was wrong."

Ethan nodded a grin breaking across his face. "Let me buy you breakfast."

"It'd be an honor."

One down, one to go. Cooper grinned as he skated off the ice, feeling better about this decision than he'd ever imagined. He rubbed his arm. That damn new tattoo hurt. Cooper held up his arm and admired the blue and green fish with a Space Needle hooked in its mouth, Mount Rainier in the background, and a space for the Stanley Cup to be inked somewhere down the road. The tattoo artist did a fine job.

Cooper was home, and it felt damn good.

* * * *

Izzy stood at the deck railing of the same tour boat where she'd first met Cooper. It was all decked out in Christmas lights for the annual Christmas boat parade on Lake Washington and Lake Union. Inside, she could see their table, complete with Riley and a few of his buddies, Tanner and a date, Cedric, Brick, a few other teammates, and her sisters.

Cooper stood beside her, hugging her close. The night was cold and clear, but not even the chilly air could dampen her spirits. She loved Christmas, and right after Thanksgiving, she'd put up a huge tree. Riley and her sisters helped decorate, while Cooper and Cedric grumbled about having to put up Christmas lights on the eaves of the house.

"Are you happy, honey?" Cooper asked, bending his head so his blue eyes stared straight into hers.

"Ecstatic." She smiled at him and pulled his mouth to hers, tasting the hot buttered rum on his lips and reveling in the warmth of his body.

He nuzzled her cheek with his rough one. "Izzy, there's something you need to know." The seriousness of his tone made her stiffen and pull back slightly.

"Is everything okay?"

"I'm going to sign a new contract effective at the end of the season."

Izzy held her breath. Oh, God, here it came. The moment she'd been dreading. "With who?" She couldn't keep the worry out of her voice.

"The best team in the NHL with best ownership, coaches, and front office. It's long-term, and I'll retire with this team."

She held his arms tightly. "What team?"

Cooper glanced out at the water. The Seattle skyscrapers and the Space Needle lit up the distant skyline. "The team that plays for the most beautiful city in the country."

"Cooper, you're killing me here."

Cooper looked so serious, which made her dread his answer all the more. He was building up their new city before he dropped the bombshell, but she'd promised, and she'd follow him wherever he went.

But damn, she'd miss Seattle.

Then she noticed a smile tugging at the corner of Cooper's lips and realized he was toying with her. *The butthead.*

"What team?" she asked through gritted teeth.

For a minute he didn't answer, as if relishing her discomfort, the bastard. He met her gaze, his blue eyes sparkling with pure devilment. "The Seattle Sockeyes. Ever heard of them?" He grinned at her now.

Izzy blew out a breath and started laughing, even though she wanted to throttle him for stringing her along. "Are you sure?"

He nodded. "Positive. I've found my forever home. In fact, I bought it, just yesterday."

"Bought it?"

"The house we're in. It's ours."

"Ours?" She loved that house, absolutely loved it. Love the funky early sixties' style and how it hadn't been modernized to the point of losing its character.

"Yeah, ours." He kept grinning, cluing her in that he wasn't done with his surprises. "And guess what?"

"What?"

"A forever house needs a forever love. Don't you think?"

Before she could answer, he dropped to one knee and all the breath escaped her lungs.

He took her hands in his and stared up at her. Oh, God, she couldn't believe this was happening. Behind Cooper stood their entire group of family and friends, every one of them smiling.

"Will you be my forever love, Izzy?" Cooper gazed up at her, his eyes filled with love and hope.

She blinked back the tears and nodded furiously, unable to speak. He put a gorgeous diamond ring on her finger, a single stone ringed with sapphires and emeralds.

"Blue for the water and green for the mountains," he explained, but he didn't need to explain. She knew what they stood for. She threw herself at him before he could stand and almost knocked him to the deck. Their friends and family cheered.

He managed to stand with her hanging all over him and kissed her possessively on the lips. She was his, and he was hers. He broke the kiss and spun her around in a slow circle, while Izzy held him tightly to her, giggling with joy. When he let her down, Riley joined them for a group hug.

In the distance, the Space Needle winked at her while Christmas lights reflected off the water on the shore, and the Seattle skyline welcomed her home.

Their forever home, the perfect place for their forever love.

~ THE END ~

Thank you for spending time in my world. I hope you enjoyed reading this book. If you did, please help other readers discover this book by leaving a review.

COMPLETE BOOKLIST

The following Jami Davenport titles are available in electronic and some are available in trade paperback format.

Madrona Island Series
Madrona Sunset

Evergreen Dynasty Series
Save the Last Dance
Who's Been Sleeping in My Bed?
The Gift Horse

Game On in Seattle—Seattle Sockeyes Hockey
Skating on Thin Ice
Crashing the Boards
Crashing the Net
Love at First Snow

Seattle Lumberjacks Football Series
Fourth and Goal
Forward Passes
Down by Contact
Backfield in Motion
Time of Possession
Roughing the Passer

Standalone Books
Christmas Break

ABOUT THE AUTHOR

If you'd like to be notified of new releases, special sales, and contests, subscribe here: **http://eepurl.com/LpfaL**

USA Today Bestselling Author Jami Davenport is an advocate of happy endings and writes sexy contemporary and sports romances, including her two new indie endeavors: the Game On in Seattle Series and the Madrona Island Series. Jami's new releases consistently rank in the top fifty on the sports romance and sports genre lists on Amazon, and she has hit the Amazon top hundred authors list in both contemporary romance and genre fiction multiple times.

Jami lives on a small farm near Puget Sound with her Green Beret-turned-plumber husband, a Newfoundland cross with a tennis ball fetish, a prince disguised as an orange tabby cat, and an opinionated Hanoverian mare.

Jami works in IT for her day job and is a former high school business teacher. She's a lifetime Seahawks and Mariners fan and is waiting for the day professional hockey comes to Seattle. An avid boater, Jami has spent countless hours in the San Juan Islands, a common setting in her books. In her opinion, it's the most beautiful place on earth.

Website: http://www.jamidavenport.com
Events Blog: http://jamidavenport.blogspot.com
Romancing the Jock Blog: http://www.romancingthejock.com
Twitter Address: @jamidavenport
Facebook: http://www.facebook.com/jamidavenport
Facebook Fan Page:
    http://www.facebook.com/jamidavenportauthor
Pinterest: http://pinterest.com/jamidavenport/
Goodreads:
http://www.goodreads.com/author/show/1637218.Jami_Davenport

Made in the USA
Charleston, SC
12 February 2016